FROM UTAH TO ETERNITY

FROM UTAH TO ETERNITY

A Mormon-Muslim Journey

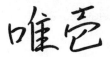

A novel by
Sarah Louise Baker

SAKINA BOOKS
OXFORD

ISBN 0953805646 cloth
ISBN 0953805654 paperback

Published by:
Sakina Books
3 Galpin Close
Oxford OX4 1PR
United Kingdom

This is a work of fiction. Any resemblance between persons quoted herein, and any real persons whether living or deceased, is purely coincidental.

Japanese calligraphy by Ryoko Imai
Cover design by Abdullateef Whiteman

Printed in Great Britain by Alden Press, Oxford

ACKNOWLEDGEMENTS

I would like to thank the following people who helped me in producing this book.

My children who took their naps regularly so that Mummy could get on with her writing.

My husband who encouraged me from the beginning, helped with the computer work and lent me his computer.

My family who encouraged me in my plans to write this book and showed great interest in it.

My friends who were all supportive and admiring; especially my fellow convert Aisha, and Robin, a source of inspiration and a great proof-reader.

唯邑

Utah, USA

Of all the places a Mormon boy could come from, Jake had to come from Utah. This had never bothered him until he first stepped outside of his home state. Before then his life had been comfortable and predictable with clear guidelines about what was expected of him and how other people were supposed to react to him. His place in the hierarchy of the church, which seemed to have been carved in stone from his earliest memories, was already set out for him. Of course he had known anti-Mormon feeling, but the church always had an explanation for that. Jake used to feel part of something impenetrable and strong and he had always seen gentiles as second-class citizens. In Utah he was one of the majority, the scrubbed, pure, well-versed majority - healthy in mind and body, confident of the present and the future, this life and the next - all sewn up. Jake had rarely questioned the church view of things. As his dad used to say, "Son! The Mormons have got it all sewn up."

So it had come as a shock to him to find when he first ventured out in the world that to be a Mormon and to come from Utah was a hopeless cliché.

"Oh no! Don't tell me. You're from Utah," or "You're from Utah? So you must be Mormon."

Even at the missionary training camp his fellow trainees would roll their eyes when they heard he was from Utah. Coming from the heart of the church, he had thought, would be an advantage, but as it turned out, as far as the other Mormons were concerned, to be a Mormon from Utah didn't take any effort. There was no originality about it. It followed that a boy from Salt Lake City would be a Mormon. Predictable! Boring! Instead of an advantage, it looked set to be the greatest barrier in his mission to persuade others to come into the church, people who could hardly have been born further away from it, in Japan.

When he first met the guys at training from the other states, California, Arizona, New York, he had been proud to be a Utah boy. Somehow he felt he had more claim to the faith, as if he was some benevolent teacher letting them in on it; but they didn't regard themselves as any less worthy than him of going on their mission, and he soon came back down to earth and tried to fit in.

Jake's training days were enlightening in many ways. He was full of anticipation about starting his assignment, and after he had found out that he had been assigned to Japan, he was ravenous for every ounce of information he could get on the place, especially on how the Japanese mind worked and how to open them up to thinking about a religion so different from their own. The training period was highly organized and compartmentalized. Jake liked this because he knew the church organizers would make sure everything was catered for: mind, body and spirit.

He was sharing a small, neat room with the other guys who would go to Japan with him. There were Bruce and Dave from Northern California and Lewis from Oregon. Dave was a Japanese-American and Jake felt particularly drawn to him, imagining him to possess some of the mystique of Japan which had somehow been passed down in his genes. Jake tended to treat everything he said with a certain reverence, hanging on his every word.

"Yeah. I'll probably get to see my folks while I'm there. One of my granddad's brothers is still alive. He lives just outside of Tokyo and he has two sons and four grandchildren. It'll be so weird to see them."

"Can any of then speak English?"

"Yeah. I guess just high-school standard but they don't really need it much for work. One of the girls studies English at Kyoto University."

"So you'll be able to practice your Japanese."

"Yeah. I'd like that. I heard from an American friend that some Japanese tend to freak out when they see foreigners or *gaigin* as they call us but they get totally confused when they see a *Nisei* like me who looks Japanese but doesn't have the behaviour to go with it. I'm looking forward to that."

Dave's American identity, it seemed, was all-important to him because he was a Mormon. He wanted to feel accepted and move up in the church without his race being a disadvantage. The truth, as Jake had often been assured in church meetings, was that the Mormons were not and never had been racist, but the slur that had been laid on them by anti-Mormons who had branded them as bigots had scared a lot of black people off. This, they said, accounted for the lack of black faces in the Quorum of the Seventy, the men at the top echelons of the church hierarchy. There was presently one Chinese member of the Quorum and this gave Dave hope. For many years now, the Mormons had been stepping up their missionary efforts all over the world to prove that the church was for everyone. Everyone, if worthy, could be a Saint.

After breakfast and silent prayer, the trainees would go for a morning run, then back to shower before the day's study began. One morning in two they would have Japanese language and culture. The teacher, Mr Sakimoto, drummed it into them that they were not to be daunted by the apparent difficulty of the Japanese language. When you had such an important message to put across as the missionaries had, you had to make every effort to learn the language of the people you were trying to reach and not be put off, especially not by the Japanese themselves, who were horrified at the idea of *gaigin* getting their hands on their precious language.

The lessons concentrated on the spoken language, so that the puzzling writing system would not be a problem at first. The students were all surprised by the end of the first lesson that they were already having rudimentary conversations in a language that sounded something like Italian. Jake was surprised that he caught on quicker than Dave whose family had never taught him a word of Japanese.

"*Watashi no namae wa Jake desu. Anata no namae wa nan desu ka?*"

"Dave. Come on Dave. Play the game. Say the full sentence."

"It's pointless. No-one does that in real life."

"Yeah, but you need the practice. I tell you. You'll be glad when you get there. Come on. Let's do the next one. You be the customer. I'm the waiter. *Irrashaimase. Nani ga hoshi desu ka?*"

"*Isu-kurime.*"

"*O kudasai!*"

"Huh?"

"You have to say please."

"But I'm the customer. In Japan the customer is king."

"Oh I'm doing it by myself!"

The students were given an outline of the education system, the nuclear family set-up, the economic organization and the vital role played by the company in the Japanese identity and sense of purpose. Jake learned to look on the Japanese as a people in direct contrast to Americans. The teacher made it simple for them. Americans found their self-worth in personal achievement and competition. They thrived on having something to set them apart from the crowd. The Japanese, on the other hand, did everything in their power to blend in, and found sustenance from co-operating for the good of the whole group to the extent of subjugating the private self. Brother Owen put it quite neatly.

"Think of America as a patchwork quilt and Japan as a cotton sheet. I think you'll get the picture."

Jake tried to internalize the information and see how it would work for his mission. The way he saw himself, as a member of the church, was that he had to sacrifice ego for the greater good of the church, so in some ways the typical American character was not suited to blending in and conforming to church ideals.

The Psychology teacher, Brother Ray Chalmers, pinpointed the best type of people for missionaries to work with. He called them "subjects." A salary man for example would be so preoccupied and tied up in the system, he wouldn't even be able to stop and tell you the time.

"What about middle-aged men who aren't salary men?" asked Jake.

"All middle-aged Japanese men are salary men," said Dave cynically. "For a man not to have gone into a company by that age would be like he was a no-hoper or something or crazy."

"So if we come across a regular guy we shouldn't try to witness him?" enquired Jake.

"Japanese men who don't conform," said Brother Chalmers, "are often not the type we are looking for. They are too contrary, never satisfied with what you tell them. Imagine! For a Japanese to break out of the system, he has to be ten times the maverick he

4

would have to be here."

Jake thought about it and decided he could at least try with everyone without prejudging them. He knew God would help him because he believed he had the truth and it was his duty to share it with everyone. Brother Chalmers said that the ideal subject for the missionaries would be a college or university student because they were their own bosses and not yet caught up in the sense of duty that would come later.

唯邑

Salt Lake City, Utah

Jake sat across from Alice and tried to keep the conversation bright. She had been delighted for him when she heard about his mission, but now that the time was looming and it looked as though they wouldn't be seeing each other for so long, she had grown quite tearful. They had been engaged for just over a year and like most young Mormons they wouldn't marry until Jake had finished his mission. It was felt that young people needed that time alone to complete their spiritual growth and set the course of their life on the right track in order to strengthen the marriage.

"You'll be distracted by Japan. You won't have time to think about me but I'll be stuck right here waiting for you with nothing to keep me occupied."

"Do you think I won't miss you out there?"

"Sure, yeah I know. But when you're the one who's left behind, you get left with all the places we used to go together. In Japan there'll be nowhere you used to go with me so you won't miss me in the same way."

"I guess not. At least you know I'm coming back though. Imagine how it was in the war! Women said good-bye to their husbands and never knew when it would end."

"Jake, it doesn't make me feel better to know other people are worse off than I am. The truth is, I'll miss you a lot and my life will be flat and dull without you. That's me being honest now." She laughed self-consciously. "Last Sunday at the workshop we took that as our theme. You have to be honest and say how something or someone makes you feel rather than pushing the blame on them. You know, instead of 'You're always trying to annoy me when you make fun of my friends,' you have to say 'I feel upset when you make fun of my friends'."

"It's brave of you to tell me how you're feeling but it still makes me feel I should do something. I don't know, like staying, or taking you with me."

"I'd love to go to Japan. No Jake, I don't expect you to give up your mission for me, not that they'd let you anyway, but I wish we could get married first and go together."

"They figure we wouldn't put all our effort in if we were married. We'd always have something to occupy us and then there would be kids to think about. It's a bit like being a monk and putting all you've got into the faith for a while."

"I hate that dorm thing though. It's so restrictive. Makes out like you're still in school."

"It's better than living alone. It takes the pressure off too 'cos they told us at training, each day can be very demoralizing. You need to come back and talk about it."

"What else do you do at training?"

"They do psychology of the Japanese mind, explain how each ward is organized, the organization of the church, brush up on scriptures, that sort of thing. We have to get close to the other guys, support them and make sure they don't get homesick or start to stagnate in the faith. This one guy, Bruce, kind of gets on my nerves. He takes it all as a big joke, even the scriptures, and says the ban on alcohol and everything is a matter of personal choice. He's supposed to be encouraging them not to drink, and in Japan it's almost a way of life."

"There's always a wise-guy in every group. They just think it's cool to rebel. Anyway if he doesn't start to get results, he won't last long."

The encounter with Alice left Jake feeling melancholy. He had underestimated her feelings about his departure. He was so familiar with the idea of sacrificing everything for the church that he assumed that she was the same. He thought she would bolster him and send him on his way with good wishes like a soldier going out to fight for the church. He didn't expect her to give him a hard time about leaving her behind. One of his teachers had told him that women never go the whole hog. That's why men made better missionaries because when it came to the crunch, women would not be prepared to give up everything for the church. Their feelings came first and if they loved a man enough, they would make sacrifices for him, not for the church.

唯色

Utah, USA

Jake was eager to return to the training. On the way back on Sunday night he fixed his mind on getting to know the Japanese psyche more. As far as he could tell, they were clean-living, hard-working people. If they could put half of the energy into the church that they put into the Japanese economy, they would make fantastic Mormons.

The others were eager to hear about Jake's weekend away, and learn his news from the outside world. The training centre was quite claustrophobic with its single building and one baseball pitch and they had spent the whole weekend playing ball. Jake told them he had had a long talk with his dad about what was expected of him and he had been taken to say good-bye to all his father's colleagues. They had really built him up and made him feel like a hero going out to conquer the world. They had all been reminiscing about their own missionary days and the way they had supported each other. They told Jake that for every success there would be a hundred disappointments, but that he had to keep a certain look on his face that said: "I've got a wonderful secret I'm sure you'd like to know." People always respond if they feel they're missing out on something.

Bruce agreed. "Yeah, you should never let them know it matters to you whether or not they listen to the message. Play it cool and they'll come running."

"But you have to put across your enthusiasm," said Vincent, another of the trainees. "I mean the Japanese are not that subtle. You have to sell it to them."

"Who said the Japanese are not subtle?" said Dave in indignation. "The Japanese have made a career out of being subtle. You wouldn't be able to tell what was going on in those guys' minds if you spent years with them."

"Yeah. I read a bunch of books," said Bruce, "written by *gaigin* who'd been living in Japan. They said you go through stages. Right, first you love the people. Can't get enough of them. Want to go around with Japanese people all the time. They say you can always tell a newcomer 'cos he'll be first to defend the Japanese in a *gaigin* bitching session. Then slowly he gets disillusioned a couple of times and he finds out the people he thought were his great pals, he doesn't know them at all, and then he gets real negative until he realizes you just have to put up with communicating on a real surface level. You could never really get to know one."

"Even if you married one?" said Jake. He'd been miles away thinking about his weekend.

"Don't get any ideas," they teased, and Jake blushed.

It was time for the evening study session. They were working through the *Book of Mormon* systematically, cross-referencing it with footnotes from the Bible. One thing Jake had always taken comfort in was the historical backing that the Mormon faith had. He was fond of reading about the latest archaeological evidence in the church magazine which backed up claims from the *Book of Mormon* about the history of the lost tribes of Israel.

In theology class the next day, Brother Palmer was dealing with approach.

"Now, gentlemen. You have spent a good many years digesting our beautiful scriptures. You are all well-versed in the Word of the Lord but your average non-Saint, least of all your average Japanese, has a very rudimentary knowledge of scripture in general and religious history in particular."

"What if we happen on the one guy who has read the scriptures or the Japanese Jehovah's Witness?" piped up one of the students.

"Well, Joe. He is a rare bird indeed. For our purposes, we have to put across our message in a simplified form, outlining the main facts."

"But you may get some wise-guy who keeps trying to catch you out," said another student.

"Gentlemen! We must not forget we are dealing with the Japanese here. The Japanese are a very quiet and taciturn race. They run from situations of confrontation. It is more likely they will nod politely and show rapt attention throughout your discourse. The question is, however, how much goes in? For this reason and for reason of language ability, you have to go low on detail, high on impact. That is you have to try to put over to them the wonder of Joseph Smith's confrontation with the Angel Moroni."

They were then asked to run through some of the highlights of Joseph Smith's career and to role-play in front of the class. Jake's part was the scene of Joseph Smith dictating his translation of the Golden Plates to Brother Oliver Cowdery from behind a screen during one of his periods of inspiration.

The session left Jake feeling quite relieved that they were not expected to go into too much detail when doing missionary work in Japan.

Later before bed, as they wrote up notes, Bruce put down his pen and looked at Jake for some time until he said:

"Jake! Do you think any of this 'anti' stuff has got through to Japan?"

"You mean stuff against the church?"

"Uh huh. You know all that cliché stuff about Joseph Smith being a fraud."

"I guess not. My dad says that's all jealousy. They see how great the church is, how it attracts people every day from all over the world. They see us living good, successful lives and they resent it."

"You mean like they wanna corrupt us?"

"Yeah. I think so. Let's face it. If the church spreads, it's good-bye alcohol, good-bye tea and coffee and then who suffers? The big corporations."

"Except Coca-Cola."

"Yeah. The President said that was OK."

"And if the President said it, it must be true." Bruce raised his eyebrows slightly, searching Jake for signs of questions ticking in his brain. "Jake, do you ever get doubts?" he said, quickly.

"Sure I get doubts. Everyone gets a few doubts, don't they?"

"I don't," said Bruce with a serious expression which cracked into a smile when he saw Jake's look of slight panic. "I must admit I get a lot of doubts."

"But the devil wants to get a hold of everyone. You just have to fight it and pray for strength and keep reading."

"Would you read anything?"

"There's nothing better than what we have. It's a waste of time. Any doubts you have, you just have to sit down and read the *Book of Mormon* and the *Pearl of Great Price* until you get back on track."

"How about anti-Mormon books?"

"I wouldn't waste my time."

Lying in the dark that night, Jake prayed in earnest. He prayed for strength for himself, and strength to support Bruce. He liked Bruce far better now. He prayed for success. Success! One day, the Church of Jesus Christ of Latter Day Saints would be established in all the world.

Breakfast was served at six every day. Eggs, toast and juice.

"You know what the Japanese have for breakfast?" said Dave. "Rice and soup every morning."

"That's weird," said the others screwing up their noses. "How could they face that first thing in the morning?"

"You know what we're studying today?" said Vincent. "Pitfalls."

"What's that?"

"Things to avoid," he said.

"Like all the Japanese attractions," said Bruce. "Anything worth doing over there, we probably won't be allowed to do."

"Raw fish," said Vincent with a look of disgust on his face. "That's something to avoid."

"Listen. If you have not tasted raw fish, you have not lived," said Dave. "It's really good. I'm telling you. When you get back you'll be down the Japanese quarter. You won't be able to get enough of that stuff."

Vincent did not look convinced. "Anyway, today's session is about advice for missionaries. Rules and everything. Where you're not allowed to go. Who you're not allowed to mix with. Stuff like that."

"You mean they check up on everyone we mix with?" asked Bruce, horrified.

" I don't think so," said Vincent. " I think it's just guidelines."

"To make your mission as effective as possible and to ensure you come back stronger in the faith than when you went out, the training committee has set rules for your protection," explained Brother Nielsen with a smile. Groans went up from the class. "Brothers, seriously, if you stick to the rules, you will get something out of Japan that no one but the Lord can give you. A fruitful and blessed mission. You won't come back fatter or slower or more cynical. You won't have any messy emotional problems to clear up. So, let's go to it. Number One. Brothers always travel and witness in pairs. Two. Never enter anyone's home without permission!"

"Sir! I would have thought that was obvious."

"Son, we have to spell it out. However, here's Number Three. You are not to enter a house where a woman is alone."

A slightly cynical laugh was audible from some of the missionaries.

"You know very well that our moral code is very tight. We want to give the best kind of impression we can. We are sending out people with respect and decency." Brother Nielsen had become annoyed by now.

"Number Four. Brothers may not enter any restaurant or cafeteria including American chain restaurants except with special permission from your President."

"Do they have American restaurants there?' Jake whispered to his neighbour."

"Yeah. I hear they have Burger City, Donut Heaven, Dixie King."

"That's fantastic!" said Jake, excitedly.

"During these sessions," Nielsen went on, "a missionary can pay for or accept one drink and up to one sundry item. Thereafter, each is required to pay his way. This is meant as a courtesy and not an inducement. Also, we cannot have our missionaries whiling their time away in cafes.

"Number Five. Cultural exchanges with Japanese families, such as picnics, trips, and so on, will be arranged by your President. There are to be no private arrangements.

"Six. Contacts with other foreigners living in Japan should be kept to a minimum beyond exchanges of polite conversation. As you already know, our main concern is the Japanese people."

Nielsen sat down, tired with the exertion of speaking. His voice became quieter. "Now, you may come across other students along the way: Chinese, Koreans, Singaporeans, Indians, Pakistanis, even Middle Eastern students. You are out of your depth with these non-Japanese. I stress. You are out of your depth and you are not to witness them without express permission from your superiors."

"I don't understand, sir, when you say out of our depth." This was Lawrence, a serious young man from Los Angeles.

"I mean," said Nielsen as if explaining to a child. He used a rather pedantic, sing-song tone. "You've been trained in Buddhism, Shinto and things concerning the Japanese. You have no expertise in other religions."

"But the Chinese are also Buddhist, sir."

"Yes, but our approach is specifically geared towards the Japanese. If you try to apply that to Chinese you'll get tied up in knots. Anyway, we've set these rules for very good reasons and previous generations of missionaries will testify to that. So we'll leave it there. Your Presidents will go into more detail when you arrive. Good-day."

Bruce was to be found sauntering along the corridor, singing 'I'm in prison' to the tune of 'I'm in heaven'.

"Sounds like it's party, party, party all the way down in Japan, guys," said Vincent.

"It's work, guys," said Jake. "There'll be free time but we've gotta remember we're there to work. Anyway it's not like we're gonna see nothing of Japan. Brother Chapman said we get taken on trips pretty often and we get to do outdoor activities, barbecues and stuff."

"Sounds like they keep a tight rein though," said Lawrence. "Sounds pretty much like the army. Only act under orders!"

"They have to keep it well-organized," said Jake. "We've got an important job to do and we need all the help we can get."

The afternoon session was to be a preview of some of the videos they were to use.

Jake had been looking forward to the Wednesday afternoon recess period as his uncle had arranged to come to take him riding on his ranch which was a short drive from the centre. From a string of summers spent at his uncle's farm, he had come to feel at home with horses.

Now he was galloping in boundless exhilaration across the open country beyond the ranch.

"Big Country!" he shouted across the plains with a frenzied grin on his face. He slowed a little as he realized he was pushing the horse too far, although he had enjoyed the free run. He looked up at the big sky and the big land stretching in all directions, and the great clouds sailing rapidly across the blue. Jake was over-whelmed with love for his country. "America is so beautiful," he cried. No-one could hear him. "Thank you for letting me be born here Lord," he prayed quietly, suddenly surprised at the need to cry. No one was around. He let the tears flow freely all over the horse's neck. It was the outpouring of mingled feelings; gratitude to God, awareness of the weighty responsibility that lay ahead, fear and panic of a new country and unfamiliar things, the premo-nition of homesickness overwhelming him, mom, dad, his brother Frank, his sisters, Lisa and Joanne, the church. He was suddenly ashamed to realize he had forced himself to remember Alice. She had had nothing to do with that welling-up of emotion he had just experienced. "But this is the girl I'm going to marry," he thought, annoyed with himself. Wasn't she always asking him: "Do you think about me, Jake? Will you think about me often when you're away? Do you love me Jake?" Her clear, green eyes flashed into his head and he reassured himself. Of course he cared for Alice. He was going to marry her, wasn't he? It was in a more reflective mood that he cantered back to the ranch, but he felt that the run on the horse and the crying session had washed his system clean. His stress had fallen away and he felt psyched-up for something good.

When he got back to the room Lewis was glum and Bruce was fuming.

"What's up guys?"

"Some overenthusiastic jerk decided we should use our recess time profitably." His tone was sarcastic.

"What happened?"

Lewis broke in. "You know Brother Steele? The one whose father's in the Seventy? He comes in while we were watching this war movie I'd brought from home, turns it off and says, 'I've got better videos to watch.' The guys all booed and hissed, so he says, 'Shall we check with President Michaels?' That's when we knew we were beat."

"So we had to sit through ex-junkie Sam and depressed crazy Karen saying how their lives had changed so much after they'd entered the church," said Bruce.

"Oh right," said Jake. "Those are the videos we had in training the other day."

"But that was just the beginning," said Lewis "They were all the same, like 'The *Book of Mormon* has changed my life! I no longer drink! I no longer do drugs!'"

"'I no longer want to attack my parents with a knife,'" mocked Bruce. "'It's so good to know there's a place in Paradise for all those people who have been blessed by God's plan.'" His tone was pedantic like a little child who has just learned to read. He pointed. "'You too can take part in God's plan if you just sign on the dotted line and give over half your salary in tithes.'"

"Ten percent," corrected Jake.

"Get it right, Bruce," said Lewis, smiling. "So that was our recess wasted," he added.

"Sounds like you guys had a raw deal," said Jake, sympathetically. "Now if you had gone horseback riding with me, you would have had a truly spiritual experience. Nothing like going back to nature." He lay on the bed looking at the ceiling, trying to recapture the memory.

"You look good, Jake," said Bruce. "Anyway, what are we going to do about Steele?"

"It's OK. He's posted to Yokohama," said Lewis.

"Yes, but we have two more weeks of this to go," Bruce groaned.

Just then Dave came in, fresh from his round of tennis. "Six - zero, six-four, six-two," he chanted.

"Sounds like you sporty guys had the better deal," concluded Bruce.

"The Japanese can't say no," announced Mr Sakimoto. The progress of the trainees had borne out his assurance that Japanese was not a difficult language to learn. Once they had overcome the psychological barrier and stopped worrying about it, they found they could master the language in small, manageable bursts. Jake had been through the first, stumbling stages, followed by a swaggering stage that made him feel like he really had it. He was almost there and then he would reach another plateau and the enormity of what was still unlearned stretched to the next horizon. But you needed that over-confident stage to keep you going to the next plateau, and the next. Everyone had been surprised when Dave had turned out to be one of the less gifted students. He reminded them again and again that he had barely heard a word of Japanese at home.

"He's an all-American Jap," said Brother Tyler.

"We don't have language like that in this school," said Sakimoto sternly.

The trainees had been reprimanded the morning after the video incident about Attitude. They were told that watching Vietnam war movies was not conducive to a positive image of orientals. Moreover they were students in training and had better things to do than watch Hollywood movies. They were in the business of minds and hearts. What was more, the supervisors had not liked the negative attitude to training videos. The sneering attitude was uncalled for because it was these very testimonies on video that had won over many a soul to the LDS.

The day's Japanese lesson was another attempt by Sakimoto to show something of the Japanese character through language.

"Say for example in English, you ask me. 'Would you like another glass of juice?' I say, 'Yes please' or 'No thank you.' Now the Japanese language does not have this blunt tool of the 'no' word. We do have '*I*' which translates as 'no' but it would never stand alone. It needs hedges on either side. It would be rather, '*Jusu wa ne! Chotto irrimasen desu.*' That would translate something like, 'Juice, hum. I don't really need that.' Never ask a Japanese a question which would leave him squirming to get out of it without offense. For example. 'Do you know the way to the hospital?' Person thinks, 'No I don't. Please let me off.' but says, 'Um, the hospital. The hospital is it? The hospital. Where is the hospital? Well, actually, the thing is, you see, that I myself am not quite familiar with this part of town. But um (waiting to be let off).' Do you get the picture brothers? To directly refuse a request goes against Japanese norms of communication. In English, think of the different ways of saying 'no' which say different things. Different kinds of intonation. You can let someone down gently by saying 'no' with a certain kind of intonation which puts across regret. This same function in Japanese is covered with more words, more politeness, because intonation is not as versatile as in English. OK. Please practice in pairs. Requests and polite refusals. Go to it."

Jake sat in the library engrossed in a book entitled *Shintoism: The Way of the Gods*.

"See here," he said to Lewis who was doing his Japanese home-work. "There's a god of umbrellas." He laughed and read on. "Lewis, there are hundreds of gods. Something for everybody."

"Well, we believe in many Gods as well, but ours are more meaningful. But I heard the Japanese don't take it all that serious-ly," said Lewis. "I heard they use religious rituals for things like weddings and funerals and stuff but other than that, it takes a back seat."

"Yeah. It says here that the priest comes to do a ceremony for new car-factories for good luck and fortune. But I've been think-ing. If like you say, they have this kind of superstitious religion that doesn't fill their life, maybe they're looking for something. Maybe they will be open to new ideas."

"Who knows? I guess we'll find out. But real life is too busy out there. They have too many distractions; college, exams, business, promotion, marriage, spending money, eating, drinking, clothes! Even the students don't have time to turn around. Can you see a student cramming for university entrance exams finding time to browse through the *Book of Mormon*?"

"Maybe that's why personal contacts are important. We have to bring them to church, talk to them, answer their questions."

"Really I'm looking forward to this, Jake. We're going to see something totally new."

"But you see what gets to me. You see all of these religions and there are so many and they're all so different. It makes me wonder how on earth there can ... I mean, how can it be that so many peo-ple are on the wrong track?"

"Yeah, even the Christians. There are dozens of them all arguing over something or other."

"I wish they would just listen to us. You know. Just look at the *Book of Mormon*, you know. It speaks for itself. I mean we're not telling them to reject the Bible or Jesus or anything. We're just saying, 'We have something to complete the Bible, the missing link, the fulfillment of the Gospel.' Otherwise how can they explain some of the prophecies?"

"Truth is, Jake, a lot of people are happy with the way things are. They don't want to be bothered with something new."

"You know what I think? I think they're threatened by it. They're thinking, 'maybe there's something in this Mormon thing.' You just can't explain away all those testimonies and the scriptures. They're just afraid of the truth staring them in the face."

"I guess that's why they tell us to witness students, before they get set in their ways."

Jake went to bed disturbed that night by the books he had read. How was he going to get to the Japanese with their Buddhist ideas? They didn't believe in God. How was he going to square that with the Shinto thing? It reminded him a bit of Native American Indians. He had once seen a beautiful documentary about what they believed. There were pictures of fields of corn waving in the breeze with a beautiful blue sky in the background. They were said to worship the spirit in nature which was divided between all living things. An old man sat serenely by a cedar tree and said, 'Can you not tell? The trees have spirits.' The Shinto philosophy was similar in that it was the worship of the forces of nature, with prayers to the different gods to bring you this or that, or to protect you from something. But it seemed too worldly, the way they used it. For example a college student might pray to one spirit to help him get through his exams and he would spend the rest of his life making components in a factory and what would he put into life? Or a girl might pray that one or other boy might fall in love with her even though he might have a rotten character. Human beings could barely see past first base half the time and they sometimes made stupid requests. For Saints it was better to wait and see where the Father wanted you to go, and do His will even though it might seem like the hardest thing at the time. Some Japanese would pray for a lot of money so that they could throw it all away on immorality. That wasn't religion in the truest sense. Where was the guiding light? After this reflection, Jake decided to concentrate on helping the Japanese see this new religion as a way of helping them make better choices which would bring them a better life here and in the next world. He fell asleep as he pondered on his strategies for opening the Japanese mind.

The remaining days of training put the students under increasing pressure to improve their Japanese, work out missionary strategies, and really have points of doctrine down pat. In scripture class, they had gone through tailor-made responses to the most common questions that usually cropped up in the history of the missions. With a patient smile or a condescending chuckle, they would deflect the favourite objections. 'But I heard Joseph Smith made it all up?' 'Well, if he had had that much genius, I'm sure he would have ruled the world. I don't think he would have spent his time painstakingly translating scripture.' Or, 'Wasn't Joseph Smith a gold-digger?' or, 'Didn't he have dozens of wives?' Questions like these were more common amongst Europeans or Australians who were more familiar with Mormon controversies. The arguments in the US had led to misconceptions and difficulties in other places, but countries like Japan were largely uncorrupted by anti-Mormon propaganda. The Japanese were more likely to object to the banning of alcohol or caffeine, or to raise questions about life after death or simply the existence of God. There were also Japanese Christians who would needed convincing of the differences, as for example, in the questions of the definitions of trinity and Christ as creator, or the ability of all people to become gods. There were points to emphasize, especially to romantic young women, such as the doctrine of eternal marriage; and for the bereaved who were concerned for their loved ones there was the concept of retrospective conversion. The psychology teacher again and again talked about the disillusionment of the youth; how they were, many of them, searching for the meaning of life, and he cited the figures of conversion to New Religious Movements, both home-grown Buddhist ones and American-based movements. He kept drumming into them, "You young men are armed with the most valuable thing in the world. The TRUTH. Are you going to bury it under a bushel? No! God has elected you to go out and spread it to all nations."

The same rousing message was echoed in the assemblies during the last week, which were held in training centres throughout the state. The students relished the chance to get out and visit new places and meet the other missionaries who were to be posted all over the world. The graduation ceremonies were high-spirited, joyful events aimed at filling the missionaries with zeal and high morale. They were allowed to invite two family members each, and the ceremony would start with prayers, then songs followed by a rallying cry from the centre president in the form of exhortations and anecdotes from generations of past missionaries. Next was the prize-giving for those trainees who had excelled in different fields. Especially important was the prize for language achievement; when this had been awarded the winner would deliver a short speech in his new language. Jake had never felt so proud as when he witnessed these sessions. It was a testimony to the power of the church that they could take so many young men, turn them around, and have them fluent in such a variety of languages within months. He was convinced that the same power given to the disciples of Jesus to speak in tongues was now radiating down through the ordinary people on the ground. How else could so many young guys end up fluent in Spanish, Mandarin, Russian, Hindi and all those other languages?

The sub-Saharan Africa training centre had its ceremony first, and when Jake entered the room what struck him first was the calm atmosphere. The audience was arranged in rows. One section was a sea of crisp, white, short-sleeved shirts and brown or blond heads with the very occasional jet-black or Afro head interspersed. Each trainee held a copy of the order of ceremony on his lap. Each one had the familiar name badge. So uniform! The guests were seated in the other sections. Most of the men wore the same white shirts and grey slacks and most of the women had on floral print dresses with white or blue cardigans. Jake had known of some LDS girls from his school, and some girls his sister knew, who had rebelled against this homey, feminine image. They would dress down in jeans and sweat-shirts and cut their hair in plain, spiky styles. They despised the prissy, floral look. Sure enough, when they had grown up and started thinking about marriage, they would go through the inevitable transformation. Plain sweat-shirts grew flowers and designs, then turned into blouses. Jeans mutated into stylish slacks and then plain skirts, gradually getting more flared, more floral, and the parents and elders would smile because they had seen it all before. The rebels always came back home with their tails between their legs.

Jake took a seat next to a student from the eastern European section. He introduced himself with a firm handshake.

"Where's your posting, Brother Eric?" asked Jake.

"Poland."

"That's neat. How's your Polish?"

"Not bad. It wasn't as bad as I thought it would be. We had a really good language teacher."

"Same here. If you'd have told me last year I'd be speaking Japanese by the end of this year, I would never have believed it."

"Japan? Wow. I guess that will be something of a culture shock."

"Yeah, the people maybe are real different but the business culture and the city life is supposed to be pretty much the same."

"But everything will be in Chinese. How will you know where you're going?"

"They say in Nagoya the signs are also in English and we get to learn a few Chinese characters. Anyway, how do you feel about Poland? I heard it's all state-run shops and nothing on the shelves."

"I think it's changing a bit. I'm curious to know what it's really like. Our professor says the streets and buildings are grey on the whole but the houses are real nice and the people are warm, pretty intellectual too. He said they all read a lot because there's nothing on TV, and no good movies or magazines, so they rely a lot on books. Many of them are crazy to get out of Poland and go travel-ling, so they welcome foreigners pretty much. I think we'll be able to get the message across. Most of them are Catholic, so it won't be so new. What about Japan. Are they Buddhist?"

"It's a mixture of Buddhism and Shinto out there. So yeah, reli-gious-wise, they're on a different planet, but they said in training that a lot of young people there are searching for a more meaning-ful faith."

The hubbub of the talk died down gradually as the missionary-training President took the stage. Jake craned his neck to look for his friends scattered among the audience.. They had been told to sit next to missionaries from the European section to get to know each other and share experiences. The President's speech was meant to make them feel proud and full of fervour to go and spread the message.

"If Joseph Smith and Brigham Young could be here today, they would be so proud to see all you young men in the prime of your lives, sacrificing two years to go and do God's work. The Church of Jesus Christ of Latter Day Saints is strong in all corners of the world, thanks to people like you. You are the footsoldiers of the Church. Australians join hands with Africans who join hands with Europeans and on throughout the world thanks to you. Thanks to you, there will hardly be a household in the world which hasn't at some time or another seen the familiar pair walking up the pathway, asking them to open their Bible, urging them to listen to the Gospel in all its fullness, reassuring them that the Lord has wonderful things in store for those who heed his word."

They were reminded of the need to stick to the rules and the discipline of the mission, for their own safety. They were warned about getting into dialogue with intellectuals, politicians, religious leaders and unnecessarily deep conversations with students. As the familiar refrain went. 'You are out of your depth with these people'. Loss of faith was the most tragic consequence of ignoring the advice of one's superiors. Some people may be capable of enticing missionaries away from the faith, their home, their family and church 'and you know what's most tragic of all?' said the President. 'Your chance of eternal life.'

The speech went on, warning of some of the disappointments, but stressing the rewards of a missionary career. They would all come back better, wiser men, more useful members of the church, more successful in business and better prepared to head families. The President ended on a rousing note and then the hall resounded with hymns.

The graduation ceremonies filled the whole week. Jake's section was scheduled for the Thursday. All the students were a little disappointed because they had hoped to leave with their families that day, but they were duty-bound to attend the last meeting of the week at the European section.

"I'm sick of this soldier, soldier talk," complained Bruce as they were getting ready for the day ahead. "You've seen one of these jamborees, you've seen them all. It's not as if we don't meet up with the same guys all week."

"I'm kind of interested in the European one though," said Jake as he began folding some of his things neatly into his suitcase. "I was talking to a guy who was going to Poland and there were another two going to Romania."

"Can you imagine?" said Dave. "A poor East European country! What are they going to eat out there? Dumplings and cabbage I guess."

"This guy Eric said the bad food is only in restaurants. The home-cooked food is supposed to be great. He said you walk into a restaurant out there and nobody moves. The waitresses all kinda sit around staring at you," said Jake.

"You'd think they didn't want customers," said Dave.

"Well they get paid anyway whether customers come or not so they couldn't care less whether you get served or not," said Bruce. "I heard in Russia everyone has to have a job because there's no unemployment, so you get two old ladies sitting at each end of the escalator, knitting."

"What's their job?" asked Lewis amazed.

"Just sitting there checking no-one gets hurt or fools around on the escalator. Most of the time they just gossip and do their knitting."

"You wanna job, Bruce?" said Jake.

"What?"

"You wanna pick up your stuff off the floor. We have to share a room in Japan and I'm not cleaning up after you."

Bruce gathered up his clothes and flung them at Jake, and an impromptu pillow fight broke out. Jake gave up, his face flushed; he sat panting on the edge of the bed. Bruce put a fatherly arm around his shoulders and said in a crooning voice, "Now Jake, you and I are going to be bosom pals in Japan. You know you can tell me anything. I'm here to support you and answer all your questions. The deal is, you do all the housework."

Jake retaliated by hitting Bruce into submission with the pillow.

"OK, we go halves," he cried, and they all made their way down to breakfast.

The day was spent preparing for the ceremony. Some were assigned to setting up the hall, others to preparing food. Some of the prizewinners had speeches to learn. There was a lot of general cleaning to be done. Jake found himself on one of the cleaning teams in the classrooms with another trainee called Greg.

"It's Europe tomorrow night, right?" he asked

"Uh huh."

"Is Turkey in Europe or Asia?"

"Asia, isn't it?"

"I thought Turkey was in Europe. My brother went travelling there the summer before his junior year and I thought he said Europe."

"I know they had Turkey in the Middle East section the other day."

"That's why I wondered. I guess it's because they're Moslem, but Jeff said they're just like the Italians. They don't wear all black and they sell beer and wine and have bars and everything."

"Do they speak Arabic?"

"No, Turkish. He said they have mosques though."

"Do they pray five times a day?"

"I think the old guys do. The young guys are into music and partying and movies."

"I think we're lucky going to Japan. Everyone says we're gonna have an easy time. Looks like a beautiful country too."

"Yeah, I wanna get in some touring if possible. Do you think we get to go on trips?"

"They say so but we have to go in groups or with Japanese church members."

The atmosphere was getting tense by the evening as everyone struggled to get ready and to get packed to leave because they would have a full day on Friday. The first job after changing into fresh shirts was to greet their guests. Jake stood apprehensively in the lobby. He hadn't been in the awkward position of choosing between a parent or his fiancée because his mom had been invited anyway as she worked in the administration section of the church which dealt with mission arrangements. She came through the door with Jake's dad and Alice, her arms outstretched to hug him. He didn't have to worry about being embarrassed in the general throng of hugging and cooing which was going on around him.

"Jake, we're so proud," said his mother, already tearful. His mother was easily given to tears at anything mildly cute or moving.

"Mom," said Jake. "If you're crying now, what will you be like at the prize-giving?"

"I know," she said smiling shyly. "But I'm just so proud."

Jake was the second in the family to go on mission. His brother had been sent to Argentina.

"You're looking good, Jake," said his father, slapping a manly hand on his shoulder. "How's it going?"

"Pretty good. We've learned a lot. Now I just can't wait to get out there and put it into practice."

"Son, it will be the best time in your life. It's all downhill after that," said his father shaking his head and then hugging his wife as he saw her disappointed expression; "until you get married of course," he added. He winked at Alice, who managed a wan smile.

"So this is where you've been hiding, Jake," she said.

The fiancées were expected to play the role of spurring on their men-folk to the challenges ahead, just like war-wives and fiancées who would send their men to war, assuring them they'd be patient and wait for them to get back, and at the same time fearful to see them going off to do their duty for their country, or, in this case, for their Lord.

The ceremony went without a hitch but was noticeably lacklustre, falling as it did before the end of the week, and the missionaries themselves had become a little fatigued by the endless repetition. The families, however, enjoyed it and it was, in any case, largely for their benefit. The prize-givings were also something special for the students. A trainee called Frank won the language prize and he gave a little speech about the significance of Mount Fuji to the Japanese and as a symbol of Japan. As always everyone was impressed by his grasp of the language, and for those who had no idea of languages it was something awesome.

Alice seemed very impressed later on, as she and Jake chatted over the buffet.

"Can you speak like that guy?"

"Pretty much," said Jake.

"Say something then!"

"Oh, people always ask you that. I can't just say something. It wouldn't sound natural."

"Say anything. Go on Jake. Don't be embarrassed."

"What do you want me to say?"

"Anything that comes to mind."

"Ah, *Watashi wa Nihon e ikimasu.*"

Alice beamed. "What does it mean?"

"I'm going to Japan."

"We know that Jake."

"Well you said to say anything!"

They were both distracted by one of the trainees called Ken. His sister was speaking loudly. "Everyone asks this and I know they get sick of it, but why are there no women missionaries?"

"There are too women missionaries," Jake chipped in.

"Yeah, but how many?" she protested. "A fraction of the group."

"No, more and more sisters are wanting to go to the missions," said Ken.

"I know, but it's so male-dominated. I mean look at this evening. We had row upon row of guys and I didn't see a single woman there."

"It's these women she's been mixing with at college," said Ken apologetically to Jake.

"If you don't ask questions, nothing changes," she said, embarrassed by her brother.

"The fact is," said Jake, "the missionaries sometimes find themselves in difficult situations and most of it, day to day, is tedious stuff; you know, walking from place to place."

Alice said, "Once they bring someone to church, especially if it's a woman, then there are plenty of sisters to greet her. I mean I agree with you. It wouldn't work if they only relied on male missionaries to get female converts."

"They need female role-models," said Ruth, "but what I'm jealous of is all that travelling. You guys get to see all those exotic places while we stay at home and bake cookies."

"You've never baked a cookie in your life," Ken burst out.

"OK," she said. "Well, you know, do whatever we do."

"Stay on the phone and EAT cookies," he teased.

None of the students was able to concentrate on Friday as the winding-down process began, which was really a winding-up process from the previous night. All their class teachers tied up any loose ends and then sent them on their way with further pep talks. Jake was beginning to feel hazy about where one subject began and another finished, but they were advised to internalize all the psychology and culture they had done and now concentrate on the application of the techniques they had learned, constantly going over them and practicing them in Japanese. Mr Sakimoto was especially concerned that in the week's vacation before the departure much could fall by the wayside.

"You have to practice every day," he urged. "Listen to your cassettes and those of you who get Japanese radio stations, tune in! *Gambatte!*" he said finally with a benevolent smile. These were his charges. He felt for them because he knew what they were up against, how even if they were fluent, their all-American looks would present a brick wall in the mind of the Japanese listener which stood against communication. But there had been many who had gone before them and had won over some souls, so again he said, "*Gambatte kudasai*," which roughly translated means, 'Please, try your best.'

On Saturday morning Jake was so caught up in the flurry of departure that he forgot to say goodbye to Bruce. Bruce's parents had stayed overnight nearby so as to take him home straight after the meeting on Friday. It suddenly stuck him that when they would meet again, it would be in Japan. The thrill of it struck him all at once, and filled him with a slight sense of panic. He had a responsibility. His first real job, in fact; and he would have to manage in a completely foreign country. It was then that he remembered his meeting with the President and his panic subsided as he thought about the organization. There would be people to cushion him at every step; there would be the reassuring comfort of dorm life and the church enveloping his own existence, the familiarity of his faith which would buoy him up wherever he was. It was all God's world, whether you lived in Utah or Nagoya, the same faith held you up. It was like railroad tracks which kept you on a straight path wherever you happened to be. This is what he explained to President Michaels when he was asking him how he felt now that his mission was imminent, and what he had learned in his training. He seemed reassured at Jake's optimism.

"You have a good attitude, Brother Jake. You know we'll depend on you to keep the other guys going. I've seen a lot of young men pass through this place and they fall into two categories, the doers and the dead-weights. You're a doer and I know you're going places. Sure to be something good come out of this, Jake, when you come back from Japan, if you live up to your mission."

"I always pray I'll do that, sir."

"About the dead-weights; we're also counting on you to keep Brother Bruce in check. He's your partner. We don't take the pairing-off of missionaries lightly. A lot of thought goes into it, so I guess you understand that you carry the bulk of the responsibility here. Do you understand Jake?"

"Yes, sir. I'm sure Brother Bruce will make progress once we get going."

President Michaels stood up to shake Jake's hand. "Well! Guaranteed I'll be praying for you all that you have a wonderful mission and that you make us all very proud."

The good-byes at the centre were excited and disbelieving, amid cries of "See you in Japan" and "See you in Nagoya." Many of the missionaries had never been overseas before. "*Sayonara, Sayonara*. Have a good vacation. See you in Japan."

唯邑

Salt Lake City, Utah

Jake had decided to spend as much of his vacation week as possible with his family. He tried to savour family meals and their regular family conference because he knew that this would be what he would miss most during dorm life. It was good to choose any room in the house and chat to whoever was there, knowing you belonged anywhere you chose and were always welcome. At other times it was good to go back to his own room to think. Both his sisters still lived at home, and although his older brother lived near his work he was coming for his farewell dinner. One of his favourite parts of the house was the breakfast bar where he would talk to his mother, while other family members drifted in and out, joining in the conversation. He sat eating potato chips while his mother made the dinner. She had been asking about Japanese food and what he was going to live on, and she told him to fill up on bread. She carried on chopping for a while, and then she spoke more quietly, without looking up.

"You seeing Alice this week?"

"Sure."

"Oh I'm so glad." She looked up at him. "She was on the phone to me yesterday wondering if you'd said anything. She figured you'd been so busy getting ready but I said you'd been hanging about the house and that you'd be sure and call her to invite her over."

"You mean before the farewell dinner?"

"Well Jake," she said alarmed, "surely you're going to want to spend some time alone before you go. You won't see her for a whole year."

"I wanted to take it easy though mom, this week, you know, hang out at home, spend time with you and dad."

"Oh, but we don't expect you to spend all day with us."

Lisa breezed in. "What's this?" she asked.

"I'm just asking Jake whether he's made time for Alice this week before he goes. You know Jake, she'll be real disappointed if you don't call."

"You mean he's not gonna call her?" asked Lisa. "He's going away for a year and he forgets to call his fiancée?"

"I already said she's coming to the dinner, so why don't you get off my back? Sorry Mom but I have a lot of preparation, mental preparation. It's important."

"OK Jake, if this is important for your mission, but I'm just telling you what she said to me on the phone. Maybe you can straighten it out with her on Thursday."

The solitude of his room beckoned and Jake excused himself.

"He's gone to meditate," said his sister in hushed tones, "and contemplate the universe before he embarks on his grand mission."

"Don't mock your brother please," said his mother. "Dinner in thirty minutes."

The farewell dinner was a disaster. Jake's mother had gone to a lot of trouble to decorate the table and to plan a special menu. She had been working for two days to get everything ready, and as he packed and withdrew often to his room, Jake's contemplative mood was taken for sulking. His father had told him to snap out of it and grew angry at him for not offering to help his mother with the preparations. As usual, his mother had not complained but had been carried away with her hectic plans. She had always taken domestic duties upon her own shoulders, treating any offer of help as an extra favour rather than as something expected. This had the effect of making all the family more willing to help. Their father was more rigorous about instilling a sense of duty, and he enforced a strict roster of chores. He was always telling his wife to relax and let the children take over the chores, but she was only happy in the hub of the house. Except during family meetings and when receiving guests, Jake had rarely seen her in the living-room. Her habitual place was literally in front of the kitchen sink. For his dad, it was either on the phone or behind a newspaper. Theirs was a big rambling house and although the children had grown up sharing their rooms, now the boys were older they had been given rooms of their own. Their parents were convinced it made for closer relationships if young children shared a room, and they didn't approve of typical non-Mormon families which featured a phone, TV and video in each bedroom. As it was, there was a private line for their father and one other phone which often ended up in the girls' room since Lisa was at the stage of going over the highlights of the day with her school friends half an hour after they'd parted. None of them had a TV set in their rooms and their dad was always trying to get them to spend time in the living-room. He had been a little disappointed that the in-depth conversations, going over emotions and relationships, that he had read about in church magazines, had never materialized. He would sometimes switch off the TV, put down his paper and ask one of them if anything was on their mind. They would say, 'No dad; can you put the TV back on please', or it would be a trigger for them to head for the door. Again his wife's laid-back style ensured that most of the children ended up pouring their feelings out in the kitchen. She was also the sounding-board for the concerns of all her children's contemporaries. It was sometimes difficult for Ray Carter to come to terms with his jealousy of her easy relationship with young people when it was he who tried so hard. He had read all the books on child development and relationships and had taken part in all the family dynamics workshops at church. He had been hurt once when Frank had accused him of doing everything by the rule book. He had told him to lighten up and get some spontaneity into his life. That was the hardest thing about faith. It gave you a sense of responsibility, so that you had to think ahead before every action and weigh it up. You couldn't do anything carelessly. If you had a divine guide, you knew the right course to follow. There was no feeling your way as you went along, as was the case with people who had no faith. It seemed all cut and dried, no dilemmas; comforting in one way, in another, boring.

The atmosphere was already strained as they sat round the table and joined hands while Jake said grace. There were the immediate family, his father's two brothers, wives and three of their children, a couple from down the block and two of Jake's school-friends, John and Lawrence, and seated directly opposite him, with the longest face, was Alice. She had said 'hello' to Jake in a clipped tone and had gone off to sit with his sister while his mom tried to jolly everyone along. Jake was angry that she hadn't even tried to hide her feelings for the evening so as not to spoil the dinner. Even his uncle Bob, who was a jovial and boisterous character, was chastened by the tense vibrations of an argument radiating round the table. He slurped his soup with a forlorn expression scanning the others for signs of explanation.

John cleared his throat. "So Jake, you must be kinda nervous."

"Yeah, nervous and excited. Now it's nearly here, I'm anxious to get going."

Glares from Alice.

"Well," he faltered, "you know the build-up is so long, what with the training session and all."

"Where's it you're going?" asked Aunt Jane, Bob's wife.

"It's Nagoya," said Jake, "there are two mission homes there."

"Na- what?" said Bob laughing. This brought a round of polite laughter.

"Nagoya," he repeated painstakingly. "It's on the Pacific about two hours south of Tokyo."

"We drop any bombs there?" asked Bob. This time nobody laughed.

"Bad taste, Bob," said Jake's dad.

"Oh, I'm sorry. Guess I don't know a whole lot about Japan."

"Jake speaks wonderful Japanese," said his mom, covering up the embarrassment.

"Oh, say something Jake," said Cindy, his cousin.

"What do you want me to say?"

"Oh, anything, whatever comes to mind."

"My mind's a blank at the moment."

"Oh come on Jake," said his mom. "you were chattering away to me yesterday in the kitchen."

"Um, *watashi wa Nihon e ikimasu.*"

"What does it mean?" said Cindy excitedly.

"I'm going to Japan."

"That was the exact same sentence you said to me," said Alice.

"So, Jake. You're caught out. Admit it!" said Frank. "You've been using the same sentence over and over, making out you were speaking fluently."

Jake smiled.

"You know they used to have Japanese characters in the old

war movies," said Jake's dad, "who were played by Chinese and I heard they would just have them repeat some nonsense word so it sounded like they were speaking, but it wasn't Japanese at all."

"I could never speak a foreign language," marvelled Cindy, gazing in wonder at Jake.

"It's not so difficult, Cindy," snapped Alice. "All the missionaries who get sent abroad learn foreign languages. What's special about Japanese?"

"Japanese is so difficult though," said Cindy. "I mean all those symbols and everything."

"They only learn to speak it," said Alice dismissively, parroting Jake's explanation to her "and it's just like Italian. They hardly learn any Chinese characters and anyway Japanese has two really simple alphabets also which are easy to learn."

"Sounds like you've been studying Japanese too," said Aunt Kay.

"No, I just told her some stuff about my training," said Jake stiffly.

Before Alice had a chance to retort, Jake's mother selected her and two of the others for the kitchen team to bring in the main course. The bustle of the passing of plates glossed over the hostile behaviour from Alice, but Cindy whispered to her sister, "She's kind of a bitch, isn't she?"

"I guess they had an argument. She keeps looking daggers at him."

"Yes, but she doesn't have to put him down in front of everyone on his farewell night."

Alice sensed they were talking about her and banged a bowl of salad in front of them.

"She's probably upset he's going away," said Laura.

"Weird way of showing it. If that was me and Tom, I'd be crying. He'd be crying."

"Yeah but Tom's not LDS. He's not likely to be sent away."

"Ssh, don't broadcast it, Laura!"

Alice seemed to calm down a little after what seemed to have been some concerned words from Jake's mother in the kitchen. The party went through the roast chicken stuffed with hazelnuts and the mood was lightened by the comfort of full stomachs. Now people had broken into little conversations around the table, and the gaping silences had eased a little. Jake politely fielded questions about Japan. Normally he relished being the resident Japan expert, but that evening he was upset and confused, knowing he might leave with an unresolved argument hanging over him.

During dessert the conversations went on and tailed off one by one until only Cindy's quiet voice could be heard.

"I don't know how he can stand anyone so clingy." She froze and coughed. Alice had realized they were still talking about her.

"If people are so rude to gossip about people at the table, why don't they just come right out and say it to my face?"

"I'm sorry Alice," said Cindy quietly trying to stop her making a scene. But Alice had decided that now a scene had arisen she might as well take it to its conclusion.

"Everyone is sitting here trying to act so darned polite and I am having the most awful time and Jake knows what it's all about, so let him tell you." She shoved her chair away and ran off to Lisa and Joanne's room now crying openly.

"I think she's a little upset because Jake is leaving," said Jake's Mum soothingly. "Jake! Joanne! Go on up and see to Alice."

Jake was relieved to be excused from the table but not to see Alice.

"You go Joanne! See if she's OK, I'll go to my room."

"Oh no, Jake. You've got to face the music. Come on!"

They went in to find Alice sitting sniffing on the bed.

Joanne put her arm around her. "Alice, I'm so sorry to see you so upset. Is it because Jake's leaving?"

Jake stood awkwardly by the bed.

"He knows why I'm upset."

"I guess it's because I didn't call her this week."

"Talk to ME, Jake," said Alice angrily. "I don't need an interpreter. We're not in Japan now."

"I know, I know. I haven't called this week and you were worried you weren't going to see me before I go."

"Excuse me for wanting to see you," she said sarcastically. "I guess I come after your whole family and all your school friends. You see Jake, being your fiancée, I just thought for a moment you might want to see me before you go."

"Alice, I've been so busy getting ready."

"He hasn't, Alice. He's been moping around the house. Jake! You could have found time to call."

"Oh thanks for the big favour," said Alice. "like you could find an hour in your busy schedule."

The sarcasm failed to hide the fact that Alice had good reason to be hurt. All the signs pointed to an unwillingness on Jake's part to see her, and she knew it. They cleared it up with apologies but Alice felt no better. Her fears that Jake's mind was far from her had found confirmation. Emotionally he had already upped and left. She would only see him at the airport. Jake was relieved to get out of the room. Alice felt a glimmer of hope when Joanne told her that his behaviour was a result of his denial that he was actually leaving. Since he could not bring himself to say goodbye, he would keep putting it off and putting it off until it was too late. Joanne loved to read books about psychology and fancied herself as something of an amateur therapist, so her words comforted Alice enough for her to be coaxed back to the table where everyone was trying to pretend nothing had happened. The party broke up as soon after dessert as was polite, when the initiative of John making motions to leave allowed the whole party to agree that it was getting late and that Jake had a lot of packing to do and they had a busy day tomorrow. Jake could imagine the conversations on the way home as he stood by the door receiving hugs and handshakes and good wishes and 'be sure to write's.

The next day was Jake's real good-bye day and he enjoyed it immensely because it was spent in everyday familiarity with the whole family at home, with neighbours dropping in all day to wish him well. His brother and sisters took turns accompanying him in his room watching him pack, and most of the conversations were about family affairs, local affairs and church affairs, all home territory. It was therapeutic to consolidate the memories and substance of his homebase life to feel safe enough to leave it. Today there was not much talk of Japan, of anticipation or speculation, but solid reflection, and this was exactly what he needed. He had time with his mom in the kitchen as usual and she was thoughtful enough not to mention Alice. Instead they talked about pleasant mundane things like all the clothes he had gathered and never thrown out and stories of the baggage the girls had taken to summer camp and the baggage she had taken on her first, long trip when she went to the east coast with her husband when they were first married. Jake even spent a dutiful hour sitting in the living room with his father. He knew that would mean a lot to him, seeking him out without waiting for his dad to have to come and ask him to sit for a talk. Predictably, he talked about other missionaries he had known and how they had all come back much more worthwhile people.

The meal they had that evening was the real farewell dinner for Jake. The row with Alice ensured that her parents had decided not to invite him for dinner on his last night. Instead, the meal of pasta with water to drink contrasting with the previous night's lavish meal put Jake in mind of a Hebrew proverb he had once heard, 'Better a dinner of herbs where love is than a roasted ox and hate therein.'

唯邑

Interlude

The long-awaited departure from the airport was finally upon them. Jake now had an unreal sense that he was actually leaving his cosy, familiar world for something very far away and very alien. Salt Lake City airport was a regular witness to the missionary farewell and homecoming committees. All around the hall stood well-groomed young men with short haircuts surrounded by huge groups of fussing relatives, rearranging their clothes, kissing them, hugging them, wiping their eyes and then all standing back stiffly after the final hug, lest another hug would mean he would never leave them, then tearful waves: 'We love you. God bless you. Be good!' Then the missionary, looking suddenly very young and vulnerable, would walk off to join the group of departing missionaries like a schoolboy on his first day at school. As Jake pulled away from his mother and they exchanged the final waves, he was struck by the realization that faith was indeed demanding. If he hadn't been Mormon he wouldn't have to fulfill this duty. He could have stayed in his comfortable environment and only travel for pleasure; but the nostalgic feeling was almost instantly pushed aside by a sense of endeavour, of rising to a challenge, which hit Jake as he joined the group and they surged forward through the barrier.

No-one spoke as the plane took off. Each dwelt in his own thoughts, for once not embarrassed to turn away and let the tears sting the eyes. This time they knew few of them would hold back the tears. Jake looked down at the stark symmetry of Salt Lake City, home of God's true church. "I'll bring some lost sheep back to you," he whispered. Take-off is always an emotional experience, a time for reflection, but as soon as the 'ping ping!' sounds the mood changes. Take-off is the past reflecting on the unknown future. Flight is purposeful, cheerful and at times unbearably boring.

So now Jake sat back with a copy of *Time,* resolved to find out something about the state of the world he was flying across. There was an article about Far Eastern companies. It explained that Japan was still very reluctant to open her markets to foreign goods and had still managed to retain a very big slice of the export cake in Europe and the US. Now she was on the lookout for new markets in Africa and the Middle East. Just recently the Japanese had had their noses put out of joint by the up-and-coming 'tiger economies', especially Singapore and Taiwan which with their populations of worker-bees and scarce national resources had realized the Japanese were onto a good thing and sought to emulate their mass-production export of consumer goods. Jake looked up from the article and thought how his dad and his friends were always complaining together about US markets being flooded with Japanese cars, and his dad had said that the traditional American car manufacturers were struggling. This was why he and his friends had always made a point of buying American. Nothing annoyed his father more than getting home with something he'd bought from a store only to find the label 'Made in Taiwan' on the back of it. 'Don't we make anything in America anymore?' he would groan. But Jake's generation was not so hung up on consumer patriotism. They were only too well aware how well-made many Asian products were. In California, he knew that shops in San Francisco were largely stocked with Hong Kong imports and the names had become as familiar as US brand names. He was pleased, though, that Japan had taken a liking to what the US did best: good food, fast, and at low prices. That apart, he was excited to be going to the land of Honda, Hitachi, Nissan, Sony: all those names which had become common currency, not least among the young.

They came down to earth on arrival at Los Angeles. For many who had been backwards and forwards to the west coast before, this was no more thrilling than a bus ride, but at least they were on their way. Home was already far behind. Their supervisor Brother Simmons told them not to underestimate the distance they had travelled and to thank God they could now do it in comfort. He told them to think of the first Mormons who were driven out of New York and migrated first to Illinois and then on to Utah. They had had to do it the hard way and it was thanks to them that the faith had been saved for posterity and brought to their generation. The missionaries, however, were not in the mood for sermons and barged their way off the plane to make their connection. Some of the Californians were meeting them at L.A., while Jake's room-mates were flying out of San Francisco. The L.A. missionaries came through with red faces, fresh from their last good-byes. The Utah missionaries were by now in boisterous mood and were teasing them, so they withdrew to reflect for a while while the others horsed around.

The next plane provided more of a party atmosphere because it was large and spacious and packed with people. Some of them looked to be Japanese-Americans and many others were Japanese-Japanese returning home after vacations in the US. There were several honeymoon couples. California had become a popular destination for honeymooners in recent years, superseding the tra-ditional destination of Hawaii. Some were even known to go as far afield as Australia. The strangest thing was that these Japanese travelled in large groups and followed meticulously scheduled tours with provision even for romantic candle-lit meals for two with all the other forty-nine couples. This was a most unusual arrangement in the judgment of American observers and the cause of much hilarity, but for the Japanese, the safest route was the one trodden before you and they weren't in the least embarrassed.

This time, as the plane took off, Jake already felt as though he was on his way. He felt a comfortable pang of pride as the American coastline swept into view and spiralled away, and then there was nothing to break the vision but stretches of ocean flecked with surf and dotted with miniature vessels. From such a distance the world looked so fragile and its inhabitants had dwin-dled into invisibility. Jake had a comforting realization that the route to Japan was almost entirely across the ocean so that if there was a crash, they'd be more likely to survive, and he actually paid attention to the life-vest demonstration.

The missionaries sat in small groups chatting and going over their arrival manuals. Some were testing their Japanese on the pas-sengers.

"We should get into missionary practice right here," said Lawrence. "They're sitting ducks."

"Now, I don't want you bothering anyone on the plane," said Brother Simmons. "They're on vacation so let them relax."

"Can't we talk at all?" asked Jason, disappointed.

"Sure! And you can answer questions about the faith if they ask, but don't witness them here. Take it easy! Some of them could be Americans."

The couple across from Jason looked eager to talk and he was bursting to practice his Japanese.

"*Anata wa Nihonjin desu ka?*"

Bursts of giggles from the Japanese bride.

"Yes we are from Japan," said her husband in clear English with a slight American twang. "Your Japanese is very good."

Jason glowed. "*Doko ni ikimasu ka?*"

By now the woman was in awe saying to her husband, 'He speaks Japanese, doesn't he?' but her husband was just as determined to show off his English.

"Ah we are returning to Japan, Yokohama actually."

"Ah Yokohama," said Jason knowingly.

"You know Yokohama?"

"No this is my first time in Japan," said Jason forgetting himself and going back into English.

They carried on asking about each other. By this time the young woman had joined in, asking her husband for a translation at each sentence and speaking through him to Jason in Japanese.

"Ask him if he's married," she said.

"No I'm not married," laughed Jason in Japanese. He had suddenly realized that in this three-way conversation, the one thing they had in common was Japanese. The guy's English was quite good but his wife couldn't speak any. So why didn't the guy respond in Japanese? He was baffled until he remembered that Mr Sakimoto had told them that Japanese people would be as eager to practice their English on *gaigin* as the other way around. The Japanese man signalled the end of the conversation with a practiced handshake and a very polite nod.

"It has been very nice to speak to you, Mr Jason, and we wish you good stay in Japan."

"Thank you," stammered Jason, taken aback by the rather formal end to their conversation. His neighbours had been listening in, impressed, and were eager to hear what he'd been saying.

"He wouldn't speak to me in Japanese though even though his wife couldn't understand."

"Yeah but remember how Professor Chalmers said that women take a back seat and are sometimes embarrassed to speak directly to foreigners," said Greg.

"I guess so," said Jason. "Did you hear my Japanese?" He was naturally proud of his first live attempts.

"Way to go, Jason!" they said, patting him on the back.

The Japanese couple seemed amused that the group was discussing their conversation, and gave friendly smiles and waves. Meanwhile Joe and Richard had made the mistake of starting up conversations in Japanese with their neighbours.

"Are you Japanese?" their neighbours asked sarcastically.

"No, of course not."

"Then why are you speaking Japanese? Never seen a Japanese-American before?" they said.

They apologized but were rather upset by their attitude.

"They must get a little tired of it, though," said Andy. "Everywhere they go at home they're taken as foreigners and when they go to their parents' country, everyone thinks they're Japanese."

"Yeah, they'll probably never feel accepted as Americans," said Jake.

"That's going to be us in Japan," said Andy. "No matter how good our Japanese is we will never be fully accepted in Japan."

"Yeah, but in Japan there's only one ethnic group," said Jason. "America is called the melting-pot. No one feels like an outsider in the States because everyone is an outsider."

"Yeah, but there is a dominant group which people think of when they think of America," said Jake. "We conform and Orientals don't. It's a hard fact but it's true."

"It may be true in Utah, small town boy!" said Vincent, "but you take a walk through downtown L.A. one day and tell them who's American."

Jake went quiet. Since mixing with Californians and East Coast people he had begun to feel a bit provincial. He had started to wonder whether his window on the world was maybe a bit narrow. He tried to read widely to gain the whole perspective; *Time, Newsweek, Washington Post, Herald Tribune*; but Mormon life, especially in Salt Lake City, was pretty much restricted to a uniform group and a lot of time was taken up with church activities.

Everyone had grown tired of small-talk in Japanese and the meal offered a welcome change. Nothing remotely Japanese yet on the menu though, perhaps because they were still closer to the US, so they had steak and French-fried potatoes with peas. On the few occasions when Jake had eaten airline meals, he had always enjoyed leaving his tray really orderly for the flight attendant, finishing up every scrap, putting the knife and fork back on the tray with the foil on top and arranging all the waste paper neatly in a cup. Even hearing from a friend of his sister whose own sister was a flight attendant for All-American Airlines that they just threw everything into one bin didn't stop his compulsion. He was smug as he looked at Jason's messy tray of half-eaten, mauled food with paper spilling over and juice spilled. Another thing he had heard from the same girl was that it was common to go into the flight cabin of any plane and find the crew dozing. The faint hum of the engine, along with the warmth and darkness and gentle motion, would lull them all to sleep. This was no cause for panic though, because any deviation from the computerized flight path would set off an alarm to wake up the crew. Other than that, piloting was so tedious that most pilots were hard-pressed to keep awake. Now the whole jet was growing quiet as the crew had designated this 'airplane night-time' and Jake welcomed the chance to sleep away some of the boredom of this, his longest flight.

Crossing the date-line had made the night fairly short and soon he was being jolted awake by the sound of the breakfast cart. The disagreeable sensation of a dry mouth and nostrils and the unpleasant fug of recycled air made it a rude awakening. Jake's eyes were aching from lack of proper sleep and his neck was stiff from lolling to the side. The breakfast was most unwelcome so soon after dinner, and only the juice revived him.

"We should have put out 'Do Not Disturb' signs," groaned Andy.

"Do they have to be so regimented?" said Vincent kneeling up over his seat. "Breakfast at 4 am?"

"Get used to it!" said Greg, fresh from the bathroom. "We gotta get up early every day in Japan." His huge teeth were gleaming. It was true that Mormons had massive, glossy teeth, and after brushing they looked even glossier.

"I'm about ready for the movie," said Jason gathering his earphones.

The movie, which was one of the *Batman* series, kept them occupied for two happy hours, and after lunch, which seemed to overload the stomach after the last two meals, Japan seemed a little nearer, but not near enough for them to get excited. They seemed to have flown back and forth in time. The sun would be gloriously rising above the clouds and within a couple of hours they would be flying through streaks of pink and purple sunset. The view from the window really did look like heaven. This was how Jake imagined heaven to be, and he thought how beautiful and awesome it must be in reality, when even the sky on earth was so fantastic. He tuned in to some classical music which seemed to go with his dreamy mood.

But after an hour Jake reached crisis point, a kind of despair where you realize there's still a few hours to go. You feel cramped in your seat. Your neighbour's asleep. There's nothing to eat, no movie and you don't feel like reading. He couldn't squeeze past Andy to stretch his legs. He flipped through the radio channels but lacked the patience to tune in for more than a minute. He looked out of the window: nothing but Pacific blue. He gazed around the cabin, which was a sea of gaping mouths and lolling heads. He started to scream inside for something to break the boredom. He had been looking forward to the trip for so long, when he would be actually be on his way, but he forgot that he would have to endure these cramped, idle hours. International jet-set travel was not as glamorous as its advertising.

At last the endless tedium came to an end as the cabin started to stir and the gift cart arrived. One of the missionaries was kidding around asking the others for drinks orders and got a disapproving glare from Brother Simmons. It was strange for Jake to be in an environment where alcohol was the accepted thing, because all his life he had been very much shielded from it, having always lived and worked in a church environment. It depressed him as he saw the Japanese passengers revive themselves from their haggard naps with bottles of whiskey and other spirits, even the young people and the women too. He had been told Japanese women rarely drank. He did not like, either, the change in atmosphere as the hitherto polite people started lurching across to talk to the missionaries again. Brother Simmons raised a restraining hand, as one older Japanese man was weaving his way to Richard's seat to talk to them.

"I'm so sorry sir, but these young men have to prepare for an important meeting when we land. Thank you so much."

The Japanese man retreated with apologetic bows and the missionaries were glad to have been saved.

"Never converse with drunks," said Brother Simmons in a low voice. "It's not worth it and you don't get anywhere."

唯壱

Tokyo, Japan

At last they were nearing Japan. Bright noonday sunshine was warming the cabin and a snake of people was waiting for the bathroom to prepare for arrival. All the young Japanese women had jumped up at once and were daintily clutching their toiletries and hair-brushes, although their thick, dark manes had hardly a hair out of place. Some of the passengers were already seizing their luggage and barging forward to the front, only to stand in the aisles weighed down with bags, until they were told to return to their seats for landing. By now all the missionaries' eyes were glued to the window as they watched Japan coming into view. It didn't look so exotic, a bit like Canada really. The Legoland of grey buildings grew bigger and bigger until they were level with the airport buildings; then thump! thump! rattle! and that moment of tension on landing when you prepare to crash, followed by the reassuring taxiing. Jake saw his first Japanese person on Japanese soil, in a neat, blue uniform with a cap signaling to the plane. 'Konichi wa!' was Jake's greeting of the man through the glass, and he wondered how many other people did likewise. The ground staff at airports had the unique position of providing the very first impression for visitors to their country.

The impatient passengers couldn't contain themselves as they grabbed their luggage and ran to the exits, only to be held up again. The missionaries were told to stay seated until the clamour had passed, after which they made their orderly exit feeling rather special as they walked together in their group of identically outfitted young men into the arrivals area, where they became the subject of many an excited dig in the ribs and giggles from passing Japanese. Most of the missionaries were too mesmerized by the scene to feel self-conscious. None of them had ever been to a place which was dominated by another ethnic group. They had all grown up in white American suburbs; the nearest most of them had got to this was the Chinese quarter of L.A.

"So many Japanese!" said Richard in awe.

"Yeah Richard. Like we are in Japan," replied Jason.

"But this is the airport," said Jake puzzled.

"Yes, a Japanese airport," said Jason as if talking to a child.

"But you would think it would be a bit multi-national, you know people coming and going from vacation, visitors, tourists. It's like we're the only tourists."

"We're not tourists," said Jason.

"There's one!" said Richard pointing excitedly as they glided along the travelator. Gliding the other way was a back-packer, a tourist who would probably have called himself a traveller. He glanced at them in disdain and showed contempt at Richard's friendly wave. Travellers did not like to be reminded of home, and certainly did not have any affinity with the likes of Mormon missionaries.

"Well how do ya like that?" said Richard, nonplussed. "Do you call that rude or what?"

"Do Japanese tourists all wave at each other in L.A.?" said Jason.

"No, but like we were saying. He's about the only other foreigner in the airport."

They laughed at how odd it was to talk of themselves as foreigners.

"Anyway we're *gaigin*," confirmed Jake, "officially, from today, *gaigin*."

As they came to the 'aliens' channel at passport control, and the mirth surrounding 'alien' jokes had died down, their eyes began to settle on the other aliens. There seemed to be a few more travellers, mostly scruffy backpackers with the deepest tans and a practiced air about them. The groups of young women that they would have taken for Japanese were actually Filipinas. They were all agog at the handsome, young Americans behind them in the line. Each of them had a little vanity case and a folder. They all looked young and seemed to stick together as if afraid of losing one another. Their leader was a swaggering man with a tight, curly perm and sunglasses and a rather bored expression. He exchanged words with the official and the girls were waved through. They followed each other like a flock of geese chattering.

"You see those girls?" said Lawrence, in the know. The others listened expectantly. "They're all from the Philippines."

"Yeah Lawrence we kinda guessed," said Jason sarcastically, "when we saw they were all carrying Filipino passports."

"Yeah but do you know who they are?" asked Lawrence mysteriously.

"College students, I guess, on a trip," said Richard.

"No, they're hostesses."

"What, you mean flight attendants?"

"No, they work in bars as hostesses. They're bussed in from poor countries to work as cheap labour in Japanese bars and restaurants. They're locked up and they can only go out with their minders." Lawrence's story was interrupted as he reached the passport official, but Elder Simmons had done the paperwork and they, like the Filipina girls, were waved through in a group.

Jake felt a little envious of the travellers, who seemed so independent and free-spirited. They dealt with their own paperwork, and could go where they wanted when they wanted. But the downside must be the struggle to find accommodation in a very foreign country, and places to eat and ways of getting around. Jake's group had it all laid on. Nothing to worry about; just follow the leader, like a school-trip. He regretted, just slightly, that the challenge was not theirs. 'Maybe on future trips,' he wondered, 'I'll get to be my own boss.' A picture of him taking Alice and their future children on vacation flashed through his mind and he quickly dismissed it, catching up with Lawrence's tales of the Japanese mafia.

"Where did you hear all this?" asked Jason.

"A book on the Japanese mafia," said Lawrence, a little exasperated at their air of scepticism. "Apparently, they have their fingers in a lot of pies and they're involved on politics and corruption and all."

"So what's new?" said Jason.

"Well, let me get back to the point of the story. These girls have a really hard time. They can't escape. They can't talk to anybody. They have to work real hard. Sometimes they don't even get paid at all to support their poor families back home."

Jake was saddened to hear the plight of the cheery-looking Filipinas. "We should try to help them if we come across any," he said earnestly.

"Yeah, bring them into church," said Richard.

"No, Jake" said Brother Simmons catching the tail end of the conversation. "If those girls have chosen that kind of life, it's up to them to get themselves out of it. Now, everyone follow me!"

The group trailed after him, snaking through the crowds of Japanese passengers, each accompanied by an upright suitcase on wheels. Not a hair out of place, not a scuffed shoe; the Japanese all looked like they had read the same catalogue on impeccable, designer leisurewear, and had bought their luggage at the same store. Brother Simmons explained, hearing a remark from Sean about the identical suitcases, that this was to save space which was at a premium in the crowded airport, especially during certain times of the year, because the Japanese took many of their five-day holidays at the same times in summer and at New Year. The Japanese certainly seemed neat and orderly as they darted this way and that, wheeling their bags before them.

"OK now," said Brother Simmons, rounding up the group. "We're about to get a bus into Tokyo. It's a fairly long trip, so if you need to visit the bathroom or get some snacks, do it now!"

Jake heard the word snacks and rushed to the nearest kiosk to find something to sustain him on the bus. He was confronted with an array of odd-looking, jelly-like objects in plastic sachets. The potato chips looked OK and there were M&Ms, Hersheys and a few unfamiliar-looking chocolates. On the whole, there was no brand recognition. At home your eyes homed in instantly on your favourite products. Here there was no way of deciphering, but he was here to gain new experiences and to learn about a new culture, so he plumped for a packet of M&Ms and one of the jelly-like snacks.

Richard was his neighbour on the bus. He had had to throw away his can of drink because he thought it was juice and it turned out to be iced coffee. 'In a can? Can you believe it?' he said. Richard looked disapprovingly at Jake as he pulled out his jelly snack.

"Decided to try the local delicacies," said Jake popping it into his mouth.

Richard watched to see his face change and saw Jake surreptitiously spit it out. He laughed. "Tasty, huh?"

"It's like dried squid or something. It tastes fishy. Too rubbery for me." But he was pleased he had eaten his first Japanese food. He had really made up his mind not to be narrow-minded about Japan. He would learn from these people and try to share in their culture.

The landscape so far impressed him. Plenty of low mountains; very green and lush, and they had passed dozens of fields. He had heard Tokyo was all high-rise and cramped flats but this seemed to be open country. Archetypal paddy workers in sun hats were bent over the fields working by hand. Jake tried to drink in everything so that he would always remember it. 'So this is Japan,' he thought. In some ways it looked completely different. One strange thing was driving on the left. That was the weirdest sensation, especially at intersections. In other ways, if you passed a stretch of open country with pylons, it could be Utah itself. But now Jake was wondering what the city would bring.

The approach to Tokyo was easy to spot because the tower blocks grew denser and and the jumble of neon was quite dazzling to the eye. Strangely, the sky looked lower. This struck Jake because at home in Utah, the sky was big, but now suddenly, going into Tokyo, it seemed to hang very low and very dull. This sky worried him, made him feel a little claustrophobic and very aware of his breathing. They were drawn closer to the centre, and the spaces between the buildings shrank, until they were in the middle of Tokyo. The neon signs were now incredibly dense and garish. People thronged the streets, many of them carrying fashionable shopping bags. Here and there Jake's eye caught an English word which stood out from what was still a jumble of Japanese for him. He couldn't imagine a day when he'd be able to decipher it.

The missionaries, who had been dozing through the country-side, were now alert and trying to get any clues they could from the new landscape as to what their lives were going to be like here. The majority of the Japanese men wore short-sleeved white shirts and suit pants while the women were in short dresses or skirt suits; but occasionally one would see a man in a smock-like jacket with characters on it, or an old lady would wear a kimono held by a large cummerbund. Then one of the missionaries would cry, 'Hey!

Check out the real Japanese lady.' 'Did you see how bent she was? She looked like a hunchback.'

"That's from years of working in the fields," explained Brother Simmons. Now the whole bus was hushed to hear words of wisdom from the only Japan veteran amongst them. Although Brother Simmons had only been coming to Japan for three years, he was deputy President of one of the Tokyo wards and it was his job to accompany the main group, guide them through their initiation and then dispatch them to their various destinations. The new missionaries arriving today would be sent to all the major Japanese cities, but their arrival meeting and orientation were to be held in Tokyo.

They pulled up in front of the LDS complex, a little way out of the centre of Tokyo. It felt like a pleasant suburb lined by rows of small shops: almost a villagey atmosphere after the neon jungle they had just crossed. As they descended from the bus a welcoming group of missionaries and locals greeted them with a traditional Japanese greeting - '*Bansai!*' - Ten Thousand Years, as they raised their arms in the air.

The newcomers were self-conscious as they filed into the hall. Jake was disappointed because everything reminded him of the ceremonies at training but he checked himself. Same faith. Same church. There were bound to be similarities, but he could see by the faces of the others that they too experienced their arrival as an anticlimax. Jake brightened when he heard that his friends had already arrived from San Francisco and were sleeping. He was eager to swap impressions with them. A very young Japanese woman passed around a tray of juice and pretzels as the missionaries settled down to meet the mission President. They all stood up as he came into the room, and began to clap as he made his way up to the rostrum. This had a little of the atmosphere of a political rally. Brother Francis turned out to have a very clipped way of talking.

"Gentlemen! Brother Francis! Good evening! Good News!" (pause for effect) "we're all members of the one true church on earth!" (Applause.) "You want more good news?"

"Yes!"

"We're gonna spread that truth all over Japan!"

Cheers and applause.

"Are you with me?"

"Yes!"

"Louder!"

"Yes!"

"You want more good news?"

"Yes!"

"I'm gonna be brief because I know you're tired."

Cheers resounded round the room.

His tone took on a more serious edge. "I want you to know that you are all very welcome here. The Lord sent you here to spread the fullness of the Gospel in this far corner of the globe. Are you with me?"

"Yes!"

"You are welcome here because soon you'll all be part of our family and we are a very close family here in Japan, and we in Tokyo keep a very close eye on all our brethren here and in other cities. We want you to know that any question you have, any worry, any fear, will be answered right here by our good brothers all around Japan. We know you've left families behind, so we want to be your family now. That's how it is, my young friends, that the church of Jesus Christ of Latter Day Saints in Japan is such a success and has remained that way. When you leave here we want you to leave your mark. What's that? Ten, twenty, thirty more new members lined up at our church doors on Sunday mornings, the blessed *Book of Mormon* sitting in thousands more Japanese homes, right next to the little shrine they have there. My young friends, seize this opportunity because it is precious and it goes fast! God bless you."

He had left them in a contemplative state of mind as he came to the end of the speech. Suddenly he snapped them out of their reveries. "Dinner and bed, in that order. Sister Masako!" he barked, and the juice and pretzel lady scurried forward with submissive nods, showing them the way to the dining area.

"Please, Please, Welcome, Please!"

"Will you look at this," said Jason as they were led into the dining hall, "No tatami, no cushions, no chopsticks. Are we in Japan?"

Sister Masako hovered at the door looking concerned at Jason's outburst. She had imagined he was extremely hungry and wanted to eat right away. She was used to the tired travellers arriving at the dining-hall fresh from the USA expecting efficiency and familiar surroundings.

"Dinner very soon," she said.

Jason quickly reassured her. "I'm sorry. Oh no I didn't mean that. I was just expecting chopsticks."

Masako looked confused.

"*O hashi?*" he tried to make the sign for chopsticks with his hands but Masako was none the wiser and she excused herself quickly.

"*Chotto matte kudasai*," she said.

"I know what she said," crowed Andy.

"Wait a minute!" chimed in four of the others.

They ate their meal in a desultory mood. None of them was hungry after the back-to-back meals they'd had on the plane, and fatigue was starting to make them feel sick.

"At least we got rice," said Jason as he toyed with the meatballs and peas.

"They'll ease us in slowly with the Japanese food, I guess," said Vincent.

They were shown to their rooms. For the first night Jake was to share with Richard, Jason and Lawrence. After that he would move in with his own friends and colleagues for the rest of the induction period. He was looking forward to seeing them. He was glad he took time to freshen up before sleeping. The others just hit the beds without even brushing their teeth. They would probably feel lousy in the morning. One of the wardens who showed them to their room gave them their instructions.

"No talking from now please. You can sleep as long as you like and you will not be disturbed. If anyone wakes up early, he must on no account disturb the others but must leave the room and come to the common area. You are excused prayers tonight."

They were too tired to talk. Jake experienced the bliss of every weary jet-lagged traveller, to lie flat at last and rest his head. He fell into a delicious and profound sleep which was the sweeter for knowing he wouldn't have to get up till he was ready.

Jake was horrified to wake up and find he'd slept all night and into the following afternoon. He sat up in bed in shock and saw the shape of Richard still in his bed. The others were gone. There was something quite depressing about having missed a large part of the day, and knowing that in only a few hours it would be dark again. Jake went to the window and saw a few apartment blocks opposite with bedding draped over all the railings. Above the buildings was that sky again, very low, grey and ominous.

Lewis, Bruce and Dave were playing pool in the leisure room when Jake went to find them. There was a round of friendly slaps on the back and greetings in Japanese. So far they found the place crowded and colourless. They too had been struck by the lack of foreigners. For Dave it was quite an experience to find a place where he could at last blend in totally even though he didn't feel like one of them inside. He just knew that on the outside he was one of the majority. But he hadn't felt some irresistible pull from his roots or a mystical sense of belonging or anything like that. Jake remembered a guy from school, Patrick, who had Irish grandparents. He had gone on a trip to Ireland one summer and described the overwhelming feeling of going back to the old country and sensing a pull of blood-roots as if he was returning to his spiritual home. He was very struck by the experience and had tried to stay there and make a living, but there was nothing in the Galway village for young people, and finally he went the way of many young Irish - to America.

"Did you get the 'You with me' speech from the President?" said Bruce with that ironic expression on his face he used when he wondered if you were thinking what he was thinking.

"Yeah," said Jake. "the usual rousing stuff but I thought the end of it was good: 'you're all part of the family' and everything."

"He's gonna start the orientation tonight," said Dave circling the table to size up a shot.

"Are we gonna get some free time?" said Bruce. "I wanna go see something."

"We can't go out till after orientation, but we have Wednesday off before we go to Nagoya. I'm going to see my folks," said Dave. "How about you guys?"

"Well we got no folks to see," said Lewis, "so I guess we'll make do with sight-seeing."

"They're organizing an all day sight-seeing tour," said Jake. I'd like to take in a few sights before we leave."

"We don't have to go with all the guys," moaned Bruce. "Come on! Have a bit of adventure. Break away from the pack and come for a real tour of Tokyo with your uncle Bruce!"

"You mean Bruce, the ace tour guide," said Jake with derision. "His first week in Tokyo and he's gonna take us around."

"Well. I want to see what I'm interested in and explore a little, maybe meet some locals."

"Anyway," said Lewis, " you probably won't get permission to go alone."

"What about Dave?"

"I had permission already," said Dave. "They're picking me up at the centre anyway so I don't have to figure out the subway by myself."

"Rules, rules!" said Bruce with a sigh and missed his shot. He tossed his cue aside in exasperation. "Game over!"

"Oh, Bruce!" they wailed, as he scattered all the balls.

By now all the groups had arrived and all but two of the newcomers had slept off their jet lag and had enjoyed a high-spirited dinner. By special request they had been allowed to sit on the floor and use chopsticks, although most of them had gone back to forks. There had already been a few 'shoe mishaps' with people forgetting to remove their shoes at the right place or forgetting the toilet slippers or worse, coming back into the dining-hall with the toilet slippers on, to the great amusement of the Japanese staff. The staff were already amused to see the young men squatting around the room in groups on a dusty floor while their comfortable chairs sat empty.

"You know Japanese many times sit on chair," explained Kumora-san, Masako's assistant. He beckoned them towards the chairs.

"That's OK sir," said Jason. "We wanted a change." Seeing Kumora's blank expression he tried to think of the word for 'change' but was lost, so he just said, *"Daijobu desu* - OK!" Kumora was impressed.

"Your Japanese is very good."

Jason gave him a weak smile and sat down. "So why not speak

to me in Japanese?" he said to the others. "What is it with these people? They refuse to speak Japanese to us."

"They look at the head," said Dave, "and they just can't figure out how Japanese words are coming out, so they just ignore it. They're so used to seeing *gaigin* in the movies speaking English."

"Anyway, how does he know your Japanese is good?" said Richard. "You only said two words."

"Exactly."

"I think they just want to flatter you," said Dave.

"Uh Uh!" said Bruce. "They just don't want you to learn any more Japanese."

Jake was surprised how quickly they had begun talking about 'them', the Japanese, and making generalizations. He was determined not to fall into this trap but to take them as individuals. Perhaps it was actually because they'd just arrived that they saw the Japanese *en masse* as 'them'. Maybe later it would be different when they began to get to know people. He had been watching Sister Masako's earnest running about, checking everything was OK for them and doing various errands for the President and his team. She seemed very sweet and eager to please. Jake hoped that was the influence of her faith.

The President's grand welcome speech washed over most of them as now they were fully accustomed to the rallying rhetoric. They heard his account of the dedication of the local Temple in 1980, but what they were really interested in were practical details about their immediate future. They had a full day's training ahead including plenty of practical work. Most of them were interested to hear the experiences of the missionaries who had already been there for a year. They also had more language classes scheduled, plus meetings with Japanese church members who were to describe their experiences. The programme even included a couple of sessions in the gym; this, the President reminded them, 'because the body is ...?'

The audience finished the phrase, 'the temple of the soul'.

The most tedious part of the evening was the introductions of the senior Japanese church members in order of rank. They went on to give lengthy speeches in mumbled Japanese about their careers and identical messages of welcome and encouragement.

"Satisfied Jason?" said Lawrence. "Enough Japanese now?"

Jason was nonplussed. "But I didn't catch more than two words. This is serious guys! We're supposed to know this language."

Jake had just concentrated on the speakers' faces and mannerisms, which was easier when you weren't distracted by the message. The speakers seemed barely to move their lips and their expressions remained quite impassive. Occasionally, they would jerk their head to emphasize a point but their arms never left the lectern. The tedium was only broken by a slightly more lively staff member who bounced onto the stage with a jovial grin, his red face beaded with sweat. He swept his hair to one side nervously.

"Hi! I'm Yamamoto," he said in rather slurred English with a slight American accent. "Pleased to meet you. I am so honoured to meet you freshmen here at the church of Latter Day Saints in Tokyo. Welcome to my city. You will be welcome in my city. I hope you feel very relax and happy feeling here in Tokyo. I attended Toyama University in 1972 and joined Mitsubishi Heavy Industries in 1976 as production line supervisor in the aeronautical engineering department."

The audience felt stultified by his blow-by-blow account of his engineering career. Jake knew that Japanese men, especially, defined themselves in terms of their position in the career hierarchy and in relation to the company, which nine times out of ten would carry them through their working lives. Yamamoto's perception of becoming a Mormon was explained in the same dispassionate way. "I joined in 19 so-and-so, entered the order of the Aaronic priesthood in such-and-such a year," without reference to any change of heart and soul. Maybe he thought it was not appropriate in front of such a large group, but Jake hoped the witnessing of other converts in the next few days would be more revealing. By the end of his speech, Yamamoto was bathed in sweat and obviously relieved for his ordeal to be over. Even President Francis was showing signs of fatigue.

"Gentlemen! You may be a little surprised at tonight's proceedings, but this is the Japanese way of doing things, and when in Japan ...?" He stopped, actually expecting a reply. After a few seconds silence the audience cottoned on and finished: "Do as the

Japanese do!"

Francis had this strange technique of going for audience partici-pation at regular intervals. It was probably to keep them awake through the stream of live resumés that they were required to listen to.

"Send it on a postcard!" droned Bruce as the last and most jun-ior church member listed the highlights of his life from Kyoto University to junior salesman at Kansei Securities. So far all the speakers had been salarymen rather than the much talked about drifting students who were supposed to be their prime targets. Most of them had joined the church after starting with a company. They seemed to talk of it as a useful parallel to their developing careers. Jake wondered how committed they really were, whether they put the church first, and whether they tried to get other con-verts from amongst their colleagues.

At last the scene changed as a spotlight was trained on the stage and an old man in a brown kimono appeared, sitting behind a Japanese harp or *Koto*. There was a hum of anticipation as he started his song. At last, something authentic and Japanese! Jason was delighted. The first few minutes of the mournful, high-pitched song were stirring, and the audience were happy to have some-thing different, but as the song went on there was more and more shuffling in seats, light coughing and surreptitious glances at watches. When would it ever end? The man would pause and they would prepare to clap, enthusiasm rekindled as it drew to an end, but then the man would launch off again into further warbling verses. This was an epic. Then suddenly, instead of tailing off like songs they were used to, he ended with an abrupt sound, some-thing like '*uh chah*!' Had he finished? It was too much to hope, but now he sat back with a serene smile on his face and the room burst into applause, not so much of appreciation as relief that it was over.

"What is this?" said Lewis as they were leaving for their rooms. "Lessons in boredom or something? I thought those guys would go on and on; and that musician!"

"That was an epic Japanese love poem," said Jason, "which ended in tragedy."

"It would have ended in tragedy if he'd gone on much longer," said Bruce. As usual he was clowning around imitating the musician, singing in nonsense syllables with long pauses followed by shrieking wails. The tension of the evening was long gone.

In the Japanese lesson they were really put through their paces, and the teacher, Mrs Watanabe, spoke only Japanese. They had graduated to a more advanced course designed for English-speaking businessmen which was to continue during their mission. They all enjoyed the introduction to written Japanese and were told to memorize the syllabic alphabets by the next day. These alphabets, *hiragana* and *katakana*, were used to write Japanese in conjunction with Chinese characters. They were surprisingly easy to learn and the missionaries were very proud as they deciphered their first Japanese words. The *katakana* was used to write foreign words borrowed by Japanese, of which there were now many, as Japanese had become westernized in a very short space of time and had imported countless words for the new concepts, not all of them used in an identical way to English. The teacher tested them by giving them syllables and getting them to say the word. It took a little getting used to, but the trick was to say the syllables quickly and the words would come out. This was because the syllabic system broke up all consonant clusters so that *st* became *suta*. The missionaries were puzzling over '*sutoresu*' and finally Andy got it. 'Stress!' he shouted and this led to the rest of the group catching on to 'McDonald's' as '*Macudonarudu*' and 'ice-cream' as '*isukurimu*' and 'price' as '*purisu*'. The other alphabet was used for Japanese words, especially grammatical endings. Jake was excited to find that he could read one of the words on the sign opposite his window: 'something *biru*'. '*Biru*' was 'building'. He looked forward to the day when all these signs would be meaningful to him. This is what it must be like for illiterate people, he thought. He had once seen a programme about a woman who couldn't read or write, who battled daily to chart her course through a society of written words. Nearly all these people shared a deep sense of shame about their illiteracy and had developed elaborate ways of hiding it, for example by learning the shapes of common words or pretending they had something in their eye when the time came to write. At least we've got a good excuse, thought Jake. Still, he was glad to know that many signs in Tokyo were also written in English.

The meetings with Japanese converts did not prove to be much more inspiring than the speeches they had heard the night before. There were no emotional testimonies of 'the *Book of Mormon* changed my life' variety, as were to be heard in the States, no grateful tales of the debauched and drunken sinner at last finding the true way and turning his life around. Most of the converts had led pretty blameless lives before joining the church. Some of them were women, who did not drink anyway, whilst two of the men said they only drank half a beer on company occasions to please the boss.

"You mean before you joined the church?" said Lawrence.

"No I used to drink a lot then. Now I have half a beer because if not, my boss get very angry."

The missionaries were shocked. "You mean you still drink alcohol?" asked Jake.

Brother Simmons cut in. "I don't think these young gentlemen realize the pressure on some of our Japanese brethren, trying to live the life of a Mormon whilst working in companies. As Brother Moriyama says, it is very impolite in Japanese to refuse a drink, especially when one is trying to impress clients."

"But the church is more important, surely!" Jake protested.

"All in our own good time," said Simmons.

One young woman, Sister Fujimora, seemed to be spiritually involved in the church in a way that wasn't apparent in the others. She explained in a soft, faltering voice how she had earnestly prayed to God to let her know if the *Book of Mormon* was true and he had answered her prayers. When she woke up, she felt what she described as a light feeling in her heart. She had opened her book randomly at any page and the word that lay under her finger as she opened her eyes was 'truth'. She had obviously been very moved by what she felt was a miracle. Later, on her way to work as a receptionist at the Sumitomo Bank (her career details were not left out), she decided that if she saw a *gaigin* coming out of the subway as she went in, she would commit herself to the church. The innocent *gaigin* who strolled out of the subway as she went in was unaware that he was the omen that changed her life. She proudly showed the page of her *Book of Mormon* with the word 'truth' highlighted in fluorescent pen. What was more impressive were her notes and other underlinings which showed evidence of serious study.

"My dream is to go to Utah," she announced.

Jake's heart went out to her as he thanked God for the blessing of having been born there. He was impressed with her studious attitude and obvious piety. The miraculous stories like this had sustained his faith at times when some people had tried to shake his faith with accusations and lies against Joseph Smith. He remembered the outcry that had arisen after the publication of a book called *The God Makers* written by ex-members of the church. His dad had been the first to hear about it and had tried to shield them from it, but one gentile from school had started taunting some of the Mormons with it. What upset Jake most was that anything that cast doubt on the person of Joseph Smith also undermined the scriptures he had received and thus the whole edifice of the church. He had prayed to God for a sign on his way home from school and it happened. He was walking along, deep in thought, when he heard a car stopping behind him. A smiling man offered him a map.

"Son! You couldn't give us directions, could you? We're looking for the Temple."

He gave them directions and was curious to know where the two couples were from.

"We've come all the way from Australia," they said. "You couldn't believe how we dreamed about this place and now we can hardly believe God has brought us here."

They explained how they were going to the ceremony to have their marriages sealed, so that according to Mormon doctrine their marriage would be valid in heaven. Jake was reeling with joy because as far as he was concerned, this was the sign he had prayed for. People wouldn't come all the way from Australia to visit a church that was built on sand. They wouldn't dream about going to a church unless they believed it was the true church of Christ and they had obviously been convinced of the authenticity of the *Book of Mormon*. As the elders had told them so many times, no one except a man inspired could have written such a book, and although they had never seen Joseph Smith, they were prepared to pledge themselves to his word and base their whole life and future life on it. It was that important. This was why calumny against

Joseph Smith hurt Jake so much.

To diffuse the rumours that were going around, they had special church meetings where the elders explained how the authors of the book had a grudge against the church and were so bitter that they had tried to destroy it, but the elders assured them that no-one can succeed in destroying God's word. They said that if anyone wanted to read about the life of Joseph Smith they had all the information at their fingertips. Many of the things Smith had been commanded to do by God were very difficult for him, but were very necessary amid the conditions of hardship they had faced; and didn't he build a godly community at Nauvoo where the people prospered, and weren't his revelations dynamic enough to have him killed, and wasn't Brigham Young devoted enough to carry the torch and build the wonderful church that now spanned the world? As usual, the comforting words of the elders had calmed Jake's fears and made him feel confident in his faith and eager to carry it into the world.

It seemed that Sister Fujimora had had an impact on the group because there was a pensive peace in the room when she had finished talking.

"I think Sister Fujimora has given us a lot to think about and reflect on," said Brother Simmons graciously. "We need more people like you, Ma'am, to support the church here in Tokyo."

She smiled shyly and sat with the others giving quick, apologetic nods to the class. One thing that Jake had noticed about the few Japanese women he had seen so far was their rather apologetic stance: those deft little bows when they came in or went out of a room or needed to reach across you for something. He was rather embarrassed whenever Sister Masako brought in the food or cleared away the plates because she seemed to apologize for breathing or even disturbing them. Most of them, having been brought up in large families, were used to helping clear the table, but she seemed mortified if one of them tried to stack the plates.

"*Sumimasen ii desu,*" she would say as she hurried to gather the plates.

"She doesn't have to apologize for doing us a favour," said Jason under his breath, but Masako was only comfortable if allowed to carry on her duties without being acknowledged.

After the morning of lessons on Tuesday most of the missionaries were itching to get out. Since the weather was fine they were allowed to have lunch in a nearby park. There was a very pleasant atmosphere down in the park with salarymen arranged on benches around the place, reading a newspaper or just dozing. Their counterparts, the office ladies, were sitting in rows enjoying their coffee and laughing girlishly. They wore neat, identical uniforms. There were also groups of hugely fat schoolgirls scoffing doughnuts to their hearts' content. The missionaries were surprised because they had been led to believe that Japanese girls were all very slight. Sister Masako and Sister Fujimora explained that schoolgirls could enjoy life and get as fat as blimps, snacking after school every day, but before they joined companies and thus became potential marriage partners, they had to go on crash diets and most office ladies ate like birds. The office ladies opposite, sure enough, were eating dainty sandwiches from a lunch-box, glancing surreptitiously in their direction, obviously wondering why the two Japanese women were sitting with such a large group of *gaigin* men. It seemed that the salary men were regulars at the park across from the missionary centre because they showed no signs of surprise.

"Now you see," said Bruce eyeing the school-girls, "they've picked up all our bad habits. Would ya look at those doughnuts."

"Yeah, I didn't know Japanese people could get so fat," said Richard.

"You know the Japanese diet is the most healthy in the world," said Dave with authority. "Not much fat, little protein, enough starch every day. Lots of fresh vegetables and fresh fish. That's why some of the oldest people in the world are Japanese."

"Unfortunately," said Brother Simmons, "the diet is slowly changing in favour of western fast food, and heart disease is on the increase. Oh yes, given the choice, most of those schoolgirls would choose Burger City for lunch."

"It has one advantage," said Sister Fujimora, who reddened when she realized they were all listening to her, "the average height is increasing."

It was true that many of the schoolboys seemed to tower over the middle-aged men. Some of them were very tall even by American standards. The schoolboys looked like old-fashioned sailors as they were all wearing black trousers and tunics with brass buttons and high collars. Some of them sported caps like the postmen wore. They were all identical. It seemed a bizarre way for schoolkids to dress. The schoolgirls were also identical in blue and white nautical uniforms, all with the same glossy, jet black hair, the salary men all in white, short-sleeved shirts and grey or black slacks. So uniform! It made it easier to tell which category of society each person fitted into. Even the middle-aged housewives, who may have chosen a different colour or design for their outfits, did not stray outside certain conventions of dress. Jake liked the uniformity. He felt comfortable as if he knew what to expect from people. He felt very comfortable in the park and he tried to work out why. It seemed to be because everyone was sitting in their own space, not infringing on anyone else's territory. Nobody was bothering anyone else or even watching anyone else. They were all engrossed in their own little group or newspaper. Jake explained this to Lewis, and David Fromer, a missionary from New York, overheard them.

"Yeah, I mean, have you ever seen a park in New York? Every kind of weirdo feels free to come over and hassle you. You got people on skates colliding all over the place, winos falling over each other, junkies selling their stuff ..."

"Religious nuts selling their stuff," quipped Bruce. The missionaries laughed and put up their hands saying "Guilty!"

"Yeah, you know what I mean," David went on, "like personal space and all that stuff, you can forget it here."

Jake reminded them of a lecture that Brother Owen had given about Japanese culture. He had talked about the lack of private space in Japanese life. Young children slept in their parents' room until about the age of five and many families all slept in the same room. Apartments were small, especially in Tokyo. In the workspace, ninety-nine percent of people worked in an open-plan office with nothing more than half a desk to call their own. Even managers did not shut themselves off into private rooms as they did in America, but sat amongst their juniors. Much of life went on in crowded subways or shopping centres. Solitude was rare but not sought after. They seemed happy with this lifestyle, quite self-contained. Maybe this was why they were such masters at remaining inside their own space wherever they were.

The missionaries finished their lunch-boxes. These were called *o bento*, traditional Japanese lunch-boxes with individual compartments containing a variety of things. It was strange that they were eating wholesome rice, egg, fish and pickles, while the Japanese were tucking into American food, except for two construction workers nearby who also had lunch-boxes. Even the construction workers were perfectly turned out in tan overalls, with not a speck of dust or grime on them. Jake felt as though he had landed in a model village where you could dress up the characters and have them walk around or sit down. Everyone was so immaculate. It was something outsiders often said about Mormons, especially in Salt Lake City. He heard one guy on the radio once say that Mormons reminded him of robots. They were so perfect, they seemed unreal. Every last one clean, healthy and fit and dressed in immaculate suits all going about their business in an orderly fashion. Jake was proud of this image though it embarrassed some, and this was one reason why he was already beginning to feel at home in Tokyo.

The rest of the day passed easily after the refreshing outdoor lunch. Most of the missionaries were in a frivolous mood, full of anticipation of the time when they would be sent out in the field. They spent the evening in the leisure room playing pool and eating potato chips trying to make sense of Japanese TV. So far the evening's entertainment had been back-to-back game shows.

"Isn't it just like home?" said Andy.

"Yeah, but they don't have so many commercials," said David.

Jason was straining to listen above the chatter in the room. "You guys!" he said exasperated. "I'm trying to work this out."

"I can't understand a word," said Bruce gawping at the screen. "It really does sound like *aso! aso! aso!*"

"Maybe if we listen every night," said Jake, "we'll get it."

"Watch game shows every night?" said Jason, as another panel of young, smiling Japanese contestants ran onto the screen, waving.

The missionaries found the air quite humid. All day there had been a rather unpleasant, clammy sort of heat and a low-lying sun was pressed against the now familiar, low, grey clouds. In fact, Jake had hardly even seen the clouds themselves. It seemed that in Tokyo there was a sky below the sky. Smog was the only explanation because even the tops of some buildings were hidden and despite the heat, the sun was always blurred. Sister Masako had told them the rainy season was approaching, which would break the humidity, but this was the most inconvenient time of year for the Japanese. The dull humidity brought night-time insomnia.

"Jake! Are you awake?" Bruce's voice shot through the restless silence.

"No!"

"Ha, Ha! I can't sleep."

"Neither can I. It's the heat. It's really getting to me. I feel I need a shower all the time."

"Hope it's not gonna be like this in Nagoya."

"They say it's hotter in Nagoya."

"You're kidding."

They tossed and turned for a while longer, each aware that the other was suffering from insomnia and probably wanted to talk.

"It must be nearly four by now."

"No it's only 2:30."

"You're kidding. What can we do to send ourselves to sleep?"

"Read the *Book of Mormon*?"

"Jake!" said Bruce in mock horror.

"Oh I didn't mean it like that. It's just the church says it's a good thing to do if you can't sleep at night, to get out the *Book of Mormon* and read. It's the best way to fill time."

Bruce envied Jake's attachment to the faith a little, and thought that perhaps some of his piety might rub off on him. "OK go ahead! You read."

Jake was surprised. He hadn't expected Bruce to be so interested, so he sat up and began to read, trying to read in a meaningful voice so that Bruce could get the full impact of the words.

And it came to pass that this man did cry unto the multitude that they might turn and look. And behold there was power given unto them and they did turn and look and they did behold the faces of Nephi and Lehi.

And they said unto the man, Behold what do all these things mean and who is it with whom these men do converse?

Jake paused and heard Bruce pretending to snore, 'Zzz, Zzz' "No go on!" he said. "It was actually powerful stuff."

Jake was beginning to realize that Bruce was one of those people who made a joke out of anything to hide their embarrassment in showing their feelings.

"Don't you feel it's speaking to us directly?"

"How do you mean?"

"You see like, 'this man did cry unto the multitude': that's like us missionaries speaking to the Japanese, or this line, 'behold what do all these things mean?', could be us hearing a strange, new language."

"Say, Jake, do you have some kind of gift or something about interpreting the scriptures?"

Jake smiled. "Of course not. I just pray a lot and I believe God speaks to me through the scriptures. He focuses my attention on one passage that seems relevant at the time."

"OK, so who represents Nephi and Lehi in our case?"

"Now that I couldn't tell you. I'm not some kind of oracle."

"Go on!" laughed Bruce.

The scripture reading did its job and the repetitions of 'It came to pass' and 'Behold' gradually lulled Bruce to sleep like a child listening to a parent reading a well-known story. Jake realized he had read for a long time as he heard Bruce's genuine, even snores. So he closed the book and turned out the light to find that dawn was just filtering through the haze.

Breakfast came, and the atmosphere was quite different as all the missionaries were looking forward to their day out. Dave was already in the lobby waiting for his relatives, craning his neck at every passing car. At last, a wiry old man came into the lobby and stood face to face with Dave, a questioning look on his face.

"Davu-san?"

"Yes!," said Dave beaming. His great-uncle's face broke into a broad grin and he put his arm around Dave's shoulder giving him a friendly pat on the back.

"So good to see you," he said in staccato English.

"Great to see you, Uncle."

"How's your father? Why he never come visit us?"

Dave was bundled into the car among his aunts and they whisked him off into the world his grandfather had left behind. He was to be Japanese for a day. The others were really happy for him.

Jake had managed to persuade Bruce to come along on the group trip to see some sights. They were being taken around by second-year missionaries so it wouldn't be so restricting, and they got to ride the subway. Stepping down into the subway brought them into an amazing, underground parallel of the world upstairs. Yet there seemed to be even more people and more shops. It was quite amazing to realise that this hidden world existed just below the street. The local station was small in comparison to those they were heading for. Jake enjoyed the sleek and smooth ride to the transfer station. The doors opened instantly and a pleasant female voice accompanied you throughout the journey. Jake was pleased that he recognized she was using the polite form of the verb because most of the sentences ended in *masu*. Chris, the second-year, told them that she would announce the previous station and then tell you 'welcome', 'mind the door!' 'hold tight!' 'take care!', and would then let you know where you were going and announce the next stop with all the connections. It reminded Jake of a Florida theme park. There, everything had seemed to run no less smoothly. No-one pushed in the queue, and everyone glided patiently about the place. Every ride you would get in, they would say, 'welcome', 'sit tight!' 'take care!' 'we are off now', and then on the way out, it would be, 'thank you', 'please remember to take all your belongings!', 'mind your fingers'. It was like having a robot mom following you around all the time. The train was quite crowded and Jake was surprised to see that most of the passengers who were sitting down dozing or reading were men, while the women stood up, some of them barely able to hold onto the straps with their little arms. He was also surprised to notice the first unpleasant smell he had smelt in Japan, a sweaty smell from the intense heat. Someone back at the centre had assured them that body odour was almost unheard-of in Japan. As usual, they were all neat and perfectly groomed. Now he was close up, he could see that the girls' hair was brushed completely smooth and was very glossy and well-conditioned, while there was not a speck of dandruff or lint on anyone's shoulders. What was more, they didn't seem to mind being stared at. Their eyes seemed to fix on a level straight through you without ever catching your eye, and you could stare at them without any sign of discomfort on their part. Somehow, despite that, Jake got the feeling that they had everyone in the carriage sized up. It was just that they had a really subtle way of doing it.

"Why aren't these kids in school?" asked Richard.

"Search me. You see school-kids around every hour of the day and night," said Chris. "I know they have a lot of extra classes in the evening, but I never know where they go in the day."

The same uniformed schoolchildren were dotted around the subway car. As they got out at the transfer station, the missionaries had to negotiate waves and waves of commuters all going absolutely purposefully towards their destination at speed, seemingly oblivious of their surroundings. To avoid breaking up the flow or being crushed underfoot, the missionaries had to sidestep to get into the stream of traffic, and then struggle to keep up with the leader, Chris, whose ginger head they used as a beacon amongst the black heads. Jake found he was very scared of getting lost, so he frantically tried to keep up. In this station there were quite a number of foreigners. Every few minutes, out of the corner of his eye, Jake would spot a figure who didn't fit in. Any dawdling by tourists looking for the way, or fumbling for tickets, was out of the question. You had to be ready. The group gathered briefly to check they were all there and then split into two groups in case they got lost. Getting on to the next train was quite another matter. It was packed but none of the passengers seemed to flinch as another improbable phalanx of humanity managed to squeeze aboard. Jake felt very unnerved pushed up against so many people, and the atmosphere of the subway car was like an elevator where it was not proper to speak. He held his breath for the three stops, desperate for some space. How could these people put up with this every day? They must get to work exhausted. Where were they all going in the middle of the morning? When they at last got off, the whole group just wanted to stand for a few minutes to get their breath back and get their orientation. Jake did not like being hustled around without knowing where he was going and he got Matthew, the other second-year, to show him the subway map. The second-years had a nonchalance about them that was a little irritating. The new boys had never been on such a journey before and needed a little explanation and prep. The second-years' job was to show them around, not lead them blindly.

"You'll get used to it," said Matthew. "Just stay close!"

"But we need to know where we're going," interjected Lawrence, who was staying in Tokyo. "Can you guys slow down a little?"

"Comes with practice," said Matthew.

"Don't you remember your first week here?" asked Jake.

"Sure! It was confusing at first but we got used to it."

Chris was waiting impatiently to start them on their tour, so they trooped a little despondently behind the old hands to be shown Tokyo's highlights.

The heat of the subway was soon forgotten as they entered the calm courtyard of the Meiji shrine. They went to a little fountain at the entrance where people were pouring water over their hands from a bamboo ladle. It was a purification ritual. Then they were allowed to wander about the building seeing its various compartments; one where a priest in a tall hat was carrying out a ritual with some kind of shaker. Jake liked the glossy, painted buildings and the gateways. A world away from the bustle outside, this superbly laid-out garden. Jake had heard a lot about oriental gardens because his mom was very keen on plants and trees. She had told him to take photos of the gardens and to buy her a bonsai tree. Unfortunately, when he had asked Brother Simmons about it, he said they retailed at about a hundred and twenty dollars minimum. It wasn't totally out of the question because he wanted to buy it for her as a gesture, but he'd have to save for a very long time.

The garden followed a pathway around tranquil ponds covered in lily pads under canopies of trees with little gazebos positioned here and there at strategic points for visitors to take in the surroundings. There were hardly any flowers, but a wide variety of bushes and trees. The only thing which spoiled the beauty of the garden was the lid on it: that sky again. Instead Jake concentrated on the pools of water and noticed a little turtle sitting on one of the rocks. It was such a perfect sight that he thought it must be a model, but as soon as he went to inspect it, the little thing blinked. Jake couldn't take his eyes off it for a long time, because it seemed like the perfect thing to be in this garden. As he saw the last of his group making for the exit, he got caught behind a group of middle-aged ladies with parasols who seemed to blend into the garden equally as well, and he kept turning to see his little friend on the rock receding into the distance.

"Change of pace!" announced the second-years and they were whisked into the fray of the *Ginza,* which meant 'golden', and this was the commercial centre of Tokyo with the highest buildings, the brightest neon, the most expensive stores and the most exclusive restaurants and clubs. Everyone on the street looked too well-dressed to be true, and the standard of dress in Tokyo generally, as they had already discovered, was pretty high. The women all had designer bags showing they had visited the various stores. Some of the guys were wanting to go into Mitzukoshi store because they'd heard it was famous. It seemed to be full of automaton-like little ladies in bus-boy outfits showing the way with a frozen smile and a neat sweep of the hand. The missionaries loafed through the cosmetics department and sauntered over to the elevators. Bruce had heard that the elevator attendants here had one of the most prized jobs in Japan. The missionaries were allowed to go around the store and meet up in thirty minutes. By now their guides were getting a little tired of being with newcomers. Jake and Bruce headed for the elevators as the attendant stepped out in her pill-box hat and white gloves. Her eyes swept the room without focusing as she beckoned her passengers into the elevator. Throughout the ride, she pressed the buttons with a flourish, stepped out to invite customers at every floor and bowed deeply to each, incoming group, all the time never halting in her set monologue. She was programmed to list the floor numbers and their contents, to thank customers and greet them; and utter nothing outside of the commentary. When Bruce asked her for the sports section she seemed not to have heard and continued regardless. She must have mentioned sport in her spiel because she didn't leave anything out. All the while her heavily made-up face was impassive with that frozen smile. Jake and Bruce got out, stunned.

"You know what the worst thing is?" said Bruce

"What?"

"I think she continues her routine even if there's nobody in there with her."

They both giggled at the thought as they went to inspect the sportswear. Since neither of them yet knew how to use the money, they were none the wiser, but they enjoyed being away from the group trailing behind the know-all second-years.

"Is that going to be us in a year's time?" said Jake.

"Yeah. I mean anyone's gonna know more about a place if he's been there longer," said Bruce. "Did you hear Chris speaking Japanese to the girl in the ticket booth? He just went on and on. I mean what does it take to ask for twenty adult tickets."

"*Ni-ju nin kudasai*," said Jake, practicing.

"Exactly! They were showing off to the freshmen."

Bored with window shopping they decided to go and have a snack in a café. It boosted their confidence to ask for orange juice and ice-cream, and it was refreshing to be treated the same as everyone else without either too much attention or too little courtesy. The café was quite elegant with prices to match, but it was good to be able to relax and feel that their Japanese career was starting.

Back at the centre, feeling a little flat after the day's excursion. Dave's friends were eager to hear about his trip. It turned out he had visited two of the same places as the others, but he had been chauffeured around by car and had the benefit of doting relatives eager to tell him all about Japanese history and culture, instead of the blasé second-years who hadn't bothered to tell them very much. Dave had been given a gorgeous Japanese dinner at their house, where his great-aunt had gone to a lot of trouble. The only awkward moment was when they had brought out the saké and offered him a cup. He stammered his excuses as best he could but it came out as 'Saké no good! I Mormon.' Luckily one of his cousins had understood and explained and there were no hard feelings as they brought out green tea and Dave had to laugh and say, 'Sorry! Tea no good. I Mormon.' Dave recognized by the tone of their voices that they were asking each other what it was that stopped these Mormons from taking saké and tea, but *gaigin* habits were so unusual anyway that they were not offended. It would be a funny story to tell the neighbours. In fact, Japanese people were a little disappointed if they were entertaining *gaigin* and nothing amusing happened. There was many a legend of the *gaigin* who came out in toilet slippers or put bubble-bath into the hot-tub which was only for soaking or who tied his *yukata* the wrong way or couldn't use chopsticks. All such incidents were their affirmation that they were a people apart and no outsiders would ever be able to understand their ways or fully fit in. Indeed, Dave's family were amazed that Dave could use chopsticks.

"We eat a lot of Chinese food," said Dave. We have a lot of Chinese restaurants in San Francisco."

His great-aunts were delighted that he appreciated their cooking and apologized that it was just a simple little meal they had put together, and they also apologized for inconveniencing him to have to come so far out of his way to eat such a humble meal. Dave knew from his dad's briefings that this was a cue to reply that it was the best meal he'd ever tasted and that they shouldn't have gone to such trouble on his account, and that he was sorry to burden them with a visit when they were so busy. Then the final apologies from the host would round off the little ritual. Dave was glad he had taken the trouble to learn these polite expressions in this case because they seemed to leave a very good impression.

Overall, he told his friends, growing up as a Japanese-American with Japanese-American parents didn't in any way prepare him for what life in the real Japan was like. Some of the ornaments in his father's home were similar but the idea of Japaneseness outside Japan was really a collection of cultural symbols. Real Japan was modern Japan which had moved on a great deal since the time his grandfather had left and there were many things about his cousin's life which were very similar to America.

"You know they're crazy about baseball over here." said Dave. "My cousin showed me some of his baseball cards and magazines. Also they have these massive comic books, thick as telephone directories, and he says he buys one every week. They're a kind of a cult among school-kids."

"Did he say all of this in Japanese?" asked Jason, eager to know the extent of Dave's progress.

"Kind of half-and-half. He learns English in school but they don't do much conversation, although he goes to a conversation class after school. I filled in the gaps with Japanese."

Jason was relieved that Dave's Japanese wasn't any better than his because he had begun to work himself into a panic about starting work the following week.

唯色

Interlude

It was time to go to Nagoya and all the other destinations. The missionaries stood in groups waiting for the bus which was to take them to the main station. Many of them would be riding the same train which went right through to the far south. They had been told to be ready to get off at their stops because the doors only opened for an instant and they didn't want the wrong missionaries ending up in the wrong towns.

Although they'd been in Tokyo a short time, the men were nervous to leave the centre and go out into the world of missionary work. Until now, everything had been preparation and training, sitting passively while others told them things. Now they were expected to go out and get results, rather like salesmen. If they weren't producing results, their mission President would put pressure on them, because they were not having this amount of money spent on them so that they could while away their time like a vacation.

The missionaries had heard much about the fabled *shinkansen* bullet trains. They were sleek and comfortable with wide windows. Jake had only been on an express train once in his life, when he rode the Amtrak with his family to Oregon one year on vacation. Americans rarely considered the train, as the country seemed to be made for the car and the explosion of airline companies meant that air travel was cheap and as commonplace as the bus was in other countries. Amid the general unfamiliarity of the experience, the missionaries stared out of the window and Bruce started to laugh at the guards. Positioned at regular intervals along the platform were spruce officials with white gloves and whistles, whose job it was to check that the doors were closed and to shuttle the passengers safely in. Then, at the head of the train, the main guard would blow his whistle with a flourish, salute the train and point his finger in the direction the train was going . Then he remained with his arm outstretched like that until the train was out of sight, and only then would he drop his arm. The same acting-out of seemingly meaningless gestures that they'd seen in *Mitzukoshi* store! This same pride in the job! It was a proud man who had graduated all the way from the local railway lines to the nation's most prestigious network. That guard would probably have stuck to the rule book if no-one had been there to see him.

"It was worth it," Bruce called to the guard, "we were watching you. I like that. Always someone there to wave the train away," and he pointed his finger towards the cities that were waiting for them, as the train moved off. The others imitated him because now it was a symbol of their leaving and their determination and sense of purpose for their missionary years which were about to begin. It was a bright afternoon and they felt optimistic. What pleased Jake most was to see that as the suburbs of Tokyo flew past, the gloomy sky was left behind, and the familiar sky that he knew from home came, and stayed with them all the way to Nagoya.

唯壱

Nagoya, Japan

It was growing dark as they neared Nagoya. What struck Jake were the neon signs flashing all over the city approaches, announcing the Brother computer company. Everywhere he looked would be a sign in English proclaiming 'Brother'. 'Big Brother is watching you', thought Jake. Five minutes before arrival the guard had begun his announcement. The main railway line journeys required the full announcement treatment with arrival time, all connecting lines and how to reach them and ongoing departure times for all the major cities nearby, plus information about the various exits from the main station and where they led. The guard had a very reassuring and gentle voice as he listed the destinations he must have repeated a hundred times before, and the sound made Jake feel welcome and full of anticipation of his new home town. The beeping of the doors signalled for them to alight, and sure enough they slammed shut again within seconds, leaving the missionaries standing breathless on the platform, their luggage in a heap. They were soon to be met by a couple of other missionaries. A pair clad in the familiar grey slacks with short-sleeved, white shirts came jogging up the platform. The group was a little anxious after its Tokyo experience, but the hearty handshakes soon dispelled any fears that they would be working below a couple of tyrants.

"Brothers! Good to meet you. Ellis Parkes, and this is Brother George Sutton." All hands exchanged with each other in a network of arms and they were taken to the taxis.

"Good trip?" asked Ellis.

"Yeah, it was great," said Bruce. "The trains are slick."

"Guess this is your first time in Japan, right?" asked Ellis, addressing them all.

"First time overseas, period." said Jake

"Me too," said Bruce.

"First time for me, though some of my folks live here," said Dave.

"That's neat," said Ellis. "Whereabouts?"

"Tokyo. I went to visit yesterday in fact."

"So I guess you speak Japanese fluently," George asked.

"About the same as the other guys," said Dave modestly. "My parents don't actually know Japanese that well, so we never spoke it when I was a kid."

"Does everyone think you're Japanese?" said George.

"So far, no. Nobody has spoken to me yet."

"You just wait," said Ellis. "We've been here a year already and Japanese people still go blank when we speak to them."

They got into two taxis and sure enough the driver turned around and looked expectantly at Dave. He gave a start as Ellis gave him the directions in Japanese in a long-suffering manner. Dave and Jake were enthralled as Ellis went on to have a conversation with the driver who was smiling at intervals and nodding knowingly.

"He says he's met Mormon missionaries before," said Ellis. "Also he had a couple of Australians in the cab only last week."

"Australians?" said Jake with a bemused expression.

"*Gaigin* are all the same to them," Ellis laughed. "The President has prepared a welcome dinner for you tonight. Hope you're hungry."

"Are we going to the President's home?" asked Jake.

"Of course, that's where we live," said Ellis.

"Really?" said Dave quite shocked. "In the President's house?"

"Yeah, as there are only eight of us, we live quite closely. He has a whole floor with his office and our rooms and the family have the other two floors. He likes us to eat together most of the time. Says it's important to feel part of a family."

Jake knew that Bruce would not like this set-up.

"What's President Ericson like?" asked Jake, immediately regretting he had asked such a blunt question so soon.

"He's a good guy," said Ellis. "He knows how difficult it is and he just expects you to do your best. He also likes to sit and talk individually with us in case we have any problems."

Jake thought of his father.

"Does he have kids?" asked Dave.

"Sure! He has two sons and a daughter at home and his oldest son is back in the US at BYU."

"Where you from yourself?" asked Dave.

"Eugene, Oregon. You?"

"San Francisco. Jake's from U-taah," he said, exaggerating the sound. "SLC, capital of the world."

Jake smiled self-consciously.

"I like the house," said Ellis. "Only thing is, there's no garden, just a small yard. You miss the open space. That's why I joined a football team, to run wild once a week. I used to play a lot of sports back home."

"Is that a Japanese team?" asked Dave.

"No it's a *gaigin* team. There are a few Americans here in Nagoya working for Japanese companies. Also English teachers from the US and other places. Why? Do you play?"

"Sure! High-school team. Nothing great but I enjoy sports."

"How about you, Jake?"

"No. I used to work out a little but I'm more of a couch potato."

As they approached the house, which seemed to be some way outside the centre of the city, they saw the door open and the whole family came out onto the front step to welcome them. It was almost as if they had gone back home because here they were being welcomed into the bosom of another family.

President Ericson was quite an imposing figure with Scandinavian looks and slightly receding blondish-grey hair. His eyes seemed to blaze behind his glasses and he had huge, tanned forearms. He sported a very wide grin and he greeted his charges like a grizzly bear with warm hugs. They were all quite taken aback and smiled weakly as his wife came forward. She was also a strapping woman with Scandinavian looks, shoulder-length, wavy white hair and a very deep tan which contrasted with sky-blue eyes. Her handshake was as firm as her husband. She was not dressed in a typical Mormon woman's garb of floral prints and court shoes, but had on a coarse denim skirt, a white blouse and a smock-type apron. On her feet were sturdy gym shoes. She looked capable and a little intimidating as she gave them a friendly shove into the dining-room.

"Ellis, show the boys to their rooms, would you, while I set the table. Come along Phil, Jane, Sam!" and the three children scurried to help her.

Bruce looked bewildered. "Are we staying here tonight?"

"We're staying here every night," said Jake in a whisper. "This is home."

"You're kidding!"

They traipsed up the wide polished stairs to their rooms. These looked like the typical family bedrooms they had left behind. Bruce and Jake's room had obviously belonged to the Ericson's other son. It still had football pennants on the walls and a few cassette tapes in the corner. Sports paraphernalia filled the bottom of the closet.

"Is that OK?" said Ellis, seeing Bruce's displeasure at the contents of the closet. "That's kinda permanent I'm afraid, from when Stephen used to have this room. That's the son who's away at college. We can maybe put it in the attic if you like."

"That's OK," said Bruce quickly, hoping his feelings were not so obvious.

Dave and Lewis had the room across the hall which was smaller but absolutely bare. Ellis and George shared one of the rooms while their colleagues John and Dennis had the last room. They were due back from vacation on the following day. There was a bathroom with two toilets and two showers between them. Jake was relieved they didn't have to share the family bathroom.

"You'd maybe like to get unpacked a while," said Ellis and left them.

"Seems like an easygoing guy," said Jake.

"Yeah, eager to please. I guess I should show more appreciation. Did you realize we'd be living in the family home?"

"I dunno. I figured there'd be some kind of annexe."

"I mean we don't have our own TV or lounge. It means we can't really relax."

"Yeah, and the President has his office up here."

"That other room is his office?"

"Uh huh." Jake was busy commandeering his closet space.

"So he's gonna be around us all the time."

"Maybe he just works in his office during the day while we're out working. Anyway, he seems a nice guy."

Bruce sat despondently on one of the beds. "It's like home. I've shared a room with Gordon all my life. I figured by the time I left home I'd at least get a place to myself."

"You'll have to put up with me, I'm afraid," said Jake smiling, as he filled one of the drawers with shirts.

"As you've taken over half the storage space, could I please have first choice of bed? The one by the window," he said as they both ran to sit on it.

"Bruce, I like this bed too," said Jake reproachfully.

"Jake, I got here first."

"We'll have to toss a coin for it." Jake looked at the other bed set into an alcove with a shelf above it and it suddenly looked appealing. "Well, we won't be spending much time in here anyway. I'll take this bed."

"Thanks Jake," said Bruce pleasantly surprised. Then he looked at the other bed. "OK I'm being selfish. You take the bed by the window!"

"That's OK" said Jake stretching out on his new bed.

"No, no really. I mean it. What's a view anyway?"

"Exactly," said Jake. "The back of a building, a brick wall and a tree."

Bruce realized he was beaten and began to lay some things on his bed. "It'll grow on me," he said.

A bell rang. The four of them came out at once wondering what it was.

"Are we being summoned?" said Lewis.

"Dinner time, I guess," said Dave. "Let's go!"

They were shown to their seats around the large, varnished table. President Ericson sat like the patriarch at one end, and his wife commandeered the other. She busied her children, calling to them to get one thing or another and serve the guests. She saw the missionaries' awkwardness at being served.

"It's OK boys. Tonight is special. After tonight you join in with the whole family. We don't stand on ceremony in this house."

This was another blow to Bruce's feeling of independence and having left home. It was the same old routine: shared rooms, family meals and chores.

"Will we be eating with the family every day?" he asked tentatively.

"Oh yes," said President Ericson jovially. "Do you think we'd let you go hungry?"

"Oh no, of course not, but isn't it a lot of trouble for Sister Ericson?"

"Not at all. Bruce, right? We like our boys to feel at home. It's no trouble as I cook for the family anyway, and I have Jane to help me."

Jane looked sheepish. She was about thirteen, and the only thing she shared with her parents was her deep tan. Otherwise, she was very slight and bony with long, brown hair and brooding, grey eyes. She was obviously not quite at ease with the newcomers. Her mother patted her hand.

"Jane takes a little while to get used to our new intake, don't you dear?" This caused Jane even more embarrassment and she rolled her eyes and started to eat with her hair falling across her face. Sam seemed to be the chatty one and he quizzed them cheerfully about their home towns, families, sports and what they thought of Japan.

"Do you go to school?" asked Dave. "I mean local school."

"Yeah I'm in third grade."

"Is that Japanese school?"

"Yeah. There's only me and one Hawaiian guy there. The rest are Japanese. I guess they're used to us now."

"How do you manage with the Japanese?" asked Jake.

"That's OK now. It was difficult at first because I went to English school at the church before this one but I've gotten used to it now."

The Ericsons had been in Japan for five years and they had become quite established in the area. Only Mr Ericson had not managed to pick up Japanese. "I'm afraid I don't have the gift for languages, but I get by with my wife and children as chief interpreters."

"What do you do in the church?" asked Dave.

"We actually conduct part of the service in English and then we have our Bishop who fills in the Japanese, and some of our circles are in Japanese and so forth. We get by. You kinda get in a rut if you don't pick up the language, where you manage to find your niche and carry on without having to speak Japanese. How did you boys do at training? Dave! I understand you *are* Japanese."

"Not exactly," said Dave. "I'm Japanese-American." He was beginning to know this explanation by heart. "You see my Grandpa came over after the war and he was anxious to speak English and fit in. Then my parents never used Japanese when they were growing up so we were never taught it, and so it was as new to me as it was to these guys."

"I'm a little afraid of using Japanese for the first time," said Jake. "So far I haven't been able to follow very much."

"I felt like that at the beginning," said George, "but now it's absolutely fine. Course it helps to be able to practice with the kids here."

"Yeah, we can help you," said Sam as George ruffled his tousled, blond hair. It seemed that Sam was a favourite with the missionaries. His brother Phil was a chubby, depressed-looking youth. He seemed to be suffering rather badly from acne and like his sister he was unwilling to participate much in the conversation. He answered their questions in short sentences and reluctantly loped up and down to the kitchen at his mother's requests.

"Phil has a lot of study on at the moment," said his mother by way of explanation.

"They push 'em hard in Japanese school," said Ellis. "He's in high school now so it's tough. You ever heard of examination hell?"

The missionaries looked intrigued.

"It's like the exams are so stressful and they're so important to the parents that the kids almost go crazy with nerves and study from dawn until midnight and weekends to keep up. If not, they miss out on the good colleges and their career is gone."

"You see," said President Ericson. "It's very important in Japan which university you get into. That determines the kind of company that will take you on and your chances of promotion. Aside from that the competition is very stiff."

"So are you kids planning to stay in Japan?" asked Lewis.

"No," said the President, "we'd like them to follow their brother to BYU and then they can decide where they want to end up. We certainly won't be here indefinitely, but with Japanese qualifications they have a good grounding. There's no American high school here in Nagoya. The population is too small. I know families in other cities who send their kids to American schools but the majority of the kids are from military families and they don't get the same mix of people. Besides we didn't want them to go away to school."

"Yeah, and we're lucky," said Sam "because we get to be bilingual." He smiled, having used a word he'd only recently learned. Jake liked his sunny personality which counteracted the rather morose attitude of the older ones. He put it down to adolescent problems and decided he'd better make time to get to know the new family members. It must be hard to have four new house guests every year. His family had once taken in a Mexican student for a year and they regarded him as a bit of an intruder at first, but by the end of the year they were crying because they didn't want him to go. Mormon families were large anyway and most of them, he knew, especially in Utah, had a tradition of taking in waifs and strays of various nationalities who were either studying or going through the Temple or coming to learn English. It was considered shameful not to offer accommodation to fellow Mormons who were new in town and expect them to stay in hotels, and this is how Mormons were used to having their families augmented from time to time. Mission Presidents' families were a special case because by the nature of the job they were assured lodgers all the time and only got a break when the missionaries had their summer vacation. As well as this, the family was the prop for all the new souls that were led to the church. It was not unusual to get people calling late in the evening to ask for a discussion with the President or his wife or to borrow books and videos. President Ericson chatted a bit about the church regulars and some of the successes of recent years. As he went through the names he would often refer to Brother Ellis, saying that that was one of his 'catches'. Ellis tried to hide his pleasure in being praised by the President but Jake could tell he was the brightest star from the previous year. George looked a bit depressed in contrast until President Ericson added a few names that were attributed to George's effort.

"George is very strong on running the study circle for the younger guys," said the President kindly. "Right, Phil?" He had been trying to bring Phil into the conversation throughout dinner.

"Right! Uh huh," said Phil despondently, who like his sister let his hair fall across his face.

"Tell them what you do in study circle!" said his mother, jabbing him in the arm. "Come on. Buck up!"

He lifted his head languidly. "I don't know. I guess the scriptures. A little bit each week."

Dave tried to save him from his embarrassment. "One thing we found helpful back home was to try and relate everyday problems we were having to what we were reading in the scriptures, kind of to bring it alive."

"How did that work?" asked Ellis, interested.

"Well for example, some of the guys in school were having problems with being pushed around or bullied by the older guys, so we would try to help them deal with that by telling the stories about how the religious people are always pushed around. Also if they were coming across kids in school who were trying to introduce them to drugs, we had to think of ways to make them feel superior to those guys so they didn't feel like wimps for refusing."

"We had something like that too," said Bruce, "for alcohol. We had the group draw pictures of how they'd imagine drunk people to be and come out with the most negative, unattractive images possible, so that they could ask themselves, 'Is this really desirable? Do I wanna end up like this?'"

President Ericson was signalling in Sam's direction to try and ask Bruce to change the subject. Bruce caught on and quickly said, "So do you have separate study circles for little kids?"

"No, they go in at age twelve," said the President.

"I take care of the young ones," said Mrs Ericson. "We do crafts and songs and creative play, rhymes and such, and we go over the basic doctrines."

"Japanese kids look really well-behaved," said Lewis.

"Don't you believe it," she laughed. "They can sure raise a storm if they want to. You know a lot of Japanese children are a little spoiled, to tell the truth, so our job is to knock 'em down to size a bit and get them to mix easily with lots of kids."

"They're cute though," said Ellis. "I think Japanese little kids are real cute. That's why it's such a shock when they act like little terrors."

Jake had some trouble finishing up his meal. It was a strange combination of macaroni cheese sauce, with Japanese noodles as a substitute for macaroni. The salad was recognizable to him but was covered with a thin, tangy sauce. He was happy to see American ice-cream for dessert.

"Can you buy American food here?" he asked

"There's a good shop in Sakae, downtown," said President Ericson. "They have a selection of stuff, especially candies and cookies but it's very expensive. We get stuff brought back from the States whenever we can but we can't ask people to weigh themselves down with too much."

"I find I can adapt Japanese food," said Mrs Ericson. "You'll find Japanese food a little dry and maybe plain for American tastes. You'll be likely to have maybe a piece of fish, a dish of plain veg separate and maybe French fries or plain white rice on the side. We prefer our food all mixed together."

"Yeah, when I went home," said George, "I was going crazy for Mexican food or Chinese food, you know, just mixed up with plenty of sauce."

"They have Mexican Restaurants here," said Sam.

"Great!" said Bruce. "I love Mexico. Do they have Burger City or Dixie King?"

"Yeah here and there," said George, "You'll find all kinds of fast food joints. Donut Heaven is popular."

Bruce brightened.

When they had all finished, they excused themselves to go and unpack. They offered to help in a perfunctory way, expecting that Mrs Ericson would refuse offers of help.

"That's OK this evening," she said, "but tomorrow we'll draw up the roster."

Bruce was going to laugh until he realized she wasn't kidding. "Welcome to the Brady Bunch," he groaned, as they climbed the stairs.

They felt better when they had arranged their rooms. Dave and Lewis sauntered in to inspect. Lewis was the only one with a decent-sized cassette player so he said they could come in and listen to tapes if they wanted. Dave could offer the use of exercise weights, and Jake was the owner of an expensive set of Japanese dictionaries. This left Bruce, who had brought his scouting survival kit. "In case of emergencies," he explained.

As Jake prepared for his first night in the house, he was still disappointed to feel that his immediate environment wasn't really like he had imagined Japan. So far the room, the family, and the food were like a make-do job of Americanizing a Japanese environment, but Ellis had said that after a day of touring Japanese homes it was good to get back to your own space. He thought about other young men his age leaving home. They would maybe have their own apartment or at least a decent-sized room in a college dorm with plenty of freedom and people around. What did he have but a bed, four drawers and half a closet and a routine that seemed more or less mapped-out? But he resigned himself to this. It was what the church was all about, making sacrifices, and if he worked hard here the credits would last him through his whole career. Nothing you did for the church was wasted. After all, he was not only thinking about worldly life. When he had thoughts like this, flashbacks would come to him from his Temple induction because that was the first time he had been brought face to face with what he had believed all his life. Before that it had been abstract, but in the Temple something had really overpowered him. He didn't like to dwell on it too much because it scared him to remember how he had felt. As he drifted into sleep he couldn't separate that sleepy feeling from the feeling he had had from the first moment they stepped into that first room in the Temple and he had a strange, blurred sensation in his head.

The three days before they started work were given over to training sessions on how the ward was run and how to use the trains and subway. Even the simple subway system in Nagoya looked really daunting at first, but the second years assured them that it was much easier finding your way underground. Some of the missionaries in the smaller towns relied totally on bikes and the Nagoya team were to use bikes on occasions, these being parked at various stations. All their instructions were written out clearly, line by line, in a transport manual which included translations of the most useful names and details of the impressive and comprehensive rail system. The teams would be spending the same day each week in a given location, with a different location every day, to provide them with some variety and to avoid saturation for the locals. They were shown the log books which contained details of all the homes and residences called and the response, along with follow-up information and a summary of the orientation of the family concerned. Most of them said 'Shinto', or 'Shinto-Buddhist'. Occasionally there was a red dot beside the words '*Soka Gakkei*'. Dave asked about that. "You'll get to know," said President Ericson. "It's a little involved so I want to devote time to that."

Jake was pleased that the Japanese lessons were continuing. Their teacher, Mrs Yamada, was a pleasant-looking, middle-aged lady with a very patient manner, and it seemed she had been taught language teaching in an inspired way like Mr Sakimoto back in the States. She had the students working in pairs and learning actively rather than sitting back and waiting to soak it up. This meant they had to concentrate quite hard because no sooner had they learned something than she would put it to the test. They were glad of this, however, because the day was looming when they would have to put it all into practice. Mrs Yamada introduced them to the Chinese characters called *kanji* and thereby unveiled a fascinating world of signs. She showed the origin of the characters from pictograms which represented simplified symbols. For example, the *kanji* for 'tree' or 'wood' could be modified by adding a few lines to become the *kanji* for 'root' or 'origin'. This, combined with other characters, coined new words. For example, the symbol for 'sun' plus the symbol for 'origin' meant 'origin of the sun', or '*Nihon*', meaning 'Japan'. What was interesting was how Japanese attitudes were reflected in the *kanji*, or at least the way they saw the world. For example, the central position of the rice-field in men's lives at the time when the writing system was first taking shape meant that the *kanji* for 'man' was made up of the symbol for 'rice-field' combined with the character for 'power', symbolizing 'power in the rice-field,' and this represented their concept of 'man'. The symbol for the female was derived from a pictogram of a pregnant figure with arms outstretched. Mrs Yamada told them about the derivation of her own name, 'mountain rice-field,' and then they practiced deciphering other common surnames from the *kanji* they had learned. The easy part was getting the meanings of the symbol but then they were told that each one had a variety of possible readings or pronunciations.

86

For each there was a Chinese and a Japanese pronunciation, and among the Chinese readings a sound such as '*ki*' could have several different meanings. This meant that a learner could sometimes understand a *kanji* he could not read. The missionaries began to feel very proud of themselves as they began to decipher *kanji*.

"I think I could really get into this," said Lewis enthusiastically as he practiced writing the *kanji* he had learned.

"Mrs Yamada, how many do we need to learn? Two hundred or so?" asked Jake.

"About two thousand at least," she said, "to read the newspaper or simple books, but educated people know close to fifteen thousand."

Their enthusiasm was suddenly deflated.

"Don't worry," said Dave. "You have to start somewhere. Remember that proverb. The journey of one thousand miles starts with a single step."

Mrs Yamada smiled in recognition and repeated it in Japanese. Jake liked that saying. It encouraged him because it was true that you could never achieve anything unless you started off. Anything looked small and insignificant at first. Joseph Smith began with just a few people who believed what he was saying, and how could he have imagined that this would be the basis for a huge, world-wide ministry? Jake thought about the new people they would be bringing to the church, perhaps in ones or twos, and yet those converts would be the building-blocks of a strong church in Nagoya.

Ellis took them for a subway ride to get them acquainted with the place where they would be spending much of their time. "Make sure you have good books," he said, "because you'll be spending a lot of time on trains." The Nagoya subway was a small version of Tokyo, with the same cheerfully informative voice-over, the same businessmen, office-ladies and school-children, and the same efficiency. No sooner were they on the platform than the train pulled in. At this time in the afternoon it was not so busy and they found seats for the first time. A old man with a creased face nodded a smile of welcome and moved his bag for them to sit. Ellis thanked him politely and the man sat, riveted to their conversation.

"It's a simple system," said Ellis. "You just use Sakae and

Nagoya as your main centres and just go up and down this line, changing at Sakae if you have to. All the main lines go out from Nagoya main station. That's where we get most of our trains. Usually, Wednesday, we stay in the city centre and go around the parks. That's usually fun."

"How do you start a conversation?" asked Bruce. "Do you just kinda stride over and say, 'Hi! I'd like to talk to you about the *Book of Mormon?*'"

"Something like that," said Ellis not realizing the irony in Bruce's question. "Did they talk about approaches in training?"

"Yeah, mostly about starting with talking about God," said Jake.

"That's it. We usually go up to someone sitting on a bench, preferably if they're not reading or chatting, so it's better if they're on their own and we ask if we can sit and talk to them about God or about our church."

"How do they react?" asked Lewis.

"About half-and-half. Some just shake their heads and wave their hands and we know that's a sign to drop it. Others are really happy to talk to any foreigner. Soon you get to recognize the ones who want to talk from the shy ones. What's good about working outside is that you can talk to women and girls. You know we're not allowed to talk to women alone at home and often the women are the most ready to listen."

"Yeah, we heard about that rule," said Lewis. "But isn't it kinda difficult if the men are out at work during the daytime?"

"Most times there are other women in the house, or the grand-father is there. Otherwise we can talk at the door or drop leaflets or else arrange an evening appointment."

"We're like travelling salesmen," said Bruce.

"In a way we are," agreed Ellis, "and that's why no one bothers much about having you call at the door. They're used to it and they kind of admire it too, you know, working on the ground trying to get support."

Ellis took them on a little tour of the system and then had them lead the way to take them back to their stop. Dave was very pleased with himself as Ellis said they were on the right platform. Then it was Lewis' turn to take them to the platform for Tsurumae which criss-crossed their home line, after which Jake had to lead them back to the main line. By this time Bruce said, "Yeah, I think we got it now Ellis, thanks. We just follow the signs."

"We just wanna be sure you know where you're going," said Ellis.

"The first few days we're with the second-years, aren't we?"

"Yeah, President Ericson's gonna decide who goes with whom to-night."

On the way back Bruce asked if they could go into a café.

"That's not really recommended," said Ellis seriously, "unless it's to speak to people specifically for church purposes. A crowd of *gaigin* attracts a lot of unnecessary attention. We prefer to keep the meetings under control as much as possible."

"But wouldn't that be a great opportunity to witness?" said Jake, "say if people were curious and came up to ask questions?"

"I'm told people in that situation are not all that interested in religion. They just want to practice their English. It's usually a waste of time trying to witness to them."

Bruce looked depressed as they passed all the interesting-looking places.

"Don't worry!" said Ellis. "You'll get plenty of opportunity to get into Japanese culture soon enough."

The next day the President took them to the zoo. It was neatly laid out and the enclosures were of a decent size. He took this opportunity to find out a little about their backgrounds and their attitudes and to see which of the four would be most promising for the mission.

"So we have an SLC boy!" he said jovially. Jake went red although he was always proud to be from the heart of the church. "Haven't had someone from SLC for four years. Boy named Jerry Fuller, you know him?"

"I'm afraid not sir. Doesn't sound familiar. When did you last go to the States?" asked Jake.

"We went back the summer before last. Much needed break, and I had the chance to go up to the convention. That was mighty rousing, I can tell you. Also looked in on your training centre, and gave some feedback. Unfortunately - no offense guys - we found their knowledge of Japanese psychology lacking. I feel they have improved things though."

"I'm hoping to major in Psychology after this," said Bruce, "and from what I've read, the training seemed to be pretty good."

"What matters in the end," said President Ericson earnestly, "is: can you communicate? Can you get behind the polite smiles and the small talk to the souls?"

It suddenly struck Jake how absurd it was that they were having this conversation in front of zoo cages. The President would sidle up to them at each cage and continue the conversation, smiling benignly from time to time at the animals' antics.

"Our professor told us that it's very difficult to get below the surface with Japanese people," said Lewis.

"That may be so until the *Book of Mormon* works its magic," said the President mysteriously. "As people start coming into church and are asked to participate and share their problems, it liberates them, opens up a whole new world and they find then that they feel more at home with other Mormons, even non-Japanese, than gentile Japanese."

At this point one of the chimps was hanging from the wall of the cage just in front of the President, prancing around for attention, and he had to stop in the middle of his discourse to wave at the creature. Then they strolled on to the elephants. These depressed Jake because they seemed to be completely listless. One of them had reached a stage where he was just swinging his head from side to side in a manic fashion, not moving or showing any interest in his surroundings. From time to time he would drag his foot backwards and forwards in the dust. For the full ten minutes they were standing there the animal continued with the same listless motion.

"Do animals get depressed, Bruce?" asked Jake as they were watching the elephant.

"I know they get distressed," said Bruce. "This kind of repetitive behaviour is a symptom of that. Maybe he's lonely or his cage is too small."

"He doesn't seem to have much space to move around," said Jake. He noticed the elephant had a sore bald patch on its side. "Maybe it's not such a good thing to have animals caged up for entertainment."

"But some species would have died out by now if it weren't for zoos," said Bruce.

Zoos always made Jake thoughtful. He often wondered how people who didn't believe in God could account for the variety in all of these animals. Just looking at giraffes, elephants, emus or rhinos made you ask how they all came about in such variety. If the evolutionists were right, how could all of these incredible creatures come about by pure chance? The odds were impossible.

His favourites were the fish. He looked at the pretty, glittering fish behind the glass in the aquarium and absorbed the marvellous colours, the fluorescent hues that could only be found in nature, and all the markings. When he was younger and he had looked at fish like that, it had been the confirmation to him that there was a God. It wasn't necessarily automatic that children brought up in religious homes ended up believing in God, but Jake had been convinced in his own right when he had visited zoos like this, seeing the fish and the birds and all the plants. Dave stood beside him, also mesmerized by the fish, and Jake told him how significant they had been in his religious development.

"It's weird how people try to explain it, though," said Dave. "There was this guy at school whose brother was a marine biologist. He took us diving one time and told us what to look for, you know, all the varieties and classes and how they feed and all and then he explained how they evolved from floating particles in the sea. At first I was pretty much convinced because this is what we studied in biology at school and when I would ask my Bishop about evolution, he'd kind of brush over it. 'All we need to know is in the scriptures', he would say. 'Don't go fretting over the whys and wherefores'. But I never found a proper explanation in the books. Whenever I went diving I would wonder though: why is it there are so many different fish?"

"Yeah" replied Jake "like I believe God gave Christ the power to create but what I'd like to know is how exactly he did it. I mean, did it just appear or did he create it in stages?"

"Exactly, I mean science has got some facts, you know, they've found the fossils and somehow you've gotta explain those."

"I suppose in the end you have to keep the faith and science separate and just say there's some things about faith that are mysterious and we can't know it all until the afterlife. In the meantime don't worry about it and live a good life! I mean you don't need to know about how fish evolved to be a good person."

They both laughed and went on gazing at the marvellous fish.

When they got back to the house flushed and sweating from the day in the heat, Mrs Ericson had some lemonade ready for them. They chatted about their day, and how they'd seen a bit of the outside world, but that zoos were zoos whether in Japan or in the States. They had all been very observant and were full of questions about what they had seen, how good the driving was (contrary to expectations), how schoolboys went zooming past on the sidewalk on bikes, and they asked about a games hall they had seen full of clanking machines.

Ellis laughed. "That's the *Pachinko* Parlour. It's a real blue-collar craze over here."

"Not just blue-collar," said the President. "I've seen salary men in there too."

"Yeah, well it's a game with ball-bearings and you have to get them around the machine and if you win you get prizes or something. It's illegal to win cash so they get prizes but they have some way of getting around it because you see them lining up at a window outside to get their cash."

"Those places are crazy," said Mrs Ericson. "Can you believe the din in there, that clanking and whirring and music? I've seen their eyes when they play. They're fixed and glazed and they stare at those machines like zombies as if their life depended on it."

"I don't want to be rude," said Bruce changing the subject, "but have you ever heard anyone accuse Mormons of having glazed eyes?"

There was silence around the table.

"I guess not," said Bruce sheepishly. "Well it's just that I hear this a lot from outside the church," he went on. "People say, 'Oh yeah the Mormons, haven't they got the weirdest eyes, blue and kinda glassy. Sort of glazed or hypnotic?' Then of course I make some wisecrack because I wear glasses."

"I think that's someone having a pop at us as usual," said the President.

Sam started looking around at the missionaries' eyes to confirm what Bruce had said.

Bruce laughed. "That's just it. I don't think I've ever seen a Mormon with eyes like that. I mean most of us have blue eyes, but nothing extraordinary."

It seemed no-one else could tune in to Bruce's wavelength. He often had this way of saying the wrong thing because, as he said, he liked to say what was on his mind. Sam broke the awkward pause by inviting the missionaries up to his room. "Come on guys! I want to show you my room."

They all obliged, appreciating his relentless cheerfulness. He managed to rope three of them into a game of '*kerplunk*'.

"You'll get used to this," said George. "I've been '*kerplunk*' champ since I came here."

Mournful sounds of rock music were coming from behind Phil's closed door. "Probably studying," said George. Suddenly Jane slammed out of her room, went into the bathroom and slammed back again without speaking. Bruce and Jake were taken aback.

"Actually," said George. "She doesn't like us coming down to the family floor. Kind of an invasion of privacy, I guess."

"Are we allowed on this floor?" asked Jake.

"Not before nine or after eight," said George, "but the President seems to appreciate us spending time with Sam."

"Does Jane complain?"

"Yeah, once in the family meeting she asked for us to be banned from this floor and her parents agreed, but we kinda drifted back because of Sam. Anyway she has her own room."

"Maybe we should bring the game up to our room," said Jake.

"No, the top floor is absolutely out of bounds to the family. Only the President can go up to his office. He says it makes him separate his work life from the family life more easily. Once he goes up there it's like he's out to work for the day."

"Well Sam, we don't want to upset your sister," said Jake. "How about if we play in the living-room?"

"She's just stupid," said Sam. "Anyway, it's my room and I let in who I like."

Jake felt sorry for Jane, as the only girl surrounded by brothers and missionaries. No wonder she felt tormented.

The next day was church day and the missionaries were curious to survey the lay of the land before they embarked on their careers. John and Dennis were waiting to meet them at breakfast. Dennis was surprisingly fat with a round, flushed face, while John was short and blond with very small eyes. He looked very young and Jake wondered which one of them was the star missionary of the team, when he remembered what Brother Michaels had said back at the centre, that the missionaries were placed in teams with one dynamic one and one 'dead-weight', as he put it. He guessed the dynamic ones were Ellis and Dave, but he didn't see Lewis, George or even Bruce as a dead-weight. Bruce might be a joker and a bit cynical but he seemed just as ready to work as Jake. Dennis was running through the highlights of his vacation and how he had impressed the folks back home in Minnesota with stories about Japan. But after a while his dad was tired of hearing every sentence begin with 'in Japan …'.

"Like I said to him," said Dennis, "I've been here for the past year so I'm gonna talk about it, you know. It gets to be a bore for them I guess, but I couldn't help it."

"What did you miss about Japan?" asked Dave.

"The trains. I love the train rides. The guys," he said grinning benignly at his colleagues. "Mrs E's cooking," he said loudly as she came up behind him and whacked him playfully on the head with a newspaper.

"Looks like you didn't suffer though," said George patting his stomach.

"Oh yeah, that! My Bishop is mad at me and says I should lose some weight when I get back."

"It does make a better impression with the subjects," said President Ericson, "grooming and physique."

"We'll go and play football, starting next week," said Ellis.

Jake liked the way they talked openly about Dennis' weight problem instead of glossing over it. They seemed to get on well.

"I spent a lot of time in the hospital," said John. "My sister broke her leg so we would take it in turns to go sit with her when my Ma was working."

"Oh, is she feeling better?" said Mrs Ericson, concerned.

"Yeah, she's out now, walking on crutches. Kinda messed up my vacation though. I didn't get to see my friends much."

"I'll be calling you guys up to go over your appraisals after church," said the President. "So be ready!" and he went upstairs.

"What appraisals?" asked Lewis.

"Like how you've done," said George, "assessments and all in the past year. You have to say whether you feel you're doing your best, where you think you can improve and think about your good qualities and improve on them."

"Sounds difficult," said Dave, "I mean to assess yourself."

"Well the President has the figures and he gives you feedback, but they say it's better if you recognize your own strengths and weaknesses first. He also discusses your partner's appraisal of you."

"You mean you have to rat on your partner?" said Bruce in disbelief.

"Well, kind of give your opinion," said Ellis, "and try to be constructive. Say, 'well this could be better'. 'This was good'. 'Are we working as a team?'"

"What if you partner gives you a hard time?" said Bruce. "Do you beat him up afterwards?"

"You see," said Ellis, "the whole point is to try and be honest with yourself so that none of it really does come as a surprise. You're supposed to be thankful that they're helping you on your way, you know. You don't have to be bitter about it."

"Jake! You watch what you say about me!" he said, wagging his finger at him.

"So be on your best behaviour!" replied Jake, wagging his finger back.

Jake could already tell that Ellis was the most successful of the four by the way he spoke for the General Authorities and church policy and how he sometimes corrected the others. But he seemed a nice enough person, considerate about the others, especially Mrs Ericson, and polite, trying to put people at their ease. Mrs Ericson seemed to favour Dennis and even Jane brightened when she saw him. Sam was more concerned with his bag to see what he'd brought for them: a large supply of Mexican food sundries and some videos of the latest cartoons. There were lots of magazines for Jane and computer programmes for Phil.

Sunday morning came around and it did seem to inject some life into the whole household.

The chapel was no different from any other Mormon chapel, just a simple room decorated in tan wood with a platform and two rows of tiered benches facing each other and a third column of tiered benches facing the platform. There was a very small organ and a baptismal room. Off the chapel were a few small meeting rooms with TVs, videos, loudspeakers and metal chairs. There was no atmosphere in there as far as Jake could tell, except perhaps the closeness one might feel with the arrangement of the tiered seats. The place seemed no more thrilling than a school-room.

The church began to fill up with Japanese people here and there, with the Americans sitting together. The Japanese were mostly alone. It was strange not to see the family groups. There was one European-looking couple. The fact that there were so many single people made the place seem more like a public wait-ing-room. Jake was surprised people hadn't got to know each other better, unless they were all first timers, but that was unlikely after the long vacation. At last a Japanese family came in with three children and the father went to the balcony. That must be the Japanese Bishop, thought Jake.

President Ericson strode in to smiles of welcome and applause. His congregation were obviously pleased to see him. He started by welcoming everyone, especially those who had been away, and then introduced the new missionaries by name, state and age. According to John, age was very important here and people could not relax until they could place you in the pecking order on the basis of your age. The women gave clucking sounds of approval as the ages were announced because the missionaries were so young to be away from home, and they smiled in a motherly fashion. Surprised 'ohs' rang out as President Ericson announced their home states. Everyone seemed very appreciative.

Next came readings from the *Book of Mormon* followed by a short homily in Japanese. Then they read some extracts from *Doctrine and Covenants*. The communion tray was then passed around and then the people were invited to share any concerns. One elderly man stood up and the congregation seemed to sink back into their seats in a resigned way. In laboured English, the old man went back over the President's speech emphasizing one point or another and adding anecdotes of his own.

"This is Murata-san," whispered John. "He always has to say his piece." After finishing his speech with a few polite phrases in

Japanese and a welcome to the new missionaries, he sat down with dignity. One of the European couple, the woman, then spoke, remaining seated. Her English was more or less fluent.

"I don't want to spoil the first meeting with the new missionaries," she said, "but I was very sorry to see so many people away in the summer. I mean the President was here most of the time and Bishop Yamaguchi was here, but with so many people away I felt maybe a lack of support, you know what I mean. I'm sorry. I didn't mean to criticize but I wonder if the vacations could be staggered a little."

Her husband looked embarrassed that she had drawn attention to them.

"I hear you," said the President reassuringly. "It's true. The numbers go down during the summer because of the Americans taking their vacations and of course, some of the Japanese like to go away during the summer, but as you say the Bishop was here most of the time and I myself try to ..."

The woman waved her hand in front of her face dismissing it. "I'm sorry," she said. "I guess I'm trying to heap this all onto you and it's my problem. I've gotta deal with it. I'm sorry."

The Japanese were shifting in their seats.

"The Greek drama queen," whispered John in his running commentary of the characters.

"I'm sorry?" said Jake puzzled.

"She's Greek."

"How about her husband?"

"They're both Greek."

"Her English is good."

"Yeah, they've lived all over the world, working their way around the globe I guess."

Some of the young Japanese men stood up and gave short speeches in Japanese. They certainly didn't seem to be as involved as the Greek woman's problem.

"They're just talking about their progress at work and with their families," said John. "In that order," he said as an afterthought.

One girl, who could have been a student, spoke in English. "My parents at first very confused. Very upset. Tell me I must concentrate on my books and my exams. After I get good job maybe think

97

about future, they say." She giggled slightly. "But soon they realize it is not problem for me. In fact more easy life. No need to stay
out late or go away every weekend. Now I enjoy very much coming to church on Sunday and please to meet many new friends."

Jake was glad her parents had accepted her new way of life. He
couldn't believe how hard it was for people who weren't brought
up Mormon, especially non-Americans, especially non-
Christians. How did their parents feel to have all of their beliefs
and traditions thrown back at them? How would they feel to be
excluded from their child's new world, new beliefs, or have them
come back and tell them that everything they believe is wrong?
He'd like to talk to one of them about that. Come to think of it they
had hardly touched on family problems in the training, and the
converts in Tokyo only talked about adjusting at work. He
remembered Sister Fujimora in Tokyo. She was probably a little
like this woman, young and single with a family who supported
her in the end.

At the end of the service, many members of the congregation
milled around in order to speak to the President and to be introduced to the new missionaries. John suddenly darted off as he saw
Murata-san heading his way. "Oh-oh! All yours, Jake." Jake
floundered but it was too late as Murata-san came over wielding
his *Book of Mormon*.

"Ah! Good-day sir. Ah, your name?" he said.

"Jake, sir!"

"Oh very pleased to meet you and welcome to Nagoya."

"Thank you sir. It's good to be here."

"Uh Jake-san? I wonder if you could help me," and he opened
his book at a certain page and started to go over a few words. "I no
understand. You help please."

Jake read the piece to him.

"Please Jake-san. Please explain."

Jake started to explain from the notes he'd rehearsed at training. Brother Murata seemed to be listening, bobbing his head and
saying 'uh uh' every few seconds like a machine gun. When Jake
had finished he went on with his own understanding of the text
and then asked for Jake's approval. "Um, maybe I am wrong
Jake."

"No sir, that's absolutely correct as far as I understand it."

Murata beamed and shook hands again. Jake noticed John and Dennis smiling at him.

"You see that guy," said Dennis, "he's like this every week. He asks for help and then you find he's the world's expert on the *Book of Mormon*. He does that to everyone."

"Maybe he's just trying to be friendly," said Jake.

"Just trying to show off, more like," said John.

Jake saw that Murata-san was now talking to Lewis.

"The guy's a character!" said Bruce coming over.

"He talked to you?" said Jake.

"Yeah, asked for my advice about some point of scripture."

"Would that be Nephi 5:74?"

"You too?"

Dave came over looking angry.

"Did you get the old guy coming up asking for advice?" asked Bruce.

"No, he's only interested in round-eyes," said Dave cuttingly. "No-one has come up to me. Do you realize that? They saw me standing there on my own and no-one came to introduce themselves. They were all too busy talking to the *gaigin*."

"Don't feel bad," said Jake.

"You didn't miss much, believe me," added Bruce.

"This would never happen in my church," said Dave. "If you see a newcomer standing alone, you should go up and welcome them. That's what we always do."

"You could go up to them," said Bruce tentatively.

"Why should I? I'm new here. I don't know the place."

"Yeah but you're a missionary now," said Bruce. "It's your responsibility. You have to push yourself forward."

"Right now I feel somewhere in the middle," said Dave cryptically.

As though he had heard every word, Ellis came over with the Bishop to meet Dave and Dave's hurt feelings were soon mended as the Bishop chatted to him in Japanese, asked about his family and told him about his visit to California. Dave came away flushed with pride at his first successful conversation in Japanese.

"It just came out," he laughed. "I knew what he was saying and I just had the answer like that!" and he snapped his fingers.

"He was speaking pretty slowly," said John caustically.

Dave shrugged and went off to speak to Ellis. Jake and Bruce went off to get their juice and biscuits.

"Is it me or do you find John kinda negative?" asked Bruce, pouring their drinks.

"Yeah, now you mention it, I think he is kinda negative. He was criticizing some of the Japanese people in the congregation, you know and kinda rolling his eyes when they started to speak, like you know - 'here we go again'."

"Ellis is kind of a goody-two-shoes but at least he tries to be nice. He seems to be like the leader. Did you get that feeling?"

"Yeah, like he organizes everyone and keeps them in line."

They looked across at Dennis who was entertaining a circle of young men with funny stories, probably from his vacation. "Looks like he's the popular one," said Bruce.

"Where's George?" asked Jake.

They saw George sitting with the Japanese girl who had spoken during the service. She seemed to be hanging onto his every word.

"Maybe she's one of his subjects," said Jake nodding in his direction.

"I guess this is one place where you can talk to girls, right!" said Bruce.

Ellis was bobbing round with a bag of snacks. "Study circles in five minutes!" he announced. "Our group meet in the room on the right. This is the one in English."

Jake and Bruce had been hoping for a break outside before the rest of the proceedings but they went in, interested to see what they would find. Ellis was leading the circle and they started by going through some of *Doctrine and Covenants*. There were no questions from the room so they moved into discussion time. The day's discussion was 'preparing for leaving home'.

"Now I know many of you have left home already. Some of you are at university or have just joined a company. Some of you guys are missionaries living away from home for the first time. Others of you will be leaving in the next year or so. So we'd like for those of you who have left home to talk about your experience and maybe some of these younger ones will have questions for us. Uh, Jake-san, would you like to kick off?"

Jake was jolted. He'd expected to sit through this meeting as an observer. "Well I guess you miss your family," he faltered, "and uh, you have to get used to a new place, new people."

Bruce, seeing he was struggling, took over. "Well, it depends on the circumstances you're going into, like say going into missionary life, I would say it's pretty regimented and I mean for example ..."

Ellis raised his hand. "Hold on please, Bruce-san. Could you maybe speak a little slower and use more simple English. These guys speak English but they're not that used to hearing native speakers talk."

"Ah that's OK," said one of the young Japanese, speaking for the group. "Please continue!"

"I'm sorry Bruce-san," said Ellis. "You were saying?"

Bruce tried to use more simple language. "At home, right, for example, I live with my parents, my brother and sister. I share a room with my brother. I go to school every day, come home, have dinner with the family, watch TV and do my chores. I go out to movies sometimes, play pool or go to the beach. I go to church on Sunday. We have 'family home evening' on Thursday. Now I leave home to come here." By now the audience was intrigued by the details of Bruce's life. "Now I'm a grown-up who's left home and what do I find? I live with a big Mormon family, eat dinner with them every evening. I share a room with Jake here. I'll be going out to mission every day, come back, have dinner, watch TV, do my chores. Sometimes I might get to go out once in a while. So you see my life has hardly changed."

"OK I guess we should talk about after you mission or say when you start work," said Ellis. "Do any of you have anything to say about that?"

One of the Japanese men began to speak. His English was clear and precise. "After university I joined Nissan Motor Company as an engineer." Jake was now used to this identification by company. "I was working in the lab all day and sleeping at night in the dormitory. We had our meals together in the cafeteria. We got up very early and had to work very late. We had free time only on Sundays. So I can understand how Bruce-san feels. In fact the life was not as free as my home. When I was at university, even though I lived at home with my parents, I felt more free."

Ellis laughed nervously. "Looks like we don't have that much advice about leaving home. You see, what I want to look at is the first step to being the head of the family yourself. So I mean going from your father's house to living independently for a while and then later you get married and have to take care of your own family. How can you prepare?"

"My father's dead," said John bluntly.

Jake wondered if this was why he seemed to have this attitude problem.

"Yes, I know John-san," said Ellis quietly, "but most of us have our fathers still alive, thank God."

"I am the head of the household," John went on putting his hands in his trouser pockets and leaning back to make his small frame look bigger. He waited for a reaction.

"Well I guess that's pretty unusual," said Ellis.

"So for me there's no transition," said John. "This is a breeze for me compared to what I have to deal with back home. I take care of the bills, the rent, the investments, everything."

"But how do they manage while you're away?" said Bruce innocently, not noticing John's icy look.

"Uh, but John-san has touched on a good point," said Ellis. "Financial affairs. When you leave home you have to take care of money and bills for the first time, except for some of us of course," he said deferring to John. Then he looked up expectantly, hoping for a contribution from the group.

"Maybe you want to have a car," suggested one of the Japanese Mormons, and the discussion at last went off in the direction Ellis had planned.

When it was over Jake and Bruce sauntered out with Dave.

"Does it bug you how he calls us all so and so-san?" asked Bruce.

"It sounds a little pretentious," agreed Dave.

"Maybe it's just to make us seem equal," suggested Jake.

"What I like about Jake," said Bruce, putting his arm around Jake's shoulders, "is that he always tries to see the best intentions in people. Come on, kick me!" he said. "I'm just a hopeless cynic."

Jake was touched by this praise and by the fact that he had made an impression on Bruce. He felt already that they were going to be a good team because although it was true that Bruce was cynical and a little negative, he was also honest. He would often come up with the question everyone else was thinking about but didn't dare to ask. He wasn't afraid to speak out in gatherings. Also, although he saw the negative qualities in people, he was usually fair. He seemed to be a good judge of character whereas Jake had often liked a person straight away on first meeting only to be disappointed later.

They went back to the house in happy anticipation of calling home. They were allowed to call home free of charge later on Sunday afternoon to catch their families before they went to bed.

"Jake!" gushed his sister Lisa, the distance filling her with uncharacteristic fondness for her brother. "How's it going?"

"Fine. It's great. We just got back from church."

"Oh gee, yeah, we're just going to bed. That's so weird like you're already having your day. Anyway, hang on while I call everyone." Jake heard her excited voice summoning the family. He exchanged a few words with each of them as they answered his questions about home news, impatient to hear about Japan.

"So what's Japan like?" asked his mother.

"Just the same really."

"Oh Jake, it can't be. Have you seen anything of the place?"

"I mean the house, the family, everything, the church, it's just like home. We met some Japanese at church today."

"Did you get to see anything yet, Jake, any sights?"

"We saw plenty of places in Tokyo, and, oh yeah, we saw the zoo yesterday."

"The zoo?" she said. "Did he tell you he went to the zoo?" she said aside to her husband. "Well, Jake you'd better go off and see something before you start work. We love you Jake. Think about you all the time. Love you. God bless!"

The glow from the conversation filled Jake with goodwill and he decided to call Alice. She would really appreciate that. But what if he dried up on the phone? No, he would write. It was better to write; he owed her that. Before he could change his mind he went up to his room.

"You writing home already?" said Bruce, who was listening to music.

"No, this is to my fiancée." He hadn't told Bruce about the bad feeling which had come between them just before he left.

"Yeah, good idea. You're gonna be away a long time. You've

gotta keep her sweet."

"Two years *is* a long time," said Jake. "That's why I want to keep in touch, you know: tell her about my life here and see how everything's going with her."

"Is your fiancée in college?"

"No, she works at her uncle's company as a secretary. He's in insurance."

"How did you guys meet?"

"Through family really. Through the church. My dad was good friends with her uncle. We used to go on trips together when we were kids. They used to tease us, you know, when we were young: Jake and Alice are made for each other."

Bruce smiled knowingly. "I had all of that 'girl-next-door' stuff, but I wasn't interested. When I eventually get married, I'm more interested in marrying an intellectual type, someone I can really talk to, you know on my level. Does that sound big-headed?"

"I know what you mean. It's real important to be on a similar level of education. I guess you're bound to meet someone in college."

"That's what I'm hoping. I love my mom - don't get me wrong - but her contacts are limited, her conversation - you know - all practical things or church gossip. I've never really had a meaningful talk with her."

"Maybe it's her generation."

"Maybe. But my sister's not that different. She likes to talk about food, sewing, home furnishings, all of that stuff."

"Can you talk to your dad?"

"My dad? No I guess it's the same. We don't talk about ideas, just like: How ya doing in school? The ball-game, the guys at work."

"My dad's the opposite. He's always trying to get us to sit and talk with him, tell him our problems or discuss things but we never seem to have the time."

"Yeah, I know like those Mormon dads they're always preaching about."

When Bruce had gone, Jake went over his letter.

Dear Alice

Well I got here at last. Everything's going well so far. We live with the President's family. He has two sons and a daughter. They're kind of quiet, but the little guy is cute. We met the other missionaries. There are eight of us altogether. We went to church today and had a study circle about living away from home. What came out of it was that for missionaries, living away from home is more or less the same routine.

I was impressed with Tokyo. It was pretty awe-inspiring, especially the high-rise blocks. Nagoya seems a lot easier to handle. Japanese people are well-dressed and everything here is clean and efficient.

Tomorrow is our first day missioning. I'm nervous but looking forward to putting it all into practice.

Hope everything's OK with you and your family. Give my love to them all. I'm sorry we left without having a decent talk but my mind was preoccupied. Write soon and tell me all your news.

Love, Jake.

Did it sound a bit impersonal? Too factual or newsy? Alice would probably dwell more on what was not in it than what was. Maybe he should have put the last section first or she would think he was too self-centred. So he rewrote it and folded the air-letter, feeling bad that it was half blank.

When the President got back from church, Bruce, Jake and the others watched as the second-years took their turns to go into his office. Whispered conferences could be heard later behind closed doors in their rooms. These appraisals were very significant in their careers as Mormons, especially if they had any ambitions in the church. If they lived and worked in LDS communities their record could also have a bearing on their job prospects because much of the hiring and future promotion was dealt with on the strength of personal recommendations. The appraisal from the mission assignment included assessment for attitude and performance. According to President Ericson, attitude was every bit as important as performance. Many of the other mission wards had targets to fulfil and would give the missionaries a rough time if they failed to meet them. President Ericson was also concerned with numbers because he had to show expanding figures to his superiors in Tokyo, but he also wanted it to be a positive experience for the missionaries so they could grow in their faith and become mature. For some of them this might be the first time they had really considered their identity as Mormons. He wanted to send them back as quality people, because no matter how many converts they reaped, the core foundation of the church in the US had to be made up of committed, capable men. They were the future of the church. This was why he would stress the importance of working as a team, supporting your partner, contributing to family life and helping to improve the community in Nagoya.

Bruce and Jake were becoming curious about the results of the assessments, so they gingerly knocked on Ellis' door. The three of them were sitting there and John was still in the President's office.

"Do you mind?" asked Bruce. "We just wanted to know what we're up against."

"Sure, come in!" said Ellis. They could tell by his welcome that he had received a very favourable appraisal.

"How did you do?" asked Jake.

"What we expected really," said Dennis. "We knew how many subjects we'd brought into church and we went over their progress, looking at how many of them were regular and who dropped out."

"So is it like performance targets?" asked Bruce.

"Kinda like that," said Ellis. "But they are also interested in church activities we've organized or the counselling we give to some people in the church."

George was going through a small notebook and seemed subdued. Jake thought he must feel overshadowed by Ellis' obvious ability and relentless cheerfulness. He looked up as he sensed the others were waiting for him to speak.

"You see," he began, "the hardest thing is keeping their interest. You may get someone who seems so interested and then maybe attends church once out of curiosity and then you never see him again. It's so difficult to get those people back. It's kind of embarrassing calling on them again because you know they've stopped coming for a reason. I don't know, but most of the people Ellis has brought in, they all seem to keep up their interest and a lot of them end up getting baptized."

"Ellis! What's your secret?" asked Bruce.

"I just follow the training, you know," he answered. "We were told always to leave on a note of suspense, so the subject wants to know more. Also I think enthusiasm counts, and then answering their questions or showing them how the church can help them out of their problems. The main thing is not to give up. That's what I always tell you, right, George?"

"But George! You did really well on language, didn't you?" said Dennis.

"Maybe you understand them too well," said Jake, and George's face seemed to brighten a little.

"You see, that's where I fall down," said Ellis. "I've never really gotten the language. When we go out, George is usually way ahead but when they come into church they usually want to speak English."

Jake noticed George's bookshelves stacked with Japanese dictionaries and language books, while Ellis' side mainly consisted of business and marketing books, bestsellers from the US about how to make a success of your life. George also had prints and calendars on his side of the room, while Ellis had lots of charts and journals with appointments written on them.

"Love your artwork," said Bruce admiringly. "Did you get those here?"

"Yeah, I love Japanese pictures," he said shyly.

Jake had seen one of the prints before. It was a picture of a blue wave in traditional Japanese style with elegant characters on the side. Another was in the shape of a bookmark with cranes on it and more Japanese calligraphy. Jake remembered that Dave had told him that in California many Americans liked to wear T-shirts with Chinese characters on them as a kind of decoration but they had no idea what they meant. He had also read that the height of fashion in Japan was to have a bag or T-shirt or notebook with English written on it, which were often any words randomly put together as if two or three sentences had been taken from three different books and combined. The examples the author had chosen had had him in fits of laughter and he had been looking for them himself since he got to Japan. The notepad they had bought at the stationer's had amused him. The logo on the front read 'Minty and her friends welcome you to sunshine writing day'. It would do as a start to his collection.

Suddenly John burst in and lay on the bed with his hands behind his head. He seemed to be in a flippant mood.

"How did it go, John?" asked Dennis.

"I thought this was supposed to be a private meeting," he replied, looking steadily at Jake and Bruce. Jake was disconcerted by the way his eyes stayed on him, defiant and challenging. He was about to get up and apologize when Ellis said, "They can benefit from this too John. Anyway you don't have to tell us about your appraisal if you don't want to."

"Do I look like I could care less about my appraisal?" he said mutinously. He had a way of making them feel foolish for taking it too seriously, or maybe he was covering up with bravado because the President had not been pleased with him. The awkward silence was broken by a furtive knock from Dave.

"Oh hi you guys! We have to see President Ericson."

Bruce and Jake were relieved to get out of the tense room and quickly explained how John had spoken to them.

"Has he got some kind of problem?" said Dave.

"Probably trying to establish his authority," said Jake.

They straightened their clothes and cleared their throats as they entered the office. It had several desks with files and trays neatly arranged. A cabinet with labelled drawers stood against the wall and there were several charts on the walls. The President was sitting in a comfortable leather chair behind the largest desk by the window, with four chairs carefully arranged in front of him. Lewis was already waiting nervously.

"Sit down boys! Glad to see you. Now I want to see you all together to prepare you for tomorrow and to take any questions or concerns you might have. Well, the first week you'll be working with the second-years who will take you around and show you the ropes. The following week you'll be working in the pairs you've already been assigned. What we hope," he said pausing to look at them intently, "is that you'll develop a very special partnership of mutual support. You'll be spending a lot of time together and the success of your mission largely depends on your ability to work together. Now," he said briskly opening a file, "You'll have had time to get to know our second-years. What I propose is that Jake goes out with Ellis, Lewis with George. You, Dave, will go out with Dennis and Bruce with John."

It instantly seemed to Jake that he had paired them off in accordance with his assessment of their ability. Perhaps Ellis was to be a role model for Jake. Jake was pleased but embarrassed to be considered the most promising of the four. At the same time he knew Bruce would feel insulted by finding himself with John. He had seen his look of horror as the names were announced. And Bruce was not about to leave them in suspense.

"Sir I hope you don't mind me cutting in at this point, but I have to say that John and I have not hit it off very well so far. I don't know that it would be the best thing for us to work together."

President Ericson gave a twitchy smile. He was clearly reluctant to be too frank at the start, but he said, "I know John Vallitt can be rather an abrasive character at times, but I'm sure that as you get to know each other things will begin to improve, and this is only for a week. As far as your permanent partners go, we have been known to break up teams and swap them around if it looked like bad feeling was going to work against the mission."

Bruce was not placated. "I found Brother George very easy to get along with," he said. Lewis, however, was not about to risk having his happy match usurped. Neither did he want to be lumbered with John.

"George and I get along just fine," he said in his slow, nasal voice.

Bruce shrugged, knowing he was beaten.

"OK that's settled," said the President. "And please don't mention any of this to the others. It would only cause unpleasantness. Now as to this week, your role will be as observers, primarily. You won't be required to take an active role in the sessions, just to act as back-up to your partner. Your job is to listen, observe the subject and start to build up an idea of different categories of people. Are they 'yes men' (or women for that matter) who just want to appease you? You'll find plenty of those. Are they curious people who are just interested to meet some English-speaking people, or are they thinking people who can take part in discussions and come up with arguments? How big a role does religion play in their lives? Are they already committed to Buddhism or to some form of Christianity? Are they business people or family people, or interested in the environment, or interested in money? All of these things help us to build up a picture. Now I'm passing out a sheet here with some of these profiles summarized to help you. You just put a check beside the different characteristics. Your partner will already have an area summary of the neighbourhood with details of things like social class and type of area: whether it's a place with people working locally or predominantly a dorm town. Anyway by the end of it we expect you to be experts on Nagoya and its people."

"Knowledge is Power", Jake's dad had once said. That phrase had stuck in Jake's mind from a conversation he had heard between his dad and a friend, Brother Carver, who worked in the missions department. It had been during a barbecue party given by Brother Carver, when Jake had flopped down to eat his meal near where they were sitting. They had been talking about the Mormon church's massive evangelizing initiative, famous all over the world. His dad had been asking about the effectiveness of the mission effort in gaining converts and keeping them, balanced against the time and effort spent on the missions. It was then that Len Carver had explained that there was more to it than that. There were of course the new converts to make the church grow. Then there were the stakes set up all over the world to make the church establish its influence in as many areas as possible. But another strategy was perhaps more important. It was to know as much as possible about the people of the world, the way they lived, how much money they had, their political and religious beliefs, above all the way their minds worked. The church had mapped out, house by house, large tracts of the world and were perhaps the only people, along with the Jehovah's Witnesses, who knew the world so well. That's when he said, "Knowledge is Power". Jake only remembered this because of the expression of slight foreboding which had passed over his dad's face. Jake had instinctively turned away to hide the fact that he'd been listening in.

Jake realized he had lost concentration, but the President was still going over forms. They definitely had a lot of paperwork to deal with.

"So!" the President went on. "What I want to see next Sunday is a stack of these profiles filled out, and then you'll be ready to step out on your own. Shall we bow our heads in prayer asking the Lord to support us on this challenge he has given us and pray that the fullness of his Gospel may be heard in ever more homes? Amen!"

That night they enjoyed a hearty dinner of Mexican refried beans brought from the States, and meatballs. Phil had prepared the dinner with help from Dennis and everyone was full of compliments. Jake went to the roster to discover his chores and found he had been put on dishes and garbage for that week. He thought that was pretty heavy, considering Bruce only had vacuuming that week. Jane was starting to get used to the newcomers and she smiled as she saw Jake peering at the roster.

"We switch it around," she said, "so some weeks you have an easy job, some weeks something more difficult." He noticed her accent was not quite American, not quite foreign, but somewhere in between. He had seen her laughing with her friends in church and it seemed to have cheered her up.

After the meal, the President said grandly, "I'd like to introduce you to my special room. This way please." They followed him, intrigued, across the polished, wooden floor. He opened a sliding door, which Jake had taken for a scroll, and waved them in. It was a beautiful, traditional Japanese room, absolutely bare apart from a display platform on one side and a low table in the centre. The President threw some cushions around the table and beckoned for them to sit down. He smiled warmly at the pleasure they took in the authentic Japanese room.

"A real *tatami* room!" said Dave in awe.

"What's *tatami*?" asked Lewis.

"This flooring," said the President, patting the straw-like matting beneath them.

"It smells good," said Jake, "like herbs and straw."

"Now to me," said the President, "that's the smell of Japan. Don't you love that smell? I love coming back to this room. Most Japanese homes have *tatami*. You see it's a set of very thick, close-fitting mats. The Japanese usually change them once a year but they're really expensive. We've kept these the whole time we've been here because we don't use it very often. The Japanese subjects and church members usually want to talk in my office or in the sitting-room."

"It's very relaxing," said Bruce. "They call this minimalist, don't they? I was reading a little about zen back home."

"Yes, I find it focuses the mind, the lack of clutter. A good place to pray, in fact, or study."

They sat for a while speaking in murmurs because the room seemed almost holy. Finally the President stretched and brought the little meeting to an end.

"Well, up early tomorrow, boys. And by the way, I'd appreciate it if you asked permission when you want to use this room."

"That was some little room, huh?" said Bruce that night.

"Yeah, that's what I always imagined Japanese rooms to be like, you know, all empty," said Jake.

"Yeah, minimalist. Remember Dave said his uncle's house had European furniture in most of the rooms and one room kept in Japanese style."

"Ellis was saying that when you get out into the more rural areas they mostly have *tatami* rooms like that, but more cluttered."

"You nervous about tomorrow? You're lucky going with Ellis. He'll probably help you out a lot but this John guy … I'm seriously concerned."

"I am nervous, but at least the first week we don't have to do much."

Jake hung up his clothes, casting a disapproving look at Bruce's things already falling around the chair.

"Bruce, you've got some closet space."

"I know but I'm tired at night, you know. I just like to crash and forget about it."

"Remember we're supposed to look well turned-out. Your clothes aren't gonna last long like that."

"OK mother!" he quipped, fussing around his clothes and folding them in an exaggerated manner.

"You'll thank me," said Jake.

Later on, when they were trying to get off to sleep, they kept managing to break the conversation only for one of them to start it up again. Bruce piped up yet again. "I know you don't like bringing this up, but you know the Temple?"

"Bruce, come on. I told you I don't like to talk about it. OK now let's get some sleep. We've got an early start."

"Is it because we were told to keep it secret?" he ventured.

"It's not that. I just haven't come to terms with it properly in my own mind yet, enough to discuss it."

Bruce didn't reply and left an ominous gap in the air as if one or the other was going to start talking again through the silence. Both could hear the other, expectant, eyes open but neither spoke again, and once again Jake fell asleep accompanied by some of the disturbing pictures he had tried to put into the back of his mind.

The workday morning took on quite a different tempo to the other days. It was as if everyone had a well-rehearsed routine and weaved in and out of each other, here packing a lunch-box, there collecting books and papers, with Mrs Ericson orchestrating their movements. That week Dennis was delegated to iron the shirts for the whole household. He had to have clean shirts for everyone every day by seven o'clock. It was up to him whether he did it the night before or rushed it in the morning. He had left it to the morning and was now trying to finish his breakfast in between the chores, with the missionaries coming down one by one looking for their shirts.

"Sister Ericson!" he whined. "Could you please help me. I'm afraid I'm gonna be late."

"You know what we teach you in this house," she said firmly.

"Yeah, Yeah, responsibility," he droned as if he had heard it many times before.

"You know very well," she said, "that when you're given a chore, it's your responsibility to do it. The whole house depends on it. It's up to you either to do it the night before or get up early enough."

"Mrs E. I'm still jet-lagged," he said, puffing and sweating as he rushed through the shirts.

But Mrs Ericson was already dealing with a new crisis over her daughter's school uniform.

The President was sitting at the dining table going through some correspondence.

"I'll be shadowing some of you today," he said, "in the car. Maybe catch up with you here and there to see how you're doing."

He seemed very upbeat and cheerful that morning, and answered their questions easily and breezily as if he was trying to calm their fears.

"Most of these towns are quiet little areas. Manageable. You'll probably get through fifty calls, all told, depending on how well you do. You and Ellis," he said to Jake, "about ten calls in the same time."

The President laughed as Jake's face fell. "Is that all?"

"Think about it," said John. "The better you do, the less calls you have to make." He waited as Jake became even more puzzled.

"He still doesn't get it," John laughed.

Ellis came in fixing his tie. "Get what?" he said.

"Explain to him, Ellis," said the President, "about quality time."

"Ellis knows all about that," said George.

"You see when you do a call," Ellis explained, "and the subject slams the door in you face or more likely over here, politely waves their hand at you, it takes about three minutes. But, if you get to go in and talk with them, it's more like thirty minutes. So the longer you spend on a call, the fewer you do."

"But," said the President suddenly, "Quality time ...?" Like the President in Tokyo he waited for them to finish this well-known slogan.

"... Does not always produce results," Ellis filled in.

"Which means," said the President for the benefit of the new recruits, "that it doesn't matter how long you stay, if they don't come along to church or follow it up, you're wasting your time beyond about twenty minutes."

"Remember," said Ellis, "a lot of Japanese people show interest just to be polite but really they have no intention of taking it any further."

Finally it was time to leave and they left the house in their respective pairs with shouts of 'good luck' from the family. They all clutched their notebooks which contained the train times.

"These times are exact," said Ellis as they got to the subway. "I've never known a Japanese train to be one second late, except one time." He laughed at the memory. "We were at Nagoya station on this train to Yokkaichi. That's out west, and a woman was taken ill on the train. I think she fainted or something. Anyway, the next minute there was an army of station people ready to help her off the train and I thought, 'that's real considerate', until we realized that they were only concerned that the train might be delayed a second or something. You should have seen them. They were so nervous, trying to bundle that poor woman off the train."

They took the subway to Nagoya main-line station and Jake tried to keep up with the directions as Ellis led him to the platform.

"You'll get it," he said seeing the look of panic on Jake's face. "Within a few weeks I'll bet you could navigate your way around Nagoya station blindfold."

"Right now it looks like a maze."

On the platform Ellis strode over to a gaunt-looking foreigner in glasses. As Jake watched the friendly greetings he realized the man was British.

"Where's old George?" said the man. "Did he not come back?"

"Yeah, this is my trainee," he said proudly introducing Jake. "Just for the first week, then we're back in the old team, but Jake will be taking over Okazaki from now on."

Jake shook hands and was fascinated to hear the clipped accent that he associated with the few British costume dramas he had seen on TV back home. He had only met a few British people before, back home, all Mormon converts.

"How do you find Japan, Jake?"

"Well, so far I'm pretty confused with all the trains and platforms. Next week we have to make our own way around."

"Don't worry. I'll help you. I get this train every Monday and I go to Okazaki on Wednesday evenings too."

"James is an English teacher," said Ellis. "He's from Bradford, Yorkshire, right?"

"That's right. Been in Japan three years now."

"You must like it," said Jake.

"It's all right. You get used to it. It's like you get home in the summer and you think, 'Right what shall I do now? I could do this or that or I could always go back to Japan', and in the end you think, 'well it's familiar, got my friends. The job's well-paid, easy life-style', and I sign a contract for another year. Anyway they're used to me now so they're always pleased to see me back. Actually though I do like the place. I miss home but when I'm there, I'm always comparing it with Japan. Yeah, Japan's great. Trains are always on time. Talking of which," he said, pointing as the train came into view. Jake was surprised that Ellis deliberately got on the train at a different section from James.

"Oh, I thought we'd sit with James." He liked James's accent.

"People like a little privacy on the train, Jake," said Ellis. "You know reading, going over notes."

"Have you ever taken the opportunity to witness him on the train? I mean this is a long journey."

"I don't know what they told you at training but we are told only to witness to authorized subjects and to make a record of all witness sessions. They said casual conversations were not fruitful and we might come across problems we haven't been trained for."

"Yeah, I remember they told us not to mix with non-Japanese students and to keep contacts with foreigners to a minimum."

"Exactly. Yeah, I mean we come across *gaigin* all the time, especially on the trains, because a lot of them travel out to teach in companies. So you know, we have a little conversation, create a good impression and leave it at that."

"But why don't they like us to witness other categories of people if we have the chance? I mean wouldn't you just jump at the chance? I just don't get that."

"I had it explained to me like this," said Ellis turning to face Jake and adopting a serious expression, "We're the juniors right? We're on the lowest echelons. We're just starting out."

"Yeah but we've been Mormons all our lives."

"But missionary work takes training. You can't just go out and talk to anyone without proper training. Now we've been trained specifically to work with Japanese people. We know their backgrounds, their psychology and what kind of arguments they're gonna come up with. Other types of people we'll learn about as we move on up in the church."

"But I mean if the scripture is there, it doesn't matter where they're from or who they are, all we have to do is explain it, explain the history and the facts stand up for themselves."

Ellis smiled in a patronizing way. "Jake, believe me. I was like you when I got here, wide-eyed, zealous, full of enthusiasm that I could convert the whole world, but I began to see from what the

President told me and the folks at home, that the official way is best. Let's face it. They've had the experience. They know what works and what doesn't work. I mean as they say, 'You don't send a man to war with a water-pistol'."

Jake was clearly nonplussed.

"What that means," said Ellis spelling it out for him, "is that missionaries, when they go into the field, need the proper tools and for us, our training specifically fits us for Japan."

"I guess that makes sense," said Jake. But he still had reservations. In fact he would have been interested to know what James would have said, how he would have reacted to hearing the Mormon message. He might never have heard anything like that before. He might not even be Christian. Jake had heard that the British, in general, were not as committed Christians as in the States. If James had brought up questions he couldn't answer, he wouldn't have been embarrassed because he could always check the answer with the President or look it up. He was eager to get to know all kinds of people on this trip. For the time being though, he concentrated on getting to know the Japanese. 'The Japanese?' He laughed inside. He talked as if they were another species, but Professor Owen at the training had told them the Japanese had a very strong sense of their own identity, as distinct from the rest of the world. Something to do with being an island and far from the mainland. That taught you never to wholly trust outsiders. What Jake was interested in was making them see that they were not different. Their marks were language and history but others shared their looks and their religion. They had more in common with the rest of the world than they thought. To make the Japanese open to the idea of the Church of Jesus Christ of Latter Day Saints, you had to accentuate what they had in common, with Americans especially. You had to show them that God meant his message to be for everyone.

Jake was preparing to recline in his seat for a while and gather his thoughts before they arrived, but Ellis suddenly snapped into action, bringing out all the charts, records and notes from his bag and all the information relating to Okazaki. The map was shaded blue for areas already covered within the last three years, green for the area currently under operation and white for uncharted territory. Then came out a list of houses, identified by occupants' names, or more often by a description of its occupants, e.g. *Okaasan* + *Obaasan* + baby boy.

Ellis explained that Japanese houses had no numbers, and only the largest roads had names. In small neighbourhoods you knew the street by landmarks. This made it difficult to identify streets or houses, so they had to map out the area themselves and identify the street by one means or another. One missionary had had the idea of naming streets and houses according to the names of visiting missionaries and the date and time, but this system was not really workable as it still did not tell you if a house had been visited or not when you actually arrived in the town. The latest system they had was a row of blanks drawn on the paper to represent the row of houses on a cross section of the town, which was labelled and corresponded to a section on the overall map of the city. George had been largely responsible for masterminding this system and it was much approved of by Tokyo. On each block there would be a sticky label, red for church visit, blue for Mormon house (which was exceedingly rare), white for interest shown, and the vast majority yellow for 'no contact given'. In addition, there were one or two black labels.

"Those look ominous," Jake commented.

"No, the black labels mean the person is committed to some other religion very strongly and is liable to counter-missionary you."

"Are they afraid we'll become Zen Buddhists or something?" said Jake.

Ellis smiled. "Well that's just to tell us it would be a waste of time going in there. But not always. Sometimes the President has us go on a special call to them, usually when he comes along. This is if they are Japanese who have, say, converted to Jehovah's or some kind of evangelical Christian branch or even just Catholics. He figures they are open to conversion. It's only a matter of discussion for them to be convinced ours is the true church. Anyway, the black square is just a warning so you're not taken unawares. And this," he said bringing out another sheet of paper, "is the detailed record the President already showed you. So say this is a black square, I go to the record sheet to get more information and I see '*Odjii-san* + *Okaasan* + two boys at school + husband ND Okazaki.' So that's grandpa and mom at home. Then I look in the column and I find 'Nichiren Shoshu rep for Okazaki'. That's serious because that doesn't mean they're just committed Soka Gakkei members. The Grandpa is actually an official quite high up in Soka Gakkei and the husband is the local representative. Then under comments we get 'religious dialogue'. This means he's happy to talk and exchange ideas but only to try and make out that Nichiren Shoshu is superior. So in a way, his mind is closed. So if we're going down this street again, we probably wouldn't go in there."

"I heard about Soka Gakkei before," said Jake. "What is it?"

"Let's just say for now it's a modern Buddhist sect, but it would take too long to get into the theology now. What's important for us though is that it's very popular, especially with young people, and attracts a lot of converts. They also have their own political party."

It intrigued Jake to think that a religion as old as Buddhism could have new sects too, but it made sense. Whatever religion it was, they must have new sects coming up all the time to attract the young people. Jake's head was beginning to swim with facts and diagrams and charts. He was by now looking forward to seeing Ellis in action and get talking to people.

For the final few minutes before they got off the train Ellis drilled Jake in Japanese and had him start a conversation and introduce himself in Japanese. Then Ellis took over with the opening statement they used if invited in. Jake had to translate back into English.

"Yeah, you seem to have gotten it," said Ellis.

Secretly, Jake thought his accent was pretty abysmal now he had heard the other missionaries and the Ericson children speaking. He sounded all-American. Then he remembered that George's Japanese was good, so maybe as a team they worked well with Ellis' enthusiasm and winning smile and George's quiet good manners and fluent Japanese.

He wondered why Ellis was credited with bringing in the converts. If they worked in pairs, he couldn't see how one person could take the credit for bringing someone in or converting them. It must be a team effort. Though he could imagine that there would be pairs in which one person would do all the work and the other acted as a back-up, he couldn't picture this happening with Ellis and George.

As they stepped off the train and followed the small army of commuters out into Okazaki, Jake was suddenly seized by a sense of panic. They would be calling uninvited on other peoples' houses at a time when most people were busy. Moreover, these were foreign houses where they could hardly speak the language. Jake had also noticed that Ellis would not stop talking. He seemed to be prattling on without even caring if Jake was listening. Jake tried hard to concentrate but he just wished Ellis would give it a rest for a minute and let him gather his thoughts. It wasn't just panic and dread which poured over him, but a sudden sense of feeling ridiculous, which was much worse than fear. It made him suddenly think, 'What on earth am I doing here, coming to tell complete strangers about something they have never heard of and probably wouldn't understand?' He tried to calm himself with half-remembered homilies about the sacrifices and hardships of the mission. They were not to feel downhearted. This was God's work and He would support them. But it was not disappointment that worried Jake. That he could handle. He had been well-prepared for it. What was nagging him was how to quell the feeling that they were just a couple of geeks muscling in onto someone else's life. Then, in a trance, he found himself following Ellis out of the station, across the road, past a factory and right into the first port of call of his missionary career.

They were met by an elderly lady who opened the door and immediately began to close it again while waving her hand and saying 'No, thank you'. Despite Ellis' polite opening phrases and requests that she take a leaflet, she waved her hand all the more, her face wrinkled as if she was smelling something bad.

"Plot this street, Jake, and mark this one yellow, will you? Put 'Obaasan' on the other list," said Ellis breezily as he went on to the next house.

"That lady was not interested at all, was she?" said Jake, feeling his thumping heart ease a little.

"Get used to it Jake," he smiled. "This is normal. Come on! Let's get going."

They worked their way up the street, encountering varying degrees of firm refusal. The most they had was a polite conversation on the doorstep with an elderly man who wanted to talk about the Americans he had met during the war. His English was good.

"A lot of the old guys learned their English in the war," Ellis explained, as they turned to give the man a friendly wave. He went back into his house, his chest swelling a little at proud memories rekindled.

Jake filled the row with yellow squares, except for one white square for the war hero. He was beginning to feel comforted by the routine. The rejection was not so bad after all. At least they didn't have to go further than the front door. Many of the people refused them in a way that made them feel they were familiar with Mormon missionaries and he began to feel a little less of a freak. By the time they reached a little park for lunch, they had scored nil.

"It's nice now," said Ellis stretching out on a bench, "but you wait till the rainy season."

"When's that?"

"Coming soon; and that is the worst time of year. Humid, wet. The damp gets in everything. And I'm talking torrents of rain here, all the time. Last year we had storms, tornadoes, everything."

"What do we do for lunch in the rainy season?"

"You just have to find some shelter or other, or else go to a chain store; but that means you have to buy something, so the President doesn't encourage it."

Jake looked about them. The small park was deserted. Some of the leaves were just turning and they gave the park a burnished glow.

"I'm finding it boring so far," he admitted suddenly.

"That's work!" said Ellis. "Got to keep going." As if to prove the point, as soon as they had finished their last crumb, he clapped his hands and sprang up. "Well, no rest for the wicked. Onto the next block!"

They made a few more calls and passed a row of shops.

"Do we go into stores?" asked Jake.

"No, they're too busy. We stick to houses and we talk to individuals when we work in the park or on university campuses. You'll like the park. That's Wednesday. We'll be going to Tsurumae this week, but you and Bruce will be assigned to Sakae downtown. These out of the way places are pretty dull."

Just as Jake was beginning to get complacent, they were invited in. The occupant, a housewife of about fifty, led them into a cluttered room with a low table by the television. The grandmother was sitting in the corner watching a TV drama. She was the archetypal Japanese grandma with an indoor kimono-type outfit, grey hair in a bun and very wrinkled skin. Her smile was sweet. The housewife offered them tea and Ellis asked for water. When they were settled he asked her if she had heard of the Mormons. She said she had because her son was currently studying at UCLA in the States and had met quite a few Mormons. He had told her about them in his letter home. She explained what she already knew about them, something about not drinking alcohol and being very clean and strict and about going to church. Ellis asked if she had any religious beliefs and she said she was just like all Japanese: Shinto. She observed some of the festivals, visited the shrine once in a while and called in the priest for weddings or funerals. Beyond that she hadn't thought. Ellis was doing well with the questions which were fluent and well-rehearsed, despite that stifling accent. Sometimes the lady had to request a repeat two or three times. The Grandma, obviously unaware he was even speaking Japanese, would occasionally smile benignly in their direction and then go back to her soap opera. Jake was trying to follow some of the lady's answers. He understood some of the questions from his briefing sheet which listed some of the more common ones. She was speaking fairly slowly and he was pleased to be able to pick up the gist. Ellis asked if her religion was able to solve most of life's problems and she said that one got by in the end whatever fate might throw at you. She said she had gone through the normal crises with her children with exams and leaving to study abroad and the usual financial problems, but nothing serious. They had enough to go on annual holidays and were looking forward to visiting the States. Her daughter was married to an engineer who had a job at a local chemical plant, and they had a baby boy. Things were working out. Jake had the chance to make his contribution when she asked a few questions about where he was from, his age, family, and reactions to Japan. Jake started to gain confidence and wanted to go on, until he could see that the conversation was not going the way Ellis was intending. It was obvious the woman had invited them in for information and reassurance that her son was in a safe place. Her interest was more in America than in LDS.

Ellis launched into questions on the Bible and began to explain that the Bible as we know it now is not complete. The woman's interested expression egged him on. He explained that the Bible in its present form was only as good as the translations that had come down to us through the ages. In good faith, those who recorded it did their best, but when so far removed from the source it was bound to be flawed. The Bible itself was replete with prophecies about the fulfillment of God's word; and now did she know there was another Testament of Jesus Christ which had been translated accurately in the modern age? The woman's look of wonder showed she hadn't heard any of this news before, so Ellis went on to explain the achievements of Joseph Smith in translating the whole *Book of Mormon* with the help of special stones. "He was entrusted with Golden Plates that had been buried for ages and was shown the location of the plates by an angel." The woman's only reaction was to repeat in a tone of wonder, "special stones, golden plates, um! um! *So desu ka?*" When Ellis had completed the first lesson he told her to think about what he had said. She said that she would get her son to find out more about it from his university friends. Ellis reassured her that he would be back the following week to follow up their lesson and by the time the woman's face had registered a look of shock, he was at the door, hand outstretched ready to wish her goodbye. Jake gave an apologetic smile as he shook her hand. He felt her small, limp hand as an indication that she had no experience of shaking hands. He wondered what she would be saying to Grandma.

"Do you get the feeling she was just listening to all the scriptural stuff to be polite?" he asked Ellis.

"Yeah, Jake," said Ellis not answering his question, "I have to tell you, you made a mistake in there."

"I'm sorry. What did I do wrong?"

"You shouldn't have kept her talking on personal matters about the States and everything and how you like Japan. We have to keep the topic on schedule as much as possible. Our time is limited."

"I was trying to build up a rapport, though. I thought that was important."

"OK, right. I understand. Just learn from your mistakes. Next time just answer as briefly as you can."

Jake felt a bit bruised by Ellis' reaction to what he had considered to be his first communication success. The trouble was, he had been more in sympathy with the woman. He had picked up the obvious signs that she was more interested in American life than the intricacies of Mormon theology. As they sailed up drive after drive, Jake noticed that even Ellis was starting to flag. All of a sudden they heard a car horn behind them and up rolled President Ericson. He looked incongruous in these surroundings. His lumberjack looks and build were more suited to a North American forest than the dainty streets of small-town, rural Japan. One or two old ladies on the way to the shops stared as they saw him clamber out of the little car.

"Hello, boys," he smiled striding over to them. "Just came to see how you're doing."

"Not bad, sir," said Ellis trying to look more cheerful. "We had a couple of people interested."

"You want me to finish any of them off for you?"

"Well there was this one woman we're booked to go back to next week."

"Aha, yes I think we'll leave that. You went over the first lesson with her? What else?"

"Yes sir, so we'll follow that one up. The other one was an older man who spoke to us on the front step."

"Any outcome?"

"Not really, sir."

"Well I think we'd better go and tie that one up, huh? Now Jake, as this is your first day, you can go sit in the car and take a rest and we'll go and see this fella."

Jake was relieved to go to the car after an afternoon spent on his feet. The sticky heat was unpleasant to work in and he felt exhausted. He sat in the car and laid his head back trying to go over the day in his mind. On the whole, it had been less nerve-wracking than he'd expected. He had found Ellis rather moody towards the end of the day but that was probably the strain of working all day in the heat without much success. Then he thought of the kind of day Bruce must be having with John and thought he wasn't that badly off after all. He looked at his papers and was pleased that he had managed to keep up with the records. Soon Ellis and the President came back to the car. Jake waited for them to say how they had done but the President just started the car and drove off. Jake asked falteringly, "How did that go?"

"Oh fine," said the President dismissively. "We'll see him next week, probably in church the week after."

"Oh good!" said Jake. "So are we finished for the day?"

"Yep!" said the President. "That's it. I came at the end of the day so I could run you home. Figured you'd be beat on your first day."

"Thank you sir," said Jake, and then fell silent as he sensed that they didn't feel like talking. Gradually he dozed off, and they hardly spoke a word all the way back to Nagoya. As they drove up to the house they saw Mrs Ericson on her knees in the garden, digging in the flower-beds.

"Did you look after Jake?" she asked Ellis.

"Oh yes ma'am. We had a fairly quiet day so he saw the usual routine."

"Yes, I was real nervous at first, but gradually got into it. I like filling in the reports," said Jake.

"That's a pretty important part of the job." She got up and stretched painfully. "Oh my poor back. Never know why I bother trying to get the garden into shape. The weather's so changeable. We'll have the rains soon."

"Ellis told me about the rain," said Jake.

"Now," she continued, bustling them into the house. "I would do the garbage now Jake because you have other things to do later and you may want a break this evening."

Jake dutifully gathered up the garbage from around the house and had a chance to peep into all the rooms he hadn't yet seen. The house had the usual large paintings of scenes from the *Book of Mormon* on several of the walls. Sam was playing with his 'Gameboy' when Jake went in and he was so intent on the game that he just raised his hand in greeting. Jane's room was locked but her garbage can was conveniently placed outside for him. Phil's room was cluttered with books piled up everywhere and papers strewn about. Phil was out at crammer school until late. Jake wrapped up the garbage and then out of habit asked Mrs Ericson if he could help prepare the dinner. She accepted his offer and instructed him to peel the potatoes and vegetables. Jake made a mental note not to offer again. He was no fool, to ask to do more than his share. As Mrs Ericson worked she would keep returning to her journal and reading it avidly. The preparation of the dinner seemed to be an unwelcome interruption for her. Glancing at the title he saw it read *Journal of Molecular Biology*.

"I see you're interested in science," he remarked.

Her face took on the zeal of someone truly dedicated. "Yes," she said, "in my previous incarnation I was a molecular biologist."

"Seriously?" said Jake. "Wow, that's fascinating!"

"Yes, I was Head of Department at Cleveland University for several years before my husband got promoted to the missions."

"Were you sorry to give that up?"

"Was I ever? And believe me, the longer you're out of the running, the harder it is to keep up. The field progresses so fast. All I can do is read the literature and keep in touch with my colleagues. I've been asked to give one or two lectures here in Japan, one at Yokohama and another at Osaka. Still," she sighed, "we have to go where the church propels us."

Jake looked at her in a new light. She was certainly unlike other Mormon women of her generation. Most women in his mother's circle were homemakers, except the few, like his mom, who had part-time jobs, but that was usually back-up work for the church. The church prided itself on raising women who put home first, and his mother had always drummed that into his sisters. 'High-flying lawyers would come down to earth with a bang', she would say, 'if after a day out in the world they came back to an empty house and no dinner in the oven'. In fact many Mormons nurtured a feeling close to disdain for career women, and could tell all manner of fearful cautionary tales of lives of spinsterhood or childless later years. In spite of that, the younger generation had followed the spirit of the whole country, and more and more young Mormon women were pursuing careers which continued even into marriage. Yet it was still only a minority who left the children with a babysitter to continue with their careers. In this context, Mrs Ericson's achievement seemed remarkable.

Jake finally got his rest before dinner. He could hear the others were home next-door but despite his curiosity he wanted some time alone at last. It struck him then that since he had left Utah, he'd hardly had a moment alone except in the bathroom. He needed time to go over the day's events and shake off some of the stress which was starting to build up. He'd had a full ten minutes of solitude when Bruce cautiously opened the door and came in grinning.

"Well!" said Jake. "Someone had a good day."

"Yeah, it wasn't so bad. You know, John's OK when you get to know him."

"So he didn't give you a hard time?"

"No, in fact he told me all the short cuts and introduced me to his favourite places in Gifu town."

"What favourite place?" Jake was intrigued.

Bruce flopped down on the bed. "I'll tell you the whole story. Right, first we get to Gifu and he takes me to the place they'd been working before the vacation. We do a few calls, all no responses. Then he says, 'come on! We've earned a break.' We go into town and he takes me to Burger City and we just sit there for a couple of hours eating French fries and watching the people. Then these two college students come up, a boy and a girl and ask if they could speak English and we have a really good discussion about college and all. John told them about the church and asked them really casually to come along. He gave them his card and they seemed real interested. Then do you know what he does? He takes one of the sheets and fills it in, 'no response, no response, no response!' all the way to the bottom of the list and then he puts one red sticker. He said that was for the couple in and he just designated any house for them."

Jake was aghast. "He cheated like that?" he said.

"That's not all. We went out again for a quick stroll, about ten calls. We got asked into this old guy's house, who also spoke English and we got him interested enough to arrange a call back next week. So John says, 'Right! Day over!' and we go back to town to a restaurant for a couple of hours. I asked him how he got away with it. He said now he had the chance, he felt like he deserved a week off before he goes back to the grind. But he was kinda right. You get more chance of meeting someone who wants to talk in a café than going up to the houses. Anyway we got two prospective church visits out of it. Not bad, huh?"

"Yeah, we only got two as well, one and a half really. The President caught up with us to run us home and he went off with Ellis to persuade this one old guy we'd met to come to church. But we worked all day for that. Nearly eighty percent no luck!"

"You see! So you could have had an easy day like us."

"But there's one problem. What if someone finds out you've been falsifying the records?"

"That's John's problem. Remember I'm only an innocent trainee. Anyway, he told me to keep my mouth shut. I'm only telling you because I figured I could trust you."

"Yeah but don't get any ideas when we go out together. I'm not risking getting caught up in any scam."

"Don't worry, Jake! You know Sister Ericson told me to do my vacuuming now. She's kinda bossy."

"Yeah, I was just helping her with dinner."

"But you're on dishes, aren't you?"

"Well, I offered to help. I was being polite but she said, 'sure', and gave me all the vegetables to do."

"Creep!"

Jake laughed. "But guess what she did before she came on the mission?"

"Sergeant-major I guess, with that booming voice of hers."

"No, she was a molecular biologist."

"No kidding!"

"Yeah, she was pretty high up in her department at Cleveland University."

"Wow! I would never have believed that. Probably why they push their kids to study and all. OK, see you at dinner. I'm off!"

There was an awkward moment at dinner when the President asked John where they'd got to. He'd driven around their territory in Gifu several times trying to catch up with them. Jake was surprised at how fluently John lied without a hint of embarrassment.

"Oh you must have come by when we were witnessing those students."

"Well I drove around for a while and waited and came back again."

"Yeah, we spent a lot of time in there because they had so many questions but anyway they said they're coming to church."

"Well I'm pleased with you two. Well done! Sounds like you had a good day. Dennis! Sounds like you drew a blank." Dennis looked sheepish. "And George! One interested. OK. Well I guess you'll settle when you get back into the routines."

Jake understood that the President meant George was not effective without Ellis to back him up, but he hadn't found Ellis to have any particular 'golden touch'. He just stuck to the rules, which Jake supposed was good. He was surprised at John's audacity in flouting the rules so brazenly and then to lie about it afterwards. The trouble with Bruce was that he would follow a bad example like that because he already had that rebellious attitude.

When dinner was over, Jake spent another hour doing the dishes, and then realized why Mrs Ericson had advised them to do their chores early, because they were called to the office by Ellis for a study session.

Bruce was angry. "Are they going to give us a break or what," he fumed. "Out at work all day, chores and then we gotta study."

"Whaddya mean, 'working all day'," said Jake under his breath.

"OK. OK. Well I thought we'd get some leisure time."

Ellis led the study group, but everyone was unresponsive and drowsy, so he broke them up into mini-workshops to discuss the lesson. Jake and Bruce sat with John.

"We had to give a character report on you guys after dinner," said John, gloating.

Jake watched John's sneer and it suddenly struck him that maybe John had encouraged Bruce to break the rules in order to test him so that he could report back to the President. He knew how important it was to some of the missionaries to get commended on their mission and that this could be one way of ingratiating yourself with the authorities. Jake could tell by Bruce's look of panic that he was having the same fears.

"Yep," John went on. "I told him you did as you were told, participated in dialogue and filled out the reports as instructed."

Bruce took that to mean that John hadn't told on him, but he was still uneasy. "I'm in it now," he said to Jake later in their room.

"Maybe you should tell him you wanna follow the rules tomorrow."

"Yeah, but he can say what he wants about me, can't he? So I may as well take it easy! I mean I can always deny it. He had no proof we spent the day in fast-food joints."

"Yeah, but the President may have told him to test you, to see if you had the right attitude."

"Yeah, but why would they do that just with me?"

"Who says they didn't try it on the others? I mean Dave and Lewis may be afraid to admit it."

"Let's ask them!" said Bruce.

"What?"

"Come on! We've gotta ask them. I'm not gonna be trapped like this."

Lewis and Dave were quietly reading.

"Hi you guys," said Dave. "How did you like the study circle?"

"Great!" said Jake unconvincingly.

"Listen guys," said Bruce. "I just wanna ask you something. Did you guys work hard today?"

"Sure!" said Lewis. "We must have done about forty calls."

"Did you take a break?"

"About thirty minutes in the bus station. We had lunch."

"How about you, Dave?"

"Yeah, Dennis said they usually took a couple of hours filling out reports in Burger City in Gifu so we spent the lunch break in Dixie King."

Bruce was relieved. "You see," he said. "Now don't say a word about this! John told me they had two long breaks, two hours in the morning and two in the afternoon."

"You're kidding!" said Lewis. "Sounds like you guys struck lucky with John and Dennis."

Jake explained. "We're just warning you. We had this idea that they may be testing us, you know, under instructions from the President, to see who'd be willing to cut corners or break the rules."

Dave looked pale. "Is that what they're doing?"

"No, I don't think so," said Bruce reassuring him. "I guess it's just that John and Dennis take it easy and Ellis and George work according to the rules. That's probably why Jake and Lewis didn't get taken for breaks."

"But anyway," said Jake. "I wouldn't go along with everything they say. Just tell them what we've been told at training and say it's better to do it properly if you don't wanna get into trouble. I mean those reports are detailed. Someone's gonna know if they're not done properly."

"Oh, we did the reports OK," said Dave.

Jake realized then that John was probably just a lazy person who didn't want to make the necessary effort. After sharing these confidences the four felt closer because Dennis had also told Dave not to say anything about their break. He had justified it by saying that you sometimes met more people in restaurants. By the end of the discussion, Jake felt that he had assumed the role of leader and that the others had already begun treating him like one. He felt he should give them good advice and not descend into rule-breaking right at the start of the mission.

"OK," he said. "I suggest we play it carefully this week. We don't want to mess up our missions, so you, Bruce, and you, Dave, should remind your partners of the rules. Tell them you want to train properly to be ready for next week. Dave! It's easier for you. Just say none of the other guys take long breaks and you're worried the President will get mad. As for Bruce, you'd better persuade John that it's better not to take so much time off during the day and you're worried because all the other guys worked on calls all day."

"But hasn't John got a good case?" said Bruce. "Is it really worth trailing up and down, knocking on doors when most of them are gonna slam the door in your face?"

"Trouble is you don't know which ones will," said Dave thoughtfully. "You have to call to find out. Plus you have to record all calls and if you haven't really called and later someone goes back to that area, they might find someone there who's interested."

"Yeah, like suddenly Gifu town turns out to be a hotbed of Mormon sympathizers!" said Bruce. "Get real! We're just wasting people's time."

Dave looked disappointed. Jake thought it was terrible to be disillusioned so early in the mission, so he gave them a pep-talk.

"Listen, we know a lot of this missionary work is monotonous, plodding on. Think of it like this! We're panning for gold. You dig and dig until you find those gold nuggets."

"Like Joseph Smith," said Dave brightly.

"Yeah, exactly," said Jake. "He had to keep on going back waiting for the angel to give him the location of the plates."

"So we keep digging," said Lewis in his deadpan voice. "Until we strike gold."

"Right!" said Jake. "If you never took the trouble to dig, you'd never find the gold."

As Jake sat thinking about it later, he found himself unconvinced that the people they'd met that first day were sincerely interested in the Mormon religion. The missionaries' appeal seemed to have more to do with America and their own status as foreigners, and what they represented. He decided that when it was their turn to go out alone next week he would really capitalize on that interest of theirs and show them how they could enjoy a life like the Mormons had. Now, his first day over, he felt much more confident that he had something valuable to bring to the people and he shouldn't 'hide it under a bushel' as the phrase went. He opened his *Book of Mormon* and checked under 'light' in the index.

'*The people that walked in darkness have seen a great light: they that dwell in the land of the shadow of death, upon them hath the light shined.*' He found the verse moving. In study circles they often looked at the subject of the light of the Word of God and he remembered looking at the verse and seeing it cross-referenced with Isaiah in the Old Testament. He remembered from his Japanese class that Japan, ironically perhaps, was the Land of the Rising Sun. But spiritually, according to their professors, they were a people who walked in darkness because they hadn't accepted or even heard of the basic truths. Many of them had never even come across the Bible and had no knowledge of Jesus Christ. He wrote the verse down on a slip of delicate Japanese paper from his new stationery set and put it in his briefcase as a kind of talisman. He would pull it out if he even felt for a moment that what he was doing was not worthwhile. He resolved to get the Japanese teacher to write it out for him in Japanese. It might even convince her to at least go and read some more.

The Tuesday routine was similar to Monday's. A different train and a different town; but it was the same endless calls and recording of the results. It was only Jake's second day and already he felt as though he was set in a humdrum routine. Once in his life, he'd taken on a summer job in a warehouse. His dad had decided it would be character-building and a chance to take responsibility for his finances. That was the worst summer he could remember. The warehouse was filled with the noise of a blaring radio playing the same few hits over and over again. He had only the two resentful full-time workers for company. There was no way they would welcome a school-kid who would vanish after a couple of months and leave them to their tedium for who knows how many years. Jake's job had been to take lists from the grocery store upstairs and move all the required goods from the various parts of the warehouse to be piled in the elevator. It was back-breaking because the full-timers were the only ones allowed to use the fork-lift. Every morning when Jake cycled to work, he would experience a sinking feeling and the whole day was eaten up with longing for the first break, followed by a longing for lunch, longing for the second break, and then home at last, exhausted, to eat, sleep, get up and start over again. The weekend was a distant beacon every week. Monday was torment. When he finally finished, the full-timers came to say a grudging good-bye and he had felt very grateful that this wasn't to be his life, that he would probably go to college and get a 'good job'; but then his father had told him that even 'good jobs' were boring. Office jobs were sometimes even more tedious. Now Jake was beginning to feel it. This was his first 'proper job', so to speak. He was outdoors with someone for company, a new country, exciting prospects, meeting new people every day and getting to talk about really stimulating things. So why was he bored already?

He asked Ellis over lunch, "Ellis, do you find missionary work a bore?"

"I wouldn't say a bore," he said. "I enjoy the dialogue, going into people's homes and getting to witness them, especially if they bring up arguments that I know how to answer. I guess it's pretty boring when you don't get a break for ages though. I like the train rides."

"Yeah, me too. I like looking out the window or just watching the people. What I like about them is that they don't mind you staring at them on the train." Jake noticed many of his sentences these days referred to 'them' or 'they', meaning the Japanese. He had hoped he could avoid generalizing about Japanese people but it was so easy and convenient, he couldn't help it.

"I like to read on the train," said Ellis, "or look out the window."

Just as they were about to finish lunch, an unkempt man with unruly hair and large glasses with quite frightening, staring eyes came up to them.

"Ah, my friends. Nice to see you again. How's everything?"

"Fine, thank you sir," said Ellis. "This is Jake."

"Pleased to meet you," said Jake. "Do you work around here?"

The man sat down, pleased they were ready for a conversation. "Ah I live in Kasugai, yes."

"What do you do?" asked Jake.

"Ah, yes," said the man smiling and nodding vigorously. "Ah, where are you from?"

"Utah!" said Jake with a questioning intonation, not sure if the man would have heard of it.

"Ah yes. Very good. Aha Utah. Mormon-san *ne?*" He smiled.

"Yes that's right," said Jake surprised. "We are missionaries. We call on people to tell them about our religion."

The man kept smiling widely. "Ah Mormon. Very nice. America very nice. I like America very much."

"Have you been to the States?" asked Jake.

"I like America," he said again.

"Well it's good to see you again but we have to go," said Ellis briskly and started walking off before Jake could protest.

"Bye. See you again," said Jake.

"That guy," said Ellis cringing. "We've seen him about four times. He always comes up and wants to talk. He's real creepy."

"He seemed kinda friendly," said Jake. "Maybe he's lonely." He looked back to see the man sitting forlornly on the bench.

"Anyway Jake, same problem," said Ellis. "Too much asking questions about themselves or talking about yourself. It's not necessary. You just go right in there with the point. But with this guy, you're wasting your time. He's nuts anyway."

This time Jake decided to keep his mouth shut and bide his time until the following week when he could do things his own way.

In Kasugai they did even worse than the day before and found just one housewife who was interested. She had been reading a lot about different faiths and had a sister in Tokyo who was a Catholic. She was herself just finding out about becoming a Catholic when Jake and Ellis came to save her. They could only speak to her on the doorstep because she was alone in the house, but it was enough time to tell her that the Bible was not to be relied on in its current state and that if she was interested in Jesus Christ, what he said and did, she wouldn't find it with the Catholics because for them, the first port of call was the word of the Pope, the word of the priests and the Catechism. Did she know there was another testament of Jesus Christ? She didn't, so Ellis imparted lesson one and then decided to invite her to church so that she could see for herself, and one of the women would be able to give her a counselling session. Otherwise, in between times, she might go to the Catholics.

Jake told Ellis later on the train about the training they'd had for Japanese Christians. For those already committed, they had to stress the courage they'd taken to make such a big step and congratulate them for recognizing the truth of Jesus Christ. Then they would introduce the *Book of Mormon* and the coming of Joseph Smith as a supplement to what they already knew so that they would be anxious not to miss anything. With those who were just interested in other Christian denominations, they took a different track and warned them of the errors those churches had made and how Joseph, when he was growing up, faced with the huge array of choices, rejected them all, and then praying to be guided to the true church, received his first vision. Japanese people, on the whole, were said to be impressed with visions.

The whole time Jake was talking he found Ellis to be unresponsive. Like yesterday, it seemed to be his habit to start the day wound up and full of energy, eager to talk on the way out, after which he would gradually withdraw throughout the day until, on the way home, he was taciturn. Jake put it down to the stress of the job and turned to watch the uninspiring scenery flashing by, the plants and factories, pachinko parlours set in isolation like silver palaces in the middle of fields, the jumbled small towns with their medium level highrise apartments. Even the smallest towns had their neon signs, looking gaudy and metallic in the daylight. The train was uncomfortable and crowded, and this time Jake felt as if the gangs of schoolchildren looked more threatening than the scrubbed soldier boys and sailor girls he had become familiar with. They had on the same uniforms but there were subtle differences. Their trousers were much wider and high above the ankle, revealing patterned socks and big, clumping shoes. Their hair was tightly permed and of a different brownish shade as if it had been dyed. Some of them had shoulder-length hair and quiffs. The girls had the same fixed sneers, thick lipstick, the same brownish hair, and they wore their uniforms with a defiant attitude, again with some subtle changes. Jake could tell they were laughing at them and talking about them so he tried not to meet the gaze of the ringleaders. He listened to their drawling talk and it seemed as if every sentence ended in '*dai yo*'. He guessed they must be the equivalent of street-wise kids back home who cut school and hung around in gangs. Though he knew the extent of rebeldom in Utah, he also knew it had nothing on other parts of the States. He himself had never happened upon the rougher parts of the big cities he had visited, but he had heard some stories, enough to make him glad of his innocence. Strange that he'd never even considered drop-out kids in Japan. This was what came of thinking in stereotypes. When they'd stepped off the train amidst the deliberate jostling of the youths, Ellis clued him up.

"I don't know if you noticed those kids," he said.

"Sure I noticed," said Jake, "but I didn't want to say anything in the train."

"You notice they looked rough, not like the average kids. They call them '*bosuzoka*'. They're like junior *yakuza*. Have you heard of *yakuza*?"

"Yeah, they're Japanese mafia, right?"

"Yeah," he said as they got into the subway. "They like to intimidate people and as most Japanese are afraid of *yakuza*, the youngsters like to get some of the reflected glory."

"Are their parents in the mafia?"

"I doubt it. They're just kids who don't do well in school. Their dads are in low-class jobs and they figure they may as well fool around in school. In the evenings they ride motorcycles, real noisy, up and down the streets and everyone is afraid to stop them. Anyway certain parts of town we work in, you find them everywhere. You just have to ignore them. They look scarier than they are. None of them has ever spoken to me. They just look. It's part of their thing to be mean to foreigners."

Over dinner, Mrs Ericson warned them about the weather.

"Rains are coming," she said with a look of satisfaction.

"It's OK for Mom," said Sam. "She doesn't have to go out."

She looked angrily at Sam. "Yes, but I would like to go out. You know very well Sam. You don't know how lucky you are, getting out into the world every day."

"Mom's got housewife blues," said Sam, by way of explanation.

"You sass your mother again and you go to your room," said the President, and Sam hung his head and carried on eating.

"The missionary routine is not as exciting as it seems," said Dennis. "I'd rather stay home and please myself."

"The calls we make seem to be mostly housewives," said Bruce. "I think they're glad of someone to talk to. That's why they stop to talk."

"Well I know of some women married to salary men," said Mrs Ericson, "who barely see their families half an hour a day. They get up early to prepare breakfast and see the husband off at about six. Then the children are packed off at seven or seven-thirty. Then she has the whole day stretching ahead of her alone at home and by the time her husband rolls home drunk from entertaining clients, it's past midnight and she's gone to bed. The kids come in after classes real late and study all evening." Now it was her turn to be reprimanded by a cough and a disapproving look from her husband. He did not approve of her talking of drink in front of Sam.

John took up the subject. "This is why you always find the rich housewives out shopping downtown or sitting having tea and cakes in cafés during the day. They have to fill the hours somehow."

"Yeah, and some of them join classes," said Ellis. "I know some of the English teachers do private lessons for housewives, and they said the housewives also have tea-ceremony and flower arranging lessons, and they can get involved in local politics or arranging events."

"Do housewives work in Japan?" asked Dave.

"No," said Mrs Ericson. "Working after marriage is considered unseemly for most women except for working-class jobs. Office girls just work until they find a husband and then stay at home. It's OK when the children are young but then they're left alone when the kids go to school. The kids even work Saturdays here so they only get to spend Sunday as a family."

"This is one of the obstacles we have to getting people into church," explained the President. "Sunday is a precious day for them to go out on trips and when they see the commitment the church requires, they get cold feet."

"We see a lot of housewives living with their folks," said George, "which I guess is a good thing for the company, or to have a sense of purpose."

"Yes but that's more common in rural areas," said Mrs Ericson. "Now more and more young married couples are having to live away from their parents because all the work is concentrated in the city."

"Do the housewives want to work?" asked Dave. "I mean do they just feel they can't because of convention?"

"No," Ellis answered. "I think they think it's demeaning to have to work. Like their husband is not on a good salary or something. At least that's the high-class housewives whose husbands have good jobs."

"My Mom says she has to work for herself," said Dave, "and we never suffered because of it."

"What does she do?" asked Mrs Ericson.

"She's a legal secretary. That's what she was trained to do and she went right out and did it."

"Good for her!" said Mrs Ericson with gusto.

"Still," said the President with gravity. "The Mormon faith does not undervalue the role of wife and mother. Most people would say that's a full-time job." His smile said the conversation was over and they finished their meal in reflective silence.

Mrs Ericson's forecast had been accurate. The next day they awoke to see the streets sodden while the buildings opposite and the trees all had a battered, drenched look. As they stepped out, they found that the air was still humid and very close. Ellis and

Jake were posted to Tsurumae Park which Ellis told him meant 'stork', or something. Wednesday morning was the Japanese lesson which they had all enjoyed, as they went over some of the characters for the local stations. Their stop meant 'eastern mountain'. They learned to recognize it. They had learnt the *kanji* for 'exit' and 'entrance'. Jake thought that the one for 'exit' looked like a devil's fork so he always remembered it meant 'exit' because he thought of 'exit to hell'. Other *gaigin* had worked out their own personal recognition systems. For some train lines it was essential to recognize *kanji* for certain destinations as they were only given in Japanese. But it was a very personal system and one person's 'man looking out of a window' would leave another person confounded. The ability to recognize them was however a great boost to one's self-esteem and to the feeling that one had mastered the place. Jake even wrote a few in his letter home to show off his new ability. After the lesson they were to spend the day in the park. Jake and Bruce were assigned to Sakae where Ellis and George usually worked. From the following week Ellis and George were to work on the university campus.

"I like park days," said Ellis on their way to Tsurumae.

"Yes, it must be great to work in the open."

"Also we get to talk to people more. People you meet in the park are usually willing to talk and listen, although you do sometimes get weirdoes like that guy yesterday. By the way, stay way clear of drunks. There are some who like to hang out in the park."

As they turned the corner after coming out of the subway for the park, Jake noticed salary men and office ladies streaming past. As quick as a flash the rain began to fall and all their arms suddenly seemed to sprout umbrellas.

"Where did all those umbrellas come from?" asked Jake in wonder.

"It's raining," said Ellis. "Wait!" and he ducked under a canopy to dig in his bag for an umbrella.

"Did you get your umbrella assigned?" he asked.

"Oh yeah," said Jake reaching for his umbrella, "but this is really strange. I swear those salary men were walking along with nothing in their hands and suddenly they've all got umbrellas."

"They must have those small, telescopic umbrellas."

"But their hands were empty."

Ellis looked at him a little strangely. "The rains are getting to you, huh?"

Jake smiled. "I could've sworn ..."

"Japanese magic," said Ellis, and they both laughed as they turned into the park. It was fairly empty except for odd people passing through in a purposeful manner. The two of them sheltered in a gazebo looking over a classically oriental lily pond until the rain had died down. It did seem better in the park because they were under no pressure until some likely candidate came to sit in the park. The downpour stopped as quickly as it had started to be replaced by a blaze of sunshine which glimmered over the pond. Eventually they saw two young women who looked like bank clerks sitting down and opening their lunch-boxes.

"Should we go over?" asked Jake.

"Wait till they've nearly finished their lunch," said Ellis. "They don't like being watched while they're eating."

When the girls were having their flask of tea, they went over.

"Are you sure it's OK?" said Jake, suddenly nervous, "just to go up to them like this?"

"We look pretty business-like," said Ellis. "They just have to answer our question and say, 'yes' or 'no'."

Jake had read the statement for use in outdoor locations and it looked fairly harmless.

"Excuse me for disturbing you during your busy lunch hour," said Ellis in everyday polite Japanese. "We are American missionaries doing a survey in the park today. We would be happy if you could take the trouble to answer a few of our questions. Is that convenient?"

The girls looked at each other warily and, putting their heads down, gave a little sound of reply, "*Uh ii desu*," they agreed.

On the sheet there was a diagram like a flow chart with possible replies. Next to 'no thank you' was a little piece which read, 'then we are terribly sorry for troubling you but we would like to invite you to our church this Sunday. There are lots of other young Japanese there and it would be an opportunity for a cultural exchange. Here is our card if you should be interested this or any other week'. It sounded much more straightforward than the house calls.

Since the girls had agreed to answer the questions, Ellis handed a reply sheet to Jake and ran through them. The girls handed over their business cards with their names, company and position. They were actually from a travel agency, which boded well for the missionaries. There followed questions about religious affiliation. Both were nominal Shintos. No, they had never read the Bible. They didn't know much about Jesus Christ. They had visited churches on a company trip to Italy and found them very charming. No, they didn't know much about prophets, only holy men. They believed in an afterlife and a spirit world and were agreed that it was important to follow moral precepts in life and to treat others kindly and not be selfish or egotistical. Yes, they would welcome further guidance on how to lead a good life. No, they were not married but both had boyfriends. They both giggled when Ellis corrected that to 'fiancés'. 'Maybe', they said together, laughing girlishly. One of them became bold and asked them if they had fiancées. Jake was about to answer when Ellis said they'd better press on with the questions and Jake held his tongue, remembering Ellis' dislike of exccessive talk about themselves. When the questions were finished, Ellis held up the *Book of Mormon* and said with meaning that God had sent guidance and that through Joseph Smith He had communicated another Testament of Jesus Christ. Also through him, He had communicated the best guidance about how to live life. Didn't they sometimes think how people wasted time, money and energy on drinking, and then ruined their health and left their wives alone? That struck a chord with the girls and they nodded vigorously. Wasn't it a terrible thing for young people to study themselves into the ground in return for a job for life in a company to which they would devote almost the whole of their lives? Wasn't it unfair to work all your life and devote yourself to a company in return for a tiny house you never got to spend time in? Now the girls' faces showed reflective agreement. Maybe their lives were like that or their families. "Human beings should have higher goals", Ellis emphasized. "Something more worthwhile to strive for".

Having run through his speech, Ellis thanked them and urged them not to miss the opportunity to come to church that week to learn more. The girls nodded and took the church address cards. Then they rushed back to work with plenty of food for thought.

Jake was impressed. "That was really something, Ellis. You

sounded really - I don't know - full of conviction. They were really concentrating and agreeing with you."

"Thanks," he said modestly. "That's why I like outdoor work best. It's a lot more satisfying."

"Why can't we do the same thing on the house calls?"

"We do use some of the stuff but we have more time. You can do call-backs with houses so you can afford to go more slowly, take time over explaining the doctrines week by week. In the park, you don't know whether you'll see them again so you have to convince them in one go."

"What's with all the questions?"

"That's for the records. Also to be able to direct your arguments to things that concern them or which may be close to home. It also helps us to approach people in the same kind of category."

"What's their category?"

"Young, single, college educated middle-class clerical."

"Pretty detailed," laughed Jake. "Do we have their shoe size?"

"It just gives an idea of what concerns are the most important in their lives right now," said Ellis, adopting his lecturing manner. Jake found it disconcerting that Ellis often didn't laugh at his jokes but kept with his train of thought quite seriously. He knew he would get on well with Bruce as a partner because already they were developing a good sense of repartee, bouncing off each other's humorous comments. He was looking forward to Bruce's assessment of his day in the park.

They had a chance to talk before dinner.

"So you think these two secretary women are gonna take you up on the invitation?" said Bruce.

"Travel consultants," Jake corrected.

"Is that what they call themselves?"

"That's what it says on their cards." Jake was already beginning to build up a portfolio of business cards, neatly filed at his office desk. They were filing the paperwork from the previous two days. "Anyway," Jake went on, "they seemed curious enough. Had a basic set of beliefs in spirituality, after-life and morality. They just needed filling in on prophecy and scripture."

"You make it sound like a shopping list," scoffed Bruce.

"Well, you know what we talked about in training. These Shinto, or shall we say nominal Shinto Japanese, have an understanding of the spiritual dimension and that the world doesn't end here. It's just that they have no concept of individual messengers being sent by God or of His Word being encoded."

"Oh, very technical!" said Bruce. "Would you look at these records? You have to do about three copies of everything. Now I've gone and filed it and forgotten to make copies."

The President came in and asked them how their day had been. He smiled as they reported their success. He was unsurprised, because he knew that most missionaries got the best results on outdoor work. One of the reasons it took place on a Wednesday was to break up the week and give them a boost amid the disappointment of the other days. Bruce had told them about their three elderly gentlemen who had had the patience and interest to sit through long debates with them. One of them, the second one they had spoken to, had been sympathetic to Christianity for many years. He had once taken two American Baptist missionaries as lodgers and had been impressed with their respectful attitude to him, their concern for his welfare and their determination to lead good lives. Both had gone on to work with the polytheists in Bali, to improve their standard of living and teach them the Gospel. The man lamented the change in attitude among Japanese youth who were going further towards a materialistic outlook on life and a lack of concern for their parents' and grand-parents' welfare in their old age. "I used to shame my son in Tokyo," the old man had said, "that he had left it up to a couple of young foreigners to make sure their old father was properly cared for." He had listened intently to Bruce and John and was convinced by the idea that Jesus may well have visited South America.

The President listened patiently to Bruce's enthusiastic accounts of the day's recruits. He nodded sagely. "You'll find, Brother Bruce, that a lot of those willing to talk are either young students or older men. The students because they have plenty of time and are interested in foreigners. They hope to travel some day, maybe work for a company that has international interests. It's also a time when they are just beginning to think about the meaning of life. The older men, I'm afraid to say, are often lonely. They welcome the chance to talk to someone. A lot of them speak very good English."

"Yeah, these guys wanted to speak English," said Bruce.

"Right, and they are at the other end of life, so to speak. Death isn't far off. They don't know when it's coming. Their religion so far has failed to answer a lot of their questions and they're thinking there must be more to life."

"So," concluded Jake, "are you saying we should try to speak to more middle-aged or working people?"

"No, no," said the President, "not at all. Keep speaking to these people! They make up the bread and butter of our congregation. I'm just saying these are the people who are most likely to speak to you, so be prepared! That reminds me of a point I want to raise with you, Brother Jake, which I think will be relevant for both of you, judging by what you've told me today. Remember you aren't really there for a cosy chat. Your objective is to tell them the facts and either arrange the second meeting or invite them to church. So with these men you've been talking about and these students, yes, build up a bit of a friendly relationship, but don't get involved in lengthy debate. Some people love to run you round in circles in debate. Let me tell you. It's a waste of time. Tough though it may sound, you are not here to befriend lonely old people. You're here, in fact, to save their souls."

Jake knew then that Ellis must have spoken to the President about his chatty approach to missioning. The other missionaries came in one by one to do their filing and briefly went over the day's achievements. The President tutted as he watched them all making copies and filing. He looked thoughtful, "It's a long job," he said, "but I've been thinking about it a lot recently. Most of this stuff is going to have to go to disk. We're building up too much paperwork."

Dennis was enthusiastic. "Great idea! It will help a lot for the future visits because you'll be able to have all the information easily accessible. You can access which houses you've visited, the replies, the follow-up notes, everything."

"So, Dennis. I can count on your help," said the President.

Dennis looked apprehensive. "You mean you want me to put in all this data?"

"Not alone, of course not. Let's say you and George here are the brains behind the project and the others will be enlisted to do the routine data-entry work. I'm sure it'll be fine if we do it methodically. But it means I'm expecting a few hours of your time every evening. Agreed?"

They all nodded. How could they possibly refuse? Now though, it seemed like missionary work and church business was eating into all their time. The glow of a successful day seemed to have faded a little and after dinner, Jake and Bruce went over what the President said.

"I think he's a little paranoid about us spending time talking with the subjects," said Bruce. "Listen to me: 'Subjects!' I'm already getting into their jargon. It's true the old guys may have been lonely but they were real interesting to talk to."

"Exactly," said Jake. "You know I told you Ellis pulled me up a few times for talking too much outside the set agenda. I think it's important. I agree with you. It's important to get the people to trust us and like us otherwise they won't want to come to our church, no matter how convincing our arguments are."

"Anyway, we're our own boss next week," said Bruce. "Don't worry! I won't report you to the President if you slip up, Jake." Bruce knelt up to look out of the window at the rain glancing off it. The window was slightly open and they could smell the air of Japan, warm and fragrant.

"Rainy season or no rainy season," Bruce moaned. "I wanna go out."

"We've been out all day," said Jake, startled.

"No, I mean out, out! Today we sat in Donut Heaven, I told you, didn't I, to talk to one of these guys. We declare that on the report as 'entertaining an interested subject.' At least it's above board if we were ever caught or something. I filled in the sheet and it even has a space for items bought for the guest plus cost. 'One strawberry donut, One *hotto cohee* for client. Two orange juices for missionaries.' He offered to buy us doughnuts, so we didn't put that down on the report."

"Can we buy coffee for them?"

"Yeah, the President says this is one exception. He said don't offer it but ask what they want first. If they ask for coffee, then that's OK."

"Do you think any of these people will actually turn up on Sunday?" asked Jake.

"Well, John says about half of the people who say they'll come actually show up. The rest you never see again." He sighed. "Are we gonna get any kind of social life?"

"Another early start tomorrow," said Jake.

"We could sneak out and no-one would know, say after 11:00pm."

"You must be kidding," said Jake. "Number one: What if we get caught? Number two: Where would we go?"

"I heard there was a Delaware Diner somewhere around," said Bruce hopefully. He laughed, shaking his head. "We really have hit rock bottom when we consider a night out at a diner as a real treat."

"What's the point wasting money going to Delaware's when we can talk here just as easily?"

"It's not the same," said Bruce. "There's nothing to eat and drink, nobody to look at."

"OK. If you're disappointed," said Jake. Bruce looked up hopefully. "I'll go and make you a cup of cocoa and get some potato chips from the kitchen."

Bruce's head sunk. "I'll settle for that," he said.

By the end of the week Jake was beginning to feel nonchalant about Nagoya. It wasn't as vast as he'd thought, and now that he'd taken main-line trains in various directions, the city was beginning to look very manageable. By Friday he had managed to find his way to Nagoya main station and up to the *Kintetsu* platforms for their journey to Shiroko. Ellis had greeted a couple more English teachers that he knew by sight, but again refused to sit with them on the train. Jake was still curious to talk to other *gaigin* to find out their experience of Japan. If along the way they got interested in the church, so much the better; but he was very conscious of the fact that the mission training professors had warned them against undue mixing with other foreigners. He couldn't really understand why. they'd said something about not jeopardizing your faith, but he felt his faith was strong enough by now not to be shaken by the questions of a few gentiles. After all, a lot of them were totally ignorant of the church of Jesus Christ of Latter Day Saints, and, in fact, of religion in general. Still, as he watched the easy banter and laughter of the English teachers in the next carriage, he wondered what kind of people they were and what they would make of someone like him. They probably didn't want to talk to him anyway. Probably thought he was a weirdo.

The scenery on the way to Shiroko was genuinely beautiful, with mountains and wide fields, and several bridges spanning rushing rivers. It wasn't as spectacular as some of the scenery Jake had seen in Yellowstone or on camping trips to Canada, or even in his home state, but it was still very beautiful. The right blend of colours and shades. The rain had been incessant throughout Thursday but was now holding itself back, and they were able to spend the day without the misery of getting drenched.

On the way back, Jake sensed a weekend atmosphere brewing and was a little disconcerted to see some of the salary men on the train with flushed faces and bleary eyes staggering between the carriages and having noisy drinking parties around their tables. Typically, it was in this condition that the usually quiet and respectful businessmen decided to take an interest in the *gaigin* and come over for a chat. One of them leant over and introduced himself in Japanese.

"Name preese," he slurred in English.

Jake hesitated. He didn't know whether answering would get him into trouble with Ellis but he couldn't just ignore the guy.

"Name preese," the man repeated, his mouth gaping open, waiting for an answer.

Ellis looked at him, shrugged, and said, "No English."

"Good ploy," thought Jake but the man carried on now he was curious to know where they were from.

"Ah *Espagnol? Francais?*" he ventured.

"German, I mean *Deutsch*," said Ellis firmly.

"Ah *Deutsch*-san," said the man nodding confirmation to his friends and repetitions of '*Deutsch*-san' went round the table.

"Ah *sprechen sie Deutsch?*" enquired one of the friends, grinning broadly.

"Oh my God. I don't believe it," said Ellis. "He speaks German too? *Nein danke*," he said waving his hand and turning away. It was the only German he knew. With their luck they may have hit upon a group of businessmen who'd been posted in Germany. The men realized they were not going to get any more reaction and thankfully got off at the next stop amid several '*Aufwiedersehens*'.

"I don't talk to drunks," said Ellis in disgust. "Kind of makes me sick to see them like that."

"Trouble is," said Jake, "it seems like the only time they really open up."

"Right! Now they've gone," said Ellis, "I want to discuss something with you." He looked serious enough for Jake to listen carefully.

"I don't know if you notice that I talk a lot in the morning on the way to a job, while on the way back I keep quiet."

"I had noticed," said Jake, pleased that he was going to hear an explanation of Ellis' apparent moodiness. It was true that Jake could hardly think in the morning for Ellis' chattering, but at the end of the day, when he was eager to go over things, Ellis would sit in brooding silence.

"We were taught this technique when we got here by the guys who were second-years then, and the President. He told us in every pair, you've got a leader who is told to keep his partner on the rails, you know, watch him and make sure he's OK. One of the important things is to make him enthusiastic about witnessing every day and reinforce it if he does well. So we were told, Dennis and myself, to psych them up every morning by talking about what we're gonna do that day and showing you're really positive about what they're doing. Then after the morning's work you tell them if they did something good, chastise them if they did anything wrong or didn't pull their weight and then on the way back leave them to reflect on the day's work themselves. They said something in the training about 'withdrawing communication' so that the partner realizes what pleases you most is if they are enthusiastic about the job and do the job well, and for that they have to be in the best frame of mind at the beginning of the day. So they become dependent on that support every morning." Ellis hesitated. "Is that clear? I've been doing it so long, I feel it's automatic now. I can't explain it very well."

"Is that what you've been doing with me?" asked Jake.

"Yeah. It's to teach you the same technique which you'll have to put into practice when you go out as a team with Brother Bruce."

"Well," said Jake shaking his head doubtfully. "You know Bruce is a pretty sophisticated guy. He'd probably see through that and say something like, 'Hey, Jake! Why are you acting so weird?'"

"It doesn't matter if he sees through it," said Ellis. "It still works. I know it works because George is always cheerful in the morning and he works hard and he gets worried when he hasn't done well, like I'm disappointed in him or something."

"What if George thinks you haven't done so well?" asked Jake.

Ellis looked hurt. "I'm the team-leader," he said. "So George falls in with my plans. We have to let them lead the witnessing at regular intervals, but I do most of the talking. Anyway, what I'm saying is George does depend on me being in a good frame of mind and looks to me for approval."

Jake was doubtful, but he said he'd try it as advised. Ellis told him that the President would go over it again at their special preparation meeting for team-leaders.

Jake felt sorry for poor George being psychologically manipulated in that way. In his opinion, it didn't seem to make sense to put on an act like that. Surely it was better for both missionaries to be themselves, to talk about what they were going to do in the morning and go over what they had done on the way back. Also it was important to have some fun and crack a few jokes. What was the harm? It was a stressful job. Again, he found himself resolving to work in his own way the following week. He preferred to have Bruce on his side if he was going to get any success out of this mission. Bruce would probably get better results if they talked openly about their daily progress, rather than one of them always being in the dark.

When they got back to the house, they were called up to the office to receive their allowances. The President congratulated them on their first week and said they would tie up a few loose ends on Sunday, but that from then on they were officially on free-time. Until Sunday morning, they had a free choice – within limits.

"Great! So we can go out!" cried Bruce excitedly.

"Uh, well," hedged the President. "I'm afraid evening outings have to be cleared with me a couple of days in advance. I'm sorry."

"Don't worry," said Dennis cheerily. "We'll get a video. I belong to the video club. It's not far. We can go to the store for popcorn and ice-cream. It'll be just like the movies."

"Yes. Friday evenings, we have a TV dinner," said the President, "because my wife goes to the theatre with her friends. I have to drop Jane off at her friend's house and then we can start the movie." The President was suddenly like a big kid looking forward to the movie as much as the missionaries.

They put votes into a hat for war, western, adventure, sci-fi, comedy or documentary. 'Adventure' won so Dennis plumped for *Crocodile Dundee* if it was in, and had a few alternatives as back-ups. They had all laughed when they pulled out one of the choices. It said *Amadeus* in brackets, under 'documentary / drama'.

"Who was that?" said John derisively.

"Me," said George. "Why?"

"I mean you're seriously outvoted," said John piling up all the votes for 'adventure' and 'war'."

George shrugged. "I'm interested in classical music," he said flatly.

Bruce was dying to be one of those who would go to the video store with Dennis but the President insisted that he could not allow more than two of them to go barging into small Japanese stores in the evening. "It could be alarming for them," he warned. So they agreed to draw lots and Lewis won.

"Some other time, Bruce," said the President.

"I feel like a caged animal," said Bruce. "I mean it's so childish. 'Daddy, Daddy, can I go to the store for you?' What are we, in short-pants?" He grumbled to Dave and Jake as they settled down in the living-room with their cheese and onion pie on trays on their laps.

"Yeah, I'm kinda shocked about how little freedom we get," said Dave. "Like we're being watched all day and then we have to have special permission to leave the house." He closed his eyes as if in a pleasant dream. "Now if I was back home, this would be me now on the beach with my buddies, a fire, some burgers and hot dogs, looking out at the ocean."

"That's what kills me," agreed Bruce. "I remember I used to stand on the bay and look out at the sea and dream about this place. Can you believe it? I used to dream about Japan, how it would be exotic and exciting and full of new experiences."

"We haven't seen anything yet, though," said Dave. "Wait till we get out and visit some of the sights."

"I mean could you believe," said Bruce, ignoring him, "that you could live without your car? I wanna go out in a car downtown, out to the mountains - anywhere exciting."

"It's weird not driving for so long, isn't it?" said Dave. "I live in my car back home."

George came down and ate quietly beside them. "Do you guys all drive?" he asked. "Wow. I never got my license."

"How do you get around?" said Dave in amazement.

"My mom and dad drive me or my sister."

"Didn't you have driver's ed. classes at school?" asked Jake.

"No, I was actually out of school for quite a while a few years ago. I was very sick."

"Was it serious?" asked Bruce.

"At the time, yeah it was. It was meningitis and it involved complications, so I spent a lot of time in the hospital and then in recovery at home."

"That must have been tough," said Jake sympathetically. "It didn't have any lasting effect though, I hope."

"No, thank God," he said. "It just meant I had a lot of school-work to catch up on."

When the others came back with *Crocodile Dundee* and the President came in in a jocular mood and sat down, George asked if he could have the key of the *tatami* room.

"Stay and watch the movie," urged the President and Dennis. They told him to unwind a little and enjoy himself.

"I'd like to take this time to do some reading," he said quietly. Jake understood his need for some privacy after a week of being with people from morning till night. The *tatami* room, with its bare simplicity and soft lighting, did seem appealing but Jake thought he'd leave George in peace and join in with the rest. There was definitely a party atmosphere in the sitting-room and he was beginning to feel quite at home.

The next day was football day for Ellis, and the missionaries were clamouring to be allowed to go with him to watch. The President decided that this would be a good break for them and allowed Ellis to drive them to the park while George, John and Lewis elected to go shopping in Sakae. He trusted them under Ellis' supervision, but reminded them not to hang around after the game but to come straight back.

"Now you boys," mocked Bruce wagging his finger. "You be sure and hurry back after the game. I don't want you hanging around those bad *gaigin*."

Once at the park, they found that their new-found freedom had put them all in high spirits. This was the nearest they had got to freedom since they'd arrived. No compulsion to go knocking on doors, no disapproving eyes or partners breathing down their necks. Even during the illicit breaks in donut shops Bruce had felt uneasy for fear of being caught. Now they were away from work in a pleasant park, with permission, and they felt at ease.

Soon a thin, pale young man came over to sit with them. "Hi you guys!" he said. "Where are you from?"

"The States," they said in unison.

"Oh yeah. Whereabouts?"

"San Francisco," said Bruce.

"Me too!" said Dave raising his hand.

"Utah!" said Jake apologetically.

"Oh, so you guys are Mormon, right?"

"You see, he's a dead giveaway," said Bruce pretending to strangle Jake. "Yeah I'm afraid so," he added, "but today we're off duty."

The newcomer looked intrigued. "So what's it like being missionaries?"

"Boring," said Dave. "Also we don't get to do much. How about you? Where are you from?"

"Wisconsin," said the young man. "My name's Andy. I'm an English teacher."

"What's that like?" asked Jake.

"Not bad. It can be dull at times but on the whole I enjoy it."

"Do you teach kids?" asked Dave.

"No: adults, companies. We go to Japanese companies and teach them English in the workplace. We have a different company every day so we get to travel around a lot."

"Right, so that's why we often see *gaigin* on the trains," said Jake. "They must be going off to their classes. So your Japanese must be pretty good?"

"Are you kidding?" said Andy. "I don't speak a word of Japanese apart from '*hotto cohee kudasai*'. No, we only use English."

"We have to learn Japanese for our mission," said Dave proudly. "In fact we use Japanese every day."

"So how long have you been here?'

"Just a week in Nagoya," said Dave. "Seems like a year already." The others nodded in agreement.

"OK, so you must be in the honeymoon phase," said Andy. "You love Japanese people and all things Japanese, right!"

"We would," said Bruce, "if we could meet any Japanese people aside from work. Seems like we just have time to tell them about the faith for a few minutes, then turn around and go on to the next one."

Andy leaned back on his hands. "I'm a veteran," he said. "Two years now and I've been through ups and downs here, I can tell you. Now I'm wise to Japanese people, I don't make the same mistakes."

"But how do you know what they're like if you don't speak Japanese?" asked Jake in surprise.

"Believe me, you know," he said with assurance. He looked at Dave sizing him up. "I guess you're Chinese-American, right!"

"Japanese-American," corrected Dave.

"I hope you don't take it personally about the Japanese," he said apologetically. "It's just that in their own country they're different. I know Japanese people back in the States and they are not the same."

"At the moment, I'm having a problem with everyone thinking I'm Japanese myself," said Dave ruefully, "and not treating me special like the others just because I look like them. I mean it's like treating all African-Americans like Africans. People do get to move around in the world."

In the distance they saw another *gaigin* couple. The man had short, curly hair and pale, freckled skin. The girl looked Mediterranean with dark, shoulder-length hair and tanned skin. "Hi Andy," they said coming over. They nodded politely to the missionaries. "Are you playing today?" asked the young man.

"I may play later," said Andy, "if they need a substitute."

"Who's winning?" asked the man.

"No score so far."

Then they sat down in a clique with Andy and began to go over work gossip. The couple did not attempt to bring the missionaries into the conversation. Jake could tell they were British and the three of them could not help listening in. He heard the girl say,

'Who are they?' raising her eyebrows disdainfully in their direction.

"Mormons," said Andy ominously.

They gave knowing nods and grimaced.

"How rude!" said Bruce under his breath. "Who does Miss British English teacher think she is? I'm going to show them," he said indignantly.

"Leave them," said Dave. "You must be used to it by now, Bruce. You know how everyone always reacts to Mormons."

When the couple left, Bruce called Andy over. "Hey, Buddy!" he said. "Thanks for introducing us to your British friends."

"Oh I'm sorry," said Andy looking embarrassed. "I guess we English teachers are kind of cliquey. They're from my company."

"Yeah we speak English too," said Bruce sarcastically. "Don't worry! We weren't going to bombard you with Mormon doctrines."

"Yeah, I'm sorry. I should have introduced you guys. Maybe next time."

Jake didn't like that feeling of being left out or considered an embarrassment, someone people didn't want to talk to. Since they weren't supposed to mix with other *gaigin*, it made them all the more curious to know about other people's lives.

"Look, here's my buddy Paulo," said Andy. "He's from Italy. He's a good guy. I'll introduce you."

The Italian came off the football field for half-time, smiling broadly at Andy. He greeted the missionaries warmly and welcomed them to Nagoya. Then they had a friendly talk about their home towns and what they thought of Japan. Unlike the Brits, Paulo seemed to have a reverence for them as religious people, much as some people treated priests or nuns. Jake would have preferred to have been treated like one of the guys but it was better than being ignored. The conversation was broken up as Ellis came bounding over and politely egged the missionaries over to the edge of the field.

"I'm sorry, guys," he said panting. "I could see you talking so intently and I didn't want you to stick around too long with the other foreigners. Remember the rule. I don't want to be a kill-joy but it's important. It's for your own protection."

"What, are you afraid we'll give away state secrets?" said Bruce.

"Look it's not my rule," said Ellis, "but as long as you're on the mission, you have to follow the rules and it's up to me to look after you guys. If you get into trouble, it's me that gets it in the neck." Ellis ran off to the bathroom and Bruce took his chance to make some contacts. He came back to the others proudly bearing two business cards.

"I've got their contact numbers," he said, "and guess what? Paulo's invited us all to a barbecue next Saturday. There'll be loads of *gaigin* there."

"The President would never let us go," said Jake despondently.

"We don't have to tell the President," said Bruce.

"Isn't that the title of a movie or something?" said Dave.

"We can't lie to the President," said Jake, appalled.

"All we have to say is; 'Can we have permission to go down-town to the stores next Saturday about five?' We don't have to say we're also going to a party. John and those guys got permission for today."

Jake looked doubtful. "Let's think about that next week," he said.

"I'm going back now," said Bruce, "I'm bored with this game."

"You can't go on your own," Dave objected.

"You mean, I need someone to hold my hand," he laughed, "in case those nasty Japanese people get me. Gimme a break!"

"You'd better check with Ellis," said Jake, "just in case. This is only our first week, remember. I'll ask him for you. Here he is."

"Hey Ellis! Is it OK if Bruce goes back alone?"

"Could you just wait till the end of the game?" said Ellis. "It's only forty-five minutes."

Bruce held his stomach and grimaced. "I suddenly felt sick to my stomach," he explained. "It must be the new diet."

"Oh well, maybe I'd better drive you back if you're sick."

"No, that's OK," said Bruce bravely. "I'll manage. Once I get on the subway I'll be OK. All this fresh air. It's not doing me any good."

"I think Jake should go with you," said Ellis firmly.

"Well I don't want to drag Jake away from the game. I'll be OK. Don't worry!"

Ellis was in a dilemna. He was responsible for them, but his teammates were getting impatient. "OK you go ahead," he said.

"Be careful!"

As soon as Ellis' back was turned, Bruce gave a thumbs-up sign. "Free at last," he said to the others. "Catch you later!"

Five-thirty at the Ericson household and everyone was back except Bruce. The President was tense, going into the hall every few minutes to check the front windows.

"You should never have let him go alone," said the President. "The boy's barely been here a week. How does he know his way around?"

"I hope nothing's happened," said Dennis. "He won't be able to ask for help."

Little Sam was worried, going up to each person trying to get more information. 'Did Bruce have an accident?' 'Is Bruce OK?' 'Is Bruce lost in Nagoya all alone?' 'Does Bruce know how to get back?' 'Did Bruce get sick?' He was shooed away by everyone.

"Just give it a rest, Sammy," snapped his father. "If he's not back by seven I'll call the police."

Six o'clock and the key sounded at the door. The whole house visibly relaxed. Bruce was going to have to have a good explanation, thought Jake. He looked fine.

"Is everything OK?" said Bruce, looking concerned. "Is something wrong?"

"Bruce, it's six o'clock," said the President. "Ellis said you left the game at three-thirty." Jake could see Bruce's brain whirring into action.

"I'm sorry," he said. "I didn't realize you'd be so worried. I'm touched really. No, what happened. I was feeling more and more nauseated so I had to get off the subway at Imaike and find a bathroom somewhere. I stayed in there for a while vomiting and then I went into Donut Heaven to ask for a glass of water and to recover. Then I got lost on the way back, would you believe it!"

"Now Bruce, it was not a wise thing to do," said the President, "to go off home on your own like that, especially in view of the fact that you were feeling sick. You should have stayed and used the bathroom in the park. Now in future I hope you'll learn from this, that there must be no travelling around alone except with special permission."

Later in Lewis and Dave's room, they heard the full story. Bruce had just wanted to explore by himself, and please himself. John had told him that Imaike was a buzzing place, so he got off there and went to look around. What he was really looking for was an authentic Japanese restaurant, but he was afraid to go in. They all looked intimidating and there was no sign of a menu outside. Most of the restaurants had replicas of plastic food displayed in the window to show what they served, but Bruce had been none the wiser. Soon the welcoming sight of Donut Heaven came into view and he had spent an idyllic hour eating from their large selection of doughnuts, listening to American 50's music and watching the customers come and go. It was an innocent pastime but he knew he couldn't have told the President the truth. As it was, he had told him a half truth. Later he admitted to Jake that he'd also had a cup of coffee.

"You broke the 'Word of Wisdom'!" said Jake in dismay.

"You know something? John drinks coffee," he said defiantly. "And tea. He says he's been drinking it for years. Doesn't know how he managed without it before then."

"Well if you wanna go ruin your body, it's your choice," said Jake. This time it was not their usual cheerful banter. Jake was annoyed at Bruce for taking the 'Word of Wisdom' so lightly, and also disappointed at him, that he felt he had to do this rebel thing at such a late age. Jake had thought him more mature than that.

"Well you're so perfect," said Bruce dismissing him. "How do you know something is bad if you've never tried it?"

"God forbidding you things saves you the trouble of finding out how bad those things are. It's for our own benefit. Remember how they always used to say in church that parents tell little kids not to touch the fire so the little kid doesn't have to burn himself to find out."

"Come on Jake. I don't need any lectures from you. I had some coffee, OK? Get it into perspective. Anyway who says God forbids it?"

Jake looked askance at Bruce. He thought it was accepted by all Mormons that the 'Word of Wisdom' had been given to Joseph Smith by God Himself. "You know it was revealed to Joseph Smith to abstain from harmful things."

"Because the body is the temple of the soul," said Bruce, in his mocking tone.

"Bruce! I'm not gonna sit here while you mock the scriptures."

"OK OK, just tell me if you agree with this," he said impatiently. "Because this is what John thinks."

Before he could finish, Jake cut in. "I don't want to know what John thinks. What do you think? When you came here you couldn't stand John. Now suddenly you're copying everything he does."

Bruce was exasperated. "Look. I thought about this before, myself. I heard it from a lot of people long before this. Anyway, the 'Word of Wisdom' is just that, wisdom. It's saying it's wise to be able to abstain from these things but it's not obligatory. It's not the end of the world if you try some coffee or tea."

"Don't you wanna be wise?" asked Jake.

"Sure, sometimes, but I'm also curious, and today my curiosity overtook my wisdom."

His tone of voice made Jake chuckle and the tension went out of their argument. He was silent for a while as they both flipped through their magazines. Then Jake said, "What's it like then?"

"What's what like?" said Bruce thinking he was talking about the computer magazine.

"The coffee."

"Bitter, hot, not bad."

"You hated it, right?"

"No, no. I guess the taste grows on you."

"Just don't drink it when I'm around, OK?"

Church day came around again and Jake and Ellis were anxiously watching the door to see if any of their catches would come in. John and Bruce hit the jackpot when their young college students from Gifu showed up, as well as the old man from the park who had had Baptist lodgers. John and Bruce looked smug as the others carried on anxiously looking towards the door. At last the dainty figure of the woman from Kasugai who was inches from falling into Catholicism came into view. She seemed hesitant and Ellis jumped up, bounded over to her and led her to a seat next to a Japanese woman nearer her own age. Jake was really disappointed that the travel agents hadn't come. He was sure they seemed really impressed by what Ellis had said, as if it was really relevant to their lives. Ellis was dismissive when he mentioned it.

"Ah, girls like that," he said. "more interested in boyfriends, travel and fashion." But Jake was sure they had struck a chord. He comforted himself with the idea that they might go on to read more about the church, and who knew, in the future come to a service. Everything was worthwhile because one word of testament to someone could be the seed of a future conversion of someone who might go on to be a really active member and a credit to the church.

The service went on more or less as it had the week before. Some of the congregation talked about the week's problems. One middle-aged woman chose this day to open her heart to the audience. Jake wondered later if this had been for the benefit of the Kasugai woman. She told of a wasted adulthood spent pushing her two children beyond the limits in terms of schoolwork, only for her son to end up as a foreman at a components factory in the northern part of Japan, while her daughter was married to a junior salesman and had two small children and was set to stage a repeat performance of her mother's empty life. This Sister had taken to drinking saké secretly at home during the day and watching daytime soaps all the time. If she did go out, it was only to gossip in tea-shops with the other ladies in her small circle. Her husband, exhausted and depressed, was a shadowy figure whom she saw at breakfast and on Sundays, and who for all she knew could have been working on the other side of the world once he boarded that express train into Nagoya to work in an insurance company. Their horizons had been limited: New Year with his family in Nakata province; at O-bon festival, four days in Singapore shopping and eating Chinese food. So how had the Mormon faith transformed her life? Now she didn't need to drink. Instead of watching TV she would study the scriptures or plan special meals to please her husband. At tea with her friends, she would try to win them over to her new faith. Sundays she would spend at church and her husband was free to sleep all day. Everyone, in short, was happy. The lady dabbed her eyes as the President thanked her for her moving testimony and encouraged her to keep on witnessing to her friends. The Kasugai lady just looked alarmed and her neighbour smiled benignly as if to indicate that there was much more in store.

Jake just wished they would spend more time on points of scripture or history or announce the latest archaeological finds like they did back home; but maybe all that kind of stuff was too advanced for a foreign church.

The Kasugai lady seemed to enjoy the hymns, and John and Bruce's old gentleman joined in with gusto. It seemed that he was familiar with hymns. After the service he greeted John and Bruce like old friends and said he had really enjoyed the service. Jake felt suddenly sad for him after what the President had said about lonely old people who liked to talk to foreigners. The college students were surrounded by Japanese people of their own age and seemed to be feeling at home. The President had delegated the Greek lady and one of the Japanese convert ladies to work with the Kasugai woman. She looked rather startled as they bundled her into one of the study rooms to watch a video presentation, assuring her that lunch would be served on the run while they were studying. The men's study circle began with an appraisal of the week's successes and an acknowledgment of who had shown up out of the total invitations for that week. Dave and Dennis were despondent as Ellis went over the list. Ellis reminded them that the following week was crucial because the new missionaries would be on their own. He outlined the main procedure for house calls and had the new missionaries parrot back to him the opening lesson for new subjects. The Japanese men helped them with pronunciation and gave very encouraging replies as the missionaries went through their presentations.

Jake was working with a young engineering student called Tsuyoshi who had joined the church about eight months ago.

"Do you have a few minutes for us to talk about religion?" Jake began in Japanese glancing at his prompt sheet.

"Certainly, young man. Come in! Are you American?"

"Yes, we are missionaries in the area. Our job is to tell you about Christianity."

"Ah, that sounds very interesting. Please sit down."

"I wonder if you know anything about the Bible."

"The Bible. Well I've heard of it but I'm afraid I don't know very much about it. Perhaps you would take the time to tell me."

If only all the sessions went like this, thought Jake. When Tsuyoshi reported back to the group, he said Jake had memorized the sentences very well but his pronunciation was still very American. The group then listened while two of the Japanese Mormons gave a demonstration of a house call in Japanese. They all felt sorry for Dave who was expected to be ten times more fluent than his peers just because of his face. The four new missionaries were then sent to the language lab next door while the Japanese men were taken through their paces in witnessing in their companies and on campus. The President took this session. When they came out of their language practice, Jake was concerned as he looked into the study room to find that the Japanese lady from Kasugai was still in there. She looked tense and weary. He thought it was too long for a first visit. They had a late lunch back at the house and he asked Mrs Ericson.

"Sister Ericson. You know we had a housewife come in today from Kasugai. I notice she's still in the study room with one of the other Japanese ladies and the Greek woman.

"Yes, it's her first visit so they're anxious to impress her."

"Don't you think that's rather long though? She looked pretty tired."

"Well, there is a lot to go over, you see. Plus I understand this woman was on the verge of becoming a Catholic."

"Yes, well, I just thought that it was a lot to take in during one visit. I wondered if it might put her off coming back."

"I don't think so. I think she'd feel very welcome here. The women make a point of welcoming newcomers and asking all about them and we always say how glad we are that they came to church. But you're right. We do have rather too many people who attend church once and then never again. There's a fine line to tread between making them feel welcome and not overburdening them on their first visit, but since this woman already knows a lot about Christianity and is thinking about joining the Catholics, it's important that we straighten out any wrong information she's been given right away."

Mrs Ericson's explanation was reassuring but Jake couldn't forget how that woman's face had looked through the little window: sort of strained. It reminded Jake of police interrogation rooms that you saw on TV.

The weather was quite fine that day and Jake went to sit out in the tiny yard where Sam and Phil were listening to a baseball game on the radio. Sam was delighted to see him and complained that his brother never wanted to play ball, so Jake let him practice his catches while he pitched for him. Dennis came out to sit and listen with Phil and they seemed to be kindred spirits, bulky Dennis and the rather lumpy Phil, who were both very languid people who liked to sit around. Sam, a wiry little bouncing-ball, made full use of Jake's attention and they sat out until sundown, a murky glow behind the trees. Then a very beautiful moon rose, the first full moon Jake had seen in Japan.

George was standing at the patio doors, admiring the moon with them. "You know there's a special moon ceremony in Japan," he said.

"Oh yeah. What's that?" asked Jake.

"I know! I know!" said Sam jumping up and down.

"Go ahead!" said George, smiling at the little boy.

Sam put on his serious adult voice. "It's when the Japanese go out in the Fall when the moon is real big and special, like about now and they watch the moon all night."

"Well, for a good long time anyway," said George. "It's called 'o mome-gari'. It's been going on for centuries. They gaze at the moon silently, sort of taking it in."

It sounded impressive to Jake. "Is that part of a religious cult?"

"Oh no," said Dennis. "It's not a cult. Nature is very important in Japan. That's one thing I really like about Japan. They appreciate nature. They mark the seasons."

"Yes, I guess it's kind of a pagan idea," said Jake.

"It's not pagan," said George forcefully. "I wouldn't say it was pagan. It's just appreciating the beauty of nature around you. You know, the spirit in nature."

Jake recalled the native American philosophies he had been thinking about before he came to Japan. It was the same kind of idea; the spirit within nature.

George warmed to his subject. "Have you heard of Zen? Well, it has a little to do with the concept of Zen. It's all about focusing on something and reducing things to their pure and simple form. Like imagine just focusing on the moon and nothing else. It helps you to meditate. And the tea-ceremony!"

"Oh, the tea-ceremony is so boring," said Phil suddenly.

"Well that's because you don't understand what they're actually doing," said George. "You see how they've turned a simple thing like making a cup of tea into an elaborate ritual where every little instrument you use and every little movement matters. That guy who is leading the ceremony is concentrating so hard on what he's doing, everything else is blocked out and the people are mesmerized by the movement of the *sensei*."

"Has anyone tasted green tea?" said Sam screwing up his nose. "It looks gross!"

The others laughed but George was not put off by this irreverence. "In fact the tea itself is not important." His voice sounded like the soundtrack of a documentary on Japanese life and culture. "It is the making of the tea that matters and the style of the drinking."

"Except if you're Mormon," Dennis chipped in, "and then you can't drink it."

"You mean you sat through that whole ceremony with pins and needles in your legs and you can't even get a drink at the end of it?" asked Phil.

"Green tea is different. Anyway American culture's not like that," said George. "That's why you don't understand."

"How do you mean?" enquired Jake.

"Well it's all about consuming. We'd eat or drink anything as long as it's quick and easy to buy and prepare."

"That's such a generalization," Dennis protested. "Americans are interested in good food too and good cooking. I know my mom is real interested in cooking."

"We can see that," said Sam prodding Dennis' stomach, and Dennis shifted his bulk slightly to bat him round the ear.

"But you have to admit," said George, "that most urban Americans have lost their powers of concentration and of doing things properly in a way that generations have done before them. Everything has to be instant in the States or it's not worth bothering with: food, music, books, TV, news, commercials, all of that."

"It depends on your way of life," said Jake. "Look at us Mormons. We sit and study in church all afternoon, spend time praying earnestly. We don't eat rubbish or waste food. We work as a community and spend time spreading the message of the church."

"But isn't that a bit instant too?" said George. "It's like, knock, knock! - here it is! Take it or leave it. On to the next one. But it really takes time for people to absorb faith. I would say it's a slow process."

Jake remembered the Kasugai lady. "But we take time out to teach them in depth if they come to church."

"They need time alone though," said George. "to go over it in their own minds, read at home and wait for some kind of inspiration."

"Yeah, that's why we tell them to go home and pray earnestly for a sign that the *Book of Mormon* is true," added Jake.

Dennis nodded reflectively. "Yes, I agree with you, George. I think it is important to take time over things, maybe appreciate things."

"The bottom line is," said Phil, "can you imagine the average American taking time out to watch the moon?"

They all laughed at the picture this conjured up. The President came out breaking the mood. "Boys!" he said. "Here you are. I've got some good news for you. Come and have dinner!"

The President was looking gleeful as they ate dinner and everyone was in anticipation of the great news. "Well," he said. "This is the Fall, the season when the leaves change, right? Well, the Bishop has announced a Fall leaves viewing trip. Have I got that right?"

The old hands looked pleased but the newcomers were still in the dark.

"What is that exactly?" asked Dave.

"You sit and watch the leaves turn brown," said John drily.

"No, no," said the President. "John isn't making it sound any fun at all. You see the Japanese like to mark the changes in the seasons, whether it be spring or summer, with some kind of celebration. In the Fall, it's a picnic in the country on a beautiful hillside with all the cascades of colourful leaves all along the hillside." The President was getting quite carried away by his enthusiasm.

"You see, like I was telling you about the moon-gazing," added George. "Well this is a similar thing to appreciate the Fall."

"Leaf-gazing," said Dennis jauntily.

The group were pleased at the idea of a picnic and a chance to see more of the country and to be able to talk to the Japanese church members outside the confines of the church.

"It's very relaxing," said Dennis. "I mean after you've climbed the hill because I remember from last time, it was real steep."

"Will that be Sunday?" asked Dave.

"Oh no. We can't interfere with church," said the President. "It'll be on Saturday."

Bruce looked up from his soup. "What time on Saturday?"

"All day," said the President.

"What time would we be back?" he asked.

"Hard to say really. Whenever. Why, are you expecting a call from home or something?"

"No," said Bruce coldly. "It's just that since Saturday is our only day off, and it's nice to have a chance to do your own thing. Is this a mandatory picnic?"

"Don't make it sound like a chore," said Ellis. "It'll be fun. We usually have a great time, right sir?"

"Oh yes," agreed the President, "and don't worry, Brother Bruce. There'll be plenty of open spaces for you to explore if you want to get up to no good," he chuckled.

After dinner Bruce was livid.

"It won't be so bad," said Dave as they sat cramped in his room looking dolefully at each other.

"I want to meet some new people, interesting people," said Bruce.

"Why, are we boring people?" asked Lewis.

"No offense," said Bruce, "but a guy can get sick of hanging out with Mormons all the time. We came here to meet Japanese people, right?"

"Dave is Japanese," quipped Lewis with a grin and Dave smothered him with a pillow.

"We meet Japanese people every day," said Jake.

"Yeah, but Japanese Mormons are the same as any other Mormons," Bruce complained. "Anyway, I also want to meet British people and Australians, even Italians."

"So that's what this is all about," Jake commented. He tried to reason with him. "Think about it Bruce. We have to have permission to go out in pairs, right? So even if I or one of the guys agreed to go with you to that barbecue, it would probably only be for the afternoon."

"Yeah, but they'd be on their picnic till late evening," said Bruce.

"You don't know that. Anyway, you can't risk getting caught again. And the other thing is, who are you going to find to go along with you? I can't speak for us all but I'd rather go on the picnic. You don't know what the other *gaigin* are like."

They were all taken aback when Lewis suddenly said, "I'd like to go along to the barbecue."

"Atta boy!" said Bruce encouragingly. "You see. I do have an ally. Me and Lewis will go to the party and you guys have a lovely time at your girl-scouts' picnic."

Dave put out his hand. "Bet you a thousand yen you don't get permission."

"Done!" said Bruce.

Jake sat a long time after Bruce fell asleep that night, gazing at the moon. It did have an entrancing effect. He was a little worried about how Bruce might jeopardize his mission, and also about how his behaviour might reflect on Jake himself since he was supposed to be team-leader. It didn't seem worth it for the pleasure of coffee and an evening with gentiles who might be living completely the wrong kind of lifestyle. They had been warned at training. Jake went over that evening's meeting with the President. He and Dave were called in with Ellis and Dennis and were told to keep the meeting between themselves. He informed them that they would often have such meetings of which the contents had to be kept strictly within office walls. He had gone over the method that Ellis had mentioned on Friday, which he called 'the psychological priming technique'. He understood that it might feel forced at first, but it was vital to the success of the team. He had added that any problems that their partners had or signs of spiritual doubts, loss of enthusiasm or behaviour against the rules, had to be reported. This was what was bothering Jake now. He liked Bruce. He didn't want to get him into trouble but if it meant his mission was on the line, or his good credits with the President might suffer, what was he to do? They were told to pray together every evening and morning and to encourage their partner to discuss concerns or problems at that prayer session 'to keep their hearts light', as the President put it: something like a confessional but without the confidentiality. Because Dave and Jake had had no opportunity to share their thoughts on these meetings, Jake was not sure whether Dave intended to follow the President's guidelines. After their frank talk about the barbecue, he had a feeling that Dave would keep it quiet, but Dave was also ambitious, and again Jake wondered whether he would risk jeopardizing his chances of proving himself on the mission. It seemed that Dave's training week with Dennis had not been a huge success in terms of call-backs and church visits. In fact everyone had been surprised to see that John and Bruce had done very well. Jake was sure that Ellis had been perturbed by their success, having been told that missionaries were ranked in terms of expectations. The President had ranked Ellis at the top and Bruce right at the bottom.

Jake fell asleep thinking about his family, realizing that he hadn't thought of them between last week's phone-call and the one today. He had heard all their trivial news and threw them off with a few general remarks about his mission. 'Yes everything's fine. Just fine. Sure, yeah we had a potential convert today. A few people were interested.' But this didn't satisfy his sister's curiosity. 'But what's it like?' she asked. 'I mean what's Japan like?' 'Nice,' he'd said lamely. 'Nice. Rains a lot, though.' She handed the phone over to their dad, exasperated and they'd had a few more words about the church and how everything was fine. Jake realized how long-distance telephone time was wasted with these banal phrases. You had the person right there, so you could say anything, just like a conversation in real life, but the distance and the awkwardness got in the way so you just ended up saying, 'Fine.' 'How are you?' 'Fine.' 'I'm fine', echoed in his head as he drifted towards sleep.

Jake's efforts to keep Bruce in line and assert his leadership failed from day one.

"Jake, why are you gabbing so much? You sound like you're about to take off. Cool it for a while! I'm tired."

At the platform for Okazaki, they met James, and before Jake could utter a word, the three of them were on the train in a cheerful group around a table. I suppose it can't do much harm, thought

Jake, and decided to try and talk as much as he could. He went on and on about what a great place Japan was and how many towns they'd already seen and all the different trains they'd taken.

"Could I have the times of those trains, please?" quipped James.

"Excuse me?" said Jake, and then getting the joke, he laughed nervously. "You're kidding me, right?"

Bruce apologized for his friend. "Normally Jake is a quiet, retiring character. I just don't know what's come over him today, but his tongue seems to have run away with him."

How could Jake possibly have any credibility with Bruce if he teased him all the time? Inevitably, the conversation went on and they heard about James's life in Japan, the politics of his language company, the night-life of the *gaigin*, the way Japanese people really are, and gossip about some of the more eccentric *gaigin* in Nagoya, like Betty from Florida, who had been there for fifteen years, who had worked for the same company the whole time and always spent her summers on the island. Then there was Burt from Nebraska who owned his own home, played the Japanese *koto*, had married and divorced three Japanese wives and whose home was open-house to all *gaigin* and their entourages. Bruce was enthralled to hear about this forbidden world. Jake was interested in what James called 'long-stay syndrome', a phenomenon, James explained, in which a *gaigin*, perhaps very plain and ordinary, ignored back home, become addicted to the idea of being different, of standing out from the crowd, of being admired or considered special. These terminal *gaigin* might be travellers who had stopped off in Nagoya intending to teach, make a few bucks and leave, but who, once they had tasted that feeling of being thought of as exotic, chose to stay and stay rather than blend back into obscurity back home. James then apologized for the fact that he was going on a bit, but Bruce urged him to continue his classification of the *gaigin*. There were, for instance, the young Westerners who were considered quite ordinary back home, nothing special to look at, who were idolized by pretty Japanese women. It was strange how some people found members of another racial type universally attractive. James said that most *gaigin* who were bit short of cash could get modelling jobs with the many companies around Nagoya or do voice-overs for shops and hotels for announcements in English. Foreign faces were preferred for many types of advertising, mainly because the Japanese, being bombarded with American films, drew most of their heroes from them. Even Western babies seemed to be preferred by the Japanese, who would shake their heads over their own adorable bundles, saying their noses were not 'high' enough, or that their eyes did not have enough folds. People were never satisfied with what they had. James left them with a cheery wave, promising (much to Jake's consternation) to meet them in Donut Heaven on Wednesday. Bruce was delighted to hear that James was also going to the barbecue.

"Don't get your hopes up about that barbecue," said Jake, as they made their way down to their pitch for the day.

He was relieved to find that Bruce cooperated very well on the house calls. He was good at mapping out the new areas of town and took his turn to introduce themselves in Japanese to the startled people. By now they felt no hurt at being turned away time and time again. The householders were also relieved that they left with a cheerful smile and a polite greeting. At training, they had been told how important it was to leave a good impression, because maybe in a few months time or even a few years, when it was time for that house to come up again, they would feel differently and invite them in. The crucial point was to go in only when you were invited and not to make them feel you were too pushy, which was even more important with the very reserved Japanese.

In due course they were invited into the home of a young man who seemed to be in his thirties. He was off sick, and as his wife worked all day, he was extremely bored. He had been to Europe but never the States, and it turned out he was very interested in religion. He was a member of the *Soka Gakkei* which Jake had heard mentioned a few times in training, but about which, when it had come up here, the President had not had time to explain much. The man insisted on speaking English because he considered it important for them to follow what he was saying. By the end of his monologue, it seemed as though he had turned the tables on them and was witnessing them.

Soka Gakkei, which derived from *Nichiren Shoshu* Buddhism, was one of the more recent sects of Japanese Buddhism and had been sweeping the country, partly due to the proselytizing zeal of its members who put even the Mormons in the shade, but also thanks to its influence in the political life of the country under the auspices of the *Komitei* party. It had charged young Japanese with the nearest thing to religious fervour they had known in a long time.

"Our purpose in life," explained the man, "is simply to attain happiness."

It seemed he had had practice talking about *Soka Gakkei* in much the same way as Jake and Bruce had been given their set texts to read in Japanese about the Mormon faith because he used quite complex words which did not fit in with his overall ability. "Such happiness," the man went on, "can be attained through three values. These values are beauty, gain and goodness. There can be no such thing as absolute truth. Only values must be decided on by the people. One of these three, beauty, can be reached through the five senses. The second, gain, can be reached through relationships with other people and with objects in the environment. Thus our lives develop for the better through beauty and gain. But to achieve happiness, we also need a happy society and this depends on the personal conduct of each person."

"But how do you agree on what is good?" asked Bruce.

"Everyone must decide together," said the man. "If they all agree, that is good for them."

"But what's good for one may hurt another," said Jake.

"This is why one must avoid unpleasantness, harm and evil," said the man, as if it was as easy as frying an egg.

They went around and around for a while on the philosophies of the truth of values but the man would not budge and finally they decided too much time had been spent and it was now time to make their own presentation.

Jake asked the man what he hoped to achieve in the Hereafter, and he said ultimately, eternal peace by blending with the essence of the Buddha which was the true reality, and then there would be no more striving and no more conflict. Jake had explained that God had other plans for His creatures. If they had led good lives on earth and followed the doctrines and covenants and been through the sacraments, they would be able to ascend through the levels of achievement to take their place among the gods.

Surprisingly, the man chuckled. "Well, that's rather a childish way of saying the same thing, don't you think? I may be Japanese but I cannot be fooled so easily," he added with a knowing smile.

Jake was at a loss so Bruce took over. "We didn't mean to patronize you," he said. "It's just that we want to discuss what God has planned for mankind, all about the prophets he has sent and the scriptures. We believe we have the truth."

The man became serious. "We are taught that only *Soka Gakkei* is the truth. All other creeds and ideologies are false." He pointed to his little altar in the corner of the tidy room. "This is all we really need to have and all we need to do is to chant our *Daimoku*. Then we feel happiness and calm and we get whatever we are asking for."

"Is that like praying?" ventured Jake.

"Maybe a little yes, but the words we say are very important. Only the words of the *Daimoku* are sufficient for man."

It seemed the man was in his own nirvana and there was no getting into his consciousness, but it had been an eye-opener. So he asked them to come back and discuss some more when they had had time to think about what he had said.

"How about that!" said Bruce as they made their way down the drive. "A subject inviting us back."

They laughed at the irony of it, but Jake was still a bit sore at the scoffing attitude the man had displayed towards their theology.

They had no time to discuss the incident properly before lunch time. Bruce had bargained with Jake to have lunch in a café for being good. Jake had to admit that he was cooperating very well and seemed to take an active part in the witnessing. He did not want to alienate him and he decided his simple request would do no harm and keep him in a cooperative mood. Also, even Jake himself was curious to know what was behind the wooden door of the little town café. As they stepped in a neat, middle-aged lady called the usual greeting, '*Irashaimase, Dozo*'. When she looked up from her coffee machine she was taken aback. '*Ah! Dozo, dozo, sumimasen.*' There was a little stirring among the customers, mostly workmen in tidy overalls, together with one or two secretaries from factories nearby. Eyes darted towards them and away again. Surreptitious whispers passed between companions.

The woman, who seemed to be the manager, sent her young assistant to deal with the *gaigin*. He sidled up to them with his note-pad shielding his face. "I'm sorry I don't know English," he said in Japanese.

"That's OK," said Jake, "*Nihongo wakarimasu.*"

The waiter visibly relaxed and waited for their order. Jake had been practicing his *hiragana* and *katakana*, and so, laboriously, they went through the menu together until they hit on, '*chizu sando*'. They ordered one, plus two hot chocolates and then proceeded to wolf their home-made sandwiches under the table, smiling every so often at the other customers, their mouths stuffed full.

"How about the *Soka Gakkei* guy, huh?" said Bruce. "Trying to beat us at our own game!"

"Yeah, I guess when you've only ever known one religion, it's hard to talk to someone who is just as committed to something else."

"I suppose it's not that different though."

"Bruce! How different can it be? Come on! They don't believe in God or the afterlife, no prophets, no scriptures."

"Well," he said vaguely. "I mean the moral thing, you know. Trying to lead a good life, do the right thing and all of that."

"But how can anyone possibly know what's right if they aren't told?"

"By intuition, I guess."

"So where did that intuition come from?"

"I don't know. From God, I guess." Bruce was not in the mood for theological discussion. He was too busy taking in his surroundings, so Jake went over the morning reports, checking to see that everything was in order.

It seemed the little café was not quite at ease with them. They were the 'alien life-force', as Bruce put it, and they imagined the scene when they had left, of the regulars talking about 'the day the *gaigin* came to town'.

"The day the history of Okazaki was rewritten," announced Bruce, grandly.

That afternoon, they had two recalls from the previous week. The first was the old man whom the President had gone back to the previous week. Bruce was confident. He felt he had old Japanese men figured out after their success the week before. The man seemed delighted to see them and this time invited them in to his sitting-room, well-furnished in what the Japanese would call 'the European style'. His kind-looking daughter-in-law sat sewing by the television and she jumped up to bring refreshments.

"Sir, really. We can't accept food or drink because we have so many calls during the day."

The man understood but he still insisted on bringing something just in case they were hungry. They asked him to go over what the President had said and he proudly brought out the leaflets he had been given.

"Did you get a chance to read them?" asked Jake.

"Ah, very interesting story. Yes, I like very much."

"Are you familiar with the Bible?"

The man sprang up with a glint in his eye and brought out his copy of the Jerusalem Bible. Jake and Bruce exchanged knowing glances.

"Yes, we can probably find you a better copy from our own church, sir. Where did you get this one?"

"My very good friend, Mr Lorenzo from Massachusetts. Very good friend after the war. We write many letters. Very nice man."

"Why did he give you the Bible?" asked Jake.

"He was my friend. I give him Japanese saké set."

"Fair swaps," said Bruce sarcastically, ignoring the old man's questioning look.

They continued with Mr Tanaka, who showed nothing but admiration for what they had to say and about the wonderful tales from the life of Joseph Smith. He was particularly fascinated by the visions that Joseph Smith had reported.

"I have seen many ghosts," he grinned. "Once at Heian shrine in Kyoto, I saw a young lady sitting by a tree. I was amazed, but very beautiful young lady. I was not afraid. We also saw ghosts in the war, on Okinawa island. I suppose dead soldiers," he said sadly.

"Yes but we are not talking about ghosts in this case," said Jake pedantically. "These were visions, Holy visions which are very special. Only shown to those chosen by God."

"I see, very special," the man echoed.

"The angel Moroni appeared many times," Jake explained, "to give Joseph Smith specific information."

The word 'angel' seemed to set off something in Tanaka's mind and he spoke aside a little to his daughter-in-law who came back downstairs presently with a dusty envelope. The man carefully pulled out the treasures inside and showed them his 1958 Advent Calendar decorated all over with Christmas angels. "Yes, *angerus*," he said nodding encouragingly.

"You've got the picture," said Bruce.

"Get the picture," mimicked Tanaka, a line he'd probably heard in a movie. He seemed to be delighted with these living representations of US culture bringing back fond memories of the post-war years. When they finally invited him to church, he had a quick conference with his daughter-in-law who seemed to be encouraging him.

"She worried," he said. "I not go out too much, like Japanese retired husband. You know what they call in Japanese 'dead leaves'. It means they are hard to get up, stuck! Too much in house."

To encourage him, they told him there would be lots of other men his own age.

He looked wary. "Japanese?"

"Yes, all Japanese. Some are Mormon converts."

The man did not seem too happy at the prospect of having competition.

"I suppose not that many," said Bruce. "Young people too," he added. "Men, women, children."

"American?"

"Oh yes, plenty of Americans." This seemed to cheer him up so he agreed to go to church that Sunday.

Next they had to call on the housewife whose son was away in the States. Jake quickly refreshed his mind with her notes and remembered that she seemed more interested in aspects of American life. They knocked on the door. No reply. Could she be out? Unlikely but possible. She knew they were coming. They had made a formal appointment. Could she be in the garden? They craned their necks but couldn't see the back of the house beyond the walls. Maybe she had just decided not to open the door after all. Jake did not like to think of her cowering inside as they kept on knocking, praying for them to go away, or maybe wondering whether she should answer or not and thereby missing an opportunity she might never have again. They went away despondent because she did not open the door, and they slipped an invitation card into her mailbox.

"She's probably thinking, 'Oh my God, not those crazy Americans again'", said Bruce, after Jake explained how she'd reacted to Ellis' rather over-enthusiastic presentation the week before.

"I was trying to talk to her about what she was interested in, but Ellis said later that was wrong. He was saying there's no time to waste and that you have to go straight in with the theology."

"I think he's wrong," said Bruce firmly. "Now he's blown it with this woman who might have been quite willing to come to church."

"Yes it's true. It's important to establish a relationship first so they trust you before you start to preach to them. They've probably never heard of this stuff before."

On the way back, Jake reflected, during their easy banter, that he felt totally at ease working with Bruce despite his sometimes irreverent comments. He liked his directness, and his good humour buoyed them up through the tedium of the day. So he decided to be himself and not to try and put on the forced behaviour that the President had advocated. He would be honest and explain things to him.

In the evening, he asked to speak to the President in his office. He suddenly felt a little stupid as the President waited impatiently after being taken away from some important calls.

"Sir, you know the talking thing you talked about?" He was tongue-tied, not making any sense.

"What on earth are you talking about?" asked the President.

"I'm sorry. You know the technique where you psych your partner up in the morning and then wind down in the evening?"

"Yes. What about it?"

"I tried it today but it didn't work. Bruce just laughed and asked me why I was jabbering on and he said to ..." He suddenly stopped, not wanting to mention James. That would drop them in it! "To, to me, to ease up and stop chattering, and then on the way back we had a lot to talk about."

"Well, Brother Bruce is a very perceptive young man. Don't worry, Jake. Just go on as you are, but I will tell you one thing. Don't go over the ins and outs of your witnessing too much. I mean talking about the subjects and what they said and the details of the arguments. Just talk about general things."

"Right sir!" said Jake, pleased to have got it off his chest, and satisfied with the President's complacent reaction. He started to go out.

"Any other problems?" asked the President meaningfully.

"Ah, no, sir. I don't think so."

"I see. Only I had Dave in here earlier on."

"Excuse me, sir?"

"That's OK Jake. Well, you go along."

Jake puzzled over these connections. Later while he was watching the TV, he noticed that Dave had fallen unusually quiet and looked nervous. It dawned on him that Dave might have felt compelled to come clean about the barbecue, but he couldn't be sure. What if he told Bruce his suspicions and it turned out Dave hadn't said anything? Whatever happened Jake was pretty sure they wouldn't be allowed to go, so he decided to forget about it for the time being.

Kasugai was a quiet day, and they had been asked to call back on the lady who had undergone the hot-house treatment at church on Sunday. She did open the door but didn't seem very comfortable. She had found the video and study session interesting but wanted to think about what she had learned. But Jake and Bruce couldn't leave it there. Ellis had asterisked her name and next to it he had written 'next visit urgent!'

"Yes," said Jake. "Think about it this week and you can discuss any questions with the women on Sunday."

"Um. There are so many questions," she said with uncertainty.

The conversation was limited because they were using Japanese.

"The people at the church have a lot more to tell you," said Jake, "so it would be very good if you could attend this week."

The woman now had to resort to excuses, the foreigners not

being sensitive to the Japanese hints that people used when they wanted to avoid saying something directly.

"The problem this week," she said slowly, "is that we have planned to take my children on a trip."

"Could you go Saturday?" ventured Jake.

"We Japanese are often very busy. Sunday is the only day we have for entertainment. Besides," she became bolder. "My husband is taking me to the theatre in the evening."

"Who will take care of the children?" asked Jake clutching at straws.

"Their grandparents," she said, looking startled.

"Well, don't worry," said Bruce. "You can come the week after."

"Well, church is in the morning." Jake was not going to let up. "Maybe you could come along and then go off on your trip. Why not bring your husband, the kids, the whole family? It'll be great."

"I'll ask my husband," she said.

Before Jake could press her further, Bruce thanked her and jostled Jake down the drive. She waved good-bye with a grateful smile at Bruce for letting her out of the bind.

"What? Was I too pushy?" asked Jake anxiously.

"The poor woman," lamented Bruce. "Do you wanna drag her into church?"

"Oh my! Was it that bad? It's just that Ellis has marked it urgent. They'll get mad if we lose this one. I mean she was willing to come along last Sunday."

"It must have been the videos," said Bruce. "Those schmaltzy videos would put anyone off."

Jake felt guilty for pressurizing the woman, but he knew that if he had taken the time to perform the elaborate dance of politeness and reticence, she might never have got the message. But then, as it was, he might have blown it anyway by being unsubtle. He would have to go more gently next time, with the housewives especially. They were so afraid of giving offense and so non-committal that it was almost impossible to get a straight answer out of them.

While they were praying that night, Jake prayed aloud that God might open the heart of that woman and give her the courage to come back to church. He also asked forgiveness for being impulsive and then asked Bruce if he had anything he wanted to clear off his conscience for the day.

"Er, nope. Don't think so," said Bruce.

"What about wanting to go to the barbecue?"

"Is that a sin?"

"Well it's breaking the rules of the mission and so the church, I guess."

"Are you the thought police?" asked Bruce darkly.

"I'm sorry. I just wanted you to benefit from the prayer."

"That's OK. I'm benefiting," he said. "Let's pray that we both get what we're looking for out of this mission."

It sounded good to Jake so they ended on that note.

Bruce decided to approach the President on Wednesday morning so as to leave enough notice for their plans for Saturday.

"Sir, it's my parents' wedding anniversary next week. I'd like to get them a gift. Lewis said there was some good crystal in the department stores downtown, so I wondered if I could use Saturday to go shopping instead of the picnic."

"Well, Bruce," said the President. The other missionaries kept on with their filing with attentive looks, showing they were awaiting the President's verdict with interest. "You know the Fall picnic really is a great time. You'd be sorry to miss it. It's nice once in a while for us Mormons to congregate in the open like this and see something of this beautiful country."

"Hmm. Sounds good and I'm torn," said Bruce, "but I'm anxious about the shopping. You see it is their twenty-fifth anniversary."

"OK. Special permission," said the President and Bruce's face brightened, "to go get that crystal today while you're in Sakae. I don't normally allow my missionaries to go shopping while on duty, so just this once as it's a special occasion." Bruce's face fell.

"OK," he said. "I'll come clean." The others looked aghast. "I was using the shopping as an excuse. The fact is I don't like outdoor events, too cold. I thought I would prefer exploring the town."

"Bruce I don't appreciate lies," said the President. "If you have something to ask, you tell me straight, OK? Now I understand your point but as you know you cannot go out alone. I made that rule very clear that two have to go out together. Remember what happened when you got lost?"

"Well that's OK," said Bruce becoming animated, "because Lewis said he'd like to come along with me."

The President looked doubtful and Lewis gave an apologetic smile. Finally he agreed, but said very pointedly, "You have permission to go to Sakae to the department stores and Meiji store for foreign supplies. I hope that's clear, Bruce."

"Perfectly clear," he replied.

Though Bruce was ecstatic about the weekend, Jake was really having doubts. "I'm not comfortable with this," he told Bruce later as they made their way to the park, "about lying to save your skin."

"It's not wrong to go to a barbecue," said Bruce.

"It's wrong to lie, though. What if the President found out?"

"It's not your problem, Jake. Anyway, you're not lying."

"I'm covering up, though. I mean I'm failing in my responsibility to report you to the President. I'm failing to protect you from adverse influences."

"Jake," he sighed, "no matter how much you try or how much the President tries, you are not going to treat me like a little kid. I'm entitled to live my own life, follow my own decisions and take the consequences."

Jake listened carefully because he had never seen Bruce so serious.

"I know Mormons," he went on. "I've been around them all my life. We had these down-home parties and picnics and barbecues all the time. So this is not new to me. We've been with Chinese Mormons, Canadian Mormons, Korean Mormons, German Mormons. They are all exactly the same. So I am not going to go wild over the chance to picnic with a bunch of Japanese Mormons. Now what is new to me is the world of gentiles who have different ideas, different pastimes, different ways of dressing and talking about the world. These are the type of people I'm interested in. Now I'm not foolish. If they have something there I don't approve of, I'll leave it. I'll do that because I want to, not because you or the President tried to prevent me."

Jake understood his point because he was himself often curious about gentile ways. It was sometimes fascinating to find out about their lives without the pressure of having to witness them all the time; but from a young age he had been brought up with the notion of obedience which was essential for the smooth running of the church and family and of his own life, and for the 'Word' to have any impact on his life. There were always people wiser and until you knew better, it was advisable to follow their advice and obey them. In the end though, Jake was persuaded by Bruce's argument. He would turn a blind eye and if Bruce was found out, he would tell the President he knew nothing about it. Bruce was sure to cover for him. He was sure of that. Their shared secret seemed to strengthen their partnership and Jake prayed he was doing the right thing.

They were due to meet James at lunch time, so they went around the park for a while. Bruce was an old hand in this park, having been there with John the week before. As they walked towards it, they noticed the road was up all along the way. There seemed to be road construction going on all over the area. By each excavation site, a neat little man in grey overalls and a hard hat had the job of guiding the pedestrians past the chaos. He spent the whole time waving people on.

"Don't you love these little jobs?" said Bruce. "You know, all these watchmen and guards, like the guys who wave the trains off?"

The guard scowled as he waved them through.

"Excuse us for living and breathing," said Bruce.

"What was wrong with him?" asked Jake. It was the first time he had felt hostility since he'd been in Japan, apart from those hoodlum-type kids. Curiosity was normal but this guy seemed to find them distasteful. Jake noticed the other construction workers busy all down the road. They all wore strange, sock-like slippers with a space between the big toe and the other toes rather like mittens for the feet. The slightly-built men with their strange slippers looked more like ballerinas than construction workers to Jake. Some of the older workers seemed to be just looking on, supervising.

Jake and Bruce were wary as they entered the park because they saw most of those sitting around having their lunch were construction workers. Two of them looked up from their *o bento* lunch-boxes, so Jake decided to take the plunge and approach them. This called for his best Japanese because it was unlikely they spoke English.

"Is it possible to talk with you for a few minutes?"

The men looked at each other laughing and exchanged colloquial phrases that Jake couldn't tune into. They were probably embarrassed.

"Ah, you America-*jin!*" said one immediately convulsing into laughter with his friend. "I English no speak."

"That's OK, sir. We speak Japanese, a little," he added, in view of their advanced slang.

Jake and Bruce made out that what they were saying to each other was something like, 'If they speak Japanese I'll eat my hat.' They were obviously not impressed with Jake's polished textbook phrases. They seemed to be getting impatient so the missionaries quickly took their leave. The next trio of younger, more surly workers proved even less forthcoming. They dismissed Jake and Bruce with hostile sneers and also very colloquial asides which clearly meant 'Where do these *gaigin* bozos get off, coming up to us in our lunch hour?' But Jake and Bruce did not let their ultra-polite veneer slip and they apologized in the most polite Japanese they could muster which only made the three companions crack up even more. Still, Jake was determined to be consistent in his behaviour whether talking to blue-collar or white-collar workers. He was convinced that they should remain beyond reproach, because the reputation of future Mormons in Japan depended on it.

"Yeah, they talked a lot of baloney but they were real polite about it," joked Bruce when Jake told him about the importance of image.

"Anyway I disagree," Bruce said firmly. "I think we should learn some of the street Japanese, you know, so we can get down on their level. Then we'd have some chance of getting through to them."

"It would sound phony," said Jake. "I've heard foreigners try to speak slang back home. It makes you cringe. I remember this one Spanish girl who stayed with us one summer. Her English was lousy and she had terrible pronunciation but she kept using slang.

He mimicked her. ' Eh you ghuys. You won go in za mall.' For the next half hour they carried on this game of speaking heavily-accented English peppered with slang. Jake was the Spanish one and Bruce played a Frenchman. They were anxious to get some luck before lunch. Otherwise they would feel bad about sitting around in Donut Heaven.

Before long they spied their quarry, a fairly old man with thick-rimmed glasses dressed in engineering overalls. He was giving them friendly nods and looked very pleased to have them come over and talk. At once he sprang up and introduced himself, warmly shaking their hands as though they were old friends.

"I am Kato," he announced. "I work at Sumitomo Bank." He didn't look like a bank-clerk, but the missionaries launched into their presentation, pleased to find a willing listener. Kato-san seemed full of wonder during the conversation. He nodded so enthusiastically throughout that Jake almost overshot the first lesson material. Kato's English was not too bad, though a bit stilted, but his listening seemed to be better when he insisted they read the presentation in English. Jake was pleased with how it went and decided to round it up.

"Kato-san," he said slowly. "How would you like to come to my church on Sunday?"

Kato continued smiling encouragingly but had obviously not taken it in, so Jake repeated more simply.

"Kato-san, maybe you come to my church Sunday;" and then he repeated the message in Japanese just to drive it home. Mr Kato was overwhelmed.

"Oh Jake-san. It's a great honour for me but I'm sure it would inconvenience you."

"It would be a great pleasure for me," Jake assured him and Bruce smiled, nodding encouragingly.

"Hmm. There are many Americans there?" asked Kato-san.

"Yes, many of them are Americans but also many Japanese."

Kato's face lit up and he accepted the invitation. It was as if his whole world had opened up, a world of Americans and people who spoke English and ate and dressed as they did in the movies.

Jake's pleasure was marred by Bruce's cynicism as they waved good-bye to Kato.

"They just nod and smile, but do you think he caught a word of what you were saying?"

"How do you know?"

"I just get the feeling he was humouring us. You can tell because if you suddenly change tack or ask a question, they carry on nodding and smiling."

Jake remembered that Kato had not at first understood the church invitation; but once he had understood he seemed to be over the moon about it.

Jake and Bruce were in high spirits at their speedy job with Mr Kato and with lunch-time coming up, and soon they went into another double act with Bruce pretending to witness as Jake played the subject.

"And so our heavenly father's plan was to send us into this world to test us to see who would earn the most rewards," Bruce began.

"*Ah so so so so!*" fired Jake like a machine gun, manically nodding his head.

"And so we took on our human bodies and I always have Cheerios for breakfast, how about you?"

Jake continued nodding and agreeing, and they were both convulsed with laughter, having proved their point.

As they walked into Donut Heaven, they were greeted with a cacophony of '*irrashaimases*' from the youthful and eager staff. A young, plump girl with two neat plaits under her cap came forward and gave a short speech of welcome and requested their order. Jake ordered chocolate doughnuts and a strawberry shake while Bruce went over to James's table. Immediately, Jake was ensconced in the warm, cheerful world of Donut Heaven with its jolly pop music, sweet food and whimsical decor. All kinds of people seemed to patronize the place, but most were school and student age kids or young working women. The women usually had a plain doughnut each and an iced tea while the schoolgirls gathered around a tray piled high with a bewildering variety of doughnuts. Jake wondered how they got so much pocket money. They probably had rich parents. Here and there, in an alcove, a lone salary man could be spotted reading the financial newspapers over doughnuts and coffee, lost in the childlike surroundings, like a father in a child's nursery.

"Sorry, I'm afraid it's the Brits," said James, as Jake came over to join them.

"Good to meet you," said Jake, smiling at James's friends.

They were introduced as Brian and Julie. "Hi, Jake. Nice to meet you. Are you a missionary too?" asked Julie peering at his badge.

"Yes, that's right," said Jake.

"Don't worry though. We're off duty," added Bruce.

"Oh that's OK. We're quite interested in religion," said Julie. "We have Mormons back home actually."

"Yeah, you'll find us in just about every corner of the globe," said Jake.

"Julie's from London," said Bruce, changing the subject, "and Brian's from Manchester, right?"

"Great. I've never been to Britain," said Jake, "but I like the TV series we get from over there. I also liked that movie, *American Werewolf in London*. That was great."

"I'm sure I saw an American film once, too," joked Brian with a mock-puzzled look on his face. He was quite young-looking with cropped, dark hair and cheerful eyes.

"I loved American series when I was young," said James enthusiastically. "I was brought up on *Starsky and Hutch*. Do you know that was the highlight of my week when I was a teenager? School and homework were so boring and I couldn't get a Saturday job. Saturday night, my dad would bring home whelks after the pub and we'd watch *Starsky and Hutch*, then *Soap*. Do you remember *Soap*?" he asked, as Julie smiled nostalgically. She had very wild, permed hair which seemed to be dyed black, and this mass of hair made her face and sharp little blue eyes seem very small.

"You see. That's why we like America," she said, "because we used to watch all your telly programs. Do you remember *Happy Days*?" The three of them were wrapped in nostalgia, going over favourite American series; and then the subject switched to favourite children's programmes.

"Do you remember *Hector's House*?" asked Brian, provoking a whoop of delight from the others at the memory. By the time they started acting out scenes from *Hector's House*, Jake and Bruce were lost, but they enjoyed the exuberant conversation and felt included. Julie could hardly catch her breath because she talked so fast.

"Where are you teaching tonight, James?" they asked.

"Nihon Denso again, in Okazaki."

"Got anything prepared?" asked Julie.

"No, have you?"

"No, it's Mitsubishi Heavy Industries. Anyway they're all half asleep most of the time these days. I think I'm boring them to death."

Bruce was amazed. "You mean you just walk into all these top-notch companies with nothing prepared?"

"We just wing it," said Brian primly, and they laughed because his accent sounded so incongruous with the phrase. "You see what it is, we have to do a lot of pair-work and group-work and games and stuff and a lot of the students just find it embarrassing, so I tend to just go through the grammar from the book. They're happy with that, aren't they?"

"Yes, plenty of grammar exercises," said James. "That's what they like. No prancing around the room acting things out."

"We have pair-work in our Japanese classes," said Jake. "I find I learn pretty fast."

"Do you have Japanese classes too?" asked Julie. "Yeah, we have two hours a week but I never do my homework. I think our teacher thinks we're useless."

"But how do you manage to teach?" asked Jake.

"How do you mean Jake?"

"I mean when you teach them in Japanese."

"Oh we don't use Japanese," laughed Brian. "God, you must be joking. We can barely speak to the Donut kids."

"Speak for yourself," said James.

"Yes, James is very gifted with languages," Brian conceded. "But then he did do Frog at university."

"Is that French?" said Bruce. He was finding their banter hilarious.

"Yeah, anyway. Can you imagine if we had to teach in Japanese?" said Brian. "Oh no, it's target language only for us," he said. "That's the technical term."

"We have to learn Japanese," said Jake quite proudly, "because we use it in our mission."

"That's good," said Julie quite impressed, "cos usually Americans are rubbish at languages. Remember Laura?" she said to the others and then proceeded to imitate Laura's rendering of Japanese with a broad American accent. It reminded Jake of Ellis, and he smiled.

"Come on then. Let's hear your Japanese," said Julie, eager to hear his efforts.

"Now that is embarrassing. We've only been here two weeks," said Jake.

"Go on, please. It's just that I'm a competitive person. I have to hear if you're better than me." She asked them a question and Jake answered and then gained confidence and went into a little monologue.

"I hate you. You are better than me," said Julie. "Right; I'm going to have a nervous breakdown."

Jake was taken aback by their blunt sense of humour, but he liked their self-deprecating manner and the fact that they treated them well, not like outsiders or freaks. It was obvious that Bruce had also been charmed by them.

"Aren't those guys hilarious?" he said as they left Donut Heaven.

"Yeah, I like them. They seem interested in us as people."

Jake realized that the lunch with the Brits had done more to boost Bruce's morale than any psychological game could ever have done. Why should they sit alone eating lunch on a park-bench, barely talking to one another, when they could enjoy interesting company in the warm atmosphere of the donut shop? As long as they kept their contact with non-Mormon *gaigin* controlled like this, he didn't see it doing any harm. In fact, it could do a great deal of good. That afternoon they went out and gathered no fewer than three potential church visitors, a student and two young salesmen who worked for a trading company. The missionaries had been told, when witnessing businessmen, to mention details of the corporate side of the Mormon church, something about its assets, holdings and interests in the US, as well as international contacts. It gave the impression of a lucrative club that any ambitious corporate person would be eager to join.

By joining the church, they had access to all this traditional structure without losing any of their Japanese identity, because they were assured that the Mormon church was now expanding fast in Japan and filling that spiritual vacuum. Why not kill two birds with one stone and have a soul at ease and a successful career assured? In fact, in their snowy white shirts and grey slacks, the two men looked like Japanese copies of Bruce and Jake.

When they got back to the house, there was a letter waiting from Alice.

Dear Jake

Thanks for your letter. Glad everything is going well for you. At least you seem to have settled in quickly. Must be nice living in a family home. I'm glad about that because I was worried about you living in a dorm.

Work is fine. Sue is leaving to have a baby. I was amazed how time flies. It seems like only yesterday they were married. Anyway, she seems real excited and Tuesday we had a baby shower for her and had lunch at Bonito's. She says she'll really miss us but she's looking forward to some free time and anyway, once the baby's here, she won't have any time for her friends.

Mom and dad are fine. They send their love. I called your mom and she told me more of your news although she says you never tell her anything on the phone.

This Sunday I'm leading a seminar on conflict with parents in the late teenage years. I've been studying hard to try and make it good and I've interviewed some of the girls. Trouble is, the people who would benefit probably won't come because they're trying to rebel.

I suppose it's easier to express your feelings in a letter but now I've come to the important part, I suddenly feel embarrassed. Well, the fact is I was upset we didn't talk before you left. I wanted something to remember while you were away. I don't know. I just wanted to feel special, like you wanted to spend time with me. I suppose you were just caught up in the panic of leaving. I know your faith is the most important thing in your life. I hope it is in mine but it doesn't mean you can't express your feelings. You don't have to be so formal with me, Jake. We are supposed to be married in two years. Sometimes I think that's a good thing because two years is a time in which one can only grow, and other times I feel envious that you're over there seeing the world and meeting so many other people while I'm stuck in the same old SLC.

Anyway in your next letter I want to hear more about Japan. Waiting for your reply.

Love Alice.

Jake could tell, as he reread the letter, that she left what she really wanted to say until the end because she had begun with polite home news before expressing her feelings. He was so glad she was honest enough to say what she felt, but he didn't like that line, 'We are supposed to be married', almost as though she couldn't believe it, because it echoed something Jake had been feeling too, that it was so soon, in a way, to have his whole future planned out. Almost as soon as his mission was over he'd be thrown into a life of responsibility and commitment. The other thing that always niggled him, and which he always tried to push to the back of his mind, was the fact that he was marrying Alice whom he'd known since he was a kid. There was nothing wrong with Alice, but she was so familiar. She seemed always to have been around. Against that sense of the unexpected which he'd often dreamed of when he used to think about who he would marry it was just a little disappointing. He thought of the phrase, 'Familiarity breeds contempt', but then weren't all friends strangers once? No matter whom he married, ten years down the line they'd be as familiar as old boots.

"Who's it from?" asked John bluntly as he prepared the salad.

"Er, my fiancée."

"Oh, when's the happy day?"

"We haven't set a date yet. After the mission sometime, I guess."

Sam's ears pricked up and he sidled up, trying to look at the letter.

"Leave Jake alone!" said his mother. "That's private."

"I wanna see your girlfriend's letter," said Sam.

"Sam! I won't tell you again and it's 'fiancée' not 'girlfriend'."

Jake was trying to suppress his blushes. He hated that affliction of his cheeks and ears flaring up when he was embarrassed. His dad used to say it was the Irish blood from his mother's side, but whatever its origins, it was a dead giveaway. There was no way a guy could look cool if he was prone to blushing. Now Sam was trying to use persuasion.

"Jake, please. Can I just take a peek? I've never seen a fiancée's letter before," he murmured, "Please!"

Jake unfolded the letter, showed it to him and then put it back again. "Satisfied?" he said.

"Actually, I think you're the only one engaged to be married," said Mrs Ericson. "John, does Ellis have a fiancée?"

"I think there's someone in the pipeline."

"Oh John, you make it sound terrible. In the pipeline. Honestly!"

"How about you, John?" said Sam in sing-song voice.

"You've gotta be kidding. I wanna establish my career first."

"Yes Jake, I wonder, didn't you consider having a few years to get your foot on the ladder so to speak. And your fiancée as well?"

"She doesn't really have a career," said Jake. "She works in an office."

"Isn't that a career?" said Mrs Ericson.

"Well, she's just a secretary."

"Just a secretary. From what I hear it's the secretaries who end up running the company. If they get sick, the whole place falls apart."

"Yeah, what I mean is she's not planning to move on at all. She works for her uncle and as far as I know, there's no room at the top."

Dave heard the end of the conversation. "Aren't Mormons supposed to marry young?" he said.

"They say it's better," said Mrs Ericson, "but I think things are changing now with younger people. If I had my time again I would have married later but don't tell that to the President. I still would have chosen the same man," she laughed.

"Well, a wife is a wife," said John flippantly. "I suppose anyone would do in the end."

"What a strange thing to say!" said Mrs Ericson. "Haven't you ever heard of romance? There's someone for everyone out there because each couple is made for each other."

"Even you, John," said Sam.

"You little rat," snarled John and Jake couldn't tell if he was angry or not until his face broke into a grin. He had that disconcerting way of pretending to be angry almost to frighten you, after which he would break the suspense with a smug smile. He was surprised how well Bruce and he had got along with each other, although since the first week they hadn't talked much. Neither had he spoken much to Ellis.

"I need to see you this evening to review your progress," said Ellis. "In the office after dinner if you don't mind."

"Is everything OK?" asked Jake nervously.

"Oh sure. It's just routine. You can iron out any problems before they get serious, ask any questions."

Up in the office, the President was chatting to the Bishop. They were having a planning meeting to organize a freshmans' welcome at the university. Bruce burst in with Dave to do the filing. They smiled at the others and got on with their jobs.

"Right," said Bruce. "We need about three BOMs to distribute this week. Are they over in the box?"

The President raised his hand at the Bishop who was in midsentence. "Excuse me. Brother Bruce, did I hear BOMs? What do you mean?"

"I need a few copies for some subjects sir."

"A few copies of what?" he said sharply.

"The *Book of Mormon*," faltered Bruce.

"I will not tolerate disrespectful language around our holy book. Do you understand me?"

"I'm sorry sir," said Bruce scratching his head in embarrassment. "A lot of the guys used to joke like that. I guess it just slipped out."

"It shows a deep lack of respect, Brother Bruce, and I will not tolerate it."

"I didn't mean it disrespectfully, sir. It's just like I say the guys back home ...!"

"I don't care what your friends back home do. You are a missionary. This book is the life-blood of our church."

Bruce was silenced and looked away humiliated as a resounding silence filled the office and they waited for the President to explode. Instead he resumed the conversation with the Bishop with an ingratiating smile as if nothing had happened.

Bruce was very down when Jake came into their room. "It was just so humiliating," he said. "I mean I was just joking."

"I suppose he just wanted you to see how serious it was," said Jake.

"Whose side are you on, Jake? That little weed Ellis been briefing you?"

"You know very well I'm with you. I'm covering for you, aren't I?"

"Couldn't he have just taken me aside, instead of bawling me out in front of everyone and the Bishop?" He cringed at the memory.

"Yeah, that was strange, because I know back home our Bishop used to call us up privately."

There had been one incident when Jake had been at an adult baptism and his friends had dared him to float some plastic ducks in the font. Baptism for converts was a very solemn affair where the person was fully submerged in the water by the Bishop in attendance, while wearing a full-length white gown. The convert herself had actually laughed heartily at the ducks, and a number of the congregation had been amused too, but the Bishop had glared at Jake and told him to take the ducks away. When he called Jake to his room, he told him in a calm way that he had ridiculed the solemn sacrament for the woman who would never have that experience again and especially offended her husband who had worked for years to win her over to the church. Jake had been taken to apologize personally and despite his attempts to blame his friends, the Bishop had criticized him for being weak-willed.

When Bruce had begun to recover from the outburst, he tried to justify the term 'BOMs'. "They are like bombs really, the *Book of Mormon*. I mean they come into your life and completely turn it around don't they?"

"Yeah, but BOM implies something negative like destruction."

"Well, it destroys the old and brings in the new."

Jake thought about that after their evening prayers. He envied

converts in a way because they had this wonderful moment of discovery and transformation in their lives. They might have been
doing all the wrong things, but suddenly they could start again.
The converts he had known during his life also seemed to be more
keen on the religion. They would talk about their lives in two
halves, 'before I joined the church' and 'after I joined the church'.
'I used to do this and now I do that'. They often had a way of
laughing at their folly and saying, 'Imagine! If I'd never joined the
church, I might be on the street by now'. For Jake, who had never
known anything else, he never remembered a day in his life when
he had consciously committed himself or felt something really
powerful and spiritual. It just seemed to grow on him or with him
like an expanding glove. It fitted his life, his family, his opinions
and he belonged in it. Maybe when he was about fifteen he started
taking things more seriously, appreciating the wisdom of the elders, really listening to the lectures for the first time. It was about
then that he'd begun to feel proud of being Mormon in a really
positive way. Before that he'd had nothing to check it against. It
had been all around him, but when he began to be aware that there
were other opinions in the world and other beliefs, other kinds of
people who'd never even heard of Joseph Smith, he saw the confusion many of them were in, the lack of focus in their lives, their
slovenly careless habits, and he felt proud that his parents had
taught him the right thing. He'd really begun to have confidence in
it. That was maybe why he'd been disappointed about his Temple
induction. He'd heard so much, prepared so much, put so many
expectations into it, that, he thought, for someone like him who
had been born into the church, it must be the turning-point similar
to conversion where you really felt revitalized and full of faith. But
for him the experience had not just been disappointing but frightening, and disturbing. Again he tried to think about something
else to quell the flashbacks; but he would have to come to terms
with it eventually. Sometimes he'd just write it off. He had just had
a bad day, maybe worked himself up too much with the stress.
When he had seen the other initiates coming out looking exhilarated, even hysterical, he couldn't understand why he felt so
shaken. Since they were not allowed to discuss it, he had never
been able to offload his fears. If at any time in his life he had wanted to avail himself of his father's counselling abilities, it was then,

but he was too afraid to say straight out what he felt. It sounded too sacrilegious, so he had hedged around it, asking whether all initiates felt great afterwards or did they feel afraid. His dad had said something about 'awe' which sometimes made you unable to speak or react, and this had sounded plausible to Jake, but he never got rid of the gnawing sense of disappointment that the high-point of his life had been something of a flop.

Jake could hear Bruce awake in the silence, probably still mulling over the scene in the office.

"Bruce?"

"Yeah?" It seemed that Bruce was glad to talk.

"I don't wanna talk about it OK, but I just want you to sum up your impression of the Temple experience as briefly as you can."

"A theme park," said Bruce defiantly. "Fairyland."

Jake was so stunned, he laughed in astonishment. Bruce waited, but he didn't reply. "Well?" he said.

"I told you I didn't wanna talk about it. Go to sleep!"

Bruce was intrigued but he didn't persist and soon fell asleep. Somehow what he said had taken the edge of Jake's sense of fear. It was irreverent but it was, in a way, just right. Again Jake walked through the rooms of the Temple reliving the ceremony and now it didn't seem so sinister or dreadful any more but kind of comical, almost farcical. Oh God, thought Jake, which is worse, to find my religion sinister or comical? He fell asleep with that question reverberating in his mind.

On Thursday, everyone was pleased to find out that there would be no activity that day because a severe typhoon was forecast and most companies and transport systems had closed down for safety reasons. People were advised to stay indoors and only venture out if it was absolutely essential.

They had an amusing conversation over breakfast as to whether their mission was essential or not. "In global, eternal terms, yes, it is more important than anything else in the world," stated the President, but in the short term he thought that they could afford one day off.

"We should go out, anyway," said Dennis, "and show the people how valiant the Mormons are, that they'd go out in a storm to spread the Word."

FROM UTAH TO ETERNITY

"No," said John, "they'd just think it was typical of crazy *gai-gin.*"

Their visions of a lazy day spent lounging around the house were soon shattered when the President decided to put everyone to work.

"An unexpected holiday must be put to unexpected use," he declared, and to Mrs Ericson's delight they were told to clean out all the closets in the house. As they worked, they listened to tapes of famous speeches by Ezra Taft Benson, supreme President of the church of Jesus Christ of Latter Day Saints, their living prophet. His steady voice mainly covered homely topics such as getting along with each other, praising the thrifty wife and the wise and loving grandparents, the kind, firm father who worked hard for his family and the cheerful, obedient children. Something must have struck a chord with President Ericson because he came up to Bruce and said, "I'd like to apologize for getting on your case last night. I was out of order to speak in front of everyone like that. My point is the same but I should have told you about it in a better way."

Bruce felt like a pauper who had been blessed by the king. "Oh, that's OK, sir. Yes, I see now I was stupid in what I said."

Bruce was still beaming when Dave came over to ask what the President had said and though the pressured atmosphere in the house had been relieved, it was at that moment that the storm hit the neighbourhood and they all rushed to the patio doors to watch the drama.

The effect was like looking through blurred goggles under water. Everything seemed to be sweeping sideways with mists of rain blurring everything. The trees were bent almost in two, desperately trying to cling to their last leaves, and every bit of loose plant or paper or even rubble was whirling about. There was a din from the street side of the house of clanking and creaking, probably gutters falling and trash-can lids falling. Occasionally there would also be the shattering of glass. Everyone thanked God they were safe indoors, except, that is, for Sam, who was desperate to get out and see what a storm was really like.

"I'll put you out there," joked Dennis, "and then we'll come and pick you up down-town later this evening, 'cos that's where you'll be when the typhoon has finished with you."

The storm was intense but soon blew over, leaving a monotonous driving rain in its wake. Men and women were beginning to venture out of their houses to inspect the damage. The President's car was a minor casualty with its windscreen wipers bent out of shape but some of the neighbours' cars had shattered windows from falling debris. Mrs Ericson was livid.

"Damn storm!" she said, stamping her foot. Luckily the President was not within earshot. "All my work for nothing." Her plants had been badly damaged and her neat lawn was strewn with rubbish. Her garden ornaments, two china cranes, were cracked and some of the flowers had been all but torn up by the roots.

"I could help you straighten it out," said Jake.

"That's very kind, Jake, but to be honest I haven't the heart to be bothered with it today. Anyway we can make use of you with the closets."

As their reward for the cleaning the President had George heat up some frozen pizzas and he gave them real American ice-cream. They all felt like kids. Then he called them to the *tatami* room for what he called 'story-time'. He said the typhoon and the small amount of damage it had done should put them in mind of some spiritual lessons.

He began by reading a passage from first Nephi which told of Nephi's people and their voyage to the Promised Land. It talked of a violent storm which caused them fear lest they should all drown and the judgment of God fall upon them. They began to repent of their sins and their prayers were answered. They were spared and reached their destination safely.

The President looked up. Sitting like a Japanese holy man, cross-legged on a cushion, he began to preach. Jake tried to get back into the reflective, detached mood he had felt during the storm, but the effect of pizza and ice-cream had rather brought him back down to earth.

"Don't we go on," began the President calmly, "following the same old routines day after day, eating God's food, walking God's earth, riding the railway? At the touch of a button, a light comes on. At the touch of a pedal, the car roars forward. I want something? I go out and get it. Now boys, you have seen today how

sometimes things don't go according to plan. Our plans are cur-
tailed by a storm. The trains aren't running. The stores are all
closed. My car is damaged. Now these are all minor hiccups
because we can be pretty sure everything will be all right tomorrow, but we ought to learn something. It's a little death," he
suddenly bellowed like a Southern preacher. "Don't take things
for granted! Don't stop striving for what is right! Don't get complacent! Depend on the Lord because in the twinkling of an eye He
could turn your whole world upside down. We are the blessed
ones. We have been given the means to do good works in time for
the Judgment. Others havn't. They're going around with blinders
on. Now it's your job to remove those blinders so that they have
the time to do their part before the storm comes. Now you see
here, Nephi's first instinct was to pray to God for help in the storm
and ask to be delivered. Boys! That's what all drowning men do."
("And women," cut in Mrs Ericson.) "All drowning men and
women," he conceded, "cry out to God at the point of drowning
because they know that there is no one else who can help them.
Well, we should make sure they call on the Lord a little earlier than
that, give themselves enough time to do His works, because when
drowning time comes it will be too late and they will have lost their
chance of an eternal home. The storm has abated," he said dramatically. "Now Nagoya sits chastened waiting for a sign."

He really is a good preacher, thought Jake. The sermon had
really made him think. In study circle tradition, they were told to
sit and write down what they would like to pray to God for if they
were at sea and in danger of drowning.

Jake thought about it. It was for their own benefit, not for the
others to read so he wanted to be totally honest with himself.

> God, make me a better person!
> Wipe out the mistakes I have made!
> Renew me!
> Give me guidance to follow the right way!'

He looked at his slip of paper for a while and asked himself why
he was asking to be shown the right way. Wasn't he on the right
way already? No, there was a lot more he didn't even known
about. He chastised himself. Be patient! He was only on the first

rung. If he waited until he worked his way through the priesthood his knowledge would grow deeper and more subtle. His questions would all be answered

Of course, if they had been required to hand in the slips of paper, he would have written something like: 'Please God. Bring all the people I've witnessed to the church. Make me more willing in my duties and my obedience. Help me be more diligent and active. Keep me away from temptation.'

Bruce was quite willing to share his private thoughts with Jake. "I wrote for my prayer, 'Please God, grant me a few more years to find out about life and hopefully that will make me a better person. Give me experience and diversity and let me handle it wisely.'"

Jake decided that in future he should let Bruce speak more when they did their evening prayers instead of always guiding him. It would give him more insight into his character and he knew that Bruce would be more open than him. He wouldn't just say, as Jake did, what he thought the President would like to hear. In fact a lot of times when he prayed Jake was more concerned with what the President would think, or the Bishop back home, than what God required of him. After all, they also needed to pray to God. Perhaps they worried about their own superiors. So what about Ezra Taft Benson? Jake wondered what it must be like to be in direct communication with God. He imagined it as something like a laser beam of light, not actual words, but that Benson could suddenly be inspired as though he had the answer to something all of a sudden. It was certain that his statements were always wise but when Jake scanned his face in magazines and tried to find signs of something special or divine, he just saw the face of a kindly, dreamy-eyed old man looking very much like the standard grandpa in all the TV dramas, white-haired, dependable and knowing. The few times Jake had seen him with his own eyes at the annual convention, he had been a pin figure in the distance and his voice had been calm and reassuring, not spectacular. Jake's dad had told him that men chosen by God did not need any fanfare or miraculous gimmicks. They had an inner serenity, a quiet certitude. That was why the millions of charlatans that flicked across the TVs on the evangelist networks or faith healing programs were so easy to spot. They were bombastic and showy. They would whoop and bawl and go into ecstasies of healing energy and then go home and count the bucks. Mormon preachers usually looked no more remarkable than TV anchormen.

The day off had truncated the week, and it was already Friday. Jake liked Shiroko. It exuded a sense of wide-open spaces, and seemed quite cosmopolitan in comparison with some of the other small towns.

As they were going up the third street of the day, with no joy to report so far, Jake noticed a black dot on the records for the next house. 'No-go area', he thought. He referred to the notes and it was written, 'Bangladeshi students - No call! Likely to be hostile.' Jake was taken aback. His picture of Bangladeshis gleaned from the TV and the church mission newsletters was of brown, smiling people, hungry but cheerful, always glad of help with one project or another. It was hard to imagine the occupants of the house snarling at them.

"A black dot means committed to something else, doesn't it?" said Bruce.

"Yeah, so in this case I guess it must be Islam."

"Or maybe Hindu."

"Maybe! Do they have Hindus out there? I always get confused between India, Pakistan and Bangladesh."

"Yeah, the borders were all messed around after the war. I read a novel about it once. It was gruesome, so much death and mutilation. They were all at each other's throats, killing trainloads of people or storming each other's temples to torch the place."

They were carrying on the conversation as they floated up and down the driveways in the now familiar routine of knock, wait, go; or knock, wait, smile politely, ask intro. question, accept refusal, go! Sometimes Jake wondered if they weren't getting a little careless about it, maybe not putting enough zest into each call as if they knew before they started that they were onto a loser. But sometimes you could tell at once by the way they opened the door and looked startled; then Jake and Bruce knew that they would never be able to get over the shock of seeing two *gaigin* at the door sufficiently to listen to what they were saying. You could tell by their faces whether they were going to be interested. Best to excuse themselves and get on with the next call. Jake knew Ellis wouldn't have approved of giving up so quickly on first sight. Nevertheless, Jake was heartened by their relative success so far, and their success on Wednesday had definitely stood them in good stead. Jake preferred to witness people who were at least receptive. It was no good speaking about something so important to a person who felt uncomfortable about you.

They were surprised when an old lady invited them in. They were going to refuse because they thought she was alone, but she said her grandson was home from school so they followed her into the house. Her grandson looked pale, sitting in his pyjamas by the TV. She hustled the boy to get up and welcome the strangers.

"Oh, please don't get up," said Bruce in Japanese. "You're sick."

"Do you speak Japanese?" said the boy in wonder.

"Yes, we do," said Jake.

To the boy, who had probably only seen Westerners in movies, this was a revelation. He reverently went to the kitchen and took the tray from his grandmother, setting it before them, and then backed away like a servant.

The lady had served noodles for them. They felt they should refuse but the noodles smelled wonderful and they were both hungry. They made the customary polite refusals but she urged them to eat, clucking about *gaigin* needing lots more food than Japanese because they had a lot more space to fill and Japanese food was so paltry.

"Do you have hamburgers in America?" asked the boy.

"Oh yes," said Bruce. "Hamburgers, hot dogs, corn dogs!"

The boy's eyes lit up. The missionaries were obviously the tonic he needed.

As soon as they had finished their noodles, Jake decided he'd better take the initiative and begin. He imagined how Ellis would have handled it. He must be doing something right since he was top of the class as far as the President was concerned. As he began the introduction to the Mormon faith, the woman seemed to catch on to the word 'religion' and nodding knowingly, she beckoned them over to her shrine. There were incense sticks burning and little offerings, a small effigy of a cheerful Buddha and photos of some elderly people.

"This is my husband," she said, smiling broadly as if she were introducing him in person, "and here are my parents, my husband's father."

"Very nice," said Jake lamely.

Then the lady knelt down and gave them a demonstration of her daily ritual at the shrine. "Now I'm clapping," she said, "to gain the attention of the gods. Then I begin to pray to my ancestors asking for fortune and good things for me and my family. My son, if he is lucky, will gain his promotion this year, if he works hard, of course. My daughter-in-law is a teacher you know. She is doing very well and of course all her pupils will pass their exams. Then there is little Matsuhito." She cast a beady eye on her grandson. "He must be a good boy in school and do well in English."

Jake decided to pick up on the interest in ancestors. He told the woman how, in the Mormon church, once a person had converted, they could baptize all their dead relatives by proxy so that all those who had died without benefiting from the *Book of Mormon* could benefit from it thanks to their living loved ones and loving ones who in the supreme expression of concern could guarantee them Paradise.

"That's very nice for the Americans," said the woman smugly, "but we Japanese do not need such things."

Don't need Paradise? thought Jake. What could she mean?

"All people who follow Buddhism well and pray regularly, their ancestors will help them and when we die, if our children are good to us, we will help them."

"But what can you hope for after death?" asked Jake.

"Yes, we have our spirit world too," she assured him. "Don't worry. We will be all right but thank you for your concern." She was obviously quite at ease with her world view and spoke as if Jake and Bruce were offering her a new brand of detergent. '*Oh that's OK. My trusty old one is just fine.*'

Jake decided they shouldn't linger but they could see the woman trying to signal to the boy with her eyes. The boy caught on and scurried upstairs bringing a notebook.

"I wonder if you could just help him with his English homework," she said obsequiously. "He's been out of school you see and he's been finding it very difficult."

Jake was torn. Were they to throw back her hospitality and refuse this small favour or should they agree and maybe risk being stuck there for ages? Bruce wanted to get away from the prospect of playing amateur English teacher, but Jake decided on a compromise.

"Yes ma'am. We'll help but I'm afraid we only have twenty minutes. You see we are working this whole street."

"Don't worry!" she said. "I'll have a word with the neighbours."

So Jake resigned himself to Matsuhito's homework, repetitive grammatical exercises that taxed even his brain. It had been a long time since he'd studied grammar. Bruce washed his hands of it and joined the old lady in front of the TV.

When he'd finished, the woman tried to rope them into regular English lessons while they were in Shiroko every Friday, towards the end of the day. Jake turned her offer down, thinking it would be too risky even though the thought of earning money appealed to both of them. One of the rules for missionaries was never to offer or accept private English lessons. It was obvious to the mission organizers that the missionaries were open to cheating while they were out all day doing who knew what. It was only a matter of trust that they spent the whole day missioning, and the authorities' main tactic of keeping it that way was to instill a sense of conscience based on faith. To back it up they had to play the missionaries off against each other, favouring one and keeping the other on his toes, making sure they reported on each other and shared fears and worries. The temptation to cheat was obvious and Jake already felt a little guilty about the long breaks and the contacts with gentile *gaigin,* but he justified it with the fact that they worked better if they had something to look forward to and they could be gaining valuable experience for the future by mixing with different kinds of people. But he drew the line at English lessons.

On the train back, Bruce was already working out how much they could make if they each taught a couple of hours a day.

"Forget it, Bruce. You're not gonna persuade me to break any more rules. Anyway, we aren't even qualified."

"Who cares? Remember what James said about backpackers

who could step of the plane from India or Thailand and walk straight into a classroom, many of them only high-school grads?"

James had said that it made qualified teachers like himself and his friends quite resentful, but then in Japan people seemed to be clamouring for English classes. Julie had even called him elitist for resenting other native speakers' attempts to make some money out of the Japanese.

Bruce was in a sociable frame of mind, looking around at the Japanese businessmen in their Friday night mood. Jake remembered the drunks from the week before and decided he couldn't handle that again.

"Just ignore them Bruce, please. They're drunk." He handed Bruce a pamphlet which contained advice for missionaries in their first weeks, telling them how to settle in and how to avoid homesickness, and how to get the best out of the experience. Bruce was very far from being homesick, but Jake wanted to keep him on the straight and narrow as much as possible.

Everyone was buzzing with excitement on Saturday morning.

"You look incredibly happy for a couple of guys missing a picnic to go on a shopping spree," remarked John, watching Bruce and Lewis cheerfully helping to make the sandwiches.

"Really you guys should come," said Dennis. "You can go to Sakae any weekend."

How were they to answer without giving themselves away? Bruce was his usual ingenious self. "I suppose you remember, Dennis, the pressure of the first weeks of your mission. You know it gets on top of you. Well this is the first full day I've had to really unwind and take stock, you know, reflect on what I've done, see where I can improve. So a little trip to Sakae suits me just fine, and then I can spend the day relaxing."

Ellis was convinced. "Yes, I guess you probably do need a little time to think about what you're doing."

"I prefer to relax in the outdoors," said Dave. "I like to lie under a tree and contemplate. That suits me."

"This is the best time of the year," said George. "The colours are just magnificent. Except spring, of course. Now that *really* is something."

There was an uneasy moment when Jane threatened to stay at

home because she wouldn't know anyone, until her mother reassured her that some of her friends were going. Bruce breathed a sigh of relief.

"It'll seem strange to Bruce and Lewis," said Mrs Ericson, "being alone in this big old house when they're so used to our noisy family."

"Yea, and don't go snooping around," said John. "In fact, I'm gonna lock my room."

"John!" said Mrs Ericson disapprovingly. "It's our ambition to build up an atmosphere of trust in this house."

"Well, John has given us an idea," said Bruce. "So Lewis, where shall we start? First we'll raid the pantry, then maybe copy all the computer files."

The President began to look uneasy. He was cleaning his running shoes.

"Just joking sir," Bruce reassured him. "We'll probably just watch TV, sit on the patio a while."

"I thought you didn't like the outdoors," said John snidely.

"Just for half an hour or so," said Bruce, worried that John seemed to be needling them.

It seemed that Bruce and Lewis couldn't get them out of the house fast enough. They were like mothers packing their children off to school. "Be sure to have fun. Don't eat too much! Take plenty of photos for us."

Jake could imagine their glee as they shut the front door. As for him, he was determined to quit worrying about Bruce, to switch off, and enjoy the picnic.

The party had hired minibuses for the occasion. Jake looked at the missionaries and the young Japanese men from church. Today they seemed to have a lot in common after all. They were all clean-cut and glowing with health. For leisurewear they had all chosen blue or black jeans and lumberjack-style shirts. A couple of the female university students were wearing exactly the same outfits as their partners. One couple were newlyweds who had just come back from a honeymoon in Utah. They had had their marriage sealed, much to the consternation of their parents. The girl's mother had hoped for a traditional Japanese wedding for her only daughter. They had been saving all her life because the average

Japanese wedding for middle-income families cost a fortune. There was the venue, the priest, the transport, the various outfits the bride had to wear during the ceremony, the banquet, honeymoon, furnishings for the new home and, to cap it all, gifts for the wedding guests to take home. But the parents were not happy to be saved the expense. They had missed a once-in-a-lifetime chance to win the social status that came from putting on such an occasion. Instead, their daughter had undergone an alien ceremony in an alien country and had cut ties with her background. The only comfort was her choice of husband, who was a very gifted student of economics and was clearly set for a great career. Slowly the couple were trying to build bridges with their parents. For this reason, some of the converts asked their families along on such outings as the autumn picnic to let their parents have a window on their new lives, to see their fellow Mormons, and to be reassured. Many of the study circles on Sunday, especially for the young converts, talked about dealing with conflict within the family. In the end, unless the parents were especially committed Buddhists or Shinto, it was usually the case that they didn't feel a huge rejection. The new values their children brought home were very much suited to modern corporate Japan, except, perhaps, the drinking ban. The Mormon regard for family life often even improved a son or daughter's behaviour towards their parents, and this enhanced family life in general. In some ways the parents' main fears about being abandoned by their children in old age were laid to rest when they heard about the importance Mormons attached to caring for the extended family.

When the party arrived at the location, the first challenge of the day was to climb a high mountain at the top of which would be the picnic site, which offered marvellous views under the shade of autumnal trees. The President encouraged everyone to walk in a pair with someone he or she didn't know very well. Jake found himself with Gregor, the Greek. He also found himself asking the obvious questions.

"How long have you been in Japan?"

"Five years," he said. "Before that we travelled. Before that we lived in the States."

"Oh really? Whereabouts?"

"Michigan. I had a small publishing business: books about travel and guide-books for independent travellers."

"Were you ever in Greece?"

"Oh yes. I lived there for twenty-five years, married there. I came to the States in '75 with my father. He went to join his brother's shipping business but I had been going there for summers since I was a kid."

"When did you join the church?"

"While I was there in Michigan. There was a church nearby. I was intrigued so I started going along. I liked what I saw and I joined up. My wife took some convincing but she came around in the end. She had already been 'born again' so she took it pretty bad changing again. But I told her it wasn't so much a change as a refinement. Plus she got some trouble from her colleagues at work because she'd been going on and on about her 'born-again' experience trying to convert everyone in sight; and the next minute she was coming in saying she had been all wrong."

"It takes courage to admit you were wrong."

"That's what I told her. I told her the brave people convert to a new religion and the bravest convert again. She seemed happy with that, but she was under a lot of stress. She felt it was my thing really and she was dragging behind, desperately trying to keep up."

"Do you think she did it for you?"

"I sincerely hope not."

Jake looked back at the trail they'd covered. They'd been walking around in a spiral. Every so often they would pass a little shrine made of wood with small flags attached to it. The path was muddy and slippery but the older Japanese men and women were striding along as though born to it.

"The old folks are going well," said Jake looking down at their heads bobbing along. All had professional walking boots and small back-packs and very hardy rainproofs.

"Yeah, they do a lot of walking and climbing in Japan," said Gregor. "It's a way of life here because there are so many hills and mountains, especially in this area. Some of my students go climbing every weekend. I like to see that, older people keeping fit. In Greece the older people tend to shut up shop after seventy or even sixty in some cases. They sit around and eat and don't keep active at all."

"Have you heard of those senior citizens' villages in the States?" asked Jake. "Each one is a whole complex of shops, condos, beauty parlours and leisure facilities designed exclusively for older people so they can enjoy their retirement."

"Are their families allowed in?"

"Yeah, but there are hours when visitors have to be out of the complex, especially young children. Most of the time they spend shopping or keeping fit."

"Fit for what?" asked Gregor.

Jake laughed. "Fit for shopping, I guess."

He found Gregor an interesting person. Now they climbed in silence for a while because the view was beginning to broaden around them. Jake was beginning to struggle. He hadn't done any serious exercise for weeks.

"I'm gonna have to rest a while," he panted.

"No, you've got to keep going," Gregor instructed him. "Then you'll build up stamina and get over the first barrier. If you stop now, you'll have to start all over again from zero."

Jake followed his advice although his legs felt like lead, his breathing was laboured and he was starting to feel dizzy. He could see Ellis and the President at the very front, striding confidently ahead with a trail of pairs snaking behind them. Mrs Ericson looked to be in her element, marching along and smiling with one of her Japanese friends. Jake decided he must get more in shape. If these old Japanese people could do it, he should be able to hold out. But Gregor was right, and soon his breathing readjusted itself and he felt he could go on for quite a distance. He liked the sound of the thin air with echoes of many people chattering. Their words seemed to cascade down the spirals to the people lower down. When they got to the summit it was clear that the effort had been worth it. The area was an expanse of grassy slopes dotted with benches and small stalls surrounded on all sides by regiments of trees of every shade. Jake had seen photos of Connecticut and New England in the Fall, and the resemblance was striking. There were ochre-coloured maple leaves like starfish everywhere, interspersed with pear-coloured leaves, plum-coloured leaves and others the colour of apples. A fruit-bowl of leaves, I would call it, if

I were a poet, thought Jake. The food-stalls were wooden, sur-rounded by banners and flags with cartoon pictures of fish and octopus to indicate their wares. The beautiful picnic site was play-ing host to dozens of people scattered in little groups, all smiling and having fun. There were also lots of small children, which was pleasant to see, because the busy weekday world seemed to be devoid of them. As soon as the church party started filing in, the other picnickers began to notice them and make whispered com-ments to their companions. They must have been surprised but reassured to see so many Japanese with the *gaigin*. Inevitably, the group aroused plenty of curiosity and the President deflected their uncertainty with hearty greetings: '*konichi wa, konichi wa!*' This was the first time Jake had heard him speak Japanese. The President even shook hands with some of the people. "We are from the church of Jesus Christ of Latter Day Saints," he explained slowly. The other picnickers were none the wiser but smiled politely and looked to the Bishop for more elucidation. "We're Mormons," he said and that seemed to be the key word because there were smiles of recognition from these people, many of whom had experienced the missionary campaigns.

The Mormons sat in a large circle to say a prayer of thanksgiv-ing for their food with their arms folded, heads bowed and eyes shut. The scene inevitably brought a hush to the whole area and the other picnickers sat in respectful silence. Then, just as quickly, the Mormons sprang up and divided into smaller groups while the monitors unpacked the food and distributed it. The mouths of other picnickers dropped open as the monitors made their way round the whole site distributing their abundance of sandwiches, rice balls, cookies and fruit. They accepted the gifts with embar-rassed apologies that they had nothing to give in return, as *gaigin* probably didn't like Japanese food. The monitors assured them that the foreigners loved Japanese food, but that they had more than enough.

After the lunch they organized themselves into baseball teams and invited some of the gentile children to play. They were obvi-ously delighted to be playing with real-life Americans, although probably only Ellis and Dave were up to it in terms of build and ability, and Dave looked Japanese anyway. Dennis with his enormous bulk, and the slightly-built John with his anemic features didn't cut very impressive figures. Jake was probably nearer to the image of the all-American athlete but in reality he was a mediocre sportsman. It was funny how people didn't end up at all like the stereotypes people had of them. Jake saw Jane, animated and laughing with her friends, and was glad for her that she'd decided to come along. George looked as though his mind was on other things as he stood around, a reluctant fielder, noticing the ball only after it had glanced past him. After the game, George and Gregor and Jake strolled round the site. George was interested in seeing the main shrine, which after all was the *raison d'être* for the whole mountain trail and location. As the laughter and conversation receded they felt as though they were entering another dimension. Certainly the shrine had a ghostly air with a light, dewy mist descending on it from the trees above.

"There are so many of these shrines in the country," said Gregor, "and you rarely see anyone in them. They're more like historical relics."

"I find them quite relaxing," said George. "Just to sit around. I like the fact they're quiet and out of the way."

As they walked through the series of gates, each smaller than the other, this being the distinguishing mark of Japanese shrines, they came to the centrepiece, a small, brown, cage-like structure surmounted by a grille. Incense sticks smoked nearby, and little pieces of paper ties were all around.

"Those are prayers," said George.

"Who to?" asked Jake.

"The gods," said Gregor. "Mostly for luck or passing exams, winning a fortune, you know, immature stuff."

"But people need something concrete they can understand," said George. "The idea of a God, a higher power is too abstract for a lot of people. It's not that they're praying to the gods as such, but they use them as a route to the main source of power."

Jake looked skeptical.

"It's not so different," said George meaningfully, "to what the Mormons believe, I mean, we believe in many gods. And we go through Jesus to reach the Father. It's just to help people understand better."

"That's not the same thing at all," said Jake looking to Gregor for support.

"I know what George is trying to say," said Gregor, "but I think Japanese Shinto have lost the idea of meaningful religion. It's not relevant for them any more except if it can change their fortune in mundane affairs."

Despite the location which was absolutely magnificent, Jake found the shrine totally dead. It seemed out of place amongst the lively beauty of creation around them. If it was meant to be spiritual, he certainly felt nothing. George, on the other hand, had found his peace and they let him stand quietly gazing through the dark recesses of the shrine to the trees beyond.

The day ended with songs as they ate the second half of their picnic. Dennis had brought his guitar and as the other people gradually made their way home, they were free to be themselves.

It was only seven o'clock when they got back, but Jake was relieved to find Bruce busy in the kitchen. He didn't like the way the President asked him pointedly, "How was your shopping, boys?" Did he know? thought Jake. How could he possibly know? Unless Dave had told him, but why would he let Bruce go along with it like that? Bruce was too full of excitement to bother about Jake's fears or even to hear about the picnic. They bundled into their room with Dave and Lewis and Bruce told them the whole story, who they'd met, what they'd had to eat, what they talked about. Jake wasn't too impressed. A rooftop barbecue overlooking a grey, polluted city didn't sound like fun to him.

"These guys party all the time," said Bruce. "They said: Come out any weekend and there's sure to be a party!"

Lewis reeled off the various nationalities they'd met, Koreans, Chinese, Italians, Spaniards, Brazilians, Brits and Irish, Australians, Canadians … Lewis also seemed to be star-struck by the glamourous *gaigin* who worked as teachers, models and dancers. One of them, the Spaniard, even owned a restaurant.

Jake was glad they'd had a good time, but felt annoyed that Bruce failed to show the slightest bit of interest in their picnic. Suddenly, John burst in after knocking once.

"Sorry guys! Is this a private conference or can anyone join?"

The look of panic that came over Bruce said the same thing that went through Jake's mind. Had he been listening at the door?

"We're just talking about today, that's all," said Dave. "It was a good time, wasn't it?"

"I guess," said John, "though maybe not as much fun as shopping in Sakae." It seemed that he knew something but was not going to come out with it. Jake began to feel that the network of intrigues was getting oppressive. X knew Y and Z were breaking the rules but did W know? It was a maze. Then Jake would forget what he wasn't supposed to know about John that he'd heard from Bruce in confidence. And so it would go on. He felt like someone who was losing a game of checkers and wanted to sweep the whole board to the ground. It would be so much easier if everyone could be frank about things. It was true: lies and deceit were oppressive.

All the next day the President carried on exactly as usual, and Jake thought he had been imagining things, until he gave his sermon. He picked up on the 'storm' theme from Thursday and reminded the congregation of the need for effort and sacrifice. He retold the story of the great migration from Nauvoo to Salt Lake after the death of Joseph Smith, under the leadership of Brigham Young. That was a terrible trial. Many got sick and died. They trudged through hostile territory in grim weather and sometimes storms threatened, but they carried on trusting in the Lord, who carried them through the tempest and brought them to the Promised Land. Had it not been for them there would be no Utah Temple, no missionaries and no church in this little corner of Japan. Jake had heard the story many times before but the newcomers were enthralled by the drama. The President then relived the picnic and told the people he was proud of them for the good impression they'd made.

"We were blessed with good weather and nearly all of our brethren were able to attend." Lewis and Bruce looked sheepish.

He thanked the Japanese Mormons for bringing their families along and welcomed those who, in the afterglow of the trip, had decided to accompany their Mormon relatives to have a taste of the church service for themselves.

"I want to end on a warning note for any of us who are tempted towards sin. You may be able to deceive some people but you cannot hide from the Lord. And that's all I want to say." The

President closed his book with a bang and his steely gaze unmistakably fell on Bruce.

"How did he know and what does he know?" whispered Jake to Bruce after the service.

"Why hasn't he confronted me with it?" said Bruce. He felt cornered. Whom could he trust? Someone had ratted on him. He didn't know who and he couldn't speak to the President in case the President actually had no knowledge of it, although that was unlikely. That sermon had been made for Bruce.

"Just wait till he speaks to us," said Jake. "Come on! We have to deal with our visitors."

Kato-san had come to church. Jake was watching him closely throughout the service, scanning his face for signs of interest or inspiration. He beamed throughout the service and when he noticed them in the crowd, he hurried forward to meet them. Bruce was so preoccupied he forgot to look welcoming, so Jake had to nudge him.

"Kato-san! Welcome. We are so happy to see you. Would you like to come and meet some of our members?"

Kato was basking in the attention and tried to monopolize Jake and Bruce, but they had other people to greet so they left Mr Kato with Murata-san, looking rather agitated as Murata rambled on. Since they were about the same age, Jake had decided to designate Murata as Kato's mentor, but Kato seemed to be more interested in speaking English.

Jake knew that the previous week had been too much for the lady from Kasugai because she didn't show up as he had expected from their conversation on Tuesday. He was sorry to have lost her because she did strike him as being a person who thought deeply about religion.

Mr Tanaka from Okazaki had accepted their invitation and had been vying with Mr Kato for attention. It was obvious that his English was better than Mr Kato's and he paraded it a bit.

"Well, Mr Jake, I like your church. It is very simple."

"Thank you sir. I hope you enjoyed the service," said Jake.

"Most informative, actually. I hear you had a picnic yesterday."

"Yes, it was fun. I hope you can come to the next one."

Kato-san was trying to follow and looked puzzled. Tanaka translated for him patronizingly and then said, "Mr Jake, you must introduce me to your President."

They had a busy afternoon looking after their charges. Jake was responsible for showing some slides of church life to the group of newcomers. It was a good opportunity because many of them were relatives of the Japanese Mormons who had come to the picnic. He started by drawing a diagram of the church hierarchy on the white-board. Then he showed the slides depicting the sacraments, the Temple back home, scenes from family life, the table set, the 'family home night' and slides of trips such as picnics and sports events. There were pictures of the main scriptures and then scenes from the life of Joseph Smith. At the same time, a reassuring American voice commented on the pictures and Jake read out the translation.

- A marriage sealed on earth and sealed in heaven.
- Rebirth for our new converts.
- Our glorious Temple at Salt Lake City, birthplace of the worldwide LDS church.
- Here we see a typical family, many beautiful children as you can see, seated around a simple table, hands joined, heads bowed in prayers of thanksgiving.

They had a short break for lunch followed by a video of testimonies from various people whose lives had drastically changed after their conversion.

- A brown face. A chubby boy. 'I used to hang out with the guys in the street, stealing cars and getting into all kinds of trouble.'
- Pretty blonde American girl. 'I used to be confused about relationships, with so many dates but never the right person.'
- An oriental face. A Chinese shop-keeper. 'I used to think money, money, money, all the time. No time for family, gambling all the money.'
- A German male student. 'Do you know what it's like to have drink as a friend?'

So it went on, short cameos of diverse men and women designed to strike a chord with many kinds of people who might be interested in the church. One of the regular Japanese church members then invited the newcomers to talk about areas where their lives were not working, disappointments or failures. There was absolute silence from the room, the Japanese guests being unused to such public soul-searching.

Kato raised his hand at last and said poignantly, "I have no friends. I am alone."

It touched Jake to hear him say that and it made him sad to think that Kato probably looked on them as some kind of hope for a fuller life.

There were two salesmen whom they'd met in Sakae. Their conversation had been so brief that they were pleasantly surprised to find that they had taken up their invitation to church. They were whisked off by the Bishop at the end of the session for a private meeting. Being businessmen they were treated as VIPs, and the Bishop knew that what would impress them would be some hard facts and figures about the Mormon church's business interests.

Just as it was time to leave, Ellis and George came out of their study room with huge grins on their faces. They had been talking privately with a young student whom they had invited to church. He had spent a year at the University of Southern California where he had first made contact with the Mormons but had not taken a decision then because of his family. To have chanced on the missionaries on campus here in Japan, of all places, was for him nothing less than a sign from God and he had decided it was time to make a commitment. That afternoon he had decided to join the church. The President came to congratulate him personally and the other converts had tears in their eyes from the memory of their own experience. The young man, whose name was Mr Ito, kept going over and over the marvellous chance meeting. It seemed his decision had hinged on this. The church members then sat in the church again and the President made the announcement to everyone. Then Sam was brought forward, along with a little Japanese boy from Sunday school, to make the presentation of a set of Mormon scriptures, all specially bound in leather and given in a presentation box. He also received a large box of exotic fruits in a presentation box from the other Japanese members. The church had a stock of them in the storeroom for such occasions. Such gifts were extremely expensive because each piece of fruit was specially selected for perfection and included such rarities in Japan as mangoes and guava.

Mr Ito didn't stop bowing and thanking everyone and assuring everyone that he would try to live up to the demands of his new faith. Everyone was asking about his parents' reaction and he just said that he'd talked it over and he was certain they were not too upset, just a little unsure, but they were glad it was quite a well-known church and not some obscure sect. Jake was a little envious that Ellis had clinched another conversion. He wondered when it would be their turn, because they had done well to have so many people showing up, but what they needed in the end was a fully-committed new member. For the moment, he tried to put these feelings aside and feel happy that whoever was responsible, what mattered was that people were coming into the church.

As they embarked on their third week, Jake felt as though he'd been there for months. The routine was established and every day seemed to be crammed full with chores, meals, train-rides, missioning, classes and meetings. The President continued to treat Bruce and Lewis absolutely normally, but it was as if he was waiting for them to own up. The uncertainty created an uneasy tension and Jake decided not to allow Bruce on any more adventures. Their meetings with the Brits were quite enough to be going on with. Also added to their workload that week was a roster system of evening visits in the city. The one perk in this job was that they were allowed to take the President's car.

They had fun trying to figure out the driving system on the opposite side from what they were used to, but Jake found most of the Japanese to be sober and courteous drivers. On the evening visits they had to call by special appointment, mostly on businessmen whom the President or the Bishop had contacted themselves. They were responsible for approaching corporations and spent most of their days either on the phone or going to companies. For these evening assignments, Jake was sent along with Dave. Bruce and Lewis were excluded from these responsibilities, and though they had wondered if it had anything to do with the episode on Saturday, in the end they just put it down to their inferior status in the ward hierarchy. However, it didn't mean a quiet evening for them. They were assigned computer work for the President, inputting the vast amounts of data.

On the evening of the first such assignment, it was very reassuring for Jake to go to a house where they knew they had an appointment. They were greeted warmly into the house and taken to a very plush living-room where they sat on cushions around a low, mahogany table. They were given a delicious stew containing strips of beef. Their host congratulated them on their use of chopsticks as all Japanese did and as usual Dave had become accustomed to the fact that most of the attention was focused on the *gaigin* whose face fitted. Dave felt at times he was there more as a back-up although some of the subjects were interested in his family history and about US life for Japanese people. 'I am an American,' he would say firmly. 'I don't know what it is to be Japanese. This place is as strange to me as Mexico.' After ice-cream, the missionaries brought out their photos and charts and gave a profile of the church organization. Then they showed a five-minute film on church history and doctrines covering the very basic points. It began with the youth of Joseph Smith and how he was dissatisfied with the churches around him at the time.

'Please God, show me the true church,' he had prayed, and he was told to reject them all because since 'the Great Apostasy' not one of the Christian churches was true. He was to be shown a new path. After his first vision where he reported that he had seen God and his son in a grove, he began to receive visions from the Angel Moroni who told him where he would find some golden plates on which he would find, in an ancient language called 'Reformed Egyptian', the restored Testament of Jesus Christ. He was given the means to translate it and with the help of his scribe, Oliver Cowdery, produced the *Book of Mormon*. To be untainted by gentile ways, Joseph wanted to set up a community apart with its own finance, producing its own goods, following the law of God as it was being revealed to Joseph. Unfortunately jealousy and bigotry spurred the local people to murder Joseph and his brother and his flock were left alone. Fortunately, leadership came in the form of one of the disciples, Brigham Young, who led them on a journey which was to test their souls to the edge of endurance and they finally found their Promised Land in the far West at Salt Lake where the community was established and then the Temple.

The next video had members of the General Authorities introducing themselves, giving a short resumé of their careers and explaining how the church had helped them. The longest slot was given to a Chinese American member of the 'Quorum of the Seventy'. Ezra Benson said his piece and the scene flashed to the annual conference where thousands of hands were shown going up. The video played stirring music and finished with the slogan, 'Who's for the church of Jesus Christ of Latter Day Saints?' Hands went up all over the meeting hall and the video finished with the words 'The church of Jesus Christ of Latter Day Saints. Building the Kingdom of God on earth.' The businessman was obviously impressed and thanked Dave and Jake. He said it looked very useful and interesting and that he would discuss it with his superiors and make a decision. They left assuring him that the President would call during the week.

On emerging from that particular assignment they felt like businessmen who had just concluded a successful contract. They were pleased with themselves, and at how professional they'd been. A job well done! Businessmen like this one and others they went to on these evening assignments usually did like what they saw in these presentations but they were unlikely to commit themselves as a matter of personal choice. All their decisions were bound up with the company and how it would benefit the company. If their superiors were not in agreement, the President would not be able to get through on the phone without difficulty and even then would be met with rebuffs from the secretaries and finally a polite refusal. 'We have been considering your proposition. I'm afraid it does not complement our overall policy at the present time but we hope to have further contact in the future.' Then in the tradition of salesmen everywhere, the name would be duly filed as a contact, perhaps to be picked up on sometime later. If, on the other hand, the company was impressed in general by the activities of the church, the member who had been witnessed would act as the representative and he would become an affiliated church member. He did not usually get baptized and rarely attended church, because of his busy schedule, but he would be associated with the Mormons, as it were, as a friendly face who would be contacted if there was some mutual benefit to be gained. This also excused the representative from the Mormon laws which would be fairly inconvenient for Japanese businessmen, such as giving up tea and alcohol. There were a few who decided to go along with the 'Word of Wisdom' however, and they had in fact been quite favourably received by their colleagues who saw them as healthy zealots who were above the frivolities and stupidities of the world of drinking.

The President was pleased with Jake and Dave when he heard of their success. He looked at his bleary-eyed computer workers and said they could now clock off. Jake asked the President for some advice about the *Soka Gakkei* member whom they'd seen again that day in Okazaki. The President shooed everyone out of his office and told Jake to sit down. Jake hoped he wouldn't use this as an opportunity to probe him some more about Bruce. Almost every other day they were called in for questions. 'How's Brother Bruce. Any problems? Pulling his weight? Seems to know what he's talking about? Good, good.' Jake insisted on highlighting Bruce's skills because he honestly did think Bruce was good at his job and had gone out of his way to cooperate. But the President and Ellis would keep making these insinuations that he was somehow lazy or lacked commitment. He wouldn't be surprised if Bruce began to believe it himself and think it was hardly worth trying.

The President listened to Jake's story about the *Soka Gakkei* man as he tried to summarize what the man had said. Jake explained how he had continued to resist their witnessing and he wondered whether it was time to give up on him. He was going to be away from work for a few more weeks after a long illness and seemed to enjoy their meetings and the chance to discuss religion since he had been house-bound for some time.

"I think you should keep up with this guy," said the President. "We have quite a few *Soka Gakkei* members on our books and we need to know a little more about them, to know how best to approach them. You continue with this guy. He sounds intelligent. Just remember to write down what he says, or have Brother Bruce write it down and put it in his file. It would be useful material for me, to size up the competition, you might say."

"Do they witness also?"

"Well, that's what I'm interested in. I hear they have a very high-pressure style of witnessing their faith that attempts to get the listener to unburden their mind of any associations and religious attachments so that their mind is empty to receive the new faith."

"Sounds more like brainwashing to me."

"I think that's what it is. They won't tolerate artefacts from any other religion, even traditional Buddhism and Shintoism. They insist that a convert throw away anything to do with his old ways. It's a kind of purification for them. It shows a certain insecurity you see. Compare it with us! We let our converts take it easy. Conversion is a big shock to the system. It takes some time for the new faith to settle and then to get rid of the old attachments and things to do with the old beliefs. For one reason or another they want to hold onto them until they're ready to let go. Then slowly they see us with arms outstretched calling them to something better and they gladly leave the old ways behind them. Do you see the difference?"

Jake nodded. He liked the President's way of talking when he was giving sermons or talking about spiritual matters.

"So," the President finished, standing up. "I suggest you let this guy witness you all he likes. Don't worry! You're immune. Just try to get as much information as you can," and he slapped Jake heartily on the back.

Jake had already become nonchalant about the regular train trips, and as usual they had descended into the cavernous regions of the *Meitetsu* Line beneath Nagoya station. The trains were so exquisitely timed that they did not have to pay attention to the stations on the way. Jake would just set his watch for the arrival time and they would get off. Once there, they recognized the stop, which was important because some of the destination names were only written in Japanese. The baffling part was getting on the right train at Nagoya because the destination would flash momentarily on the board and the trains came thick and fast, all going in different directions. Jake had learned to recognize the Kasugai train by its character which looked to him like a bear at a picnic table under a roof although Bruce was absolutely baffled trying to make it out. As soon as it flashed on the screen, they piled in and endured a crushed train journey with the school-children giggling and smirking around their elbows. When Jake's alarm went off they didn't notice anything unusual until they were walking along the platform. They checked their maps. The place looked totally unfamiliar. They asked the ticket collector whose job was to mechanically clip all tickets with his metal clippers like an automaton. The clippers would still be clanging away even when no one was there, in anticipation of the next passenger.

"*Sumimasen. Koko wa doko desu ka?*"

He waved a surly hand at the notice-board.

"*Sumimasen. Wakarimasen.*"

"Utsumi," he said.

"Oh God I thought so," said Jake clasping his forehead. "We're hopelessly lost."

Bruce chuckled. "Great. Let's explore."

"C'mon," said Jake. "We'd better call the office to find out what to do."

"Jake," said Bruce excitedly. "I can see the ocean. Let's go check it out. C'mon. It won't hurt."

"You are kidding aren't you? You wanna get us into more trouble?"

"Look. No one knows we're lost. We've got the whole day to go around Kasugai. We'll find our way back. If not we can just fill the reports in and make up someone who was interested."

Bruce was like a little devil egging him on to disobedience.

"No! No! I've had it with your scams. We've got to get back. We'll get found out. I know it. Anyway we've got to do this properly. It's really wrong to falsify the reports."

"Why? No one will be going over those streets again for around ten years."

"I'm just convinced we'll be found out. I want to play it by the book from now on and as I'm responsible, I'll make the decision, OK?"

"But I wanna go to the beach," said Bruce pretending to sulk like a child kicking in the ground.

Luckily, when they called the office the President found it amusing. "You guys," he said. "Didn't you pay attention to the signs? Well, it happens to nearly everyone some time or another." Jake could hear him telling the Bishop about their predicament as he flipped through his train schedules. "Well boys. It looks like you'll have to go right back to Nagoya and then out again. Now be sure and ask, 'Is this the right train for Kasugai?' before you get on.

It doesn't hurt. Right, well, hmm. You have an hour to kill because the next fast train to Nagoya doesn't go out from there until 10:12. You have chosen an out-of-the-way place to get stranded. Walk around a little if you like! Don't do any calls though! We don't have much on that place. Good luck!"

"Good news," said Jake turning to Bruce. "You got your wish. President says the next train is at 10:12 so we have an hour to kill. He said we could take a walk."

Even Bruce enjoyed things more when they had permission so he had a spring in his step as they headed off towards the shore. It looked deceptively near from the station and they lost sight of it several times as they tried to follow the smell of the air and their instinct that it was getting nearer.

When they finally arrived at the beach they looked in disgust. The shore was lined with smoking factory chimneys and rusting metal slats. A vile smell of chemical reactions filled their nostrils.

"What the hell do they pump in here?" said Bruce in disgust. It was a foul, metallic smell, very pervasive and from its smell alone, obviously toxic.

Jake covered his mouth. "Maybe we should go. It could be dangerous to breathe these fumes." But then they saw lots of blue-clad figures walking around the compound of the offending factory.

"Ugh! I'd hate to see the state of their lungs," Bruce remarked. "Imagine working here every day."

Even the sea-birds looked sickly and had oily residue on their feathers. The grey sand was scattered with metal fragments and lumps of putrid seaweed. "Don't they eat this stuff?" said Jake, toying with it.

"I wouldn't eat anything from around here," said Bruce.

They walked closer to the shoreline and stood for a while gazing out to sea. Despite the ugliness of the beach and the platforms out at sea all around the coast, the sea itself, as ever, looked magnificent and inspiring. It had a way of making everyday concerns seem trivial. It was the way the life of the sea went on relentlessly whatever happened on the land. It seemed to say, 'Who cares what else is happening? I'm still here.'

"You know I used to stand on the shore back home," said Bruce dreamily. "I would look out at the ocean and dream of Japan on the other side. 'Soon I'll be there!' I thought. 'I'll see what's been waiting for me across the ocean.' And now I'm on the other side and I'm standing here wondering what's going on over the other side." He laughed at the irony of it.

"That's neat," said Jake smiling. He also loved the ocean and loved sitting and thinking with the sound of the waves in the distance. He was glad they'd gone to this place by accident. What a nice turn of events, to be sitting gazing out to sea rather than tramping the streets of Kasugai. They sat a long time and didn't speak, each aware that the other was thinking in the stillness.

During their weekly Wednesday session at Donut Heaven, Jake felt like the outsider as the group went over their party on Saturday, remembering the gossip about local *gaigin* and competition for private English classes, comparing rates and all the good deals. James had one 'private' as he called it, where he was picked up from the station in a car, provided with a full dinner and then paid 20,000 yen per hour, which was a huge amount considering some were willing to work for 5000 yen per hour or less.

"I just don't know how you can justify that," said Julie in disbelief.

"I don't think I'd have a hard time placating my conscience," said Andy, the American they'd met at the football game who also knew the Brits.

"But it's not fair," Julie went on, "if you charge too much and they give you dinner and everything."

"They are rich," said James. "Anyway, I need the money more than they do."

"Oh yes," said Brian in derision, "to feed your family of five who are languishing in the gutter."

"I think 2,500 is fair for students," said Julie, "and 5,000 for housewives or businessmen."

James snorted in derision. "Look, if they want private lessons, they've got to pay for them."

"I think it's good if you're trying to save," said Andy. "I know teachers who've been able to put the deposit on a house back home from the money they make here, or travel for another two years."

"Yeah," said Julie, "but the cheapskate travellers could travel for ten years on the amount they spend. It's pathetic! They go to India or Thailand and play 'living like the natives' for a couple of years and spend about 50 pence a day. You know Tom who came here from Borneo? He didn't spend much more than that."

"What's wrong with that?" said Andy. "At least they get to know the locals."

"Yeah, but can you imagine," said Brian, "two bedraggled *gaigin* turn up at your mud hut where you've just scraped out a meal for your family from a pot of broth and you invite them to share a meal out of politeness and they accept." The others began to laugh. "It's true," he went on. "I've spoken to loads of travellers who did that, sponging off the locals for months. Hotels? You must be joking! Nothing less than authentic local accommodation."

"Yeah, there was this girl from university I knew. She went to Nigeria 'for her holidays' one summer," said Julie, rolling her eyes. "She met this bloke in a coffee bar and he invited her to his village to eat at his home with his family. Anyway, she ended up as the guest of honour sitting, laughing and joking with the men and then she couldn't understand why the women were being so offhand with her. She said it was just so embarrassing. She started to try and make conversation with them and they just started to hiss at her. They were probably jealous, thinking, 'who's this western floozy coming in on our territory?' Anyway, the women ended up doing all the work while she sat there like Lady Muck. I mean she didn't like it or anything because she's a bit of a feminist, you see, 'expressing solidarity with third-world women,' that sort of thing, but they were having none of it, so she refused the invitation to stay overnight and asked for a taxi. The blokes thought they'd offended her or something."

"Now I could tell you some stories from my travels," said James, reminiscing.

"Shut up, travel bore!" said his countrymen in unison.

Jake and Bruce always felt buoyed up by their meetings in Donut Heaven. Jake liked the fact that they were interested in languages too, and James and Julie enjoyed hearing about their Japanese lessons and comparing notes about the new *kanji* they'd learned. Jake was fond of the lessons and wondered if the President would consider offering them more hours with the Japanese teacher, or at least allow them to study part-time at the university like some of the English teachers.

"I'm afraid we can't spare you during the day," said the President at dinner, "so that only leaves Saturday. If you could arrange something for Saturday, we might consider paying for it."

"Oh, Jake. We were counting on you to join the team," said Ellis.

"Me?" said Jake. "But I'm not that good at football. Dave will join."

"Sure, yeah. I'd like to play but it would be good to have us all in the team. We need something physical at least once a week."

The President agreed. "Dave's right. I'd like you all to keep fit and play some regular sports, so I'd like you all to join the team. Then after study on Sundays we could maybe organize basketball."

The prospect of sports didn't appeal that much to Jake. He'd had his fill of sports activities and team games back home. These days he found himself more interested in the world of the mind, quiet academic pursuits, and now he found himself in Japan it was a golden opportunity to really improve his grasp of the language. The introduction to *kanji* had really set him thinking and he already had dreams of learning enough to be able to read a newspaper.

"That's settled, then," concluded the President, even though Dave was the only one enthusiastic about sports. "Ellis, would you please organize basketball for this Sunday? My wife will help you with calling around to buy the equipment."

Then Mrs Ericson had an idea. "Well, my Japanese is not perfect but it's not half bad," she said. "How about if I teach you an hour a day either before breakfast or on evenings when you don't have appointments?"

"Oh, I'm sure that'd be too much for you," said Jake.

"No, no. I really enjoy teaching," she said. "It would also save the church money and we could bring in some of the church members for conversation practice from time to time. Even Phil and Jane could help us. They're using Japanese every day."

"And me!" said Sam indignantly.

"Yes, Sam too," she agreed. "In fact," she looked at her husband. "Isn't it about time we all really got down to some serious study? I'm sure it would benefit you, dear."

The President smiled wanly, but he thought her idea was good, and he agreed to Japanese lessons for the missionaries two or three evenings a week to keep up the momentum, making sure it didn't encroach too much on missionary duties and 'family home evening'.

That Saturday Jake was glad he'd plumped for football after all because he joined the team and began to feel exhilarated when he proved an asset to them right from the start. Their team was made up of Ellis, Dave, Lewis and George along with some other American and Australian *gaigin*. The other side were a mixture of Europeans and South Americans, most of whom were more used to soccer, so Jake's team already had an advantage as well as having all the burliest, broadest players. There was one Australian named Roy who was taking the whole thing incredibly seriously and would rage and grimace whenever they lost the ball or someone made a wrong move. George told Jake at half-time that he was one of the few *gaigin* who actually worked within a Japanese company and he had quite a lot of influence regarding contracts they were making with Australia. George added that he spoke flawless Japanese and Jake was anxious to sound him out and find out how he had managed this, but he seemed a very aggressive, uncommunicative person and difficult to approach. George pointed out his Japanese girlfriend who was cheering them on from the sidelines along with a friend of hers. She was said to be devoted to Roy and proud of her enormous Australian boyfriend who had a big-shot job and could play the best football; but despite her attentive behaviour he seemed almost to ignore her, and at the end of the game he strode off to the car with Akiko tripping behind him trying to keep up. It struck Jake that she had found someone who looked and sounded impressive but in fact had no real personality. The other players were polite but distant, seeming to recoil instantly at the idea of socialising with Mormon missionaries. They had respect for the Mormons as players but didn't seem so interested to find out how life was for them in Japan or how they spent their days. The exception was, however, their clear interest in Dave, as they wanted to find out how it felt to be taken for a Japanese all the time. They all seemed to have Japanese girlfriends.

"Were those the guys at the barbecue?" Jake asked Bruce back at the house.

"I think so. There were quite a few American guys there but I mostly spoke to the Brits and to the Spanish guy."

"Did you talk much about the church?"

"Uh uh! We decided to keep quiet about that unless anyone asked. We get sick of the same jokes and comments. Sometimes you just need to take off your Mormon front and be yourself for a while."

"Isn't being Mormon part of being yourself?"

"I guess what I mean is all this kind of 'perfect ambassador for the church' kind of façade. Yes, I am a Mormon. I try to live like a Mormon but that's not all there is about me. I have other thoughts or other ideas outside of what the hierarchy has set out. Anyway, people get offended if you strike up a good relationship and get to like a person and then you find out they had an ulterior motive all along, and that they were just trying to convert you."

"Is that bad?"

"Well it kinda devalues the relationship. It's like, for example, someone finding out that their friends only like them because they have money and as soon as they lose their money the friends disappear."

'I don't see it like that," said Jake. "I mean like you're betraying them if you make friends just to convert them. What you're offering them is the most valuable thing they'll get in life. It's like, if you have something valuable, you'd want to share it with people you like. Trouble is some people don't appreciate the value of religious truth and they think something like that is worthless, whereas we think it's the most valuable thing life has to offer."

Bruce looked up, vaguely disturbed. "Do we?" he asked.

That Sunday witnessed the baptism of Mr Ito. He had had an intensive week of study with the Bishop who found he knew a lot already from his time in Southern California, and he deemed him ready to take his first sacrament. Mr Ito did seem to glow as he came out into the chapel where the congregation was waiting. This, of all the newly-baptised Jake had seen, looked to be a man who was certainly convinced of what he was doing. The white baptismal robe looked very dramatic. The President made the usual speech about reviewing your own commitment to the church and thanking God for bringing another member to the flock. Then the Bishop dunked Mr Ito bodily into the pool in such a swift movement that one could almost have missed it, and Mr Ito emerged with his sins dripping away and his face cheerful. There was nothing like a full ritual baptism to mark the end of something old and the beginning of something new. Jake thought it was a powerfully effective initiation because it really made the convert think and made him realize he had made a serious decision. For this reason, he imagined people would not be inclined just to drift into the Mormon church.

The baptism was inspiring for the other visitors and it was not uncommon for some who might have been dragging their feet suddenly to be overwhelmed with religious fervour and to decide, themselves, literally to take the plunge and get themselves baptized into the church. Mr Kato was one who needed no prompting, and later he shyly beckoned Jake over into a corner and said, "Jake-san, can I join your church?"

"Certainly you can. Do you feel ready? I mean, have you read the books we gave you?"

"Oh yes. Very wonderful. I decide. I like your church very much. Mormon people very kind. Yes, may I join please?"

The way he said it made Jake of think of someone joining the library. He seemed impatient.

"Perhaps you'd like to see the Bishop."

"Or maybe the President?"

"Or the President. But someone has to give you your training and it's better if that's in Japanese."

"Yes I'm sorry. My English is no good."

"Oh no," Jake reassured him. "Your English is fine." Kato beamed. "It's just that this is an important step. It's better to be sure you know exactly what you're going into."

Jake was a little disappointed that no one seemed to make such a fuss of Kato-san. When he asked the Bishop, he seemed to be too busy to deal with it and the President said it would be better to put him off until the following week. Maybe he wasn't important enough in their eyes. He wasn't a businessman. He wasn't young. He didn't have much influence. A widower with a grown-up son in Yokohama? It turned out Kato-san was a janitor at the bank where he worked and no-one seemed to be in a rush to rejoice at his conversion. He was Jake's first success and he felt protective of him but also anxious to make sure it was credited to his progress chart. Tanaka was a 'no-show' that week so Jake thought he must have come along merely out of curiosity. Otherwise there were no other really promising prospects. Kato-san hung around until the last activity was over and was even anxious to come along to the basketball game, but Ellis told him activities were over for the day and that they were looking forward to seeing him the following week. Jake watched as his hunched figure left the building. 'God bless you,' said Jake softly, and then wondered why he'd said that.

The following Sunday Jake was very surprised to find that Kato hadn't shown up.

"It's unusual for him," he confided to Ellis. "I hope I didn't upset him last week by not making a big deal out of his conversion, but everyone was busy."

"Yeah, he seemed real interested," said Ellis. "Maybe he had something else he had to do. We can give him a call later."

Jake was anxious to claim this one as his own. "Right. That's OK, thanks Ellis. I'll follow it up later."

Jake kept looking towards the door all through the service but there was still no sign of Mr Kato. He was despondent. He had seemed the most hopeful of all their prospects.

That week a couple with a baby had come along to church. Jake and Bruce had witnessed to them on Thursday in Toyota City. The man was preparing to go abroad and he seemed very eager to invite them in to quiz them about the States. They had found it difficult to keep to the point but by now Jake had begun to realize the varying motivations of people who were coming along to church or who had shown an interest. Apart from the rare few who were spiritually oriented and rationally convinced of the truth of the church, you could divide the others into two broad categories: lonely people for whom any attention was welcome, and people who had an interest in things foreign. The man in question, along with his family, had been sent to California by his company and was set to spend at least five years there, so he was eager for information. He was a computer technician who worked in the design department of a subsidiary of Toyota Motors. When Jake had seen his distracted manner as soon as he mentioned the scriptures, he decided to answer his questions on the States and call him into church where he was likely to be siphoned off into corporate affiliation. He got along very well with Bruce since he had never heard of Utah and saw Bruce as an ambassador for California. His wife had sat supportively beside him, showing exaggerated, polite interest. When Jake had the chance to speak with them at church, she seemed very impressed with the arrangements for children. A young Japanese woman who had converted along with her husband some years earlier led a workshop about child-care and bringing up children. She had reached the toddler stage in her discussions about child development so Mrs Nikita was dispatched to the mothers' meeting while the Bishop eagerly led her husband to speak to his peers who had already come under the spell of the church.

Jake called Kato's home later when he got back to the office and he got no reply. He tried several more times but with no more success. He waited until Monday and called Kato's work. The telephonist coughed and said, "I'm terribly sorry. Kato-san is not here any longer."

"I see," said Jake. "Did he leave?" He was puzzled. He knew that the likelihood of a Japanese leaving his job before retirement was remote.

"Are you a friend of his?" the young woman asked.

"A friend? Yes. I was expecting him at the weekend but he didn't come."

"Yes, you are worried. I understand. I'm very sorry. It's very sad."

"Has something happened?"

"Sir. Maybe you haven't heard the news. Kato-san died on Wednesday."

"I see. Thank you. I see." He put the phone down slowly. Poor Kato-san! How sudden! He had seemed so well. His mind went back to the last time he had seen him. He had looked alone and a little rejected. If only they'd taken time out for him last Sunday. Maybe he would still have died, but he would have died happy and, perhaps, fulfilled.

Jake had to wait to tell the President because he was almost late for his train. They spent a desultory day in Okazaki, and even Bruce felt rather sorry for Kato.

"Shall we call in on Tanaka and tell him about Kato?" he asked.

"Yeah, we should. I mean, they weren't friends but I feel I should tell someone. At least someone might have cared about the old guy."

Tanaka invited them in rather guardedly and apologized for missing church. He also said that family commitments meant he could not attend regularly, but he thanked them for a most interesting experience. He was shocked to hear about Kato in the way one might feel when one had only recently seen someone alive.

"But we saw him that Sunday, no?" said Tanaka, aghast. He was speaking Japanese now as his mind tried to take it in. "He looked fine; and then who would have thought he would be dead within the week?"

"I wonder where he is now?" mused Jake and Tanaka looked at him as if he were mad. "Not the ghosts again," he said looking around anxiously.

His daughter-in-law was trying to ascertain who had died.

"Oh, an old man from Fushimi, dear. You don't know him. An employee of Sumitomo Bank." The daughter-in-law relaxed and went back to her TV drama.

They asked what they should do and Tanaka suggested they pay their respects at Kato's home.

The President seemed distracted when Jake told him the news, not overly concerned, and this made Jake angry. Feeling a sudden assertiveness he said firmly to the President, "Sir, I feel I should visit Kato's house and pay my condolences. I believe he only had one son. I'd like to let him know about Kato's interest in the church."

"Quite honestly, Jake, I doubt very much if they'd be interested. Probably wonder who in the world you are."

"It's important to me, sir," said Jake, surprised by his forcefulness. He reddened. "Well, I feel responsible for him somehow. I feel it's as though he was meant to come to our church so soon before he died."

The President could see Jake was serious.

"Where did he live?"

"Fushimi, sir. It's not far."

"When do you propose to go?"

"Now, sir."

"Now isn't it a little late? Shouldn't you call first?"

"I can go in the car. It wouldn't take long."

"Oh no. I'm sorry. The Bishop and I have an appointment this evening. You'll have to take the subway. Or," he thought for a moment. "Can you ride a bicycle?"

"Yes sir."

"You can borrow Phil's bike. It'll get you down there in about forty-five minutes if you're fast." Jake could tell the President thought he was crazy to go out late in the dark to the house of a man he hardly knew to meet relatives who might or may not be home, but he felt a strong compulsion. The others were amazed he'd been allowed to go out alone.

"Jake has an important personal mission," said the President.

"Me, too," said Bruce. "Donut Heaven is beckoning right this moment."

The President was in a reckless mood. "If two of you want to go for doughnuts now, you have permission, but come right back!"

Bruce and Lewis jumped up like excited children. "Thank you, sir!"

It was strange to be on a bike after years without practice. Jake decided to stick to the sidewalk like the other cyclists and he took care to dodge the pedestrians. Occasionally he would see a schoolboy careering along wildly with a friend perched on the handlebar or suspended somehow over the rear wheel. It was strange to see people of all ages sailing along on bicycles, even businessmen in their neat suits. He passed several brightly-lit shops and restaurants, and sometimes the sound of drunken laughter or *karaoke* singing would drift out onto the street. Julie had told them about *karaoke*. She and her colleagues were often invited to restaurants and bars with their students. With their inhibitions gone, the Japanese, so sober and reserved by day, would turn into a bawdy, singing rabble. They would take it in turns to sing the lyrics to well-known songs in time with the background music. The lyrics and accompanying illustrations turned everyone into hopefuls for an audition. The Japanese were said to have surprisingly good singing voices. Julie and her colleagues were invariably called on to sing the Beatles or Elvis for them, not that they shied away from songs with English lyrics.

The snippets of various songs were like a mournful background to Jake's thoughts. As he neared the house in Fushimi, he began to feel apprehensive. The street was badly lit and the address was not very specific. Going up and down the tiny streets of the little neighbourhood, there was nothing to distinguish the houses. Jake was beginning to feel foolish when he decided it was time to be brave. He had come all this way. He would ask. There was a small restaurant with tiny blue lanterns on the corner. Jake opened the wooden door and saw a dingy little restaurant serving noodles on Formica tables to a few working men. The owner looked quizzical but said, '*irrashaimase*' and beckoned Jake to a table.

"Thank you, no," said Jake. "I need some help." His polite Japanese was coming out well by now after so much practice. "I wonder, do you possibly know a Kato-san? I'm looking for his house."

The owner blanched a little. "Kato-san *wa né?*" he said obviously wondering what he should tell Jake. "Well, let me see. There are a few Kato-sans."

"Kato-san of Sumitomo Bank. I know he died recently. I've come to offer my condolences."

By now the whole restaurant was involved. An old man came forward. "Yes, I know Mr Kato. Let me take you to his house. Would you like some noodles first?"

"Oh, no thank you, sir. You go ahead. I can wait." But the man insisted on bustling him down the street. Jake was glad of someone to introduce him to the family and pleased he'd taken the initiative to ask for help. This was his first real adventure.

Kato's house stood out from the rest because of the arrangement of black wreaths by the front wall. Tall bunches of artificial flowers were suspended on stands. The old man knocked and a young man came to the door. The old man introduced Jake and then went back to his noodles.

Jake felt awkward. He had obviously come at a sensitive time because Kato's son was sorting through his things.

"I didn't know my father had foreign friends," he said. "I've been in Yokohama."

"Oh, I only knew him a short time. You see I'm a missionary. I met your father in the park and told him about our church and he came these last two Sundays. Uh, I wanted you to know that he decided to become a Mormon the week before he died. It's just we didn't have the chance to baptize him."

Kato's son scratched his head, a little embarrassed. "I see. Mormon." He repeated the word a few times. "I didn't know my father was religious."

Around the room were the remnants of Kato's possessions. His glasses looked forlorn, sitting on the table, his boots and shoes stood in neat rows, his clothes all folded ready to be taken away. Jake wanted to learn more about him from his little house, but he felt like an intruder.

The son shifted awkwardly waiting for Jake to excuse himself.

"Well, if you find his *Book of Mormon*, please keep it. You may like to read it yourself." He sat for a brief moment scanning the room and then stood up, much to the relief of Kato's son. "Well, I'm sorry to have disturbed you. I should go now. Thank you for your time."

The son seemed seized by a sense of duty then as Jake was leaving. He probably couldn't imagine why he was showing so much interest in his father but he felt obliged and so he said, "Maybe you'd like to attend my father's funeral. It's on Thursday morning."

Jake hesitated.

"It would be a great honour for us if you would come," the son added.

"I have to work," said Jake, "but I'll try. Thank you."

"Just here, Fushimi shrine at 10:00. Thank you for coming all this way."

As Jake rode back through the dark alleys of Fushimi, he couldn't come to terms with the fact that Kato's death had hit him so hard. This had, he realised, been his first direct experience of death. He couldn't remember the death of his grandfather, which had happened when he was eight; and whenever he met someone who had lost someone close, it hit him hard. He remembered how he had felt bad for John when he'd heard he'd lost his father. It slightly mitigated his objectionable character. Jake couldn't imagine losing such a close person himself. Yet he couldn't come to terms with the strength of his feelings about death when his faith had such an optimistic view of death. The whole of church doctrine pivoted around the promise of the life to come, a wonderful re-creation where the good Mormons would have a purified and perfected spiritual existence and gentiles who had never heard the 'Word' would be given the chance, while the nonbelievers had a world of their own making, not anything close to hell but far removed from the elevated world of the righteous. So whatever way you looked at it, the outlook was more or less optimistic for everyone. If this was what Jake believed, why did the reality of death fill him with such uncertainty? He wanted to be certain that Kato was OK, to know where he was, to think he himself had had a hand in getting him there. It was a pity he wouldn't be able to attend the funeral. Jake passed a workshop with its lights still on amid the dim houses. It was a *tatami* mat workshop. The wonderful smell of the *tatami* renewed Jake's optimism. It was a very natural, all-pervading smell, delicate but pungent at the same time. Jake was filled with determination. He would go to the funeral. One way or another. Bruce would back him up.

So that Thursday for the first time, Jake wilfully broke the rules. Instead of going straight to Toyota City, they took a detour to Fushimi. The funeral was to be held at a large local shrine. Bruce decided to bow out of the funeral in favour of some window-shopping in the electronic stores, so they arranged to meet up later.

As Jake entered the shrine, he noticed that all the mourners were dressed in black. He wondered if his white shirt and anorak were suitable, but then he was a *gaigin* anyway. Kato's son greeted him furtively, obviously surprised he had come along. "I would appreciate it if you didn't mention my father's religious feelings," he said.

Jake nodded, but was a little put out. He took off his name-badge and put it in his pocket. The secret would remain between himself and Kato.

The service consisted of the burning of incense, mournful gongs and chants. A priest performed rites over the body with a shaker which looked a little like a magic wand. Some of Kato's colleagues and his boss from the bank gave short speeches about his quiet life. Jake didn't bother to follow what was being said. He just concentrated on Kato's soul and tried to project messages to him by a kind of telepathy. He assured Kato that he would baptize him by proxy. He imagined he was the only one in the room who really understood Kato's wishes. He flattered himself thinking it was essential he was at the funeral, the only one who was tuned in to Kato's spiritual needs.

The mourners filed out as Kato's son thanked them. When it was Jake's turn, the son looked uncomfortable. "There is a small reception," he said with an expression which pleaded for him to decline the invitation. Jake took the hint. He was now attuned to Japanese sensibilities.

"Thank you, Mr Kato but I have to go to work. It was good of you to invite me."

He shook his hand warmly and accepted a designer carrier bag which contained the customary gifts for those attending the funeral. There was a box of candy and a brush and comb set. Upon opening the last package, Jake was disappointed to find Kato's leaflets and his copy of the *Book of Mormon* all returned.

Thanksgiving came around towards the end of November, and the church had planned a dinner as a public relations exercise in a nearby public hall. They wanted to be seen to be the main ambassadors of the US in Nagoya, and had invited other influential Americans in order to deflect competition. These included all the senior staff of the language companies and some representatives of Japanese companies from the States, as well as other well-established American residents. From the Japanese side were invited many of the senior staff of Japanese companies who had affiliations with the church, and local politicians. Jake was one of the welcoming party who stood in rows to shake hands with all the guests, offer them juice and *hors d'oeuvres* and show them to their seats. The banquet was laid out on several horseshoe-shaped tables all looking in on a central table which was reserved for the President and Bishop and their families. The Bishop's wife was busy welcoming the wives of the important guests who were regular visitors to the annual dinner.

Jake's mother had been delighted to hear that he would not

miss out on Thanksgiving. She burst into tears and talked about his empty chair at the table for the first time. Never before had a family member been far enough away not to make it home for Thanksgiving. Even Frank had managed to get home from Argentina when he was on his mission. Jake's mother had seen countless movies about people who had moved heaven and earth to get home in time for Thanksgiving and she had entertained a faint hope that Jake was storing up a surprise for her, but he had had to be firm on the phone.

"Mom, it's out of the question! We don't get time off. Plus I don't have the money and in fact it wouldn't really be worth it for one day." He realized afterwards that he shouldn't have said that, but still when she heard about their own special party she was happy for him and told him to be sure and take lots of pictures.

The women had worked hard to prepare the food and Jake was amazed to find it was absolutely authentic. It was the best meal he'd had so far in Japan. All the missionaries had been assigned to different tables so that they could socialize with the guests and not get cliquey. There was a rather objectionable character on Jake's table, a rotund, slobbish, middle-aged man from Florida named Craig who was the manager of a small language company.

"Well this party's going with a swing," he said. "Thanksgiving with no alcohol!" He was incredulous.

"It's not unusual for us," said Jake curtly.

Craig started exchanging private jokes with the Japanese men at the table about the lack of alcohol and they agreed nodding vigorously and then doing mock toasts with their glasses of juice. 'Kampei!'

"What's that?" asked Brendan, an American consultant for Hitachi who had just arrived in Japan on a fact-finding trip.

"You mean you haven't been initiated!" said Craig with a loathsome smirk. "It means 'cheers', 'good health'."

"Shouldn't that be 'bad health'?" quipped Jake. He was surprised at his own wit; and then it was his turn to exchange nudges with one of the Japanese Mormons who was sitting with them.

Craig then got involved with giving Brendan lots of old-hand advice, leaving Jake to carry on a more polite conversation with the guests. He wanted them to leave with the impression that Mormons were sober but friendly people, people who refused to join in foolish behaviour but were capable and efficient in business and public affairs.

The President stood up to give a speech, which was on the theme of thankfulness. He said it was a useful day to stop and give thanks for the majority of Americans but it shouldn't end with the turkey. It should be an ongoing thing. 'If people are truly thankful,' he said, 'then they will be thankful every day and the Mormons humbly try, through their efforts, to show gratitude for their many gifts by calling others to share in them.'

Craig had his head in his hands by the end of the speech, much to the bemusement of the Japanese guests who were waiting for the Bishop to translate.

"This is so embarrassing," he said lifting his head. "Lord save us from the God-squad."

"You didn't have to come along," said Jake. "I guess you knew it was a Mormon event."

"Yeah, I'll know better next time," he said, "If I'm still here."

Jake wasn't that used to blatant mockery of the church, and this made him feel uneasy. He'd known people to be indifferent or full of strange questions or even hostile but it was unsettling to think that someone else took everything you believed in and thought important in life to be totally ridiculous. He didn't mind intelligent argument and curious questions. He'd been taught how to handle that; but complete derision was something different. There was no way of coming back at it. Craig obviously regarded the Mormon church or religion in general as his last port of call. Why couldn't he just dismiss him as ignorant and forget about it? But it brought the old feelings to the surface again. Did they seem ridiculous to other people with their short hair and Elder badges and tales of visions and golden plates? He didn't mind being hounded for what he believed in or having to make sacrifices or having someone quiz him about doctrine because then he was being taken seriously. What he couldn't stand was to be thought of as an idiot or someone not even worth considering, to be treated like a child who had fallen for a fairy story. His prayer that night was intense and earnest, to strengthen his faith and make him once again proud of what he stood for.

Jake felt he needed some kind of boost to his faith, and on

Friday evening while the others were watching a video he asked for the key of the *tatami* room. In a way, he resented the fact that he had to make so much effort to get some peace. He would have enjoyed a light-hearted comedy to lift his spirits. That night they were watching *Airplane,* but for the moment, some solitude and reflection were more important to Jake and he decided it would be better to miss the noise and make the most of it.

As soon as he stepped into the room, he felt as though he was entering another world. There was something special about stepping on *tatami* and something liberating about an empty room. The room was meant for activities that needed no props. It was a place for conversation, meditation or even martial arts exercises. Even the presence of books seemed to impinge on the empty space, so Jake just sat on a cushion for a while and thought about the future. For the first time he planned, and for the first time he gained an important insight. He was his father's son but he was not his father's property. He belonged to the church of Jesus Christ of Latter Day Saints but he wasn't their slave. He was a respected member of the mission, not an automaton who only said what he was supposed to say and went where he was supposed to go. Now he realized where the uncertainties were coming from. The fear of being made ridiculous was because he hadn't yet really made his own choices. He hadn't chosen to be born a Mormon but he had grown to believe it himself. Neither had he chosen Japan. The mission authorities had chosen it for him, but he was glad he was there. He went to the towns he was designated to cover and followed the guidelines as he had been taught, and he was grateful for the opportunity to spread what he believed in. So what was wrong? He felt himself straining to get out of the comfortable straitjacket he'd found himself in. There was nothing wrong with the choices other people had made for him, but maybe now it was time to start making his own choices. He could see what Bruce meant about wanting to expand his experience. It was like being imprisoned in a comfortable home thinking there was nothing else, until you looked out of the front door and saw what was on the outside; something much bigger than you had ever imagined, waiting to be explored. But obedience, obedience kept nagging him. He was brought up to value obedience. If you obeyed your superiors and did your part to make things work, one day you would enjoy and deserve the obedience of others. But his sense of himself and his own capabilities was beginning to overwhelm him. He had his own mind and his own will. It made him feel suddenly very optimistic, like he had discovered some secret treasure but he wouldn't tell anyone about it until he had decided what to do with it. His newly-discovered will was a fragile thing and had to be exercised with care. He started on the first step. Within the limits of the mission, he would do what felt right to him. He decided to take a leaf out of Bruce's book and start to think for himself.

George had seen the light on through the paper sliding door and he put his head around the door gingerly.

"Oh it's you, Jake. OK you go ahead!"

"It's OK. Come in! I was just getting some time to myself. You know what it's like in this busy house. Is the movie finished?"

"No. I haven't been watching it. I had some letters to write home."

Jake decided George deserved some peace, so he gathered up his unread books.

"Do you like to study the scriptures alone?" asked George.

"Well, I was just thinking actually, kinda reflecting."

"Do you mean like meditation? That's what I use this room for. It's good for meditation."

"I don't really know the difference."

"Between what?"

"I mean between thinking and meditation."

"Do you want me to explain?"

Jake nodded.

"OK, sit down! Get into a comfortable, relaxing posture. I don't mean like yoga or anything, just whatever feels comfortable."

"I still haven't gotten the knack of sitting on the floor."

"OK. Just lean against the wall and try to follow my instructions. Meditation is a way of getting inside your own head. It's a way of forgetting everything from outside. That's why this room is so good, no clutter, nothing to distract you. Now, you can either focus your eyes on one point in the room or else close your eyes."

Jake decided to close his eyes. George's voice did have that hypnotic effect that people associated with therapists.

"Now, what you do is conjure up any image you like, something pleasing to you, but nothing too mechanical, preferably something in nature."

Jake searched through the crowded images in his head to pick on something. "The *Book of Mormon?*" he suggested.

"Jake," said George, a little irritated, "The President's not here now."

"Well, that is special to me."

"OK, I think you've misunderstood me. I'll give you some examples. Maybe a tree, a star, a fountain, a pool maybe, a flower, something in nature, a clear, bright light, the ocean?"

Jake liked the image of a fountain. There was one in the piazza outside the Temple back home. He had always loved that fountain, sparkling and spraying in the beautiful sunshine with the sounds of joyful chatter echoing around it. "OK. A fountain," he said.

"That's better. It will work better now. Are you concentrating? Focus absolutely on that fountain! See every drop of water in absolute detail. Hear the sound of water running. Smell the fresh air and the feel of the water in the air. Feel the air all around you. Absorb yourself in that fountain and think of nothing else!"

Jake felt at ease and went along with George's suggestions. He didn't fight his words, though he remembered he had once read about a mental patient who had nothing wrong with him and had desperately resisted the hypnotist's words, struggling to maintain control over his thoughts. That story had fascinated Jake and he had always wanted to try it, to test the strength of his will. But now he wanted to see where the fountain led him.

After a while, as he concentrated all his senses on the fountain, he began to feel light-headed, and outside concerns began to recede.

George continued to talk him through. "Now unload all your cares and worries and let them pour into the fountain, pour away. Anything else that comes into your mind, just empty it! Now your mind is focused on the fountain and what it represents, nothing else. Your mind is free and empty. Now watch the fountain for a while and enjoy the peace of mind!"

When he came round Jake felt wonderful. It felt like he had spring-cleaned his mind. His muscles felt relaxed and his tension and stress had been lifted. It was the first time it had occurred to him that the mind also needs a vacation.

"Now do you understand meditation?" said George. "You have to do it to understand it."

"Do you meditate often?" asked Jake.

"As often as possible."

"What do you visualize?"

"I meditate on a phrase actually, a repetitive sound that reverberates in the body and signifies eternal truths. I don't have a picture anymore. I've actually gone beyond pictures."

"What's the phrase?" asked Jake, imagining it to be very powerful.

"It's secret," said George. "It was given to me by a Japanese on the understanding I keep it a secret."

"I respect that," said Jake piously. "Well I'm gonna use that again for sure. It's great for helping with your problems."

There was nothing much else to perk Jake's spirits up through the weeks approaching Christmas. He had lost his enthusiasm for missioning. They were getting nowhere with the *Soka Gakkei* member from Okazaki who continued to use their visits to try and convert them, and Jake found himself losing concentration as he tried to take notes as the President had asked. Mr Tanaka had made various excuses over why he could no longer come to church, and was inattentive as they continued lessons for him at home. He seemed to enjoy their visits, but Jake felt it was futile. They never had any further reply from the lady in Kasugai. She was likely to be Catholic by now. The couple from Toyota City were being dealt with by the Bishop, and other than that, each week would bring one or two interested parties, usually from the park in Sakae, while they would be lucky if even one new person attended church each week. The President was expressing concern about Dave and Lewis' progress. When he had to report on what was now regarded as his team, Jake always made a point of saying how he thought Dave had a great attitude and that Lewis plodded along but was a quiet person and probably didn't appear forceful enough. Since Dave looked Japanese and Lewis looked like a mouse, it took away some of the *gaigin* glamour which so often got the missionaries their first foothold, and this seemed a likely reason for their lack of progress.

Dave felt bitter about the situation, which also caused him to panic about his position in the mission and whether he'd end up with a good report to take home to his Bishop. He and his family had a dazzling career mapped out for him, perhaps something in the line of finance or insurance. His best subjects were mathematics and economics but to get anywhere in the church insurance or securities companies you had to be a high-flier in the church. In his frustration Dave would blame it on Lewis and this put a strain on their relationship.

"He's just so dumb," he confided to Bruce and Jake one evening. "It's like having a lap-dog around. He just never takes the initiative. I make all the suggestions and he just nods and says, 'I guess so' or 'whatever you say, Dave.' It starts to get on your nerves."

"You should tell him then," replied Bruce. "What's the use in telling us?" His relationship with Dave had also cooled since he had been narrowed down as prime suspect for giving away the barbecue secret. Dave went quiet as though the thought hadn't occurred to him.

Jake repeated one of the lessons they'd done in personal development and relationships. "Bruce is right. If you have a problem with someone, it's better to confront them with it in a mature and diplomatic way. I mean you've both got an interest in improving your mission."

Dave decided to take the advice and Jake did feel a little sorry for him. He was very committed and enthusiastic. He saw that when they did the evening visits. He put so much effort into them. It was unfair that it was all wasted because his face didn't fit. George didn't agree when they discussed Dave's problem. "If they think he's Japanese on first sight that's even better. It tones down the shock of finding two *gaigin* on your doorstep. They need a Japanese as a kind of buffer, a go-between to introduce them to the *gaigin* and interpret.

"But Dave isn't Japanese," said Jake.

"Yeah. I guess that's the problem. He looks Japanese but when he opens his mouth, they realize they've never seen anything like this before, a Japanese with a weird religion who even speaks like a foreigner. They need an authentic Japanese if they want to have a role-model, if they're interested in joining the church."

"Do the Japanese Mormons go missioning?" asked Bruce.

"That's increasing, but it's been mainly on campus or in companies, usually with people they already know. It isn't normal for Japanese to come up to a complete stranger without an introduction. That *Soka Gakkei* thing for example, which is the nearest thing they have to missioning, goes on a personal contacts basis. For example a member is introduced to X through Y so that the one who makes the introduction takes some responsibility and this makes the person who is being witnessed feel more comfortable. I really think it's better to have that intermediary. The way we do it, you know, going in cold like that, it's really a slim chance if you look at our progress."

Jake and Bruce nodded in agreement. Their achievements did seem like small returns for a lot of effort, but Jake's Bishop had told him that the experience was as much for the missionary's benefit as the subject's. It taught patience, perseverance, endeavour, humility and communication skills, which were accomplishments not to be sniffed at. It also furnished population information for the church, as Jake remembered from what he'd pieced together over the years. It also got them a foothold in places where they could be established and known.

The first time the Donut Heaven conversation got around directly to matters religious was a week later. Jake had grown very attached to the saccharine comforts of the place and the easy company of their British friends, along with their assorted 'mates', as they called them. Today's mate was a fellow American from Iowa. He had been in Japan for about a year working for the same company as the Brits. His name was Frank, and at first sight he looked very intense. He sat smiling nervously, while the others exchanged their usual chat about the week's events and news from home. As soon as there was a break in the banter, which was infrequent given Julie's constant stream of ideas, Frank leaned forward.

"I heard you guys were Mormon, right?"

"Yes, but we're on lunch break," said Bruce. The Brit's irreverence had rubbed off on him over the weeks and he had become somewhat flippant about their activities.

"So I guess you're not all that serious about that stuff," suggested Frank.

"Outside of lunch, yeah, you bet we're serious," said Bruce. "We wear our shoes down pumping the streets of Nagoya, calling the lost souls to come and join us." He became over-dramatic because he knew he had an audience in the Brits who liked his distinctive sense of humour. They treated him like an interesting specimen of Americanness who reminded them of some of their favourite sitcoms.

"But it must be difficult to keep up the enthusiasm," Frank went on.

"It becomes very routine," said Jake casually. "You get to expect a lot of slammed doors in your face but we average about four people a week."

"You make it sound like a sales job," said Frank.

"You really work hard, don't you?" said Julie. "It must be boring but you always stay cheerful, don't you?"

"Anyway, come on Frank," James chided him. "It's time you showed your true colours." He gestured as if introducing someone on stage. "Meet Frank," he said, "Nagoya's resident born-again Christian."

Frank coloured and coughed a little. "Yes, that's right. I was born again at 11:30am, May 7th 1985." It was strange how people who were born again could always remember the exact moment when they were touched by the spirit.

"Which church do you belong to?" asked Jake.

"It's actually a Baptist fellowship."

"Come on, Frank," said Brian. "Tell them your usual spiel." He looked at Bruce and Jake. "He's always trying to tell us what we're missing," he said by way of explanation. "Not just us, the whole company, aren't you, Frank? I'm afraid we're all a bunch of hopeless heathens."

Frank didn't look all that eager to go into details. He probably felt out of his depth in the company of trained missionaries. "It's just that it changed my life so much, I feel I want to share it with others."

"Yes, you don't get into a conversation with Frank," said Julie, "or his mate, Paul, he's another born-again Christian, without getting onto the subject of Jesus."

"It's good to be enthusiastic about what you believe in," said Jake.

"I'm always inviting these guys to my church," said Frank, "but they always have an excuse."

"Frank, you know we never go anywhere on Sundays," said Brian. "We don't even see Sundays. We have no Sundays. It's the social life," he explained to Jake, pulling the bags under his eyes. "It takes it out of you. Now you see at least you Christians are clean-living folk. You don't have the pressures we have."

Now Frank had to speak his mind. He was getting ready to leave and looked quite perturbed. "I'm Christian," he said with emphasis. "They're Mormon. There's a big difference."

The Brits looked at each other and at Jake and Bruce wondering what could account for the little outburst.

"Who rattled his cage?" said Brian, as they watched Frank leaving.

"It's just some theological differences," said Bruce. "You guys wouldn't understand. You know how it is. The closer people are in belief, the more they want to distinguish themselves, so their greatest enemy is the church up the road."

"Oh, I know," said Brian. "Like the church of Jesus Christ, Scientist as opposed to the church of Scientology of Jesus Christ."

"Or the church of Jesus Christ, physicist," quipped James.

"Yeah, it was the same at uni," said Julie, her words coming faster with the memory, "when we had the Socialist Workers and the Socialist Action, and what was it? The Worker's Revolutionary Party and Revolutionary Communists and they hated each other. They spent so much time bashing each other's brains out they had no time to fight the Tories."

Bruce had developed an annoying habit of picking up on any new words or references and asking to have them explained, but the Brits seemed to enjoy being chief exponents of British culture and were happy to explain some of the intricacies of British politics.

The Donut Heaven meetings were an important focal point amid an otherwise humdrum routine. No less significant were the Japanese classes which Jake really looked forward to, which now included the lessons with Mrs Ericson. She seemed to take easily to the role of teacher and had quite a strict, disciplinarian style of teaching with lots of drills and things to memorize after each class. While Mrs Yamada's lessons were more relaxed and they were given plenty of time to practice dialogues at leisure, Mrs Ericson expected much faster results, but her method was effective, and Jake found his vocabulary and his grasp of the *kanji* increasing very rapidly. Mrs Ericson seemed to enjoy her new role, as if it had revived some hidden talents and untapped energy.

Meanwhile Jake continued to practice his meditation and became more and more introspective as he discovered for the first time a world inside his own mind and a volition more powerful than he had imagined. Now that he had discovered that he could think for himself there was no turning back.

It was amusing to see a Buddhist-Shinto country like Japan entering fully into the Christmas spirit. Now that Christmas was approaching, festive window displays began to pop up all over Sakae and everything was gift-wrapped in red and green paper covered in colourful tinsel and ribbon. Even during the rest of the year, one couldn't buy a cake or a book in Japan without having it elaborately wrapped with loving skill. Dennis fancied himself as something of an environmentalist and he was forever saying in stores: 'That's OK, I don't need a bag', but the salesgirls would look so wounded that he always succumbed to their need to wrap everything. George loved this Japanese sense of perfection that went into the presentation of everything from food to gifts. Everything was displayed to please the eye. The prospect of shopping for Christmas gifts was no headache this year. It was Japanese souvenirs for everyone.

One Saturday in December the missionaries left their football practice to shop for gifts for their families. Jake chose a fan for his mother, a folding screen for his father, Japanese dolls for his two sisters and writing and painting sets for his brother. He was delighted with his choices, though not with the expense. Bruce followed his lead and found a doll for his sister, a fan for his mother and wooden ornaments for his father and brother. In fact all the missionaries opted for variations on the doll, fan, ornament theme, although Dave chose Japanese bath-robes, or *yukata*. Everyone was surprised to hear that no one in his family owned a kimono. John was the only one who opted out of the obvious choice of gifts and without even glancing at anything else he went straight for the boxed handkerchiefs: three sets of those and he was done.

It was only when Jake was dealing with all his packages down at the post office that it suddenly struck him he had bought nothing for Alice. As he had noticed before, he only guiltily remembered her some time after. Still, he thought in self-justification, he was young. It was natural that his immediate family would come first. In his mind's eye he delighted in the picture of their pleasure at opening his well-chosen presents. But the thought of buying something for Alice hadn't even crossed his mind. She was bound to assume that he would send her something particularly special as a token of his feelings for her, to show how much he cared. He could hear her voice directing him on how men were supposed to conduct themselves 'these days', an instruction manual on how to handle his emotions. 'I read in such-and-such' or 'I heard in such-and-such' or 'so-and-so says that men are supposed to do this or that' or that 'women expect that from men nowadays'. As with much of his behaviour, he had begun to realize that he often tried to do his best to go along with what other people advised him to do. It was part of the automatic obedience he'd learned over the years. Now he began to wonder whether he was being honest with himself or with Alice. Was it right to send her a gift to show feelings that he didn't possess? Maybe he was supposed to have them but he didn't. Maybe it was time to stop pretending. He would send her a card.

The President liked to keep surprises for his team until the last minute.

"As you know, boys, Christmas can be a very difficult time. For some of you, it may be the first Christmas spent away from home. The Japanese don't tend to go crazy for Christmas itself. Their big bash is New Year. Well, a big vacation by their standards anyway. They'll maybe take five days off. So what we propose is a trip for the team during the vacation to see something of Japan."

There were beams and excited replies all around the table.

"Where are we going?" "Are we going by train?" "Do we get to stay in a hotel?" "Can we go skiing?"

"We propose to take a trip to Kyushu island, which is in the south of Japan. We thought we would take in Beppu which I'm told is interesting, Kumamoto, a famous castle town, and Nagasaki."

"Nagasaki?" they echoed. "Wow!"

"We'll be travelling with other missionaries from Osaka and Hiroshima and the south, and we figured it would be a good chance for you to compare notes and socialize a little."

"Where will we stay?" asked Dave.

"In a Japanese *ryokan*," said the President. "That's a traditional inn with *tatami* floors, Japanese baths, full Japanese menu, the works."

The excitement about the trip buoyed everyone up through the last weeks of December which to everyone's surprise became bitingly cold. Jake was fascinated by all the gadgets the Japanese had devised for keeping warm, everything apart from central heating. There were heating panels under carpets, quilted jackets, strange objects which looked like giant tea-bags filled with metal filings which warmed up when shaken, which they put in their pockets. Then there was the *kotatsu*. This was Jake's favourite. It consisted of a low table with an electric heater underneath. A blanket was spread over the table and you could warm your feet beneath it. The Japanese followed the principle of warm feet, cool head. In the winter, the President put a *kotatsu* in the *tatami* room and Jake liked nothing better than to huddle in there and read or think.

Since he had been in Japan, Jake had often heard Japanese people proudly announce: 'In Japan we have four seasons'. He had felt like saying, 'So what! Doesn't everybody?' But now he knew what they meant. Like scenes in a children's book, the different seasons in Japan were marked by all the classic signs. Sticky heat and sunshine in summer, gorgeous leaves and winds in autumn, cold and snow in winter. He wondered what the springtime would bring.

唯壱

Interlude

At last the time of the Kyushu trip came around. They had been told to travel light and not to buy Christmas gifts for any of the family or other missionaries. They all paid into a central fund managed by the women's section, which would then buy a selection of varied one-price gifts so that everyone got something. This did away with the burden of shopping for people they didn't know well enough and the envy of vastly differing gifts.

The Brits made no secret of their jealousy of Jake and Bruce. They lamented about how when one had been in Japan a while one grew complacent and settled to the extent that one could hardly be bothered to travel, besides the fact that most of their salary went to pay their overdrafts back home and to finance their never-ending social lives. James was going to ski with some Japanese friends, while the others had to make do with a Nagoya Christmas far from home, probably to be spent in the local Delaware Diner.

As they had dropped people off on the *Shinkansen* when they had first arrived, so now they took their old friends back on board at Osaka and Hiroshima. There were cheerful smiles and pats on the back. They all had amusing stories to tell and surprisingly similar impressions of the country. Osaka was like a larger version of Nagoya, a bit more sophisticated, a bit more cosmopolitan, but nowhere near as big as Tokyo. The Tokyo missionaries and those from the ward in the north were bound for Hokkaido, the opposite pole from Kyushu, where it would be very cold and thick with snow. Being cocooned in the world of Nagoya, although they'd ventured to quite a wide radius around, Jake had forgotten that the Japanese might not be the same in other parts of the country. He still hadn't grown out of the habit of talking about them *en masse*. Vincent and Joe, who had been posted to a rural part of Japan, said the people were incredibly welcoming and friendly, eager to include them in local events, and regarded their activities with wry humour. They received a lot of attention as the only *gaigin* for miles around, and sometimes felt as though they had walked onto a movie set. The first few times they rode into town, a minuscule hamlet with three shops surrounded by fields and mountains, the locals would do double-takes and stare and stare. Jason had found the Osaka people to be typical city folk in a hurry with no time to talk. They worked in a city square one day a week instead of the park and people just darted past them, hands raised in refusal. There were not even any benches where they could sidle up to people. David, the New Yorker who was in Hiroshima, found the place dull beyond belief. Aside from its fame as Japan's holocaust town, it was just a grey, industrial city. The others quizzed him about the Peace Park to get a foretaste of Nagasaki. Jake could hardly take it in when the train paused at Hiroshoma station. 'So this is the place?" he said in awe, wondering what they would find in Nagasaki.

"People always expect to find the place in ashes," said David, "but as you can see it's a regular industrial city."

The second and first-years had formed their own separate groups. The training session back home had forged them very close, as had the shared experience of arrival and finding their bearings. At the far end of the railway carriage, which seemed to have been reserved almost exclusively for their party, sat the Presidents. They seemed to be engaged in very serious conversation. The Japanese staff had stayed behind to hold the fort and two of the Presidents had brought their families with them. President Ericson's family had already travelled extensively in Japan and were spending Christmas at a specially arranged party in Osaka. They didn't seem to mind spending Christmas without the President. "It kind of loses its sparkle after a few years over here," was Mrs Ericson's comment.

Among the second-years was a lone woman. She was what they called an 'experiment' in the Asia region. Her name was Carole, and according to Jason she had definitely won some success, but this had been outweighed by the unwanted attention she had received from many of the potential converts, and the mission department had not elected to send any more females, except in rare cases where a married couple applied. Carole was working alongside her twin brother which helped matters, but the church authorities reckoned overall that mixed missions had proved a mixed blessing.

唯色

Kyushu, Japan

The group took a ferry ride across to Kyushu, but it was only a few intrepid souls who ventured out on deck to stand in the raw and rainy air. Kyushu was a summer island, definitely warm in summer but only a few degrees better than the mainland in winter. Yet there was a marked difference in vegetation and a very slight tropical feel to the place. The *ryokans* were superb, just what the missionaries had been waiting for. Since Jason had already made friends with a Japanese family who took him away on weekends he had already stayed in several *ryokans*. The *ryokan* regime was quite strict. Dinner was at six in the main dining-hall, served on low tables while the diners sat on the floor. They all used chopsticks to eat the meal, which included plenty of specialties from the region, all served on individual little dishes with sauce to dip into. A full Japanese meal rarely included anything one might call dessert, and the style of food was designed more to delight the taste-buds than to fill the stomach. The missionaries, who had so far been fed on quasi-American or international cuisine back at the mission home, had to keep asking for more rice before they were satisfied.

"It's like a doll's tea party," mumbled Paul, a mountain of a man, who was working in Hiroshima.

Jason was busy telling them all exactly what they were eating.

Baths were to be taken at eight. This meant scrubbing the whole body at the taps arranged around the bathroom wall, and then soaking for about ten minutes in a shockingly hot tub which contained local spa water, said to relieve aching joints while simultaneously boiling the skin, as many of then complained. Then with red faces and smelling of soap, they dressed in *yukata* bathrobes and sat talking until lights out. The bedtime ritual was very interesting. The chambermaids came in and took the futons from the cupboard, then laid them out on the *tatami* floor for the guests. The futon was firm and fragrant, the pillow filled with straw, a very unusual change, but it had the same foresty smell of *tatami* and Jake fell into the most heavenly sleep he had ever known.

The Kyushu itinerary turned out to be a three-stop tour in the Japanese tradition of getting as much seen in the least possible time. Brian had told Jake and Bruce about his students who completed fourteen-day, fourteen-stop visits to Europe, manically getting on and off buses and clicking their cameras. The only proof of their having been places were the photos, so it was essential to be snapped in front of everything. Julie had laughed about a time she had been to an Impressionist art exhibition in Tokyo and was horrified to see Japanese visitors filing past the paintings in a jam, more intent on pushing on the line ahead than seeing the paintings. Each one got a cursory glance, and many postcard prints were purchased on the way out.

At the beach town of Beppu the missionaries took a look round a luxury liner which stood at the docks, and most of them spent the whole time playing arcade games on the ship. The main attraction of Beppu, however, was a resort high up in the mountains amongst dense woods called *jigoku,* or 'the hells'. It was a series of sulphur pools which created thick, smoky mists of varying colours. The pools bubbled like geysers, giving off sulphurous smells. Since the Japanese had thought this to be a fair representation of hell, they had decorated the location with a range of plastic ghouls and devils. But the true vision of hell on earth for the missionaries was the pitiful zoo at the top where starved-looking animals sat forlornly in the swirling, sulphurous mist. The atmosphere was damp and chilly and Jake wondered why the animals were required to suffer to give a more realistic vision of hell. It was not convincing, and they all had a much more edifying time in Kumamoto, which was the home of a very famous castle. Jake had read something of Japanese history to prepare for the trip and had since picked up something of the feudal atmosphere of ancient Japan from the daily historical soaps which usually featured peasants cowering and kow-towing before a fierce *shogun* who looked and acted with the proper ruthlessness. The castle was interesting and had a large moat beside which they could sit and ponder how life might have been for the inhabitants.

Sometimes Jake would wonder, when he thought about history, about the youngness of the Mormon faith. That was one of the most common questions people asked. 'But what about the people before Joseph Smith's time?' He knew retroactive baptism accounted for a lot of them but there were so many other people one barely thought about. He was always aware of the South American peoples because their history was contained in the *Book of Mormon*, but what about all the others? He had satisfied himself with the explanation of the scattering of the twelve tribes of Israel. Joseph Smith had come to restore the true Gospel which had already been communicated to the people who had gone before.

The *ryokan* at Kumamoto was exactly like the other one apart from being lit more dimly, and offering slightly different food. What caught Jake's eye was a painting on the wall of the corridor in the *ryokan*. It was of a black cube-shaped structure around which figures like white specks were circulating. He looked at the title, a black splodge in the corner written in *katakana*. He read: '*Kaaba*, Mecca.' Yes, he'd heard of Mecca but he never knew about the black cube. Interesting! It seemed to strike him every time he passed by.

As they entered Nagasaki Jake felt the same thrill as in Hiroshima, the city of the bomb. What would it be like? But the place was as pretty as a picture, a cheerful harbour town with slopes curving down towards the bay. The streets were wide and clean, the sky crisp and blue. There were plants in the squares and even a few flowers.

"Can you believe this place was blasted to hell?" said John.

"Language please, John. Anyway, it was quite a long time ago," said President Waters from Osaka. He was their guide in Nagasaki. He told them the story of how, during the closure of Japan to the outdoor world, Nagasaki had been one of the only outlets for trade to the outside world. It was through these trade contacts that Christian missionaries maintained contact with Japan and this was why there was such a high proportion of Christians in the city, especially Catholics. There was a fledgling

LDS mission here but they were competing with the other church-es who had more of a foothold.

As Jake was growing up, he remembered hearing a lot about Pearl Harbor and not so much about the atomic bomb. The story went that the Japanese had become so unruly with their grandiose plans that nothing less than an atom bomb in their back garden would bring them to heel. It was justified because the war came to an end and the world was saved from colonization. If a few Japanese civilians had to be sacrificed, the price was worth it. The event had never troubled Jake's conscience before until he saw that back garden. Superficially it seemed very ordinary looking park, but in one corner was a commemorative plaque, below which a crater bore witness to what had happened there. The most poignant part were the cranes, garland upon garland of colourful paper cranes adorning the monument. The park was called the Peace Park and the cranes had been adopted as the symbol of peace because of the realization that after the ultimate act of aggression, when violence had reached its mad climax, one could only turn and look towards peace.

The missionaries stood quietly around the monument in silent reflection, all trying to come to terms with the fact that they were actually standing in the spot where the bomb had dropped and devastated the city. Dave couldn't believe it: 'It can't have been here,' he kept saying. 'I mean look at the hole in the ground. It doesn't look that big. Are you sure this is the actual place?'

"That's what the plaque says," said Dennis.

"But look at this park!" Dave protested. "It's so pretty, and all the buildings are intact and the air is clear."

"It was fifty years ago," said Jake, but he too had expected more evidence of the scale of destruction.

The museum gave them more details about the events both there and in Hiroshima, in words and pictures. There were the famous images of the shadows in the ground, all that was left of the people caught near the epicentre of the blast. How could that be? What did it feel like to have your body disintegrated to become a mere shadow on the ground? The testimonies of the survivors explained the three stages of a nuclear detonation. First the sear-ing heat, then the air pressure, and then the blast which deafens, incinerates and annihilates everything within its grasp. 'Did we do this?' thought Jake grimly, as he looked at the faces of the people who had been the victims, their flattened homes, piles of rubble with a pair of broken shoes here, a child's toy there. Even the knowledge that photographers sometimes planted poignant totems at accident scenes, such as a child's teddy bear, in order to get good pictures, did not stop Jake from feeling great emotion, something near remorse. But it wasn't anything to do with him. He hadn't even been born. His father would have been a child. The feeling came from his sense of pride at being an American, a US citizen. 'Of course it had been justified,' he told himself, but had there been there no other way, with fewer casualties and less destruction? Jake looked around at the Japanese visitors in the museum and felt a wave of sympathy. They were such little people. They looked so harmless. He was left with the question as to why his church hadn't done something, said something, spoken out. The museum ended on a more upbeat note as it told the story of the world's peace activists and the campaigns for nuclear disarmament. The story of the cranes, it appeared, was that a young child who was a victim of the bomb had kept his spirits up while in the hospital by making origami cranes and they had since been adopted as a symbol of peace and hope that in the future, the new generation would create a better world. Jake knew the Japanese word for 'crane' and the *kanji*.

The missionaries soon forgot about the bomb in the flurry of Christmas, but Jake felt it in the back of his mind, like a bad smell cropping up, threatening to ruin the season. What bothered him most was that it made him feel pretty ignorant of history and politics and the world in general. His life had been so focused up until now, so church-oriented. His world was Utah, and the world outside was full of potential Mormons. He had learnt something from the training but only insofar as a certain country or people were so many steps away from the church. Wider issues had hardly impinged upon his experience.

Their Christmas celebrations consisted of a special church service with carols and readings from the Gospel. This was followed by a stroll by the harbour and then a hefty lunch accompanied by special prayers for new converts and prayers of thanks for the year's successes. They pulled their crackers and put on their party hats to watch a local Japanese school which had come to perform a nativity play for them and to sing some Christmas songs. The little mission in Nagasaki had made every effort to make something of the holiday and everyone was given a gift. Jake got a new journal and an orientation set. It turned out that everyone had been given a journal in which to record the following year's events and most of the other gifts were on the boy-scout theme: binoculars, first-aid kits, survival manuals and rain-proof foldaway raincoats.

The members of the mission had prepared a very interesting and professionally-produced play, telling the story of the first Christians' arrival in Nagasaki and the persecution of Christian Japanese who were brave enough to take that step.

Towards night-time every phone in the building was in use by missionaries calling home, although most of them had enjoyed the day so much they hardly felt homesick at all. Jake was met with tears from his mother who got so worked up she could hardly speak, except to say, 'We love you Jake. We miss you.' His father took over and told him they would probably have a fun time but it would be tinged with sadness because they missed him. His sisters were much more warm and sisterly than usual without a hint of sarcasm, and his brother was eager to find out about Christmas in Japan.

"Do they have Christmas there?"

"Well, kind of."

"What do they eat: sushi for lunch?"

"No turkey, turkey! We had turkey."

They all thanked him for the gifts which they said were sitting under the tree ready to be opened after church, and Jake's mom wanted to come to speak again now she felt more composed, but Jake's father shooed her away, not wanting to leave Jake on a depressing note. Nagasaki had made an impression on Jake and he had wanted to tell his family more about it, but he was afraid to upset them. Imagine something so terrible happening to your family! In his whole lifetime, neither he nor anyone he knew had ever suffered any significant problem or hardship more than a broken-down car or a flood in the bathroom. No death, no loss, no injustice, no heartache. Thank God, he added to check against tempting fate. Thank God; but it was a little boring.

唯壱

Interlude

As they hurtled home to Nagoya on the bullet train, Jake was considering the world that was opening up both inside and outside his head. He felt optimistic, as though he had just dived into cool water. It seemed the New Year was going to be special for him. This was the most unusual New Year he'd ever known: a different country, different experiences; but he smiled to himself, 'Your faith stays the same. It follows you wherever you go.'

They were passing the snowy peaks of Nagano prefecture shedding missionaries on the way, wishing them all the best for the coming year. The *shinkansen* was full of skis and skiers. Japanese skiers took sports fashion seriously, and everyone was dressed in the most up-to-date ski wear. The industrial landscape announced the approach of Osaka and then Nagoya, and Jake felt a warmth towards his adopted city. 'Now, what would the year bring?'

唯邑

Nagoya, Japan

Work quickly got back to normal after the vacation. The Japanese had returned from their New Year celebrations in which most of them visited their hometowns in the country. The snow looked fabulous on the peaks from the trains, but close-up it made tramping the streets that much harder. The cold weather seemed also to make the inhabitants of the houses hole up in their dens as though they were fortresses. They didn't want any *gaigin* in big anoraks and boots shattering their cosy peace by bringing the outside into their enclave. For this reason, January proved to be a very lean month. It also took some of the households time to settle back into a routine after the excitement of the vacation. Many of those Jake and Bruce did get talking to, especially on Wednesday if anyone decided to brave the park, were people who had travelled during the vacation and wanted to re-live the memories of the wonderful time they'd had, even if they'd been to Europe. They met a group of three women who actually approached them, who had been on a trip to Italy. Jake and Bruce knew as much about Italy as they did about Japan but this did not stop the girls from going over their holiday memories. The girls actually followed them into Donut Heaven where they were to have their weekly meeting with the Brits. When they saw the table full of *gaigin*, they backed away, embarrassed, but Julie called them over and they had a very enjoyable chat about things European.

Jake issued the church invitations, remembering why they were supposed to be talking to the girls and told them there were no Italians but there were Greeks at the church, if that was near enough.

Bruce suddenly remembered Paulo. "Hey yeah. We know an Italian. Paulo. He's a good guy. Do you wanna meet him?"

"Pauro," said one of the girls, dreamily.

"I guess one of these guys could introduce them," said Jake

quickly, not wanting Bruce to get involved with the other *gaigin* friends again.

When the President delivered his sermon that Sunday, it was as if he had heard Jake's questions about Nagasaki. He mentioned Nagasaki and how moved they had all been by it. He told them about the museum where they saw for themselves the extent of the human suffering. He went on to say how relations had healed between Japan and the allies and that the best form of healing was a shared faith, and which was the aim of all their activities in their modest community in Nagoya: to heal old wounds. The Japanese listeners certainly seemed satisfied with what the President had to say because they themselves as a nation were intensely uncomfortable talking about the war. They knew that the world expected them to atone for their wartime crimes like the Germans. The Americans, as ever, seemed to get away with everything scot-free, so that these words of the President's were like balm for the Japanese.

George had got into a little disagreement over the bomb. He had bought some pacifist posters from the museum and stuck them on his wall along with his Japanese calligraphy and prints. One was of a mushroom cloud and beneath the caption read: 'What if they held a war and no-one came?' It was very striking. The other was a picture of a red rose against some barbed wire on which was written: 'Violence ends where love begins.' For some reason Ellis took exception to the posters, mainly, he said, because they were not on a Mormon theme. George was offended and the President was called in to arbitrate. He was diplomatic and said that it was not conducive to a positive mood always to be reminded of something so catastrophic when you woke up every morning. George saw his point and sadly put the posters in his suitcase.

Jake and Bruce also found out, when they brought up the questions of war and nuclear bombs, that the Brits were decidedly anti-American in their politics, or were at least anti-American policy. Jake was offended to hear his country castigated in this way but Bruce found it refreshing. They always made the point that they weren't getting at them personally but at how America behaved in general, swaggering around getting involved in other countries' affairs. As they listened they could not deny the truth of what the Brits were saying about the recent adventures of the US. But as always, Jake comforted himself with the thought that the church must be doing something about it. When America was attacked, he at least as a Mormon was trying to do his part to change things, so he could wash his hands of the collective blame. He felt frustrated that he didn't have the facts to come back at them with, something that wasn't so great with Britain, but they seemed equally scathing of their own country.

They had gone against the rules now and became quite involved with the Brits. Bruce had managed to spend two afternoons with them on Saturdays, one playing baseball and another at a house party. They regarded them as their friends, but the church warning about mixing with other *gaigin* was given for good reason, because now Jake could see that he didn't feel on safe ground with some of these political discussions and sooner or later a bombshell was bound to descend.

One Wednesday they came into Donut Heaven, the backdrop for all their political and philosophical discussions, to meet with their usual warm welcome from Julie, Brian and James, stalwarts of what they jokingly called the 'café society' of Nagoya where intellectuals would come to discuss ideas. This particular day the born-again Christian, Frank, was there looking tense. By his side was a clean-cut, confident looking young man who was introduced as Paul.

"Frank told me about you guys," he said shaking their hands as they sat down warily. "I was looking forward to sharing some thoughts."

"And what thoughts would those be?" said Brian jauntily.

"Well I guess you guys wanna enjoy your coffee for a while." He stopped. "Oh sorry, of course. You don't drink tea or coffee, do you?"

"We're fine with juice," said Bruce, eager to keep the conversation off the Mormon faith.

But Paul had come for a purpose. "It's funny," he started off, "that you guys come under the Christian umbrella, because from what I've read, Christ had very little to do with it."

Jake was taken aback. "Jesus Christ is central to our faith," he said. "That's actually our proper name as you probably know. The church of Jesus Christ of Latter Day Saints. We call the *Book of Mormon* another Testament of Jesus Christ."

Brian giggled. "It sounds like a film sequel doesn't it: And now from Mormon Enterprises: Another Testament of Jesus Christ!"

Jake and Bruce knew by now that the Brits couldn't take anything seriously. Bruce was similar in that respect, retreating into humour when things were getting heavy, but Jake was confident with born-again Christians. He had met several of them back home and was happy to be able to answer their questions.

Paul stuck to the point. "If the person of Jesus Christ is central to your faith then why have a prophet? I mean, I am right when I say you revere him more?"

"Of course we revere him, but Jesus is different. Jesus is God. As St Paul says, 'In him dwelleth all the fullness of the Godhead bodily.' The head of our church says the same thing: 'Jesus Christ was and is the Lord God Omnipotent.' Joseph Smith was communicating God's message and if it weren't for him, we wouldn't know God's will."

"We have the Bible," said Frank. "I don't see how you would need anything else."

James chipped in. "Now, evangelical Christians!" he said. "Are you Bible literalists?" James had spent a summer in Oregon taking some literature courses and had met some divinity students who explained all the finer points of theology to him.

"We believe the Bible is the true Word of God," said Paul firmly, sounding like a stereotypical southern preacher although he himself was from Detroit.

"Praise the Lord!" said Brian. He and Julie had short attention spans and were soon bored with the theological conversation and had already moved on to other topics. Bruce was grateful for the chance to join in their conversation. Jake was left holding the fort as the spokesman for the Mormons. "We believe the Bible is the true Word of God insofar as it is translated correctly," he said. "This is why the *Book of Mormon* is so valuable because it filters out what is important for us in the Bible, and the teachings we should live by are in *Doctrines and Covenants*."

Paul had a spiteful look on his face. "All your deeds are like filthy rags in the sight of God. Only faith will save you."

Jake hated that phrase. He had heard it many times before, but he remained polite and composed as he had been taught to handle himself in difficult arguments. Remaining polite kept you on the moral high ground and enhanced that all-important good image. "Then what is the purpose of life?" he asked. "If good deeds are irrelevant, then why did Christ come to us and why did he shed his blood?"

"So all might be saved and enter God's Kingdom," said Paul. "God doesn't need your works, your mission," he spat, "your abstention and your precious sacraments. He doesn't need anything from you. All you have to do is to have the humility to accept His free gift of His only son and dedicate your life to him and then you'll be saved."

"So when you say, dedicate your life to him," said Jake, "doesn't that include following his teachings?"

"Yes, but they're not specific like you've made them. They're general. Love God and love your neighbour as yourself! When you've given your heart to Jesus, it just comes naturally."

"We're your neighbours," said James.

"I'm sorry?"

"Do you love us? I don't think so, otherwise you wouldn't have a go at Jake like that."

Paul gave him an ingratiating smile. "Of course we love you. We love you all. That's why we want to share our faith with you. We want you to be saved from sin. Otherwise you'll be trapped in a cycle of trying to escape from your sinful selves and you'll always fail unless you be born again."

"We love you, too," said Brian.

Paul could see he was not making any headway, so he started trying to dismantle the Mormons. "I suppose you've heard of *The God Makers*," he said.

Bruce turned round with a start on hearing the name of the infamous book written by two apostates from the church who had rehashed many of the old charges that people used against the Mormons, about Joseph Smith's life and works and the intricacies of the church hierarchy.

"Have you read it?" asked Bruce.

"Why do you wanna know?" asked Frank.

"I'm just asking to see if you know what you're talking about or whether you've only heard rumours."

"People always attack what they're afraid of," said Jake.

"Did your President tell you to say that?" said Paul, "or was it Ezra?"

Jake was surprised they knew the name of their living prophet and revelator.

"Ezra Taft Benson to you," said Bruce sharply.

"Doesn't he call God on the phone?" said Paul. "He has a direct line I hear. Any deal the Mormons want to do, they just leave it to Benson and it's as good as done. How is it that the Mormon church has some of the most powerful men in America?"

"They work hard," said Jake. "They do what's required of them and those whom God has favoured enjoy success in many areas of life, family, career, everything."

"But the allegations in that book. They must have shaken you a bit, huh? Joseph Smith, wasn't he a bit of a gold-digger in his spare time; and no-one ever saw those famous golden plates! What was it? Those who witnessed seeing them later withdrew their testimony. Wasn't Smith flung out of town several times on fraud charges?"

"It's easy for anyone to leave the church and make a lot of money out of slandering it," said Jake coolly.

"But these allegations were made several times by different people. Many of the church documents were shown to be frauds."

"How do you explain the *Book of Mormon*, though?" said Jake, with some agitation. "Why would someone who was only interested in money produce something like that? It's impossible. There are things in there Joseph Smith couldn't have known."

"Maybe someone told him," said Frank.

"Yes, an angel showed him where the plates were and he translated them by inspiration, using special glasses," replied Jake.

"So how come no one was allowed to see him when he was receiving the revelation or doing the translation?" said Paul. "Even his scribe had to sit on the other side of a curtain. Then when he finally did show them the plates, the people looked inside and couldn't see anything and he just said it was lack of faith. The guy was clever."

The Baptists didn't seem to have any regard for religious sensibilities. Even the Brits for all their flippancy had never ridiculed

Bruce or Jake for their faith or scoffed at it. Still the Baptists seemed somewhat frustrated that they hadn't got anywhere with the Mormons. Paul stood up and shook hands all round as if shaking on a fight. "Be seeing you around then," he said.

"Yeah," said Jake without conviction.

"Be seeing you around, Paul," said Brian in his mock American accent. "Not," he added when they were out of earshot.

"You poor things," said Julie. "If I'd known what they were like I'd never have invited them for lunch. They were so rude to you."

"We're used to it," said Jake. "A lot of people take offense against Mormons."

"They're just jealous," said Julie.

"If that's what being born again does to you," said Brian, "I'd rather stay dead."

Jake felt like he wanted to go over the arguments with the President to see where he had spoken well and what he could have improved on. From early experience in the church for most Mormons, evangelicals were their specialty, but of course how could he mention their meetings with the forbidden *gaigin*? He decided to say it was a Japanese student they'd met in Sakae. He hated to lie so he comforted himself to think that Paul was indeed a Japanese student, in the sense that he was a student of Japanese and they had met him in Sakae.

"Did you invite him to church?" asked the President.

"Uh yes, but he laughed it off," said Jake, uneasy at the ease with which he lied.

"So what is it you're worried about?"

"Just some of the things he said about Joseph Smith, you know the old things about him being a fraud, *The God Makers* and suchlike."

"The people who wrote that confounded book are going to have a lot to answer for on Judgment Day."

The President gave him a few comforting verses to read in the *Book of Mormon* and told him not to take it too hard about the evangelists' tactics. He had known several in his time and he believed their excessive attacks on the Mormon faith were a sign of insecurity. "They're all at sea," he said, "with nothing to anchor them or keep them on track. They have so much competition, what with the Pentecostalists pulling one way and the faith healers another. You must have seen them on network TV. They're getting lots of support, cash support, and you have all of these new ministries popping up all over the place. What do the Baptists have to really make them stand out in the market? Very little really. That's why they look at us and they see that we're radical and dynamic and we practice what we preach and we have our own networks, our own media. While they're blustering on about being born again, we're quietly winning souls all the time, all over the world, and that gets to them."

Jake always felt good after one of the President's pep-talks. He had also suggested that Jake speak to Maria, Gregor's wife who had moved on after being born again. She had joined a Methodist church.

"What finally convinced you?" asked Jake as he discussed it with Maria after the service that Sunday.

"Well I saw Gregor so alive and enthusiastic and I asked myself what it was that made him like this. So alive! Before that he was always very calm, lazy really. At first I really resisted it because it had been so emotionally stressful for me to join the Methodist church, when I was born again. I'll never forget it. It really filled my soul. It was a convention and this guy was calling, calling for people to come forward and be saved. I felt something so strong in my heart and I saw all these people crying and going to the front and I felt, 'I belong with these people'. We put our arms around each other like little children and we just cried and cried and the preacher was crying and he said: 'Welcome back to Jesus. His lost children have come back and we are so happy to have you all come forward today'." Maria was obviously re-living the moment because her eyes were brimming as she spoke. "You know," she sniffed. "This feeling stayed with me for a long time. I lived for the church meetings. I went to Bible study. I got involved and whenever I thought about it and tried to reason it out, I would always go back to that convention. I remembered how I felt. I still feel it now and I thought that must be something very, very powerful to move me like that. Gregor was never too upset about my faith or very interested. He saw it like I had my own thing, like he had his water-skiing, you know. But when he became Mormon, he came at me all the time with so many questions and we had so many arguments. He used to say, 'You can't build your life around a feeling in your heart. You have to have something concrete.' I said I had my Bible and then he would come out with all these historical arguments about the Bible. I started to think I had nothing practical to go on with my faith. My faith! It was like a beautiful silver jar with nothing in it. I realized that my experience had been real. It was from Jesus but it was like a preparation. It was preparing me to have a useful life, to build a good family and a good society."

Jake was enthralled by her story. What she had said illustrated just what he was coming to know, that faith and action go together. You couldn't just go on a feeling. You had to have facts and evidence. Surely the Mormons had that in abundance! And it was true that Jesus expected human beings to act out the faith and become better people, so that one day they might turn into Gods themselves.

Maria liked to talk, and she found a willing ear in Jake. "I like you because you listen," she said. "Gregor is very good but it is difficult when you have so many problems you share, you know. If it wasn't for my faith I couldn't go on. You see, we've been trying to have a baby now for several years. So many procedures. So much waiting and hoping, then nothing. Anyway a few years ago, I decided: no more. Maybe God has decided that this woman will not have children. We decided to leave the States, do a little travelling, a little missioning, spread our energy somewhere else. Now we're here in Japan and we have new interests, new friends. We have our church and we are happy."

"I'm so sorry," said Jake. It was the first time he had heard a story like that. Mormon babies usually followed Mormon marriages as night follows day.

"That's OK," said Maria. "You're a good person, Jake. A sensitive boy." She smiled. "I'm always telling Gregor. It's not fair. You should find yourself another wife who can have children. Leave me to be a big career woman. Maybe I'll open a chain of boutiques. You see if they had kept the polygamy laws like the Fundamentalists, he could have had the best of both worlds."

"I don't think they practice that much polygamy any more," said Jake.

"I'm just joking." She smiled and thanked him again for listening. "Any questions you have, Jake, I'm happy to answer them."

Jake had only heard of the Mormon Fundamentalists just before he went through the Temple. He had been shocked to hear that there were other groups who called themselves Mormons and were just as fervent about Joseph Smith, but were divided by political differences. The Fundamentalist movements were the most hardline of these. But there were other, larger groups as well. After Joseph Smith was murdered in Nauvoo, one group had organized around Joseph's immediate family including his widow Emma, and developed the belief that the leadership should go to Joseph's blood relatives as if there were some spiritual connection between Joseph and his son. However Brigham Young had emerged as a natural and able leader and it was he who led the pioneers out to establish the Temple in Salt Lake. The Reorganized church would have no truck with Brigham and clung to the memory of Joseph and his family. They were now custodians of Joseph's grave and those of his family members and the house where he had lived, and some of the important sites in Mormon history. As for the *Book of Mormon*, they had no particular interest in it. The Utah church, however, held the book to be at the centre of their faith, and after Brigham, continued the line of living prophets and revelators until the present day. It was they who established the prosperous world-wide church known today, while the Reorganized felt that they clung to a purer version of the faith preached by Joseph and were closer to its roots. Thus they remained an embarrassment to the church at large.

Jake had often wanted to visit their centre to see the graves and the grove where Joseph had his visions, but the church never actively encouraged that. They would say: 'We have the Temple; and that's all you need.'

The church told them about their rivals in order to preempt any confusion if they happened to hear the story from someone else, as often happened when they went away to the missions and happened to meet someone who was particularly well-informed about the Mormon church.

Mrs Ericson's Japanese lessons were paying off, and by the spring, Jake, Dennis, George and Bruce were eligible to take exams to give themselves a sense of recognition for their efforts and a goal to work towards. The mission had agreed to pay the fees for the exam. So one Wednesday morning in April, the group made their way to Nagoya University. If they had thought September was beautiful in Japan, they had never seen spring. Spring brought copses and avenues of gorgeous pink trees. There were petals all over the grass and the air smelled electric, charged with vitality. This was the famous Cherry Blossom time, and the trees transformed even the dullest street into a dreamy, pink wonderland. Carefully-planned avenues had been planted all over the city so as to flower in long tunnels of pink, forming a canopy over the heads of pedestrians or cyclists. It transformed the day-to-day missionary work into an extraordinary pleasure.

They had expected to see many other *gaigin* in the exam room, but everyone looked Japanese until Dennis got talking to them to find that they included Chinese and Korean students, all looking incredibly nervous. When the examiner arrived, they all adopted an extremely apologetic and subservient pose. Jake and Bruce had learned from James, who had one or two Korean friends, that they were treated very much as second-class citizens in Japan. The Chinese had it even worse. The Japanese liked to think of themselves as the kingpins of the east with their history of dominance, their affluence and their aloofness, which set them apart from the rest of the region. James's friend hated the fact that every time he entered a shop or restaurant, although he was the customer, he felt inclined to adopt a cringingly over-polite form of Japanese. Jake wanted to know how they could recognize Koreans because he found that they looked so similar. James said that if he had been in Japan long enough he would begin to see the differences in features. Koreans had much higher cheek-bones, very chiseled faces, and narrower eyes, while Chinese had fuller faces with more whitish complexions. Also you could tell by the clothes. James had explained another injustice, that second and third generation Koreans were never fully integrated into Japanese society with passports and other such benefits. They compared that with Dave's situation in the US. In terms of lifestyle, language and privileges, it seemed there was no difference between Dave and themselves.

The exam seemed to go well for them, and Jake came back very pleased with himself. He had been able to deal with most of the questions. It was nice to feel he was good at something academic. He had always been fairly average in school but now his first steps into the world of the mind were proving successful. He imagined himself in a few years being able to read erudite Japanese books. In the evenings, Jake and George often spent a companionable hour in the *tatami* room going over their *kanji* together, if the President hadn't captured them for computer work. They were all expected to contribute a few hours each week, and now they had two study evenings for scripture, feedback interviews, and, from time to time, a home visit so that their time was being eaten up more and more.

On Thursday evening, they had been studying the theme of the Holy Ghost and references in the *Book of Mormon* to the Holy Ghost who was named as: 'a gift of God unto all who diligently seek Him.' They learned that it was through the Holy Ghost that the mysteries of God were unfolded and that by the power of the Holy Ghost, Christ himself was manifested in the believers. The Holy Ghost strengthened faith and gave gifts of speech. Jake was convinced that this accounted for the linguistic gifts he and all the other missionaries had achieved so quickly. It accounted for how he suddenly became eloquent in some of his discussions after being tongue-tied. Ellis read out another verse from the *Book of Mormon*. 'The Lord prepareth the way that the residue of men may have faith in Christ, that the Holy Ghost may have place in their hearts, according to the power thereof and after this manner bringeth to pass the Father the covenants which he had made unto the children of men.'

John interrupted the proceedings: "Holy Ghost? Makes him sound like some kind of spook. Can't we say Holy Spirit?"

"Yes, I prefer that," said George.

"It's not a matter of what you prefer," said Ellis testily. "In the *Book of Mormon*, it's written right through, 'Holy Ghost', period."

He ended the session and Jake scribbled down the last reference which came from the Bible in the Gospel of John: 'These things have I spoken unto you, being yet present with you, but the Comforter which is the Holy Ghost whom the father will send in my name, he shall teach you all things and bring all things to your remembrance, whatsoever I have said unto you.'

That weekend the President announced the next big surprise. They could tell when he had good news for them because he seemed to be bubbling over with excitement. He felt that the missionaries were rather put upon and did lead rather humdrum lives, so he enjoyed times when they could be taken out to enjoy themselves. After all they were still young.

Sam knew the secret and he was dying to tell. "It's something to do with trees again," he announced.

"Trees?" The first-years were intrigued.

"Can you guess?" said Mrs Ericson. "Look out the window!"

They turned and saw the pink vision outside the patio doors.

"Another picnic?" ventured Bruce.

"That's right," smiled the President. "And this time I'm taking no excuses. The spring picnic is really special."

"Oh sure," said Bruce. "I'd love to go. It's warmer now and I heard how good it was in the Fall."

The church were going to have their Cherry Blossom picnic in a couple of weeks after Japanese tradition, but without the *saké* and the drunken singing.

That week Jake and Bruce were glad to be working outdoors because the trees were so beautiful and the spring air so exhilarating. This time they took one refusal after another in good spirits.

On Wednesday they got into a lively dialogue with some cheerful Japanese students in Sakae who were all eager to come along to church that coming Sunday. They were all exchange students planning a trip to Canada in the summer and were eager to get some links with foreign culture.

As they went into Donut Heaven, Jake was waiting to pay for his lunch when he felt a light tap on his shoulder. '*Sumimasen!*' When he turned in surprise to see who it was, he didn't recognize the shy-looking oriental man smiling at him. He had a fairly dark complexion for a Japanese and very large, brown eyes. He looked different. Jake quickly checked through his mental files of all the people he had witnessed but the face didn't register.

"Ah. You don't know me," said the young man, smiling broadly. His English sounded fluent, although with an accent. "I saw you at Nagoya University last week at the exam. Do you remember?"

"Oh I see," said Jake a little flustered. "Well, I'm sorry. I don't think I noticed you. I guess I was too nervous about the exam. Anyway, good to meet you. I'm Jake."

"Nice to meet you, Jake. I'm Suleiyman." Suleiyman had not stopped grinning for a second.

"Suleiyman," said Jake. "Is that Japanese?"

"No, no," he laughed. "I'm from Indonesia, Jakarta. I'm here as a student."

"Indonesia?" said Jake. "I guess I don't know much about Indonesia. I'm from Utah in the USA."

For about the first time in Jake's life, the man didn't say: 'Oh, a Mormon.'

"Oh, you're American. It's interesting that you're studying Japanese. How did you find the exam?"

Jake was tempted to make a 'Bruce joke': 'I looked down at the table and there it was', but he resisted. "Actually I was pleased. I hope I've passed."

"*Insha-Allah!*" said Suleiyman. "Yes, it wasn't too bad."

As they'd been standing awkwardly at the counter Jake felt compelled to invite Suleiyman to join them.

"Oh I'm sorry," said Suleiyman. "I don't want to disturb your lunch with your friends."

"That's OK. We're a little group who meets here every week."

Suleiyman shyly followed Jake to the table, nodded to all those seated, and then sat at a neighbouring table seeming somewhat flustered. Jake joined him, though he didn't know what they were going to talk about without the easy flow of conversation from the others. "So why are you studying Japanese?" he asked.

"I'm working for a Japanese company in Jakarta and I need to have Japanese to liase with our bosses."

"What company is that?"

"Honda. I don't know if you've heard of it."

"Oh yeah. They're real famous all over the world. What do you do?"

"I'm a factory inspector at the moment but I hope to get promoted to a more senior position after this course."

They sat silently for a while gazing at the table. Then Suleiyman asked, "How about you?"

"I'm a missionary. I'm learning Japanese to improve my mission."

"A missionary?" Suleiyman's eyes were wide. "A Christian missionary?" It was as though Jake had just told him he was an undercover agent.

"Yes, I'm a Mormon."

Suleiyman shook his head for a while. "I see. Well I would never have guessed. I thought you were working for a Japanese company in the States. Some of the people at the university are working for Japanese corporations in the US so I just assumed ..."

"Is it that unusual?" asked Jake. "To meet a missionary, I mean."

"No, it's just that they're not usually so open about it. I mean the missionaries I've come across."

"Well, it's not as if it's a crime."

Suleiyman laughed softly. "No I don't mean like that, but usually if they tell people too early they're from a church, it puts them off. People are fearful. So for the time being they make good use of the private clinics and private schools and small enterprises, then the people come to know them and trust them. Then they talk about Christianity."

"We tend to be more direct," said Jake, "and no frills as far as I'm aware. I mean we just have the church and some sports and activities for the members but mostly we're interested in spreading the message."

Suleiyman nodded for a while, stirring his coffee as if trying to take it in.

"So what church do you belong to? I mean what religion are you?" asked Jake.

"I'm Muslim."

"Oh really. I thought Indonesia was Buddhist like China. Is that unusual then, Muslims in Indonesia?"

"No, actually it's very common. There is a very large population of Indonesians who are Muslim, *al-hamdu li'llah*, but we also have a few Buddhists, Hindus, animists, a few Christians."

"Do you know of any Mormons?"

"Mormons? No I'm afraid I haven't heard of that church. It's Christian, right?"

"Yes. There are Mormons all over the world."

"Also in Muslim countries?"

"Now that I'm not sure. I know we had a Middle Eastern section at our training centre but they said it wasn't so easy working in those countries. Only some of them accept missionaries."

"You had a training centre?" said Suleiyman impressed. "That is good. It's good they take religion seriously. I wish it was the same for Muslims. We have so many people with so much to tell the world but what we're lacking is some organized way of doing it, you know like the Christians have. There are a lot of Muslims back home who fast and pray and go to *Hajj* and then they seem to forget about it. I think they forget about spreading the message."

Jake was surprised at this fervour. His image of the Muslim religion was that it was something more or less imposed on the people which they deeply resented. It had never seemed to him to be in the same league as the Mormon faith, a message to be spread. It looked like he had competition. "Perhaps," said Jake tentatively, "God helps the true faith to be spread."

"There's no doubt about that," said Suleiyman firmly. "Allah has told us in the Qur'an that he will make His true religion prevail in the end. He will show the truth to anyone who will open their hearts to it."

Jake hadn't expected such an answer. He had been hinting that maybe Mormon missionaries were more successful and organized about propagating the faith because it was true and God helped them. "So the name of your God is Allah?"

Suleiyman smiled. "My God and your God, Jake. Everyone's God. Allah is THE God, the One and Only. That is His name."

"I suppose the name in the end doesn't matter," said Jake weakly. "But I just thought Muslims worshipped a God like the Hindus, who is not the same as the Father, Son and Holy Ghost."

"*Astaghfiru'llah!*" said Suleiyman.

"Excuse me?"

"It means, 'May God forgive me'. No, Jake. Maybe you've been given a wrong impression. When I say Allah, the One God, I mean the God who created all things and all humans, the God who is Eternal, Self-Sufficient, who is the All-Powerful One. I don't know if that's what you mean by God the father."

"I guess so, yes," said Jake who was reduced to stammering by now. Where had his eloquence gone in the face of this unassuming young man who came out with these statements as if they were self-evident? Where was the Holy Spirit now? He performed a short prayer for inspiration. "But we believe it was God the Son who had the power to create the earth."

Is that possible?" asked Suleiyman. "Allah tells us in the Qur'an that if there had been more than one God, there would surely have been chaos in the universe. There can only be One supreme God."

"But what I'm saying is that Jesus was given the power by God."

"But Jesus himself was created. How can he create the earth?"

"He was a son, and he gained that power. Even God the Father was a son once. He was a man just like us, but then perfected himself." Jake had the text off pat: "'God Himself was once as we are now, and is an exalted man, and sits enthroned in yonder heavens!'"

As the conversation became more animated, the others on the next table started to overhear them.

"Sounds a bit deep," said James.

"Yes, we're discussing religion," said Jake.

"Trying to win a new convert?" said Julie. "Good luck!"

Jake was embarrassed. He hadn't intended to witness Suleiyman. It just turned into that kind of conversation.

"I think we have different assumptions about the godhead," said Jake, hoping to close the conversation because now the words from his training were reverberating in his head. '*You are out of your depth with these people.*'

"Could I just know where you get your beliefs from?" asked Suleiyman.

"The church. I mean the *Book of Mormon*," said Jake, "and Prophet Smith."

"Prophet Smith?" said Suleiyman, bemused. "You have a prophet called Smith?"

"Yes, the *Book of Mormon* was revealed to him through the Holy Ghost."

"Ghost?" echoed Suleiyman.

Jake was aware that to the absolute beginner, the Mormon points of doctrine sounded like magical fairy tales.

"When was Mr Smith born?"

"1805, in New England," said Jake, the date etched in his brain.

"Did he claim to be a prophet?"

"Yes, and he proved it by producing the *Book of Mormon* which was translated by inspiration from golden plates containing an ancient language."

Jake wondered from Suleiyman's expression whether the Holy Ghost was working in him and making him want to learn more about this book he had never heard of before, which had the power to transform his life.

"I'm sorry," he said. "I just haven't heard anything about this before. I know about the belief of the son of God, but most Christians I've met believe in Jesus and the Bible."

"Oh, so do I," said Jake quickly. "We believe the Bible to be true in so far as it's correctly translated."

"Did Mr Smith also translate the Bible?"

Jake laughed. "I'm sorry. I'm not making myself clear. Before Joseph Smith's time, we only had the Bible but after his time the original testament of Jesus Christ was restored and through him the fullness of the Gospel."

"So that book contains more of Jesus' words?"

"Ah, not exactly. It contains stories and witnesses from the lost tribes of Israel who settled in South America. They witnessed the appearance of Jesus Christ there and learned many spiritual lessons."

"Israel?" said Suleiyman. "Does it have something to do with the Jews?"

Jake could see he was getting more and more confused. "Perhaps it would be better if we spoke again and I'll have time to prepare properly."

"Yes, that would be fine," said Suleiyman. "We can invite you to our residence if you like. There are quite a few of us there from several countries."

"The fact is," said Jake, looking guilty, "we have to have special permission to go out outside working hours and actually I'm not even supposed to be talking to you."

Suleiyman laughed. "Why, what's wrong?"

"It's just that we're supposed to concentrate on Japanese people, Buddhists, you know." Jake suddenly felt embarrassed.

"Don't I pass for a Japanese?" said Suleiyman standing to attention. "Well, anyway, I'm sure we'll meet up again. *Insha-Allah.*"

All Jake's instincts told him to close that particular door and retreat. The warnings from the trainers were reverberating in his head, about mixing with foreign students, and he knew that Muslims, particularly, were taboo. He would be in hot water if he sought to build up a relationship with Suleiyman, but instead he found himself saying, "I'd like that very much. What's that '*insha*'?"

"It means 'God willing'."

"Oh I see. We meet here same time every Wednesday. See you again, God willing," he added.

Nothing could have prepared Jake for the storm that burst in his head after that first meeting. He felt as though he'd been launched in the middle of an ocean without an anchor, asking himself basic questions from scratch. Suddenly the *Book of Mormon* and the life of Joseph Smith and the church looked puny against these large questions he was grappling with. These, unbelievably, were questions that he, who had always regarded himself as a religious person all his life, had hardly even touched upon. He felt that Suleiyman had somehow lit a spark in his head but the endless round of questioning was coming from an immensely powerful source. He felt as if his brain was being moulded like putty, and it filled him with a sense of panic. 'It has to be the Holy Spirit,' he said, trying to calm himself as he sat on the subway. The crowded environment and the constant interruptions from the announcements could not shake his mental processes.

He was distracted for the next few days, and longed for the night when he could lie peacefully and try to sort out the confusion in his head. At the table with the family all around, all day with Bruce by his side, he felt fearful of entertaining these new thoughts as if he was afraid they could read his mind. On Friday evening, Mrs Ericson even remarked that he was looking distracted. By Sunday he had made the decision to talk it over with the President. He wouldn't be shocked. He wouldn't tell him the whole story, just explain he had been going through a period of spiritual questioning. However, after church, his answer came in the form of a study circle which seemed to have been made for him at that time. Ellis was talking about how sometimes men's faith was shaken and they began to have doubts. 'This is meant as a test from God and the believer has to withstand it with patience'.

"How does one overcome the doubts?" asked Jake, hoping the desperation in his voice did not show.

"By praying and by studying the scripture," said Ellis, as if it was as easy as falling off a log, "and by seeking good counsel."

What set Jake's mind at rest was that Ellis went on to say that it was the most righteous people, whom God has specially chosen, who were tested most severely because their faith had to be strong in order to lead others. 'Wasn't Jesus tempted in the desert?' he reminded them.

Had he been specially chosen, thought Jake that night? It seemed rather arrogant to presume so. Did God have some special purpose for him in the church? His mind began to run away with itself as he imagined himself scaling the church ladder. Was he one day destined to be a member of the Seventy, or the Twelve, or suppose, he hardly dared imagine, to be the living prophet himself? How was one to know if one had been chosen by God?

The stress and shock had been building up in him so quickly that he decided to practice some meditation. This was partly because what he was experiencing was so abstract. There was nothing really concrete about it at all. He didn't feel at all able to communicate his feelings to Bruce. Also he was afraid Bruce might trivialize it or dismiss it altogether. For the time being he kept everything locked inside his own head. It was between him and God.

He focused on the fountain, and imagined his burdens being carried away on stronger shoulders. He let the water wash away the clutter of his ideas and his usual assumptions. It was a little frightening to let go of the comfortable, familiar ideas, as though he were throwing away much-loved possessions from the past, but it had to be done if he was to get to the bottom of these doubts he was experiencing. First, dismantle your mental construction, in order to build it again on firmer foundations. More than likely it would turn out exactly the same but with true conviction. He felt optimistic now, and he examined the empty space he had left in his brain. All his thoughts had receded and only some of the mundane things like food or trains impinged, like sparks, on his consciousness. Otherwise there was only the fountain. All he had been thinking about since Wednesday was God. The question of God had filled his mind until he felt he would burst in trying to comprehend it. Now the first thing that entered his mind was the idea of God. He imagined his familiar picture of God, the Heavenly Father in robes with a white beard, the author of this divine plan, who had communicated with humans through time. Jake realized he was parroting the familiar doctrine that he used in missionary work. He wanted his own understanding of God if he was to work with it, to come through personal conviction and not blind obedience to the church.

But He can't be like that in reality, thought Jake. That's kid's stuff. Like Santa Claus. But he came back to the familiar verse of the Bible, that God created man in his own image and likeness. Joseph Smith had stated it clearly, as usual: 'If you were to see Him today, you would see him like a man in form – like yourselves, in all the person, image, and very form as a man.' Is that likely? thought Jake. A God of flesh and blood? Then he remembered that Ellis had told him what to do when beset by doubts. First he should pray. Instinctively, he began to pray to Jesus, but then he checked himself and began: 'Oh Heavenly Father. Show me Your essence. Teach me what You are like. If You are like a picture, show me a vision!' Again Jake felt a little arrogant, demanding visions on cue; but this was a crisis and he was serious. He waited, and nothing happened. He just had the question in his mind. He saw no picture, no image, no dazzling light. He knew only the word, God, the name of God. The word 'God' hung before his eyes inside his head like a space waiting to be filled. He waited a while, and the waiting calmed him. Perhaps it had been nothing at all. As he opened his eyes the dark shadows of the room looked strange and he blinked, feeling disorientated for a while. The meditation over, he let his thoughts crowd in again and take up the familiar places in his mind. Suddenly one memory from the conversation with Suleiyman hit him in a flash: 'My God, your God, Jake. Everyone's God. Allah is THE God. The One and Only. That is His name.'

Jake was in no doubt that this memory had been a direct answer to his prayer. So this thing was serious after all! He tried to sleep, disturbed.

Jake decided to try and put his theology out of his mind and concentrate on practical things. He needed to get back to normal after this mental shock, and he was uncertain about going to Donut Heaven on Wednesday. Bruce seemed to live for Wednesdays, however, so he didn't see how he could get out of it. He found his attitude changing. When they met James on Monday for their usual train-ride to Okazaki, he had no patience with the *gaigin* gossip. He tried to get the conversation onto future careers and finishing up in Japan.

"I don't know how long I'll stay, really," said James wistfully. "Every summer I decide, 'Yes, this is the last year', and then by September I can't wait to get back."

"You can't stay here forever with no proper goals," said Jake snappily.

James seemed a little offended. "I do have proper goals," he insisted. "They're just short-term at the moment. I do enjoy the job. It's just that it's strange always to be the foreigner. You never belong one hundred percent. As far as going back home is concerned, I do like it, but lots of things annoy me, and when I go back I keep thinking, 'Oh, that's much better in Japan'."

"Why not have both," suggested Bruce, "summer in Britain and winter in Japan?"

"I never thought of that," said James. "Yeah, that is a possibility." He looked out of the window at the cascades of spring blossoms. "But look at that, eh! You couldn't spend spring anywhere but Japan."

Jake's heart began to ache as they crossed the beautiful landscape. The world was so beautiful. Who could have dreamed up such a thing as cherry blossom? Creation was so exquisite, yet so easy to take for granted. Jake had always thought of God in relation to man, God who created the bodies of the human race. He had only occasionally thought of God as Creator of all nature, of the universe as well, until now, and he was overwhelmed with the splendour of it.

Jake's reaction in his missionary work was to become much more aggressive and forceful in his approach, as if by insisting on it to others, his faith would come back crystal clear and untroubled as before. He lingered too long on the doorsteps, knowing that further insistence could not budge them. He had learned weeks before when 'no' meant 'no'. Bruce noticed the difference.

"Has the President been pressuring you or something?" he asked as they went to the park for lunch.

"No, why?"

"You just seem to be wasting time with people who we normally leave alone. Remember what you said about maintaining our good image. You said we shouldn't be too forceful."

Jake wondered if he was becoming like Ellis. Maybe Ellis had also had doubts and was trying to work twice as hard to dispel them.

"It's just something I figured for myself," said Jake. "If we wanna do better we've got to get into more houses."

"C'mon, Jake. You know it's a waste of time. Why waste twenty minutes witnessing to a non-starter when we can leave them at the door, unless you wanna taste some more home cooking."

Jake knew Bruce was right, but he felt compelled. Probably it was better if he remained the same so that nobody would suspect anything was different. Bruce hadn't even remarked on Suleiyman, so he was OK on that score.

"Maybe you're right. I just feel like we're wasting time going up and down the streets of some of these towns. We'd even be better off doing one public meeting to the whole town and calling it quits."

"Are you daring to question church authority?" said Bruce, pretending to be outraged. "The door-to-door method has never failed them yet."

Jake leafed through the endless reports on the neighbourhoods they'd visited and suddenly felt a powerful sense of futility. What on earth would they do with all that information on how the whole world stood in relation to the *Book of Mormon*? He thought about some of those Muslim countries who wouldn't let missionaries in. He decided to ask Suleiyman about that on Wednesday. He had so many things to ask him now. He would go, he decided, and get to the bottom of this Muslim thing.

It was dinner-time on Tuesday night, and Phil was unusually talkative. He had been working hard on his physics and math and had got into a discussion with his tutor who was helping him with preparation for his exams.

"He wanted to find out more about the church," said Phil, "and he asked me how I could believe such childish things now that I was beginning to understand science."

"Well it's just when you begin to understand science that you begin to see the wonder of the world," said his mother.

"How did he explain how science came about?" asked Dennis.

"He was talking about physics and all of that and how particles and atoms are automatically drawn together to form matter."

"So where do they get that compulsion from?" asked Dennis.

"He just kept going on to bigger and bigger things and the new particles they've discovered which are already a microcosm of the smallest particle yet and how they keep discovering bigger and smaller things all the time. He said basically that it's hard to believe that God put all that together on a rainy afternoon."

They all laughed at the image.

"So did you answer him?" interjected the President.

"I just said that because the universe is so incredible and because the probability of all this just coming right by itself is so unlikely, then all we can conclude is that someone meant it to be like that."

"Thank you, Professor," said John.

Phil blushed. He was not used to dominating the talk at dinner.

"You said the right thing," said his father. "As I've said many times before, we don't expect a movie to make itself so why the universe?"

"Some people say the universe and everything in it is part of one great force," said George.

"Buddhists, I think you'll find," said the President.

"I don't know. I read it somewhere," said George. "They say that whatever goes on in one part of the universe will eventually have an effect in another. You can't escape the consequences of your actions in the end because something will happen somewhere in the universe as a result of it."

"But imagine if we were left entirely at the mercy of the consequences of what we do," said the President. "We'd have destroyed the planet by now. Our Heavenly Father, in his mercy, gives us a chance and sometimes clears up after the messes we make. Otherwise where would we be?"

"Well there are good people and bad people in the world," said

George, becoming animated. "Some people are very selfless and want to help others. I read this anyway," he added quickly, "and they repair the harm done by the selfish people and help others who are seeking it to find enlightenment."

"Where does the enlightenment come from?" asked Dave.

"Experience I guess. Contemplation, other lives."

"But I guess what's enlightening for one person may not do any good for someone else," said Dave.

"I guess it's tried and tested after many lives," said George.

Jake lingered over the cleaning-up amid the comforting, down-to-earth atmosphere of the kitchen because he knew that if he went to his room he'd be beset by endless questions. He offered to play a game with Sam but he had too much homework, so he sat down with Jane, trying to immerse himself in a soap-opera about young career girls in Tokyo, whose only problems were where to go on vacation and what to buy in the stores. Jane told Jake about this new, rebellious streak in Japanese young women, especially in Tokyo. They were spoiled and rich and they wanted money and action, travel and glamour. They had turned their backs on the sweet shyness which was supposed to be the ideal of Japanese womanhood. They had also turned their backs on marriage, at least for the time being. Behind their beautiful faces was a snarling, caustic sense of humour and a feeling of scorn for anything soft and emotional. They revelled in defying people's expectations of them. Jake got immersed in the story and enjoyed listening to the more colloquial Japanese for a change. These days he listened as much as possible to the conversations on the train and was pleased to realize how much his understanding had improved.

In the end Jake couldn't stop the clock and night-time came. He drank hot milk in an attempt to make himself drowsy but his mind came alive and kept him awake. To silence the voices he even resorted to borrowing one of Bruce's music tapes for his personal stereo. He had to be desperate because he hated Bruce's taste in music. Julie had taped him some contemporary British stuff that he was always raving about.

'We're running wild. We're running wild,' screamed the singer. 'We won't slow down. Can't slow down. You won't stop us 'cos we're in top gear.'

This wasn't working. Jake switched off the machine and abandoned himself to the questioner in his head.

If the universe was so intricate, so vast, so awesome, how could it have been created by a God who was like a man? A miracle, he answered. *But how could Joseph Smith have seen God and his Son standing there in front of him like two men?* God can do what He likes. He had chosen Joseph Smith especially. It was a special blessing that God had revealed His own form to him. *But what about Jesus?* thought Jake, remembering another thing Suleiyman had said. Was it possible for him to be created and creator at the same time? That had always been a mystery. You weren't supposed to be able to figure out these things until you were more experienced in the church. Jake felt calmer. He wasn't losing his faith, just trying to understand it better. God was helping him to stand on his own two feet. He was bound to feel a little unsure at first. That must be what the mission was all about. This was what they meant when they talked about your faith growing.

Jake couldn't settle to serious witnessing all morning in the park on Wednesday. He let two people slip through his fingers and Bruce was bemused.

"You're losing your grip," he remarked.

"I'm just a little preoccupied," replied Jake testily.

"What with?"

"Personal matters."

"Is it Alice?"

"Actually yes," said Jake. That was easier and somewhat true.

"Do you wanna talk about it?"

"No."

"Did you get a letter?"

"Yes, I mean no. We spoke on the phone."

"Things not going well?"

"Some problems, that's all. We'll sort it out."

"I won't ask you again but if you want to talk about it, I'm here."

Jake had forgotten how much he valued their friendship. He shouldn't take his personal angst out on Bruce. "Thanks, Bruce. You're a good person."

When they arrived at Donut Heaven for lunch, Jake felt as though he had an appointment with his analyst. He had so much to ask. But he decided he should play it cool. As they sat at their usual table and the lunch hour began to tick by, Jake felt himself grow tense. He wasn't coming after all. All that psyching himself up, and this Suleiyman wasn't coming. He tried to get into the Brits' conversation, which was something about Japanese disregard for the environment, but he felt even that seemed trivial in the face of the huge questions he was grappling with.

Then coming toward him like an angel of light was Suleiyman, his face shining with the apologetic beam Jake remembered from last time. Jake welcomed him like a long-lost friend. Since Suleiyman seemed hesitant to join their table, they sat to one side as before. The others hardly missed Jake's voice in the conversation, and gave a few polite nods to Suleiyman. Then they huddled together to carry on their private talk as though they were members of a select club. It seemed that on the strength of these weekly meetings, Bruce had definitely become one of them.

It seemed a mistake to go straight for what was bothering him, but there wasn't much time left. He didn't have to see Suleiyman again, so he decided to be honest.

"Somehow what we talked about last week really made me think," he confessed.

"*Al-hamdu li'llah!*" replied Suleiyman.

"Excuse me?"

"Praise be to Allah. He guides whom He wills and leaves to stray whom He wills." Suleiyman had begun talking like a preacher.

"It was just a case of clarifying a few things in my mind," said Jake. "About God. Don't get me wrong. We are great believers in God. We spend half our time trying to get others to believe in Him. What I'm thinking about is how to know more about what God is really like. I feel that when I understand that, my faith will be stronger."

"You're right," said Suleiyman nodding gravely. "I'm sorry. I haven't offered you some coffee."

"Actually Mormons don't drink tea or coffee."

"Really? That's interesting. Is this also the word of Mr Smith?"

"Actually yes. It's called the 'Word of Wisdom'. Our prophet taught us that to avoid alcohol, tea and coffee is better for the health of the body. The body is something to be honoured."

Jake felt on more familiar ground here, but was anxious to get the juice and doughnuts ordered so they could get back to their discussion. "That's OK. You get something for yourself. I have something, thanks."

Suleiyman came back with his lunch. "Does it offend you, Jake, if I drink coffee in front of you? I'm afraid I love coffee."

"No, no. Go ahead! We're used to it when we bring people in here to talk about our religion."

"Yes, you wanted to talk about your ideas about God," said Suleiyman. The chirrupy surf music reverberating around them didn't seem to fit with the subject matter. Somewhere like the *tatami* room would have been ideal, but Jake had grown to love Donut Heaven.

"You see," said Jake, "as I'm getting older, I feel that there is so much more to God than I had realized in the past. I'm just trying to get to grips with what God is really like. Maybe it sounds childish but I want to know what He looks like."

"*Astaghfiru'Llah*. May God forgive me. Allah does not have an image. Allah is not like anything in His creation. We say in Islam: '*Allahu Ahad, Allahu Samad*.' 'He is One. He is Unique.' Nothing else is like Him. These words come from a little verse in the Qur'an which has such a deep meaning which is Allah telling us about Himself."

Suleiyman recited the verse and gave Jake a rough translation:

"*Say, He is One, the Unique, the Absolute. He is not born, nor does He give birth, and there is none like unto Him.*"

"Pretty profound," said Jake. "What language are you speaking there?"

"Arabic."

"Do they speak Arabic in Indonesia?"

"No but we study Arabic because it is the language of the Qur'an. The Divine language. It can't be translated properly and it can never be changed."

"How are people supposed to learn it?"

"Allah makes it easy for us. We recite it in the original and the words give us power and then we can read a translation of the meaning in our own language. There are some good ones in English."

Jake changed the subject. "Are you familiar with a verse from the Bible, that God created us in His own image?"

"No, I'm not."

"Well, that is what we believe. So how can you explain that if what you say is true? Doesn't God look like us?"

"Maybe it's true in a spiritual sense. For example we say one of Allah's attributes is mercy and He has given each of us some of that mercy or love or bounty or something. But it's impossible to imagine Allah as having some image or shape, or being in a place. It's impossible, really. He created everything." Suleiyman's voice grew higher with the effort of explaining. "We will never be able to imagine Allah, ever. This is why we are warned in Islam about making religious objects or pictures because it spoils our understanding of God and makes us go astray."

"Yeah, we don't have images in our church, no crosses or anything like that. Probably you'll find idols and all that with the Catholics."

The time was running out and Jake felt like an interviewer with an agenda to cover.

"I just wanted to ask about some of the Muslim countries like Saudi Arabia. Why don't they allow the Mormons to come and preach?"

"I really don't know. Maybe they just don't want them to mislead the people."

"Don't you think it could be because they're afraid?"

"Afraid of what?"

'That the people will discover the truth. They don't want them to even find out about anything else."

"I'll tell you something," said Suleiyman. "Missionaries have been working in our countries for many, many years and have never got more than a handful of converts. They even taught us. I went to a Jesuit school you know, but it is very, very unusual for a Muslim to turn his back on Islam and go for Christianity. Sometimes they do it for material reasons, you know, a better standard of living, better career prospects, etc., but in their hearts they haven't really accepted it. I believe once you're convinced about Islam, it takes a lot to change your mind."

There was something very self-assured about Suleiyman despite his awkward shyness. Jake felt clumsy beside him. Bruce was ready to go. He was talking about the picnic.

"I wish we could invite you guys, but it's against the rules," he said sadly.

"Yes, the wicked *gaigin* might corrupt you," said Brian.

"Just tell us where it's on and we'll come along," said Julie.

"We don't know yet. They haven't told us."

"You find out," said Julie, "and give us a ring and we'll come along."

Jake turned to Suleiyman. "Perhaps you'd like to come too?"

"That would be great. When is it?"

"This Saturday. Give me your number and we'll call you."

"*Insha-Allah*," said Suleiyman.

"God willing," laughed Jake.

As the others were saying goodbye Jake took Suleiyman aside and said, "Would you mind doing me one favour?"

"What's that?"

"If anyone from my church asks, say you're Japanese. They wouldn't know the difference. I told you I would get into trouble if they find out you're Muslim. Maybe we can talk some more."

Suleiyman smiled. "I don't know if my Japanese is that good. Also I'm rather dark for a Japanese."

"Really if I tell them you're Japanese they won't know the difference. Anyway, there'll be lots of people there."

"OK, you call me and I'll try to join you. Here's my number, and oh, here, I brought you some leaflets in case you wanted to learn more."

"Thanks," said Jake, rather taken aback. So as not to be outdone, he fished in his bag for some of their own literature. "'Bye, take care!"

On the way home Bruce was in frustrated mood. "I hate that we have to lie and scheme like this to get the simplest things, like a little freedom to choose who you want to mix with. These are my friends. I want to spend more time with them than an hour snatched at lunch-time. It's real frustrating."

"I think it actually might work against them. If they try to restrict us so much, we might end up rebelling."

"Yeah, I'd love to come clean, to talk about my friends, see them maybe on weekends and feel I wasn't having to deceive anybody. You see there's this weekend away they've invited me to. It's a weekend in a mountain lodge with lots of activities, some fishing, some water-sports and tennis. That is something I'd love to do but: 'A', can you imagine me getting Sunday off? And 'B' can you imagine the President letting me go on a *gaigin* weekend in a lodge?"

Jake suddenly felt mischievous. "Let's try and work out a plan," he said.

That evening, in their room, they tried to draw up a scheme. "What you need," said Jake, "is a Japanese Mormon family to cover for you, to invite you on a weekend so that you can get permission from the President. On the day, you call sick to the family but don't tell the President that it's cancelled and you go off as planned."

"Jake, you're getting devious. What happened? By the way who was that Japanese guy you were talking to in Donut Heaven?"

"Just someone who's interested to know more about the church. I've invited him to the picnic."

"Where did we meet him? I don't remember him."

"He recognized me from the Japanese exam when we were in Donut Heaven last week."

"Why's he doing Japanese exams?"

"Well, his father's Indian. He wasn't brought up here," Jake explained. He was becoming too good at lying. "Anyway, how do you like my plan?"

"It's great, but how do we find the Mormon family to take me away for the weekend? They would have to miss church and they would have to be established, trustworthy members of the church to get permission to take me, which makes it unlikely they'd skip church."

"We'll look out for one at the picnic."

Jake had hidden the Islamic leaflets in his shirt drawer, hoping to forget about them, but they wouldn't go away and every time he opened the drawer there they were, staring him in the face. He had decided not to read them. He was afraid to be caught in the clutches of some evil influence that would take him over and try to make him lose his faith.

He had decided to use the opportunity on Saturday to win Suleiyman over. He didn't know enough about the church to reject it. Maybe when he discovered more, he would become convinced. Jake was by now convinced that his faith was being tested and he now had to rise to the challenge. He sometimes felt guilty for lying and scheming for the first time in his life, but he justified it by saying it was worth it to win those souls for the church. Otherwise how else would they find out about the Mormon faith? The Brits trusted Bruce and knew he was a good guy. It might actually win them over when they found out what he believed in. Suleiyman would learn to trust Jake and then start to learn more about the church. Jake knew he would be impressed by the picnic, to see how church people behaved. It was an enormous relief to realise that the turmoil of the week before was over.

On Thursday in Toyota City, they happened upon their first family of Jehovah's Witnesses. Jake thought the woman seemed particularly eager to invite them in. She was a stout woman with beady eyes. Waiting in her living-room was her mother and another middle-aged woman whom she introduced as her sister. The sister was a widow who lived with them.

"Mother, Big Sister! These men have come to talk to us about their church."

The two sprang to attention. Jake should have known there was something unusual because they never got such a favourable reception so quickly. They waited politely while Jake launched into his explanation. It had become so automatic now. His Japanese when doing the presentation was by now faultless which often gave the Japanese subjects a false impression of his overall ability.

When he had finished he thought it polite to wait for questions. The women were bursting to speak. "Could you please tell us the name you have for God?" asked the woman of the house, with a smile which told she was trying to catch him out.

What was this again with the name of God, thought Jake? Was it so significant? "Uh 'God'," he said lamely. "I don't know. 'Our Heavenly Father', or something."

"The name of God is very important," said the grandmother. "It is Jehovah!" she said triumphantly.

Jake and Bruce did not need to hear anything else. "Witnesses!" said Bruce, cringing under his breath.

"Are you Jehovah's Witnesses?" asked Jake.

"Yes," smiled the first woman. "We have our Kingdom Hall in Nagoya. We would like to invite you."

Jake was embarrassed. "Well, the fact is we have a lot of differences with your church. Perhaps we could come again to discuss it. We come to this town every Thursday."

"Wonderful!" said the lady. "We would love to discuss. We have few opportunities to discuss. We love to share our faith with everybody."

"So do we," said Bruce. "Isn't that strange?"

So they made an appointment for the following Thursday and put a big warning asterix beside their name on the report.

When they told Ellis about the Jehovah's Witnesses in the evening during filing he felt it best to check with the President. He didn't seem happy about them going back. When the President came in, he was not in any doubt.

"Don't go back to them! Waste of time."

"Well sir, they wanted to compare doctrines with us," said Jake. "I figured if they were open to the Witnesses they may be open to something else if it's properly explained."

"They're hard nuts to crack," said the President, "because the fact is, do you know they brainwash them?"

Jake and Bruce were astounded. "You're kidding!"

"No, it's God's truth. That's what happens down at Kingdom Hall. It's a well-known fact back in the States. Parents have had a heck of a job getting their kids out of that."

"So what should we tell them?" asked Jake.

"Don't worry! I'll have the Bishop call them tomorrow and cancel the appointment. He'll say something like 'we regret you won't be in town for a few months but maybe you'll call later in the year'."

They nodded and made to go out of the room.

"Boys!" The President called them back. "If there's anything you need to know about the church, or anything at all, come to me! OK?"

They nodded agreement and left.

That night Jake had the strange sensation of feeling himself get up out of bed, open his drawer and take out the leaflets. In his mind he knew he was looking for the name of God. It was only when he opened his eyes that he realized he was still in bed. He only hesitated a few minutes until he consciously got up to get the leaflets, and re-enacting his dream gave him an acute sense of *déja vu*. He shuddered and switched on the lamp. The first leaflet was plain and grey. No pictures. 'The Concept of God in Islam'. He began to read: 'The first part of the Muslim confession of faith is the basis for the concept of God in Islam. The Muslims bear witness that: There is no god but God, or no divinity but the (one) Divinity. The revealed scripture of Islam, the Qur'an, is like a vast commentary on this simple statement, drawing from it all its implications for human life and thought. This conception of the Deity is strictly monotheistic and unitarian. God alone has absolute being, totally independent and totally self-sufficient. Whatever exists or ever could exist does so by His will. He has no partner either in creating the universe or in maintaining it in existence. He is not only the first Cause but also ultimately the only cause and He is Himself uncaused.' Then the leaflet went on to repeat the words Suleiyman had told him.

Jake wasn't used to such profound, philosophical language. Church literature tended to be more simple and folksy because it had to reach a lot of people, but he couldn't deny that this was the answer to his question about the nature of God. The phrases, 'totally independent', 'totally self-sufficient', 'no partner in creating the universe', stood out. This was quite different from what he believed, from what the church taught. His heart began to race as it had the week before. He looked up at the small window. Bruce always insisted on leaving the curtain open. The light outside was quite eerie. It cast a mysterious spell over the room and as he watched the light of early dawn creep onto the bedroom wall, it seemed almost green. My God, thought Jake. This is some kind of black magic. He tossed the leaflets aside and reached for his *Book of Mormon*, praying furiously. It was like a talisman to protect him from an unknown force. He scrabbled through and opened it at the first page he came to: Mormon 8.16:

And blessed be he that shall bring this thing to light, for it shall be brought out of the darkness into light, according to the Word of

God, yea, it shall be brought out of the earth, and it shall shine forth out of darkness, and come unto the knowledge of the people; and it shall be done by the power of God.

'What light?' thought Jake, trying to calm himself. 'The coming of the scriptures unto the people of all generations. According to the Word of God.' It was OK. He took deep breaths. He had the word of God. But then he remembered the Qur'an. Suleiyman was claiming that Allah was speaking through the Qur'an. Now the dawn was breaking and the things in his room looked much more reassuring in this light, more real and concrete. It made him feel he could cope better with any troubles life was throwing at him. Now he felt foolish. What harm could reading a leaflet do? What could be better than to educate himself as much as possible on the faiths of others? It was bound to help his mission. He opened the leaflet once more. There were several words in italics. That must be Arabic, thought Jake. His eyes scanned over them: '*Al-Ahad* - The One, absolute unity.' They seemed big on this idea of one. '*Al-A'la* - The Most High.' '*Al-Aziz* - The Almighty.' '*Al-Jabbar* - The Irresistible.' That was true enough. '*Al-Haqq* - The Truth.' '*Al-Alim* - The Omniscient.' '*Al-Awwal* - The First.' '*Al-Akhir* - The Last.' Name after name and Jake's mind was reeling. But he had wanted to know the identity of God, the name of God. He was learning. He would take it in small doses and assess it against the Mormon scriptures. He looked in the index of the *Book of Mormon* under 'name'. 'Name of the Lord.' 'In the name of Almighty God I command you not to touch me.' 'Israel swears by the name of the Lord but not in truth'. 'I will not suffer my name to be polluted.' Nothing very enlightening here. He scanned a little. 'Messiah's name shall be called Wonderful Counsellor, the Mighty God, the Everlasting Father, the Prince of Peace.' That was more like it but wasn't that referring to the Messiah? That was Jesus. Jesus - The Mighty God? Then he read, 'Worship the Father in Christ's name!' It was there, clear as day.

Jake ended up confused. He couldn't get away from it. The Islamic descriptions of the names of God were so straightforward, so logical, so sublime. That's surely what God was like, the Most High, the Most Merciful, the All-knowing, the All-Powerful. How could the Muslims have gotten hold of something like that? Why was there none of this in Mormon scripture? His mind swimming, Jake fell asleep, but he fell asleep in prayer and for the first time in his life, he felt real communication. His prayers before seemed to have been an enormous sense of willing something to happen that would almost come from within himself. This prayer seemed to be reaching outside himself. He felt he was growing closer to God.

Throughout the day Jake was preoccupied, making little bargains with God. 'God, if you show me the truth, I'll work for you. I'll put everything I've got into it.' Inwardly he hoped the truth was not Islam. He could see himself giving his all for the church. That was what he'd always been prepared for. 'If Islam is true,' he said, 'let a Muslim person be the next to get on this train.' He remembered the young woman in Tokyo who had used this technique to make her decision about being a Mormon. They were on the express to Shiroko and he watched the commuter rush of people cramming in, businessmen, office girls, schoolkids, all Japanese. What a relief! 'If Islam is true,' he began again, still not satisfied, 'Let that businessman get up and give his seat to that schoolgirl.' Nothing happened. Jake knew he was being silly, expecting these instant signs. Even if what he asked for did happen, what would he do? It was a classic case of 'best of three', if you lost the toss of a coin. This ride out to Shiroko was one of the most spectacular, traversing mountain scenery and several wide rivers. As the train sped over the first of these, Jake noticed the older bridge in the distance. It always reminded him of the bridge in the movie *Bridge Over the River Kwai*. Before he came to Japan, he had derived many of his mental images of the Japanese from that movie: they were cold, ruthless, slave-driving, emotionless. They weren't like that at all, he decided, as he looked around him at the pleasant, unassuming faces around him. They just wanted to do a day's work and lead a quiet life. Jake remembered a talk one of the Presidents had given in Nagasaki. It had been to a small group of missionaries, some first and second-years, with no Japanese people among them. President Waters had said that Americans in general and Mormons in particular could learn a lot from the war. This had shown that the Japanese, though passive and amiable in peace-time, had a capacity, *en masse* and when they had a unifying goal, to act with absolute cold ruthlessness. Their single-minded quest for expansion during the war had now been replaced by an equally determined quest for the economic colonization of the whole world. 'They may look innocent,' President Waters had said, looking slightly menacing, 'but behind the façade lies a very determined streak. Now we are happy to have them come to work with us, and cooperate with us, but we won't let them buy us out.' One of the missionaries had suggested that if they became Mormons they would lose their conquering zeal and work side by side with Mormons all over the world. 'I'm afraid,' said President Waters, shaking his head, 'they are Japanese first and last. The war showed us that.' Those present at the talk were told not to spread it to anyone outside but just to bear it in mind. Jake didn't see it as such a bad thing. The Japanese worked hard. They deserved their success, but then there were a lot of guys back home being put out of work because of the decline in the motor industry. As long as it was fair it didn't trouble him. What did trouble him was President Waters' insistence that even converting to the church couldn't change the Japanese allegiance to emperor and country. It contradicted what they were always saying about the truth being a great leveller.

After a quiet morning in Shiroko, Bruce and Jake made their way to a noodle shop for lunch. It made them feel very local to saunter into a noodle shop and nonchalantly order in Japanese. Now they were more self-assured they didn't get treated so much as aliens. They even knew how to eat the noodles properly, slurping them noisily across the spoon. They were not sure if the President would be angry if he knew they were eating in restaurants, but they had to break some of the rules. They always had to remember to eat their picnic lunch on the way home. As they came out of the noodle-shop, a dark man was coming towards them with a young boy. As he passed them he flashed a smile revealing gleaming teeth. "Hi," said Bruce, not noticing Jake's look of astonishment. Jake looked back and saw the little boy looking back smiling shyly.

"They weren't Japanese, were they?" said Jake.

"No, they could be those Bangladeshis on the report. They looked Indian," said Bruce.

Jake nodded. It was very likely they were the Bangladeshis from

Shiroko who they had on the list as 'no call'. "Bangladeshis?" he said trying to sound indifferent. "Are they Muslim or what?"

"I'm not sure," said Bruce. "Hindu maybe or Muslim."

It was strange, thought Jake, to see them just now when he was going through this Muslim thing. They were probably Hindu. He preferred not to think about it.

On Friday night everyone was settling down to a video, but Jake needed something active. He offered to vacuum the house.

"Why on earth?" said Mrs Ericson. "It's not your turn. Besides, we don't expect you to do the whole job in one go. You're very busy."

"It's OK," said Jake. "I feel like doing something active. I don't want to be a couch potato."

"You have to be kidding," said Dennis. "We're on our feet all day. One thing I don't need is physical exercise," and he ambled off to the living-room with his stack of potato chips and cookies.

Jake insisted, and soon he was vacuuming the rooms. It was therapeutic to have something to do and to busy his mind at the same time. He made a mental revision of the unusual coincidences that had happened in this short space of time. A: The chance meeting with Suleiyman, B: the leaflets, C: the dream about the leaflets, D: seeing the Bangladeshis: maybe not so unusual after all but why now? Why on earth was he learning about Islam now? Why did it seem so plausible? He would see Suleiyman tomorrow, hopefully, and ask him some more questions. The he remembered he hadn't even called.

He managed to get through to Suleiyman and told him the picnic was in Tsurumae Park. Bruce had already told the Brits and they said they would try to make it. Jake put the vacuum away and noticed the lights on in the *tatami* room. George was there as usual in his quiet reveries.

"Doing any meditating?" asked Jake.

"No, actually I'm writing poetry."

"Poetry? You're a poet too? Can I see?"

"I dunno. It's not very good. I'm trying to write a *haiku*."

"What's that?"

"It's a specific style of Japanese poetry. Very succinct. Very brief. Three lines usually, I think. They're usually about the seasons. As you know the Japanese are very proud of their seasons."

"Can I see your *haiku*?" George was covering it like a child hiding his exam paper.

"Really. It's not even a *haiku*. I'm just experimenting."

Jake tried to take a look so George sheepishly gave him the paper. He had drawn a beautiful watercolour of a branch of cherry-blossom and beside it, in beautiful calligraphy, he had written:

The Cherry Blossom
is so beautiful this year,
now that I have eyes to see it.

Jake couldn't really make out the meaning but he felt compelled to make some critical comment. "Yeah, it's good," he said.

"I'm not sure," said George. "I'm trying to translate it into Japanese but it doesn't really scan."

"Are you talking about yourself?" asked Jake.

"What do you mean?"

"I mean, 'now that I have eyes to see'. Is that you?"

"Oh I see. Yes it probably needs some explanation, but the point is to let the reader figure it out for himself. The poem has to be kept simple in form but with several layers of meaning."

"So what does it mean?" asked Jake.

"What do you understand in it?"

Jake scratched his head. "I dunno. Maybe a blind person who had an operation, but that's not you, of course."

George chuckled. "It's not quite that literal. I wanted to express how this year I have more spiritual awareness. I can understand things more. I mean things look more significant. Like last year, for example, the cherry blossom was just a pretty flower. Now it has a lot more significance than that."

Jake wanted to hear more. "Have you found your faith has got deeper on your mission? I mean have you had any special experiences?"

"I've learned a lot more about spirituality. I've begun to think more deeply. Take the cherry blossom. What the Japanese say is that the beauty of the cherry blossom is very precious because it is so fleeting. A few weeks and everything is gone. It's a metaphor for human life. It's so transient and fleeting but so poignant. You have to savour every moment because it's so fleeting."

"But the blossoms come again the following year," said Jake.

"Yeah, I guess so," said George, thinking for a moment. "Jake, you must be an optimist."

The picnic under the cherry blossoms was like a vision of Heaven. The sky was a perfect blue, contrasting with the perfect pink of the trees. The ground was a carpet of pink. The trees were a canopy of pink. Everything looked perfect. The air was crisp and fresh and the sounds of the peoples' voices tinkled on the breeze. Jake imagined this was the sort of place where people had mystical visions. He could imagine an angel shimmering in the distance amongst the trees. Jake strolled with a Japanese couple from the church up to a little gazebo by the lake.

"How you like spring in Japan?" asked Mr Koyama, as if he were showing Jake around his own garden.

"It's really beautiful. I love this pink."

"Yes, we enjoy the cherry blossom every year. Lots of picnics and outings. We also have special food for spring season."

"How long have you been with the church?" asked Jake.

"Four years," said Mr Koyama "I was contacted at my company. The missionaries came and told me all about the church. It sounded very wonderful. We had never heard of anything like that before in Japan." Japanese people had this habit of speaking on behalf of the whole nation.

"How about you Mrs Koyama? How did you come into the church?"

Mr Koyama broke in. "I'm sorry. My wife does not speak English."

Jake repeated the question in Japanese and Mrs Koyama turned her face away in confusion. He seemed to have offended her husband who continued in English. Speaking foreign languages was a matter of prestige to Japanese people and they did not like to lose face, especially in front of their wives or subordinates. "My wife agreed with me that it was a good idea," he announced and quickly translated for her. She nodded vigorously.

They watched the lily pond for a while. Pools of blossom were gathered at the edges as the trees shed their beautiful loads into the pond. Jake would have preferred to have been there alone, though the scenery was made for couples. Alice would certainly like it here, he thought. Now his family and home seemed even further away from the mission life. He felt remote from his familiar life although nothing had changed. He would tell Alice about the trip in his next letter, about the beautiful setting, in detail in the way she liked and he would tell her he had been thinking of her. At least this time it would not be a lie.

There were lots of other picnicking groups at the location. A few company groups were becoming quite rowdy as the saké went around. The consumption of alcohol was a real disease in Japanese society. The businessmen, especially, seemed to live on it. The Mormons were rather disgusted at their undignified cavorting around. They were used to seeing them in formal mode. Some of them had brought portable *karaoke* machines for the occasion and were taking it in turns to croon to the group. The *gaigin* group obviously attracted attention and one after another, Japanese picnickers full of Dutch courage would be egged on by their friends to approach them. The Mormons remained courteous but refused to get into conversation.

"It's a shame," said Mrs Ericson. "This place is so perfect and the people don't fit at all."

She was right. It was like having sinners in Paradise.

Jake went over to Gregor and Maria. He enjoyed chatting with them.

"Isn't it perfect?" said Maria, leaning back as if to sunbathe in blossom.

"Yes, it's really beautiful," said Jake. "How's it going?"

"Fine," said Gregor. "A little teaching. A little writing. Maria's shop is doing OK. The missioning is going well?"

"Yeah it gets a little monotonous but we're hanging in there," said Jake.

"We're taking a trip soon," said Gregor, "out in the mountains."

"That sounds good. Doing some climbing?"

"Yeah, some serious climbing. It's good for the soul. You should try it yourself some time."

Suddenly a spark went off in Jake's mind. Bruce's weekend. For some reason, he felt he could come clean with Gregor and Maria.

"Listen, I wonder if you could help us out."

"Sure," said Maria. "What is it?"

"It's a little complex and it involves a little bit of deceit."

"A little bit?" said Maria.

"Hang on a minute!" He went to get Bruce and hauled him over giving him the garbled message. Bruce didn't know what was going on.

"I'll explain," said Jake. "Bruce has these friends who've invited him for a weekend away." Gregor and Maria nodded. "The problem is they're *gaigin*."

"So are we," said Gregor.

"You know the rules about missionaries and *gaigin*, I mean gentile *gaigin*. We're not supposed to mix." Bruce looked worried but Jake reassured him. "It's OK, these guys won't tell."

"Don't be so sure," said Gregor with a smile.

"So anyway, we wondered if you could invite Bruce to go with you and let him go off with his friends."

"Is this really important to you?" Maria asked Bruce. She obviously suspected some love interest.

Bruce made light of it. "Nah, not really. They just asked me to come along. I figured it would be better than another boring weekend in Nagoya."

Maria patted his knee. "You come with us, OK? It's settled."

"You mean you'll do it? You'll cover for him?"

"Sure," said Maria.

"Yeah, you guys need to get away in a while," said Gregor, "but what are these people like?"

"They're OK. They're British," said Bruce.

"So they *must* be OK," laughed Gregor.

"Yeah, I mean they're nice people. We got to know them in Donut Heaven. In fact they're supposed to be coming today. We have a lot in common."

"All I want to remind you," said Gregor, "is that I'm taking responsibility for you on this trip. Huh? I'm trusting you. You know the limits, right? If they start going crazy, I don't know, go for a walk or something."

Later in the afternoon Jake felt a tap on his shoulder. He turned around. It was Suleiyman, beaming as usual.

"Oh hi, you made it!"

"Yeah, it was a bit difficult to find you in all this crowd. It looks busy."

"Here, sit down and have some food!" They were rather too close to the President for comfort. The President leant over to Suleiyman, hand outstretched. "And this is ...?" he asked Jake.

"Oh this is, uh, one of the people we met in the park. He was interested in what we had to say so he agreed to come along today."

Suleiyman greeted the President in Japanese. "Very pleased to meet you, sir."

"Now you don't look very Japanese," said the President, sizing him up.

"Er, Sanjé's father is Indian, sir. But he was brought up here." Where on earth did he get the name Sanjé from? "That's why he speaks fluent Japanese."

"Oh, what does your father do?" asked the President in English.

Suleiyman looked to Jake for translation. He was acting well.

"He doesn't speak very good English, sir."

The President tried again in faltering Japanese.

"Oh he's a teacher," said Suleiyman, "at Yokohama University, of chemistry."

The President smiled. "So you must be, what Hindu? Buddhist?"

"Catholic," said Suleiyman quickly in Japanese and then the President left them alone.

"I did that for your benefit," said Suleiyman, spitting his words onto the ground. "*Wa'llahi*, it makes me feel quite sick."

"I'm sorry I asked you to lie," said Jake, feeling guilty.

"I mean, to say I was Catholic. I've never done that before." He spat a few more times and then repeated a chant, '*La ilaha illa'Llah; Muhammad-ur-rasulu'Llah*', over and over.

"What are you saying?" asked Jake. It was like he was going into a trance.

"It's the *shahada*, declaration of faith. 'I believe that there is no god except the One True God and Muhammad is the Messenger of God.' It's to cover what I just said."

"God knows what you're thinking," said Jake.

"Yes you're right," said Suleiyman, feeling calmer.

Jake wanted to make him feel better. "I read the leaflet you gave me."

"Oh yes? What did you think?"

"It was really interesting. All those names for God."

"Oh, did you read the ninety-nine names of God?"

"Ninety-nine? Wow, as many as that!"

"Yes. Allah has revealed His attributes in the Qur'an and when we pray we can call on any of those names."

Jake was reminded of his confusion. "After I read that leaflet, I looked at the *Book of Mormon* and I read, 'Worship the Father in Christ's name!' It was strange that I happened to read that particular line. I know it sounds strange but I felt it was God speaking to me by making me read that line."

"I don't really understand what you mean by 'in Christ's name'," Suleiyman confessed.

"How to explain?" said Jake with a sigh. "I guess to get through to the Father, you have to go through Christ, I guess like a messenger."

"No, no, not at all." said Suleiyman emphatically. "Everyone has the right to worship Allah by himself from rich to poor, everyone, no matter how intelligent they may be or how powerful. We don't need anyone in between. Allah is listening to us all whenever we call on Him."

"I'm sorry," said Jake, "but I can't agree with what you're saying. I have a firm belief in Jesus Christ."

"I'm not saying, 'don't believe in Jesus Christ'. No, no. I'm just saying that we don't have to worship Allah through Jesus Christ. Jesus Christ has given the message but he never said he was God."

"So you do follow Christianity to a certain extent," said Jake with a look of triumph.

"You may call it Christianity. We call it Islam."

"Well it's obvious you'd want to give it your own name but you just said that you believed in the message of Jesus Christ."

"That doesn't mean we're borrowing from Christianity, though. We have it independently through the words of the Qur'an. In fact, we know what Jesus really said. We don't have to rely on faulty scriptures."

They were quibbling a bit now but they seemed to be getting to the root of their differences.

"We don't have to rely on faulty scriptures, either. We have the *Book of Mormon*."

Suleiyman looked hesitant. "I don't like to tell you bluntly but perhaps I should so you know where we stand as Muslims. We believe that the Prophet Muhammad was the Last Messenger of God, the Last Prophet and he told us himself that there were no more Prophets coming after him. Also, Allah tells us that the Qur'an is the last Book of God. No more books or prophets are coming until the Day of Judgment so I'm afraid we can't accept your book as scripture since it came after the Qur'an."

"Ah well, it was translated after the Qur'an but the plates themselves existed for thousands of years. When was your Qur'an revealed?"

"It was about the seventh century of the Christian era, year one for us."

"Year one. I like that."

"But did Mr Smith claim to be a prophet?"

"Yes, he was in contact with God."

"Yes, so in that case, I don't want to offend you, but according to our religion he was not telling the truth or maybe he was confused."

"Confused? I don't think so. Maybe you should take a look at the *Book of Mormon*. Anyway, how can you be sure that your Prophet was a prophet and how can you be sure the Qur'an is from God? Same argument."

"Then you should take a look at the Qur'an," said Suleiyman smiling.

Jake smiled back. It was like a competition. 'May the best man win,' he thought.

"Let's make a deal," said Suleiyman. "You give me your book to look at and I will take a look. I will give you a copy of the translation of the Qur'an *insha-Allah* and you can see what you think."

"OK, yeah, sounds fair," said Jake.

The deal of his life had been struck here, under the cherry blossoms.

"I'll bring it on Wednesday, *insha-Allah*. Now let's talk about something a bit more trivial. My brain is hurting with all this *da'wa*."

They spent a pleasant half hour discussing Japanese people, the Indonesian car industry, Japanese language. They had both passed the exams and were studying for the next module. Jake was still a bit tense that anyone would hear them speaking English so he suggested they use Japanese as much as possible.

Bruce was despondent on the way home.

"What's up?" asked Jake.

"Oh nothing. Yeah, it was a great day. So your buddy showed up. What's his name again?"

"Sanjé."

"You guys seemed to be having a heart-to-heart."

"Yeah, well, he came on his own so I figured I should speak to him."

"Yeah, I was just making polite conversation with the Japanese Mormons."

Lewis had received a good deal of attention from the Japanese Mormons as he had rounded off the picnic with some renditions of Beatles songs to the accompaniment of Dennis' guitar. Like many shy people, he came into his own when singing.

"What did Sanjé think of the picnic?" asked the President from the front of the bus.

"Oh yeah, he was impressed," said Jake. "He liked the companionship. Also he liked the fact we don't drink because he knows how crazy the Japanese are about drink."

"Oh is that so? Is he teetotal?"

"Well yes he's …" Jake stopped himself just in time. "He's had some contact with some other American church people who don't advocate drinking. I believe Catholics drink quite a bit and he doesn't like that."

Jake went back to conversation with Bruce. "Did the Brits come? I didn't see them."

"No, they may have come and not been able to find us, I don't know." It wasn't difficult to see Bruce's look of disappointment. But maybe it was a good thing that the President didn't find out about their secret friends. He seemed pretty sharp about spotting Suleiyman. But not even the prospect of his weekend away seemed to cheer Bruce up.

The Brits were there waiting for them as usual on Wednesday. It was as though they lived in Donut Heaven, and Bruce and Jake only intruded on their world during that one hour.

"Where were you guys?" asked Bruce.

"When?" asked Brian. "Did we miss something?"

"Our spring picnic at Tsurumae. Don't you remember? I left a message with you guys."

"Oh yeah, that," said Julie. "You know Friday night and all that. We didn't get up till lunch-time and then by the time we'd got dressed, it was time to go out again."

They didn't seem at all bothered that they had let Bruce down. In fact they didn't seem to realize.

"I may be able to come to the lodge after all," said Bruce.

"Oh, how's that?" asked Brian. "I thought you weren't allowed out."

"Let's just say we managed to fix something," said Bruce mysteriously. "So what are the arrangements?"

"Oh, give us a ring later in the week," said Julie.

If Bruce was going to fit in, he would have to get used to their easy-come, easy-go attitude.

True to his word, Suleiyman arrived at Donut Heaven. He couldn't stay long because he had a class.

"I came to bring you a copy of the Qur'an," he said quietly. "Could you come over?"

He never liked to sit with the others. He just smiled apologetically.

"It was good of you to take the trouble," said Jake.

The book was wrapped in a piece of cloth inside a plastic bag.

"Just one thing," said Suleiyman. "This is the Book of God so if possible keep it covered and in a high place, say at the top of some bookshelves. Also I would ask before you begin to read to have your shower first."

"My shower?" said Jake puzzled.

"Yes. One has to be pure for reading Qur'an, even touching it. So as you are not yet a believer, you need full purification."

"I see," said Jake. "No such ceremony for this," he said handing over the *Book of Mormon*. "I would just say, read it with an open mind!"

"Yes, you too," said Suleiyman. "Read it with a fresh mind and forget anything you may have been told about Islam."

"I've never been told anything," said Jake, "not that I can remember, anyway."

"That's even better. May God guide you," he said and was gone.

Jake felt the irony of it; that he was a fully-trained, confident missionary, coming to preach the word of God and this Muslim guy was saying, 'God guide you'. It was strange. He had always felt superior in religious matters. This came from constantly teaching and preaching faith to others. Now it felt odd to have the tables turned. At the same time, it was good to have someone available to answer his questions.

As soon as he got home, Jake placed the Qur'an on top of the books on his bookshelf. He felt like being defiant and placing a *Book of Mormon* on top, but changed his mind at the last minute.

Bruce had decided to have Gregor approach the President about the weekend. He knew they had known each other for a long time and Gregor was a trusted member of the church. The President seemed to think he was particularly good with young people because he often chose him to run workshops for the teenage groups. Gregor had an informal approach which made him seem more like a big brother than an adult and the young people were inclined to open up to him more than to the other senior church members. Also, as a convert, he had an interesting perspective and the President loved to have him tell his story over and over. It was proof that some people were attracted to the truth of the Mormon faith purely by God's grace without any intervention on the part of missionaries or other Mormons.

The moment of truth came for Bruce when he was called up to the President's office before the study session on Thursday evening. Jake was asked to come too.

"I've had a call from Brother Gregor."

"Yes sir." Bruce wasn't sure how much he was supposed to know.

"I hear they're going to the mountains next weekend."

"Yes, sir. They mentioned it."

"They have asked me if they can take you two with them."

"That's real kind of them, sir."

"Yes, they said you'd benefit from the air and the peace and quiet. Maybe a chance to reflect." He looked meaningfully at Jake and Jake felt uneasy. He had this way of making you think he knew everything about you.

Bruce remained quiet waiting for the President to continue.

"Well, boys. What do you think? Do you want to go?"

"Sure!" said Bruce. "It sounds good. See more of Japan."

"Jake?"

"Me, too, sir. I love the mountains."

"The question is, can I spare you on Sunday?"

They looked at each other. "Yes, well. That's a problem I guess," said Jake.

"I'll tell you how we can get over it. I'd like you to spend a good part of that weekend in a kind of retreat, reading the scriptures, discussing them with Gregor, thinking about your mission and how you can improve it. You're doing OK so far but there's plenty of room for improvement."

Jake had almost forgotten that Bruce wasn't going. How he would be spending the weekend was a far cry from what the President had in mind.

"Will you do that for me?" asked the President.

"Yes, sir," they chorused.

"Jake? Thank you Bruce, you can wait outside." Jake was left sitting in front of the President. "Nothing bothering you, Jake?"

"No, sir, why?"

"You've seemed a little preoccupied lately, like you've been worrying about something."

"Oh really. You think so?"

"Yes, it's my job to keep an eye on you boys. Please don't feel you have to bottle things up."

Should he tell the President anything? If so, how much? He couldn't even articulate his thoughts. He could hardly sort them out for himself. No, he decided, he would leave that for his conversations with God. He decided to rely on his trusty old excuse. "There is one thing sir. I'm a little worried about my fiancée back in the States. Fact is we argued on the phone last time."

"Anything you want to talk about?"

"No, it's a silly thing really. Something made her mad, that's all."

"You two should sort it out this Sunday. There's nothing worse than an argument over the phone when two people are far apart. It leaves a bad atmosphere. OK! Sort it out, will you and go back to the cheerful Jake we've come to know."

Jake smiled shyly. "Yes sir. Thank you sir."

The President strode out to wave in the missionaries for their study circle.

Jake wanted to open the Qur'an that night so he took a shower as requested and even put on clean pyjamas. Bruce was restless that night worrying about his weekend and Jake was anxious for him to fall asleep so that he could begin to read.

"I don't know, Jake. Do you think we'll get away with it?"

"Who's gonna know?"

"You, Gregor, Maria. All the *gaigin* at the lodge."

"Do you think they'd tell?"

"It could just get out and I would be in serious trouble. Probably enough to get me kicked out. Maybe I shouldn't risk it. What's a weekend at a lodge anyway with a lot of people I don't know?"

"You know James, Julie and Brian."

"Yeah, but they'll be with all their friends. They'll probably be thinking, 'Who's that guy over there not speaking to anyone?'"

"You're just anxious. When you get there you'll have a great time."

Jake didn't know why he was encouraging Bruce to break the rules and put his mission on the line like this. A few months ago, he would have really warned him against it. Now he felt different. Let Bruce do what he felt was right. He would try not to push him one way or the other.

"You've got a week to decide anyway so forget about it for a while." Bruce sensed Jake wasn't in a talking mood and he soon dropped off to sleep.

Jake had been pretending to be asleep for quite a while when he felt safe enough to lift his head and check on Bruce. He could see his eyes were shut and the shape under the blanket was rising and falling. Jake felt like a naughty child who wanted to read in bed after lights out. He switched on his lamp and covered it with a towel, watching Bruce for a while to check he was really asleep. Then he brought down the Qur'an. First he prayed: 'God please protect me if this is something evil. If not, please let me get out of it whatever I need to know.' He decided to do his usual thing of opening it at the first page he came to. That gave it an element of the hand of fate guiding him. He noticed the two columns side by side; on the right a spidery script with lots of markings. That was the Arabic. In verse form was the English.

Do ye not see that God has subjected to your (use) all things in the heavens and on earth, and has made his bounties flow to you in exceeding measure, (both) seen and unseen? Yet there are among men those who dispute about God, without knowledge and without guidance, and without a Book to enlighten them!

When they are told to follow the (Revelation) that God has sent down, they say: "Nay, we shall follow the ways that we found our fathers (following)." What! even if it is Satan beckoning them to the Penalty of the (Blazing) Fire?

Whoever submits his whole self to God, and is a doer of good, has grasped indeed the most trustworthy hand-hold: and with God rests the End and Decision of (all) affairs.

It was the most uncanny experience. It felt as though God was addressing him directly on the page. He couldn't deny it. Was he 'one who disputed without knowledge or guidance and without a book?' He had a book. And then the next part, 'they say we shall follow the ways that we found our fathers following.' It was true Jake had followed his father's religion. At first it was because he was brought up that way. He may have followed blindly at first but now he was trying to make the religion his own. But that was just it. If you questioned, you got answers. And then the next part: 'Whoever submits his whole self to Allah.' Well maybe not completely but he thought of himself as a doer of good. The part about Satan and the blazing fire was disturbing. There was very little talk of hell among Mormons. Those who rejected the message outright either in life or at the point of death were consigned to a rather inferior life after death but nothing like the Hell of popular imagination. This couldn't be true, he thought, if God is merciful. But the other words were so relevant to him personally. He flipped to another page:

(Before this,) We sent Moses The Book, and appointed his brother Aaron with him as minister;

And We commanded: "Go ye both, to the people who have rejected our Signs." And those (people) We destroyed with utter destruction.

And the people of Noah,- when they rejected the apostles, We drowned them, and We made them as a Sign for mankind; and We have prepared for (all) wrong-doers a grievous Penalty;-

As also 'Ad and Thamud, and the Companions of the Rass, and many a generation between them.'

It was talking about Moses. So the Muslims believed in Moses, too! But it was only a few lines and then straight on to Noah. They must have gotten that from the Bible, Jake thought, but they had left out most of the story. Then *Ad* and *Thamud*. He had never heard of them. It was the question of Jesus he wasn't clear about, so he flipped to the index and read the list of points under 'Jesus': 'a righteous Prophet, birth, messenger to Israel, disciples, taken up, like Adam, not crucified'.

Not crucified? This he had to read:

That they said (in boast), "We killed Christ Jesus the son of Mary, the Apostle of God"; but they killed him not, nor crucified him, but so it was made to appear to them, and those who differ therein are full of doubts, with no (certain) knowledge, but only conjecture to follow, for of a surety they killed him not:

'They killed him not'. The Muslims were quite certain on that point. Jake thought about the Christian churches. There were so many of them and it was true; they did wrangle a lot over the points of Jesus' life. Jake decided he would have to go over the gospels again to check things out. He went back to the index. His curiosity now overwhelmed his fear of what he might discover. He was for the moment fascinated by what the Muslims were saying that contradicted Christianity. 'No more than a Messenger, not God.'

Back to the text again:

The Jews call 'Uzair a son of God, ('Who was he?' wondered Jake) *and the Christians call Christ the son of God. That is a saying from their mouth; (in this) they but imitate what the unbelievers of old used to say. God's curse be on them: how they are deluded away from the Truth!*

Jake drank in the last few items of the index: 'sent with Gospel, not son of God, message and miracles, prayers for table of viands, taught no false worship, disciples declare themselves Muslims.' Well they would of course. This was the Muslims' book. And then: 'mission limited, followers have compassion and mercy, disciples as Allah's helpers, as a sign, prophesied Ahmad.'

It was a lot to take in. Jake supposed it was obvious that if the Muslims perhaps saw Jesus as a rival to their own Prophet, they would have to write their own version of Jesus' life. But he looked over some of the verses. They seemed to speak with such power and authority. It wasn't like a story. It was like someone speaking to you. It made you sit up and listen. Jake decided that this was enough for the time being. There was no pressure on him. He would take it slowly and see how things unfolded. He would study the scripture hard on Sundays and in their own groups in order to prepare some answers to his questions. He couldn't help thinking that what he had just read was more relevant to him than a lot of what they studied in the *Book of Mormon,* about all the tribes and stories of ancient times. The stories were fairly deep though. He had always been told you needed someone to explain the deeper meanings. He decided he would read one more verse of the Qur'an and then try to get some sleep:

Alif Lam Ra. These are the symbols (or Verses) of the perspicuous Book
We have sent it down as an Arabic Qur'an, in order that ye may learn wisdom.

There was no doubt. It was speaking directly to him but why 'we'? If they were so insistent about one God, why did it say 'we'? He would have to ask Suleiyman.

As the usual mission routine continued, Jake decided to cut his mental and spiritual activity off from his daily life. That was the only way he could cope with the doubts that crept in every time he started to witness. It was hard to convince others when he had lost at least some of his conviction. So he decided to work on automatic pilot. He would repeat the well-known lessons and answer the familiar questions in the same way that a person selling a product would describe that product and persuade the person to buy it. That was the best way until he had begun to answer some of these questions and get the facts he was looking for. Summer wasn't that far off. He resolved to spend a lot of his vacation time in the library studying Mormon history in more depth.

On Sunday at church they confirmed with Gregor and Maria.

"Thanks for inviting me along," said Jake.

"The President insisted," said Gregor. "He wouldn't allow Bruce to go alone."

"But it's OK if I come along with you?"

"Oh, I see. You're not going with Bruce?" He looked at his wife nervously.

"I thought you'd go along with him," said Maria.

"Oh no, it's his thing. Hey, but you guys don't have to worry. I'll amuse myself."

"The thing is," said Maria, "we wanted to have a romantic weekend. You know just the two of us? We've been so busy lately we hardly ever have time together anymore."

Jake felt awful ruining their weekend. "I see, OK I understand. I'll go with Bruce. It's no problem."

Maria smiled. "I knew you'd understand. Anyway, you can keep an eye on Bruce."

Jake didn't relish the idea of going along with Bruce, and was worried he would cramp his style anyway.

On Wednesday Suleiyman didn't appear at Donut Heaven, and he called to apologize that evening. Luckily the kitchen was empty when Jake took the call and it was Jane who answered. The President was watching TV so the coast was clear.

"I'm sorry I couldn't make it today, Jake. I was busy."

"Oh that's OK. I had lots of questions for you but they can wait."

"Did you read the Qur'an?"

"Yeah, there's a lot I want to ask you."

"It's a shame you can't come to the hostel and visit us."

This was Jake's chance. "As a matter of fact, I have a free weekend coming up. Maybe I could visit then."

"Sure, you're welcome any time."

"The thing is I would have to stay over. I'm supposed to be away all weekend."

"That's no problem. We have spare futons. That'll be great. We'll prepare Indonesian food especially for you."

"Oh, you shouldn't go to any trouble."

"We enjoy it. Do you know how to get here?"

"Yes, I have the address. I'll look it up. We're used to going all over town. See you Friday night then."

"*Insha-Allah.*"

Jake was surprised at his own recklessness, to find himself pretending to be going away to the mountains with Gregor and Maria while in fact he would spend the weekend with Muslims. He thought about it. The options were: a weekend playing the odd one out with Gregor and Maria, a weekend with the *gaigin* in a lodge doing who knows what, or a weekend with Suleiyman and his friends asking vital questions. There was really no contest. He went to join the others in front of the TV and his attention was only half on the news. The President gave him a few paternal smiles. He felt that now he knew what was bothering Jake he ought to make him feel that he could come and talk about it whenever he needed to. The weather reports came on.

"It's OK Mrs E. Tomorrow is a laundry day," said Dennis.

Mrs Ericson looked up from her journals. "Oh, good. I'll give everything a good airing."

Japanese people liked to wash their clothes in very cold water, and since dryers were a rarity, they put them out to dry. They liked to air all their bedding, and one of the familiar sights of the neighbourhood was housewives beating the dust out of the futons as they hung them over the balconies or out of the windows or wherever there was space. Every evening the weather reports gave washday advice with the percentage probability of rain and the degree of good drying weather.

George was right about the tragic beauty of the blossoms and their brief life, because by Friday it was as if someone had taken down all the decorations after a party and almost all the blossoms were gone. The green budding shoots that took their place didn't look half as pretty.

Bruce was on edge all day, and Jake had been deliberating how much to tell him. In the increasingly complex scenario he didn't think he'd be able to sustain the lie that he had in fact stayed with Gregor and Maria. The truth was bound to come out. Bruce was now quite keen on him coming to the lodge. He was beginning to lose confidence in his social skills outside of a church environment. His sense of humour, so far a hit with the Brits in Donut Heaven, might not transfer well to a new bunch of people. Imagining them to be much more sophisticated than him, Bruce was afraid they would think he was a jerk. But at least some of the people from the barbecue would be there.

"I'll think I'll go off alone," said Jake, dramatically.

"Where are you going to stay? In a hotel? You don't have enough money."

"I'll stay up. It'll be an adventure."

"For two nights? You're crazy."

"It's OK. It's not so bad on the streets in Nagoya. You've seen the folks who live on the streets."

They had often laughed at he way the homeless Japanese made their homes in doorways. They made their little corner as neat and tidy as a little house with a *futon* laid out on newspaper, a lunchbox placed at the side and their shoes laid out on newspaper next to the bed. Oblivious to passers-by, the vagrant would prepare for bed, eat his meal and open his newspaper as if he was in a house with the walls removed for all to see.

"They always have real good *futons* and blankets," said Bruce. "You'll have to raid the *gomi*."

One of the most fascinating finds for *gaigin* was the *gomi* pile, or garbage pile. Japanese rubbish was strictly segregated into glass, metal, paper and organic matter but large consumer durables were placed in certain designated locations to be removed once a month. There was no tradition of 'good as new' sales in Japan, and on the whole the Japanese did not go in for second-hand goods. Also the rate of development of consumer products was so rapid that certain items had to be replaced regularly. This was why the disbelieving *gaigin* would be amazed to come upon this treasure trove of TVs, ovens, refrigerators, radios and all manner of other technological cast-offs, and they were even more delighted to find them in good working order. The thoughtful owners, when throwing out bedding, would even have wrapped it to protect it from the weather. A whole apartment could be furnished like this, and it was a common sight for a foreigner, unburdened by the social shame this involved for Japanese, to be seen bringing home his booty piled high on a stolen or borrowed bicycle. James's friend ran a service of searching for high quality *gomi* items for people and stealing bikes to order.

Bruce was still not happy. "C'mon Jake. You can't roam around all weekend."

"Maybe I'll drop in on Sanjé," said Jake, as if he'd just thought of it. "He's always inviting me."

"Yeah, that's a great idea. It'll be a good break for you." Bruce seemed to rest easy knowing Jake would be safe. He had made arrangements to meet the Brits at Nagoya Station that evening. Gregor and Maria were supposed to be picking them up from the house after work.

That evening found Bruce pacing up and down the kitchen. Gregor and Maria were late.

"This is it," he said through clenched teeth. "They're not coming. I knew it. It's cancelled. Well, maybe it would have been a waste of time."

"Relax Bruce! They've probably just been delayed."

"But if I'm late to meet the guys, they'll think I'm not coming and they'll go without me."

"Don't you know where the lodge is?"

"No way! I couldn't possibly find it alone. We're supposed to be going in cars from Nagoya with some of their Japanese friends."

"Don't worry! We'll do something if they're late. We'll go off on our own." Jake still hoped Bruce would make it on time. He was looking forward to his weekend and didn't want to spend the whole time with Bruce, since they spent nearly twenty-four hours a day together as it was.

The ring at the door came at last. Gregor took their bags to the car and assured the President they'd be well looked after. Gregor didn't look at all guilty about deceiving the President.

As a concession to Lewis and Dave, who had been outraged at the unfair prospect of Jake and Bruce going on this trip, the President had arranged for them to go to stay in the country with a Japanese Mormon family the following weekend. So they joined in waving them off cheerily.

"Don't break a leg!" shouted Dave.

"Take a lot of pictures!" shouted Mrs Ericson.

They would have to do something about that.

"Where do you guys want to be dropped off?" Gregor asked.

"Nagoya Station's fine."

"Now you guys take care. I'm responsible for you. There's no phone where we're staying so I want you to be here waiting for us 5 o'clock on Sunday, OK? No excuses. Whatever happens, be there or I can't help the consequences."

Jake and Bruce nodded and then they were free. They'd been together so much recently that to Jake it felt like seeing your child off on his first day of school. He wanted to be sure the Brits were waiting for him at Nagoya.

"Eight o'clock and no sign of them."

"Don't tell me they went without me," said Bruce, his voice shaking with disappointment.

"We'll wait a while."

Jake tried to distract him but he was perturbed. "We're waiting in the wrong place," he said. "You wait here and I'll go and see."

"No, this is where you told me," said Jake. "Wait a while longer!"

They stood a while in impatient silence surrounded by a myriad varieties of glaring neon, watching the scurrying workers moving from office to night-spot, hopping in and out of taxis and disappearing into the subway. The time went by and they were distracted for a while, but when 8:30 came, it seemed to be getting more hopeless.

"So why the hell did I rush to get here?" Bruce raged. "I was sweating over this and it looks like I've been stood up."

Jake looked at his friend's face contorted with frustrated anger and then saw it smooth into a look of sickly pleasantness.

315

"Julie, you're here at last. What happened?"

Julie, as usual, was oblivious. "Why are we late? We just had to pick up a few people." She looked uneasily at Jake. "Now there's a load of us squeezed into this car."

"Oh that's OK, I'm just hanging out with Bruce. I'm going somewhere else."

"Oh OK. Well, don't worry! We'll look after him, make sure he doesn't get up to any monkey business."

Bruce clearly felt like one of the gang as he was bundled into the car with James, Julie and an Australian teacher named Tony. In the front was their Japanese friend and his girlfriend. It was a beautiful car for such a young driver. A convoy of similar white cars had pulled up behind with all the other weekend trippers. Jake waved them off and they hooted and hung out of the window like teenage hoodlums. He would be happy when Bruce was safely back on Sunday.

Now Jake was alone. He looked around him at the huge, bustling city. He didn't have to go to the hostel. He could go anywhere in all Japan. He had a little money. But then the prospect of sightseeing alone filled him with trepidation. How could he make all those arrangements himself? He had never travelled alone in his life. That was the lot of Mormon people. They were very rarely alone. Finally, he couldn't even be bothered to work out the route to Suleiyman's hostel. The heck with it! He would get a taxi.

This was luxury, to glide across the city in the comfort of a taxi. The driver had asked the customary polite questions. 'Your Japanese is very good. Where are you from? What company are you with? Can you use chopsticks?' Lots of praise, lots of approval. The taxi drivers often wore white gloves and drove with a stylish precision, handling the controls with a flourish and returning the hands immediately to 10 to 2 on the wheel.

Jake arrived at the hostel, which was in a quiet area of town nearer to his own part of the city. He rang the buzzer. A young woman who had been using the phone opened the door and tannoyed for Suleiyman. Suleiyman appeared in a blue track-suit, looking more casual and relaxed than usual.

"*Irrashai, Irrashai,*" 'Welcome', he said in Japanese. "We've been waiting for you."

"I'm sorry I kept you waiting. I had to see a friend off. I hope you haven't gone to any trouble."

"No trouble, no trouble," said Suleiyman, ushering him into a small common room. On a low table was spread a lavish banquet of many varieties of food. The corridor sprang into life and neat little women in long skirts and headscarves bustled in and out with little dishes, putting them on the counter. Around the table were a group of eager faces. Jake was led to a place at the head of the table.

"You don't mind sitting on the floor?" asked Suleiyman.

"Not at all. I like it. It's different." Jake was hoping that this was not all for his benefit, that other guests were coming, but everyone was looking expectantly at him smiling encouragement.

"*Dozo, dozo!* Go on, please eat!"

"Oh that's OK, I'll wait till everyone's sitting down."

Suleiyman took up his place next to Jake and the other men began to pass food to him.

"Shall we wait for the ladies?" said Jake.

The men giggled. "Oh, that's OK. They've had their dinner. They're just helping out."

Jake spent a chaotic half hour having all the dishes described to him in detail and watching food being piled high on his plate. No sooner had he finished something than it was replaced with something even larger. His stomach was getting more and more uncomfortable. The food was delicious but very spicy for his taste. He could taste coconut and nuts and sweet and sour sauce and then a rush of burning for about five minutes. The milky drink they gave him soothed his mouth, and then he would begin another round. This style of eating was totally new to him. Such variety and such quantity! Mormons prided themselves on their simple, frugal habits, and when it came to eating, simplicity and hospitality were in a fine balance. This was incredible. They had to have been working for days. After five refusals they accepted he could take no more and he sat back for a while to get his breath.

"That was a wonderful meal, but I'm not used to eating such a lot at one time. How is it you guys are so slim?"

"Oh we don't usually eat like this," said one of them. "It's just you're a very special guest."

Why? thought Jake. Were they trying to impress him? Win him

over to Islam through food? It could work, he thought.

Suleiyman went around introducing all his friends. There were some other Indonesians, some Malaysians, Singaporeans and one Chinese. Another was from Syria, one Libyan and two from Iraq. Imagine meeting guys from Iraq and places like that, thought Jake. Places he'd only heard about on TV where the people were supposed to be pretty scary. Suleiyman told Jake's story briefly and the key phrase, 'Jake is interested in Islam.' Throughout the meal, small children of various ages ran in and out, sometimes sitting on their fathers' laps and then scurrying off again. Some of the Indonesians and Malaysians were married. It seemed to have been their wives who had done the cooking. They busily cleared the dishes and the Syrian man brought in some coffee.

When Jake refused, Suleiyman remembered and said, "Oh I'm sorry Jake. I forgot. Can we get you something else?"

The Syrian began to pick up the cups again but Jake stopped him. "Please, no, it doesn't bother me if you drink coffee. It's part of my religion, that's all. Please go ahead! Have coffee! I'll have milk. That's fine."

After the coffee, the serious talk began. The group began by comparing experiences of Japanese life, and the problems they experienced when trying to fit in as Muslim students. One talked about how his superior had disapproved of him praying in the lab. Another student had caused offense by refusing to join a departmental social evening because there was drinking involved. They laughed at some of the questions Japanese people asked about their religion and the general ignorance about Islam. Jake felt more comfortable with the conversation as an observer. It was embarrassing to have all the attention focused on him. Then they began to include him in the discussion, asking about his impressions of Japan. They were fascinated to hear about his experiences as a missionary and the various people he'd met on his house calls. Only the Chinese man and two of the Malaysians had ever heard of Jake's church but the others were quite in the dark. Jake decided not to go into it. He didn't want to cause any rifts after their hospitality. Plus, he had the whole weekend to go. He just gave a few bland facts about figures, dates and numbers. He felt he ought to talk about what would interest them.

"I had a look at the Qur'an last week," he said.

Those were the magic words. All eyes were on him, their faces aglow and eager with little phrases being repeated, something about Allah. Jake smiled nervously.

"What did you think about the Qur'an?" asked the Libyan.

"Ah yes. It was real interesting." He felt he should be more specific. "I got the feeling it was sort of talking to me personally."

More cries of that phrase they kept repeating.

"I was particularly interested in the passages about Jesus. For example you say he wasn't crucified and he wasn't God and all of that."

"Yes, what do you believe about Jesus?" asked Suleiyman.

Jake looked sheepish. "Well, I'm a little outnumbered," he said smiling.

The group laughed. The Libyan was reassuring. "Don't be embarrassed. We're here to help you if you have any questions."

"Well, for a start I was surprised to find Jesus in there anyway. I thought it was just the Christians who believed in Jesus. Also, I saw some other names we have in the Bible like Noah and Moses. But there wasn't that much about them."

"Oh, there is," said the Syrian. "Many times in the Qur'an Allah, *subhanahu wa ta'ala*, mentions Musa, *alayhi's-salam,* and *Sayyidina* Nuh."

"I'm sorry?"

Suleiyman intervened. "You have to explain the Arabic terms, Salih."

"Oh yes, it's very simple," said Salih. "We say for example after the name of a Prophet, *'alayhi's-salam'* which means, 'peace be upon him', as a mark of respect. After mentioning the name of Allah, we say, 'exalted is He, the Most High.'"

"I see," said Jake, "so did you get these stories from the Bible?"

The Libyan smiled. He seemed to be the senior of the group and the knowledgeable one. "At the time the Qur'an was revealed to the Prophet Muhammad, peace be upon him, people used to laugh and say he made it up. They used to say, it is tales of ancient times, copied from the olden texts. But there were things in the Qur'an, miracles, that the Prophet, peace be upon him, could never have known, details about the Prophets who were not in the Bible, messages from the lives of the Prophets that no-one else had ever thought of. There are scientific facts that have not been discovered until today, about the sun, the moon, the mysteries of water, the baby and how it grows in the mother's womb."

"Yes," said Suleiyman. "When the Europeans were in the dark ages, the Muslims had all this scientific knowledge."

"I'm not European," said Jake.

"No, no. I don't mean to speak against your people. I just want you to see how Islam was modern and scientific and it all came from the Qur'an. Now, one man could never have imagined all that by himself. It must have come from Allah."

"I have done some research," said a Malaysian, warming to the theme, "as part of my physics thesis and I have used many verses from the Qur'an which talk about the laws of physics. We know that in that time such facts were not known by anyone."

The group soon got carried away with the scientific wonders of the Qur'an and then Jake asked, "Was it just Prophet Muhammad who had the Qur'an revealed or others too?"

"Only the Prophet Muhammad, peace be upon him," said the Libyan.

"Perhaps Jake needs to hear some of the basics," said Suleiyman. "He's only just come across Islam."

"OK," said the Libyan. "I'll tell you about the Qur'an and then I think you're tired, yes? After that we'll leave you in peace."

"Yes, that's the way we do it," said Jake. "One major point per lesson."

With a mixture of love and drama, the Libyan told the story of how the Prophet Muhammad, a man well-liked and trusted in his community, suddenly was visited by the Angel Gabriel in a cave on a bare mountainside where he often used to go to pray. He was told to read by the angel and insisted that he could not read, but the angel overwhelmed him and revealed the first few verses of the Qur'an:

Read in the name of thy Lord who created,
created man from a mere clot.
Read - and thy Lord is most Bountiful,
He who taught the use of the pen,
taught man what he knew not.

Muhammad had been afraid at first and could not believe what had happened, but his wife believed in him as the chosen

Messenger of God and reassured him. From that time on the Qur'an was sent down to the Prophet at many times in many places, piece by piece, instructing him, warning him, reassuring him and giving him the guidance he was to pass on to mankind. The Prophet established a community based on this guidance and the verses of the Qur'an continued to be revealed when they were immediately memorized by the Prophet and his companions and written down by his scribes.

Jake listened to the story like a small child. It had similarities with the story of Joseph Smith, like the vision and the angel, but it he couldn't help feeling that it sounded a lot more plausible than the Mormon story and somehow more human. Jake was used to the idea of angels and always pictured them as he'd seen them in the thousand paintings that adorned Mormon houses and chapels and meeting halls everywhere. The description of the Angel Gabriel as a being of light which seemed to fill the whole horizon was spiritually impressive, but was also the sort of thing even a sci-entifically-minded person could believe. Some people rejected anything at all supernatural but this Islamic story somehow made the supernatural seem more likely.

Jake was getting tired. "You've given me a lot to think about," he said. "I think I'll just sleep on it and maybe we can talk some more."

"Yes, I'm sorry," said Suleiyman. "We always go on too much and talk until past midnight. But there's so much to discuss. Would you like to go to your room now?"

Jake was grateful for the chance to sleep. He felt mentally exhausted after the intrigues about their weekend and the worry about Bruce, followed by all this new information piled upon him on top of a very full stomach. He shook hands warmly with his new friends and thanked Suleiyman many times over for the meal and the hospitality.

"We are Muslims," said Suleiyman. "We love to practice our faith."

They did drive the point home a bit much at times, thought Jake. He was very pleased to find he had his own room. He looked around thinking it was a spare room, and then he saw the closet heaving with belongings. Obviously someone had given up their room for him. Now this was hospitality gone mad. He was about to protest but he decided against it. He would enjoy a night or two in a room to himself. For the first time in many nights, Jake fell straight into a deep and refreshing sleep with no restless questioning or going over and over things in his mind. It was exactly what he needed to prepare for the rest of the weekend.

Breakfast the next morning was a much more modest affair and Jake took the chance to ask Suleiyman for his impressions of the *Book of Mormon.*

"Yes, quite interesting," he said tactfully.

"Were there any bits you found particularly striking?"

"Um, not more than any other book. It seemed to be a story or a history or something. There were lots of dramatic pictures."

"Not as good as the Qur'an though, huh?" said Jake.

Suleiyman looked at him quite seriously. "The Qur'an is not an ordinary book, Jake. You can't compare other books with the Qur'an. Not even the Bible. This is the *kalam Allah,* literally, the direct Word of God. It cannot be equalled. It cannot be compared."

Faced with this uncustomary seriousness Jake did not like to argue, but he carried on quietly with his breakfast. "Look!" he said finally. "I appreciate the way you're looking out for me and everything, telling me about your religion. I admit there's something in it. I never knew before what Muslims believe and believe me I'm impressed, but I have my religion. I believe it helps me to be a good person. I believe it's gonna bring me salvation."

"It's a hard thing to face, Jake, but everyone at some point or another has to question and to be sure they're following the truth. It's what God requires of us."

"I know. I prayed about the truth and I feel I've found it. I'll take a look at other religions but I was born Mormon, I believe it and that's how I wanna stay."

"It doesn't matter what you were born with. Take my case. I may look like a very devout Muslim now, but there was a time when I was in school, I seriously thought about Christianity. The missionaries there were very insistent but *al-hamdu li'llah,* when I began to study Islam in depth I began to get more and more convinced of it. You see I didn't come from a particularly religious family and so I was always searching."

"Who's to stay the searching will stop?"

"I believe it stops when you find the truth. I mean you never stop learning and deepening your understanding but you end up at some time finding what you're looking for. In your case, Allah is giving you a chance to continue your search and He is offering you Islam."

"Me, a Muslim?" Jake nearly choked. "I mean, I mean, I'm not an Arab or anything."

Suleiyman's eyes became even wider. "Am I an Arab?" he laughed.

Jake realized how ridiculous it was. "No I guess not but you couldn't help where you were born. I think you learn about the religion that's nearest to you."

"No that wouldn't be fair. Allah is Just. He gives all people a chance. So, maybe this is your chance. You know there are many converts to Islam all over Europe, all over the States and Africa. That Chinese brother you saw last night, he converted."

"We know all about converts," said Jake. "A vast number of our members are converts because we are still a young church."

They were interrupted by two of the Malaysians who were going off to play tennis. "What would you like to do today, Jake? How about some sports?"

It was a good idea. He needed physical exercise and something to clear his head of its sense of theological overload. When they got to the tennis courts, Jake concocted a little game of his own in his head. As he and Suleiyman had reached deadlock in their debate, he would let the tennis match decide. He would play a bout with Suleiyman and if he won he would forget about this Islam altogether. If Suleiyman won, he would take it as a sign from God that he should find out more. Suleiyman was small and wiry but Jake was the more powerful of the two. Suleiyman's friends kept score meticulously and acted as ball boys. Jake played the game of his life because he felt that so much was resting on it. He won easily and Suleiyman congratulated him warmly, with no hint of resentment. Instead of feeling triumphant, however, Jake felt disappointed that he'd put this abrupt end to a journey of discovery that had just begun. So the Mormons were the victors, he thought; but he still wasn't satisfied with the outcome. He walked along gloomily behind the others until it dawned on him that he didn't have to bow to this one twist of fate. 'Best of three!' he said, smiling inwardly.

Jake's religious instruction continued throughout the weekend. At sunset the Muslims, who had all been watching TV, turned it off, rose as one, and gathered to pray on the other side of the room. Jake felt like the odd man out as they all stood shoulder to shoulder and prayed in perfect unison. The words sounded quite beautiful but the way they crouched with their faces on the floor looked strange, like they were in awe of some great king. It reminded Jake of the Japanese soaps when the peasants would kow-tow before the local shogun and grovel for favours. Yet they all seemed quite absorbed in their prayers. It seemed unlikely to Jake that God required this ritual of standing and bowing, up and down so many times. For Mormons, it was simply a matter of closing one's eyes and bowing one's head. You didn't need to make any big show.

"What were you saying there?" he asked when they'd finished.

"In every prayer," explained Sayyid the Libyan, "we recite the first chapter of the Holy Qur'an followed by other verses of the Qur'an, and then when we bow and make prostration we are all the time praising Allah, and then when sitting, we ask for blessings upon His Messenger Muhammad, peace be upon him."

"Why do you have to say the same thing every time?"

"This is the ritual prayer which has all the essential elements to remind us of the important aspects of life. We repeat this five times a day in obedience to Allah and to show our submission to His will. Like this, we draw closer to Him by using the words he has given us. At the end we can make *du'a* in our own words, and that is saying any specific or personal thing."

"Does it get a little monotonous? The prayers, I mean."

"For a very pious Muslim, and I'm afraid I cannot be described as such, it is an experience of light, but for others of us, who are struggling to be good Muslims, it brings us another chance to have communication with Allah, to ask for His guidance and protection and to praise Him and ask for His forgiveness."

For a person who wasn't pious, Sayyid looked pretty saintly with his gentle expression and kind eyes. The others seemed to respect and like him, except the Syrian, who often seemed to be competing with him to show religious knowledge. What got all of them animated was discussion of politics and Middle Eastern affairs. All of them seemed to have some problem back home with lack of democracy or infringement of rights of free speech. When Jake tried to join in by praising the climate in the US of freedom of speech and democracy, instead of agreeing with him they all laughed cynically.

Sayyid noticed Jake's look of confusion. "I must say," he said, "that it is true that in the West, we are able to meet and discuss religion and organize ourselves openly whereas in our own countries we cannot even meet like this."

"Why not?" said Jake. "You should demand your rights."

"It's not so easy as that, I'm afraid," said Sayyid.

"But it is the policy of the western powers that keeps the regimes in the first place," said the Syrian. "They may enjoy some freedom at home but they don't like it for us."

Jake noticed Suleiyman flash a warning look at the Syrian as if to silence him, but Jake urged them to continue. "It's OK. You go on. I'm interested in what you have to say. I've just never heard much about politics before."

"Let's talk about something else," said Sayyid. "Jake, tell us about your family."

Jake told them his family history. Names, jobs and various details and the brief story of his educational career. When he tried to explain to them something about the Mormon church, they seemed to switch off a little and only home in on certain points of argument as if Jake himself were responsible for the scriptures.

"But what evidence have you got that Jesus is God?"

"Eyewitness accounts for one. He also said he was God."

"Where? Where?" said the Syrian rushing to fetch a copy of the Bible from the bookshelves. "Now show us where it says Jesus is God."

"Well as I told you, we believe there are mistakes in the translation of the Bible so it cannot be as accurate as we would like but there are various verses such as 'I and the Father are one', or for example, 'In the beginning was the Word' - that's Jesus – 'and the Word was with God and the Word was God'."

"What's Jesus?" asked Suleiyman.

"The Word."

"But how can the Word be Jesus?"

"Yes, surely the Word means Word," said the Syrian smugly.

"As I said, insofar as it's correctly translated," said Jake. He was not used to discussing the Bible with people who knew about it and disbelieved in it. With Buddhists, they disbelieved, but they knew nothing about it. With Christians of other denominations you were on common ground because they believed in it in one way or another, but these Muslims were trying to tie him in knots, asking him to find evidence in the gospels alone. They would have nothing to do with the letters and epistles or the Acts of the Apostles. Most of Jake's well-rehearsed verses on the Incarnation, Blood Atonement, Crucifixion and Resurrection were in other parts of the New Testament. When he explained the sightings of Jesus after his crucifixion as evidence of the resurrection, they argued that it was more likely Jesus was seen alive, not because he was resurrected but because he hadn't actually died. What was exasperating for Jake was that if it was in the Qur'an, that was the end of the argument as far as they were concerned, so if the Qur'an said Jesus wasn't killed, he wasn't killed. Ditto for the blood atonement and the divinity of Jesus. They seemed to enjoy the debate immensely.

Sayyid gave Jake a clear explanation of the history of prophethood. He told him that Allah sent Prophets with guidance to every people from Adam until the Last Prophet, Muhammad. They all taught the same message: the oneness of God, certainty of the Day of Judgment and punishment or reward in the Hereafter. They all came to warn mankind and teach us responsibility as moral creatures who have been given free will. He said how Prophets were all rejected and ridiculed in their own lands, but the suffering was part of the mission, and Allah always supported each Prophet and his followers.

Jake tried to illustrate this with stories of Joseph Smith's life where he was hounded by the people he preached to and persecuted until he had to migrate with his followers to Illinois and how he was finally killed for what he believed in, but Salih, the Syrian kept insisting that the Prophet Muhammad was the Last Prophet. "You know he is even mentioned in the Bible," he said. "There are prophecies for him there."

"But I thought you didn't believe in the Bible?"

"No doubt some parts of it are true. Some parts are from Allah. If it is in agreement with Al-Qur'an we can say it may be true. Allah knows, but we have the Qur'an. This is the final book, you see, which confirms previous scriptures and points out what is true and what is false." He gave some examples from Deuteronomy which told of the coming of a Prophet, *'like unto Moses who would speak every word that God would put into his mouth'*. The prophecy did seem to have many elements which fitted the life of Prophet Muhammad very well.

"There is another one, here," said Samir, one of the Iraqis, "in John's Gospel. *'I shall send you the Comforter, the Spirit of Truth and…'"*.

"But that's the Holy Ghost!" interrupted Jake.

"Holy Ghost?" they echoed.

"The third person of the Godhead. Joseph Smith says: 'The Father has a body of flesh and bones as tangible as man's; the Son also; but the Holy Ghost has not a body of flesh and bones, but is a personage of Spirit.' They are different persons, but share the same will, the same outlook, if you like. It's like when Jesus was in the Garden of Gethsemane, he prayed to his Father, not to himself. They are quite different. And the Holy Ghost is different again."

"No, no. There is no trinity," said Samir, as if speaking to a slow pupil. "Only Allah. God is One. Now, this Comforter can be translated into Arabic as 'Ahmad' which is one of the names by which the Prophet Muhammad was known. We know from the Qur'an that 'Isa, *alayhi's-salam,* foretold the coming of Prophet Muhammad, peace be upon him."

It was strange, thought Jake, that he had come across that very verse in the Bible quite recently. It definitely rang a bell in his mind. It disturbed him because more and more he felt that things were happening despite himself. All these things couldn't be pure coincidences; or was he just looking out for them? For example, this opportunity to speak to Muslims for such a length of time and to find out so much. But by Saturday night, after another wonderful meal, this time prepared by the Arabs, he was feeling weary of being lectured to. Now he knew how some of the subjects felt when they were given welcome sessions at the church. His brain hurt and he needed time to sort it all out. Their hospitality was warm but overwhelming. He felt like he was being honoured by virtue of being American but then he remembered how they had criticized America in their political discussions. It was probably because they hoped he would convert to Islam. He decided to leave early on Sunday and explore Nagoya on his own.

His departure met with a flurry of '*insha-Allah's*' and '*masha-Allah's*' and 'see you agains'. 'Don't hesitate to contact us anytime. Don't lose touch.' How could he? They sent him on his way with a bag full of Islamic books and cassettes. He gave his last thanks to Suleiyman and then he was let loose by himself upon Nagoya.

The first place he went was a place he'd wondered about for a long time from the first time he saw it in Sakae. It was a revolving restaurant at the top of a large building which housed various department stores and banks. He was greeted at the top after a long, smooth ride in the elevator by an uneasy waiter. He was shown his seat by the window and looked at the panoramic view which took in the TV building which looked somewhat like the Eiffel Tower, and the familiar park which was now filling up with Sunday fathers. Sunday? How strange not to be in church on Sunday! It made him feel both guilty and excited at the same time. He wondered if people ever watched them from up here when they worked in the park on Wednesdays. From this height, everything looked insignificant. There was the beloved Donut Heaven and the familiar street along by the park. It was his favourite place in Nagoya. The restaurant was nearly empty and the waiter seemed put out that he had only asked for juice and a slice of cake. Mood music flowed around the plush interior. The ambience and the view were especially for him. Jake stayed a long time, taking in the atmosphere, too long for the waiter's comfort and when his chair creaked ending the uneasy stand-off between them, the waiter was too quick to guide him to the elevator. Jake sighed. Only certain kinds of people were welcome in expensive places. He knew where he was going, a place where he felt at home, among friends, a place that was open twenty-four hours a day. His sights were set on Donut Heaven.

Gregor and Maria were right on time at Nagoya. Bruce made it by the skin of his teeth. His friends, ever reliable, had taken it very easy about getting back and he was the only one who had a dead-line. After he'd gotten his breath back, Jake could tell by his expression that he'd had a wonderful time.

Gregor and Maria briefed them about their mountain hide-away to report to the President and thoughtfully handed over some landscape Polaroids they'd taken. Bruce at least could con-fide in Jake. Jake, however kept much of his experience to himself for the time being. Bruce had met a Japanese girl, Fumiko. They got along very well and had a lot to talk about. Bruce was eager to see her again and had decided to pass her off as a church hopeful the following week. Jake told him the basic facts about his visit to the hostel and the wonderful food. In the meantime he wanted to mull everything over by himself.

Back at the house everything seemed alien to him, as if it had been left far back in the past. The last month before the summer was going to be a difficult one.

During the missionary days everything he said on his calls raised questions in Jake's mind. He was forever making notes about points of doctrine that came up and questions people asked and then going over them late at night in his room. He was hungry for information as never before, and he read the Islamic books voraciously. The fear and dread he had felt at first had vanished, thanks to his weekend. He wanted to know, and now he plunged in at the deep end to see what God would throw at him. He partic-ularly enjoyed the cassettes. They consisted of a dialogue between a Canadian convert, Hamid Rashid and an Egyptian scholar called Jamal Badawi. The series was called 'Islam in Focus'. The Canadian would ask Dr Badawi questions which westerners in particular would like to know and Dr Badawi gave answers backed up by texts. With his lifetime of meticulous scripture study, Jake found the looking-up and cross-referencing perfectly natural. It took him further into the Qur'an and Rashid acted as Jake's own spokesman. He seemed to come up with the very ques-tions Jake wanted to ask.

Bruce turned out to be no more focussed on his mission than was Jake. He became increasingly exasperated with the control of their time and the lack of freedom. He wanted to meet with Fumiko more often but after her initial visit to the church she had been overwhelmed and did not want to go back, so their contact was rationed to the Donut Heaven hour and the occasional Saturday meeting when Bruce could find an excuse. He was so preoccupied that he hadn't noticed the changes that were coming over Jake, except that he seemed to be always studying. Jake used to pretend he was working on his Japanese, but after a while he started to feel a need to tell someone about what was happening to him. Bruce should know. He was the closest person to him at the moment.

"Remember once you asked me if I had doubts?"

"Yeah, I remember."

"Recently I've been having lots of doubts."

"You're kidding!"

"No, really. It's the weirdest thing. It was after I started talking to Sanjé. You know his name isn't really Sanjé. It's Suleiyman. He's Muslim."

"Yeah, so?"

"Well, I figured if the President found out he'd go crazy. Anyway he argued with me about religion and at first I was so confident I could knock him down but a few weird things happened."

"What weird things?"

They didn't seem so weird after all but Jake couldn't put into words. "I can't explain, just kinda supernatural."

"You're kidding!"

"Not supernatural. It was more kinda like God showing me something. That's the only way I can explain it. Anyway Suleiyman gave me the Qur'an."

"The Koran?"

"That's the Muslim Holy Book and it was real - I don't know – mind-blowing. I found out some incredible things in there and then you know that weekend ..." The whole story came out in a garbled rush, and Bruce sat open-mouthed.

"You, Jake. Mr Ace Mormon turning Moslem! I don't believe it."

"No, hold on! I'm not turning Muslim. That's crazy. I'm just saying that it made me doubt and ask a lot of questions. So what I intend to do is to spend the vacation studying hard and trying to get rid of these doubts. Then I can come back stronger next year."

"Next year!" Bruce groaned. "Another year. You had me worried then, Jake. Imagine you turning Moslem after all that."

"Yeah," Jake laughed, joining in the joke. "Imagine. Hah, hah!"

唯壱

Interlude

Flying out of Nagoya, Jake felt a terrible wrenching he couldn't explain. He felt something near grief to be leaving this place where he'd learned so much and experienced so much. But he would be back. He felt like he'd lost his footing and was suspended in mid-air without any support, but then he had an overwhelming sense of comfort. Someone was there to hold him. For the first time he was fully aware of the presence of God and it was much greater than he'd ever imagined. He waved to the land. 'See you again, *Insha-Allah*.'

唯邑

Salt Lake City, Utah

After the 'welcome back' visits and meals, Jake quickly settled back into the old home routine. It was strange suddenly to
have so much free time but he resolved not to waste it. Since the
first couple of weeks were spent with his own family with all the
continuity that entailed and in the most thoroughly Mormon
place in the world, his Islamic preoccupations took a back seat.
Maybe he'd been taking it too seriously. It would probably go
away after all. Everything about Japan seemed to lose its immedia-
cy, but it was difficult to be among people who didn't have a real
clue what you were talking about. Beyond general things like the
weather and the people and the food, people didn't really identify
with 'overseas'. Soon his sisters would complain: 'Every sentence
begins with "In Japan this, in Japan that!"'

"Well, I've spent the last year of my life there," said Jake.
"What do you expect?" At first he had immediately thought about
Suleiyman and his reading when they asked about Japan, but he
managed to suppress the urge to talk about it and instead tried to
conjure up things from his memory that would interest them.

The main hurdle to get over was his formal meeting with his local
Bishop, Brother Morris, who would report on President Ericson's
assessment of him so far. He was a genial man who had known Jake
almost all his life. He had always told Jake he would never need to
worry about his future in the church. He was a fine young man from
a fine family and they had always been valued members of the ward.
Bishop Morris glanced at the papers in front of him.

"No worries here, Jake, I'm glad to say. The President's been
pleased with your progress and your support of the Plessey fellow.
Just a bit down in the dumps towards the end wasn't it? The
President says here, 'personal worries'. Everything all right at
home, Jake?"

"Oh yes, sir. It was just an argument I had on the phone. It kinda worried me for a while. Also I was worried that we weren't bringing in enough new people towards the end."

"No, no. According to your assessment, the President and the Bishop are very pleased with the rate of new referrals. No, you have no worries at all on that score. No worries and please God you'll continue to stride ahead next year."

Jake smiled to himself. If he'd been Muslim he'd have probably said '*Insha-Allah*' instead of 'please God'. The Bishop patted Jake's shoulder and led him to the door. "I've told you before, Jake. You've got a bright future so you just do your best."

That's what Jake would do. His best, according to his own conscience. He had to live with himself for the rest of his life and he didn't intend to spend it in denial, in mental turmoil.

The next significant hurdle on the horizon was Alice. He went over to her house and her parents welcomed him like a soldier returning from the war. Alice looked cool but pleased to see him. He asked her about herself to please her but she was embarrassed.

"Come on, Jake. I've got nothing to tell. You know, boring old Salt Lake, boring old work. Nothing happens. It's you who's been travelling everywhere."

"Just Japan," he said modestly. He told her all the highlights and repeated the funny stories he'd told everyone else. Her father, who had been in Korea during the war, could not resist comparing everything Jake said with Korea. 'Yeah, that's like Korea. Yes, in Korea we did that.' Alice's mother seemed pleased that the Bishop had spoken to Jake and told him he had a good report from the mission. For prospective career prospects a good mission was vital in Salt Lake City or any other Mormon community.

Alice had been impressed with Jake's last letter about the cherry blossoms. "That was so unlike you, Jake. It was really beautiful."

"Is that a compliment?" he asked.

They went for a walk side by side, and sat down in a café, and the conversation was pretty much like it used to be; but he couldn't take in the idea that they would be a married couple. That had seemed worlds away but now it was growing nearer. After the mission. 'After the mission' had seemed to be in the inconceivable future, but now it was only a year away and the first year had gone so fast. Jake could imagine Alice's reaction if he were to mention his Muslim friends. Friends? Well, he'd spent that one weekend with them and he met up with Suleiyman nearly every week. Alice's family were a little racist in their outlook and some of it had rubbed off on her. Arabs? You must be crazy. They're dangerous people. If he really wanted to send her through the floor though he could tell her he was getting interested in their religion too. It seemed absurd now that he had ever entertained the idea of Islam. But it had seemed so important to him back there.

As before, Jake was happiest at home sitting in the kitchen companionably with his mom. She loved to have him back home and in her usual relaxed way would enjoy having him sit and talk, sorting out his problems as they came up, not complaining if he went off somewhere else for a while and came back. Whatever he decided was OK with her, whereas his father would bawl at him as he got up after a half-hour chat. 'Hey, where ya going? We were just getting into some interesting conversation.'

Jake had been over every detail of the missionary day with his father and his father reminisced about his own mission and all their family's and friends' missions. If Jake could have told anyone about his religious worries he would have told his mom but he didn't want to worry her. With his father he decided to tackle some of the fundamental points he had been thinking about and talk about them as if they were coming from a third party. His father was always flattered when he came to him with religious problems.

"There was this question," Jake began, "from a pretty intelligent Buddhist guy about the nature of God. It was a tough one and when I said Joseph Smith had seen God the Father and the Son in a vision he just threw his head back and laughed."

"Well, we Mormons have gotten used to that by now, surely. Ridicule for everything we believe in and slanders on our prophet."

"Yeah but the point was I couldn't answer his question about the nature of God."

"Well, prophet Joseph described it as two personages whose brightness and glory defy all description."

"And those paintings of the Father and Son standing side by side in white robes. Is that what he saw?"

"Well, I guess no one could represent the full glory as Joseph saw it. Those paintings are just representations of something that Mormons imagined but no-one but Joseph knew what he really saw."

Jake was silent for a while. "You see more and more, from what you hear over there, from say Buddhists, I mean the more educated ones, is that God is something invisible or indescribable, say like a force, not like a person."

"But God said He created us in His own image and likeness."

"That's what I always used to answer but they would say it was impossible that God, as powerful and majestic as He is, could have a body or even a family like us."

"These things are for us to see in the next life, Jake. We can't expect to have all the answers now. All we can do now is accept the teachings of the church and follow them to the best of our ability. There are wonderful things in store for us to find out, Jake."

Jake smiled. His father's words seemed naive now in the light of what he'd been reading in Islam. He had found it all eminently logical and plausible so far: a single, all-Powerful, Loving Creator, indescribable by His creatures but Who speaks to them through Prophets who were also creatures, real human beings but special, who brought books that everyone could see and read and gave teachings which they followed themselves and which teach humanity morality and how to please God and win His reward in the next life. God would judge everyone on that Day with mercy. That was it. A child would have no difficulty with that. Jake was afraid about the doubts creeping back, but pleased at the same time that the whole Islamic episode in Japan had not been an illusion. He knew it was no illusion. He had never been so profoundly affected by anything in his life as he had by what he had learned in Japan.

"Did you ask the President about these points?" asked his father. "I'm sure he could answer them better than I could."

"Sure, yeah. We discussed a lot of things but he was so busy most of the time. We didn't have that much time to talk in depth."

"Well, I'm sure when you go back this time, he'll be glad to talk to you. That's what he's there for."

Jake soon began to feel a little redundant at home. His mom

wouldn't let him do any chores. The girls had their vacation jobs and his brother was at work. After he'd gone around doing the thousand and one errands in Salt Lake that his ward in Nagoya had requested, he began to twiddle his thumbs. After having barely a minute to himself in Japan he was now faced with these long summer days of sloth alone in the house after everyone had gone out to work. He almost wished he'd set himself up with a job. They always needed people in the archives department or as guides at the Visitor's Center or on the Friendship Committee or in any of the hotels and restaurants around the city. It kept nagging him that back in Japan he had been itching to get into the library, but now he felt he could hardly be bothered. The days were so hot and the refrigerator was so full. It had the effect of deadening his brain. With no regular missioning or study circles or reading to keep him alert, he had just deteriorated into a numbing lethargy. The philosophical questions no longer had the urgency they'd taken on in Japan. Did it really matter what was the absolute truth? Life went on anyway, eating, sleeping and working. You would find out soon enough when you died. All he had to do was accept the version of the truth that he had been brought up with and do his job, finish his mission and then see what the future brought for him. People just went along with what worked best for them. If you were born in a Muslim country that was what worked best for you, but then he thought: 'so why drive ourselves crazy trying to get new converts all the time?' What about people like that Canadian who became Muslim? Well, there were always people who liked to be different. Jake had read a few of the testimonies from Muslim converts, Americans, Scandinavians, Irishmen, all Christians who had begun to question the idea of Jesus as Son of God and Saviour of all mankind. But there were plenty of people who questioned and ended up not believing in God at all or the Hereafter. Where would it lead if you started on that road? He remembered one testimony of an Irishman who had worked in a clinic in Afghanistan. He had always been troubled by the injustice and inequality in the world and had tried to resolve it for himself by first becoming a revolutionary socialist. But he found that whatever system came into play, human nature was at the root. There had to be something more powerful than material comfort or social harmony to motivate man to rise above greed and selfishness. Then among the injured and dispossessed of Afghanistan, he found God. He explained that only belief in God and hope in the afterlife was enough to transcend worldly concerns. He found it the only secure base on which to build a life. From faith one would build a family, friendships and communities, then nations. As a socialist he used to join in the taunt against all religious people: 'Don't build your hopes on pie in the sky!' Now he understood what kept those people going. He had come to know God. The signs were everywhere. He said that he had been starving his soul and his soul had rebelled as surely as a stomach growls for lack of food.

Jake switched on the TV. Game show, game show, soap, Western, commercials, news bulletin. He watched for a while but it was mostly local news and state news from California and Oregon. American TV seemed harsh and bright after its Japanese equivalent and the length of items seemed incredibly short, so that you were just tuning in when it would zap to commercials. Jake continued channel-surfing until something more substantial came up on the screen. It looked like a hospital. The nurse was speaking. She had a British accent and Jake smiled, thinking of his British friends. She was disinfecting a baby's crib. 'Yes, it's very hard when we lose babies. This is the difficult part when you disinfect a cot for the next one. It's like you've scrubbed away every trace of the baby, even its smell. It's not supposed to happen like that, is it?' 'What do you mean?' asked the interviewer. 'Well, I mean usually with babies in hospital, say back home, you see an empty cot, it means the baby's gone home with its parents. Making up the beds is a happy occasion because you know there's another baby being born every hour or so.' She finished making up the crib. 'There, all ready for the next one. Poor little things. They've no sooner come into this horrible world, then they're out of it. Probably the best thing really. Gone to a better place, as they say.' The credits began to roll and as he watched, moved by the story of the dead baby, a wave of amazement came over Jake. 'Filmed in Afghanistan'. That was too much. Too much of a coincidence. He sprang out of his lethargy and was in the library within half an hour. The curiosity and thirst for information was back. He began to draw up a comparison list of the two religions for clarification and he divided a large sheet of paper into two columns heading one 'LDS' and the other 'Islam'.

唯邑

Colorado, USA

Jake's family took a vacation together and visited Colorado. They drove out in two cars and on the way out of Utah they dropped by Jake's uncle who had the ranch near the training centre. They spent an idyllic day out on the horses and Jake thought about how much things had changed since the time he'd been riding before the mission. But they weren't changes that anyone could see. They were changes within that had to remain hidden. It was marvellous to gallop through the air which had been so close and still these past few weeks, and enjoy the breeze.

They spent two days exploring the Grand Canyon. The sight was vast and awe-inspiring, enough to dwarf the significance of all human civilization. Jake thought about the nations he had been reading about that were mentioned in the Qur'an. Some he had never heard of like the 'Ad, the Thamud, the Madyan people of Salih. Others he was familiar with, the people of Lot, of Nimrod and Pharoah and the Jewish tribes. Some of them had built incredible civilizations and reached heights of amazing material sophistication but they had grown away from the teachings of God and had become arrogant and greedy. Then their civilizations were destroyed and there was a line that often came up in the Qur'an which reverberated in Jake's head as he gazed at the empty, cavernous silence of the canyon: '*Canst thou even see a trace of them now?*'

唯邑

Interlude

The second farewell was not as dramatic as the first because Jake's family knew he was settled and Alice knew she was getting nearer to her wedding. A year had already passed, but for Jake it was a time of mixed feelings. He felt comfortable with Japan. He knew what to expect now. He liked everyone he worked with. He got along with Bruce. He was eager in a way to get back to his study of Islam. He seemed more at home with it there. But he had slotted right back in at home and it felt warm and familiar again. Over here he could take a rather more detached view of religious arguments, as an observer, rather than being right in the centre of it. Also being back home, surrounded by his family and memories of the past in Salt Lake City, with Mormons everywhere, he feit rooted in his faith. What would he do now going back and letting himself venture again upon oceans of uncertainty?

唯色

Nagoya, Japan

It was difficult for Jake to adjust to life back at the house when he came back and remembered that Ellis, George, John and Dennis had left. Ellis had been a little oppressive at times but he was a good leader and enthusiastic. He had liked Dennis' happy-go-lucky temperament and had even managed to see something good in John, but he felt George was the one he'd really got to know and respect. George had never boasted about it, but his Japanese had been better than anyone's, and in his quiet way he had been a valuable member of the team. He had a love and respect for Japanese culture which had made Jake see it in a different way, and he had helped Jake benefit from the first year. Jake decided he would carry on his tradition of reflections in the *tatami* room. The second-years had been to Tokyo for their finishing ceremony, and Jake had not been able to attend because he had booked his flights a little earlier for the vacation. So it made him feel quite sad that he wouldn't be seeing them again. The next thing was wondering what the new first-years would be like; and then there was the worry of Jake's new responsibility as team leader. The President and Ellis had made it clear throughout the first year that he was to step into Ellis' shoes. Dave had been doing as well as Jake towards the second half of the first year and was always trying to prove his ability by volunteering for duties at the church and giving up more of his time for the President's computer data entry project. Jake thought that in all fairness Dave deserved to be the team leader more than he did. He certainly had leadership qualities. At the back of his mind Jake also felt enormously hypocritical taking on this position when he had been having such basic doubts about church doctrine. He remembered Ellis had said that was part of the maturing process of making the faith one's own, but Jake's faith was fragile at that time and he knew he would feel more comfortable working in the background.

When he was summoned by the President for his first briefing he spoke up for Dave.

"Sir, I don't know if I'm fully capable of taking on such responsibility. I've noticed Brother Dave has been working very hard and he has a kind of dynamic character. I don't know. Maybe he'd make a better team leader."

"That's very modest of you, Brother Jake; but no, we're satisfied with your record and you seem to fit the bill."

"Is it anything to do with Dave's looking like a Japanese?"

"Just between us, that is a factor. You see a lot of Japanese people quite like the image, shall we say, the glamour of having American church leaders. Also, the majority of Mormons are still Caucasian, but having said that, regardless of race, you are still the better candidate."

"Thank you, sir."

The President then lugged Ellis' files from the cabinet and deposited them on the desk in front of him. 'So this is where we start.' And Jake was filled in on his duties and responsibilities for the coming year.

Bruce was sure where he wanted to be. The summer had been long and fairly dull back in California and he had been eager to get back to Nagoya to see his friends again, not least the pretty Fumiko. They had kept in touch by letter. Bruce had almost forgotten about Jake's spiritual crisis and Jake didn't want to remind him now he was supposed to act as motivator-in-chief. Dave managed to hide his disappointment well when he found out about the new assignments, but the President had made a point of giving him a few extra responsibilities and plenty of praise. Jake had been quite shocked to find out that Ellis' files contained very detailed information about each one of them, their family background and highlights of their school record, their home Bishop's report and Temple ordinances confirmation as well as the dynamics of their progress throughout the mission. Tantalizingly, Jake had not been allowed to read his own file. Bruce's file mentioned under 'Social Notes' his quick sense of humour and wit and tendency to complain a little more than the rest about mission life. 'Has been dishonest once or twice.' This probably referred to the episode over the Fall picnic when he'd tried to get out of it, but there was no indication of whether the President knew about the barbecue. 'Speaks his mind and likes to be frank,' the report concluded.

As Bruce and Jake went off to meet the newcomers they reminisced about the day they had arrived and their first impression of Ellis and George, and then of the family.

"Remember how mad you were when we heard we were gonna be living in the house?" asked Jake.

"Yeah, I remember, and then when we saw the family and found we were going to be eating together and everything."

"Actually, I've enjoyed that part," said Jake. "Sitting together and talking. I like them as a family. It must be difficult for them to adjust to the new missionaries every year."

"Yeah, it must like having foster-children."

They waited expectantly, and off the train stumbled the four new recruits, and they could have been transported back a year. The same haircuts and clothes. The same apprehensive faces and eager questions. Bruce and Jake took them in two taxis, just as they had travelled the previous year with Ellis and George. They resisted the temptation to tease the new boys and answered their questions as honestly as they could and impressed them with their Japanese and their easy confidence about Japanese life.

It was Jake's job to introduce them to the family and show them to their rooms. "We have Mark from Idaho, Christopher from New Jersey, Neil from Los Angeles and Oliver from Kansas." Jake quite enjoyed the way they looked up to him and hung on his every word.

"I'm afraid you'll be sharing," said Jake, as he showed them into the first room. It had been Ellis' and George's room and now it looked sad and bare. He'd liked the way George used to decorate it with Japanese prints and posters. "Oh, this is OK," said Christopher. "I thought it was gonna be like one big dorm. But don't you guys get sick of each other, working together all day and then sharing a room?"

"It's OK, I guess, if you get along OK, but you tend to be almost unaware of the other person in the room after a while, you get so used to it."

"In training they were saying how the partnership between the missionaries is vital for a good mission," said Mark.

"Yeah, I think that's true," said Jake. "You have to cooperate."

The missionaries were full of questions, except Oliver who looked rather downcast. He seemed very shy and did not look you straight in the eye but furtively from under his eyelashes. He was a pale, freckled young man with gingery hair and looked very young for his age. His hair was pressed right down as if his mom had fixed it for him. "Is there anything you'd like to ask?" asked Jake kindly.

"Ah, I guess not. They told us a lot in training."

Jake could already tell that Mark and Christopher were the leaders. They were both confident and well-informed about missionary arrangements. Neil's comments showed that he felt pretty sophisticated as a big city boy among small-town guys. He kept making little digs at Kansas, and Jake hoped he was right and that Neil would not be working with Oliver. He would only make him more awkward than he already was.

Jake was right about the group dynamics. The two teams were made up of Mark and Oliver and Christopher with Neil. For the first week, Jake had to work with Christopher. He decided to be on his best behaviour that week so as not to show Christopher any bad habits. He took Christopher to lunch in the parks. When they went to Tsurumae on Wednesday, Jake treated him to a half-hour lunch at the Delaware Diner. He had told Bruce who'd been working in Sakae that day not to go within miles of Donut Heaven unless he wanted to blow his friendship with the Brits. Christopher was quite good company. Like Jake he was interested in languages, but the problem was that during the witnessing, he had a tendency to try and butt in while Jake was speaking about some point. Jake told him off as politely as possible. "You're only required to listen this week, Christopher. I know you're probably eager to practice but it's important we speak one at a time." He hoped he didn't sound pompous but Christopher's Japanese was just not good enough yet. Jake tried not to be a know-it-all about Japan and tried to remember that Christopher was seeing everything for the first time. Somehow he and Bruce had managed to stumble through those first weeks.

Bruce had spent the first week working with Neil and they hadn't got on too well. Bruce found him arrogant and smug. He had this obsession with Los Angeles and with coming from Los Angeles, and he kept running down San Francisco. He also had a tendency to boast about his father's electrical components company and all the places he had travelled to. He had been to Japan before 'on business' with his father and was supposedly knowledgeable on most aspects of life there. 'Of course a lot of them eat with spoons and forks a lot of the time', he would say. 'More and more Japanese families use sofas and tables and chairs. You're more likely to find a burger joint than a sushi bar in most Japanese cities these days.' 'Thanks Neil. Like I've been here for a year,' said Bruce, exasperated as he went over the story with Jake on Thursday. Lewis, himself a very retiring person, had been finding it extremely difficult to coax poor Oliver out of his shell and had confided to Jake that he thought Oliver might be homesick. To help cheer him up and bring the others into the fold, Jake suggested some kind of entertainment at the weekend. The President was wanting to take them on the annual visit to the zoo and then he conceded to Jake's suggestion that they finish it off with a trip to a bowling alley. Neil was not at all impressed with the idea of going to the zoo.

"I'd like to stay home if that's OK with you. I have a few calls to make."

The President was expert at putting people in their place. "Brother Neil, we do things as a team around here. What's more, your call allocation is one long-distance fifteen minute call a week except in emergencies."

So Neil moped around the zoo; but for Oliver it did the trick and he began to feel more at ease.

Jake found the new job demanding. Every Sunday he was expected to log in all the newcomers who visited the church. He had to arrange welcome groups for them after the sacrament meeting and follow-ups for ongoing cases. Sometimes he would have to do the lessons for newcomers himself. Also he had to prepare and lead the study group for the young men and take study circles two evenings a week. He often had to do calls to corporate subjects in the evenings and make reports on the missionaries' progress by interviewing them all and checking their daily reports. Despite his attitude, Neil turned out to be good at missioning. There was a little rivalry between him and Christopher, but after Jake explained to them that it wasn't a competition and that they could only succeed if they supported each other, they began to work well. In fact, during the first semester they did better than any of the teams in the previous two or three years. The President was delighted and began to groom Christopher for the following year.

Now that he had seen the cycle once, Jake began to look forward to the changing Japanese seasons. First there was the humidity, then the downpour, then the changing leaves, and soon it was Christmas again. Jake had been so busy he'd hardly had time to read. Instead he would listen to his 'Islam in Focus' cassettes on the train and he continued to meet Suleiyman every week in Donut Heaven to talk about their favourite topic: religion and more religion.

Bruce had lost all enthusiasm for missionary work now that he had been eclipsed by the dynamic newcomers, and Jake seemed to be always the front man organizing and taking over. Bruce felt redundant and, as he put it, 'robotic'. It was death to the mind to churn out the same stuff day after day, going over and over the same book in study circles. Bruce wanted new books, new ideas, the chance to express himself. Jake knew what he meant about reading the same old book and he tried to get him interested in some of his Islamic books, but Bruce had had religion up to the eyeballs and for all Jake's protests that Islam was more than just a religion, for the time being his mind was sealed up. There was a passage in the Qur'an that Jake had noticed a few times, about the people who refused to listen to the Message that the Prophets were trying to transmit. Then God would put a veil over their hearts.

And We put coverings over their hearts (and minds) lest they should understand the Qur'an, and deafness into their ears: when thou dost commemorate thy Lord and Him alone in the Qur'an, they turn on their backs, fleeing (from the Truth).

Another passage of the Qur'an that had really struck Jake was talking about people in the past among the 'people of the Book', which was the Qur'anic term for the Jews and Christians, who had received scriptures in earlier times. It said that they had falsified the scriptures: '*they write the books with their own hands and they say it is from God but it is not from God.*' The Qur'an itself was filled with arguments as to how it could only have come from God, how if it had come from any other source it would have been full of contradictions. It mentioned how the Prophet Muhammad had been unable to read and write and had never known any of the things he was now speaking about. There were all the scientific facts that Suleiyman's friends had told him about, and he had read a leaflet about science in the Qur'an which talked about facts in the Qur'an which were scientifically correct which appeared as part of the revelation in the seventh century and had only been discovered in the modern age. There was proof that not a word of the Qur'an had changed since it was first revealed. Suleiyman told Jake about how many Muslims had committed the Qur'an to memory from beginning to end. Allah had made it easy for people to learn and recite. Suleiyman said that if a group of Muslims were sitting reading the Qur'an together, the slightest mistake would be corrected so that all believers acted as guardians of the scripture. The evidence was mounting up, but Jake didn't want to accept it. Sometimes he would gaze at the list of articles of faith for Muslims: belief in Allah, the angels, the Hereafter, the Divine Decree, the Day of Judgment, the revealed Books and the Prophets. He believed in nearly all of them and now all he needed was to accept the truth that the Prophet Muhammad was indeed God's Messenger and the Qur'an the Book of God. But that would automatically cancel his belief in Joseph Smith because the Prophet Muhammad was supposed to be the last Prophet. He had said: 'I am *al-Aqib*, the last; there will be no other prophet after me.' One of them was wrong. Which one?

Suleiyman seemed to be convinced, the more they talked, that Jake was coming round to Islam, but that he needed a few things to be sorted out in his mind. He kept telling him that he should do his *Shahada* if he believed in Allah and His Messenger. 'That's all you need to do, *shahada*. If you believe there's no need to delay.' Jake could not convince him that it was impossible. He was in too deep with the church. He could no more give up the Mormon faith than kill himself. Jake tried to justify his resistance to accepting Islam with the thought that there had been some mistake and that another Prophet was expected because America had been somewhat isolated from God's plan. But the Qur'an was clear on this. Islam was the complete religion and the definitive religion. Nothing new was required after this.

唯邑

Kyoto, Japan

The Christmas trip that year was to Kyoto, the famous history city of Japan. The shrines and temples provided Jake with serene relief from the titanic struggle between Islam and the church that had seemed to fill his daily thoughts. The most celebrated city of Japan was packed full of sights, and the missionaries, along with their counterparts from Osaka and Hiroshima, were split into two groups to approach the city with different maps. Most of them were delighted with Kyoto. This was what Japan was supposed to look like. This was the city of temples and rock gardens and kimono-clad women and tea ceremonies. The place was packed with tourists and this meant that in going through a shrine and its precincts one couldn't linger unless one wanted to hold up the snaking line. But it was generally the case that the Japanese tourists would obediently follow the most obvious well-trodden routes through the sites while the missionaries were quite happy to wander through the uncharted areas. The site that made most of them stare in amazement was the Golden Temple. One minute they were trudging through wooded gardens on gravel paths and the next, as they turned a corner, they were confronted with a lovely golden pavilion shimmering on a lake. This was one place where people lingered and where all the cameras came out. Jake stood drinking in the view for a long time. The camera would only be able to capture a façade of the experience. He concentrated on taking in the sounds and smells of the place. The Silver Temple, by contrast, was a little disappointing, although its gardens were beautiful. It was a rather sooty grey colour and was growing quite shabby. Another favourite was the *Kiyomizu*, a beautiful, tomato-red pavilion in the pagoda style with vast, well-ordered gardens all around and a spectacular view of the city. Jake loved to conjure up the history of places. It was mind-boggling to think of the people who had

348

walked through these temple precincts and gardens down below and away in the streets of Kyoto. He imagined the place before high-rise and before neon. He had tried to master some aspects of Japanese history but the names of the dynasties didn't really stick in his head. All he knew was that there was a feudal stage when the vast majority of the people were terrified peasants, and then a time when Japan was cut off from trade and from all contact with the outside, followed by a gradual opening up. 'What about Japan and religion?' he thought. He had once had a long discussion about Prophets with Suleiyman, how God had said that He had sent Prophets and guidance to every nation, wherever they were. He knew the Middle East had been well-served, but Suleiyman was saying that it took some time for populations to migrate to the far-flung areas of the world from the central area where people were all once concentrated. He knew Islam had reached China but he knew nothing of Japan. All he knew was that Allah had guided every nation in one way or another. Suleiyman had also heard an argument that the Buddha had been a prophet and that his teachings had been distorted over time to serve people's interests as had happened to the teachings of Jesus, but the present-day teachings of Buddhism were so far removed from Islam that it seemed hard to prove. There was no mention of God in the Buddhist teachings. Jake thought that as he was in the market for religion he should not ignore Buddhism and he had put together a kind of picture of it from his visits to places like Kyoto and from discussions with Japanese people about the little remnants of Buddhism they had retained.

唯亯

Nagoya, Japan

Towards the spring and the return of the cherry blossoms, Jake pondered the verses of the Qur'an which used the concept of the rebirth of plant life, year after year, after the ground had been dead and barren, as an argument against those who disbelieved that Allah could raise men up again after death. '*Cannot He who created you the first time repeat the process once more?*' More and more Jake was being pointed in a certain direction. He remembered what George had said the year before about the brief, beautiful life of the blossoms and so of men, but with his own eyes Jake had seen evidence of rebirth. What the Mormons had always taught about the Hereafter was not all fantasy after all; but maybe the way they described it was too childish. Whatever happened, the rebirth of the blossoms confirmed Jake's faith in that other life and he was elated.

George, being the thoughtful person that he was, wrote to Jake around that time. The letter contained startling news.

I've been thinking about Japan now that it's spring over there and how I'd love to be back. I'm taking a year off working at an accounting firm before I go to college. My mother said I should get some experience to stand me a better chance of getting a job when I come out of college.

I was afraid to tell you at the time but being in Japan really had an effect on me and while I was there one of the subjects told me about Soka Gakkei and how it was the only true religion. I read as much as I could about it and while I was home in the summer I met with some converts who live in the US. To me it answered a lot of questions I'd been asking about the church and I began to move away from some of the church teachings, in fact, a lot of them.

In any case Soka Gakkei began to put pressure on and said one of the requirements was to renounce all aspects of other religions.

I felt I wasn't prepared to do that. At least being in the church helped me to live in the real world whereas what I believed inside, my own philosophy which was in line with Soka Gakkei, I felt that was truly me.

I'm glad I've told you this Jake, because I needed to tell someone else. I hoped you aren't too shocked and that you'll write back. Good luck on the mission.

Best regards,
George

'Poor George!' thought Jake. What a schizophrenic existence! To believe one thing and live by another. That must be terrible. But what about himself? There were so many similarities with his own situation. Wasn't there a message for him in this? He thought about it long into the night, George with his new convictions but tied to the church and what people expected and his mom's ambitions for him. Could a person live with himself or really be happy if he did not live by what he believed? Suleiyman was always telling him that belief in Islam required enormous commitment. It was not enough to play with the faith. If you believed it, you had to follow it. You had to come down on one side or another. The Qur'an was full of stories of people who professed to believe in the message but when it came to any hardship or time to make sacrifices they would make excuses and run. But his case was different, Jake reasoned. God would understand. He couldn't help being born Mormon, being a missionary, and now having this important job. Anyway he didn't want to jeopardize his career. It was OK for Suleiyman in a Muslim country with a Muslim family. Jake could remain a secret Muslim who believed it but also accepted some of the church teachings. He looked again at his comparison list. More and more the side of plus points for Islam was growing at the same rate as the list of doubts about LDS. So far, every question he had asked had been answered by Islam. He couldn't deny that he believed it. So was he Muslim now? Jake began to feel afraid again as if he was poised by the side of a pool, afraid to dive; and then he had an overwhelming sense of his will telling him what to do and an overwhelming urge to pray in the Muslim way. He wanted to submit himself in prayer, body and soul. It didn't matter which direction Mecca was. A magnetic force was pulling his head to the floor and he prayed properly for the first time, and felt renewed and strengthened. Before he had time to doubt what he was doing he read the instructions on how to do *shahada*. He couldn't go to the bathroom for a shower now in the middle of the night but he didn't want to delay. He wanted to commit himself. Allah would understand his intention. So he washed himself quickly at the basin, sat on the floor and began his private ceremony. He read through the list of beliefs. Yes, he believed them all. Then he said the simple word: '*La ilaha illa'Llah, Muhammad-ur-rasulu'Llah.*' He felt daring and elated, and brand new.

The next day he wondered if he'd been a bit of a fool but he had committed himself now. He couldn't wait to tell Suleiyman. He decided he would pray for the time being and try to get used to it and keep it to himself. It would be like an adventure. He had done the first prayer before sunrise while Bruce was still asleep. Somehow he would find places to do prayers number two and three. Then by the time he got home he could sneak off and pray four and five in his room or maybe the *tatami* room. No-one went in there if someone else had asked for the key. Jake kept giggling to himself on the train and repeating it over and over. 'I'm a Muslim, I'm a Muslim. I can't believe it.' He persuaded Bruce to take the lead with the witnessing, arguing that he had done it all last year and Bruce needed the practice. Plus Jake had so much else to do. He needed to hand some of it over to Bruce. Bruce, however, was in a rebellious mood.

"I'm getting pretty sick of this stuff, you know. I really am. You know James was talking about me getting a job as an English teacher. He said he could fix it up for me."

"Bruce, you can't leave your mission," said Jake horrified; and then he wondered which was more false, a Muslim masquerading as a Mormon missionary or a missionary who wanted to teach English.

"Why not?" said Bruce defiantly. "It's my life. While I was at home I talked it over with my parents and they said maybe it would be better to finish the mission and stay on afterwards but I want to throw in the towel now, Jake. I've had enough."

Jake was getting anxious. This would reflect on him. "Listen

Bruce!" he pleaded. "We have about four months to go. Can you hold out?"

"Why? What do I need to finish off for? It's not what I want to do. I see the other *gaigin* here and I think they're having a great time. So many options. We're old enough to make choices for ourselves."

He was right; his argument was, after all, what had finally compelled Jake to commit to what he believed in, but he was nervous about this rebellious talk. It was all moving too fast. "Listen, Bruce, if you throw off your mission, where will it leave you in the church? You'll never be able to get anywhere in the Mormon church. A lot of doors will be closed for you."

"Do I look like I care? There is a world out there you know, outside the Mormon church."

"You're thinking too short-term. What about later on when you have a family and you need a stable job? Then what?"

"Teaching is a stable job." Bruce was adamant and belligerent; and he was clearly fed up with missioning. So they spent the rest of the day talking it over in a coffee shop. Jake had noticed that Bruce had turned into an avid coffee drinker. His rebelliousness excited him in some ways but on the other hand filled him with dread. "Do you want me to talk it over with the President?" asked Jake.

"Yeah, come clean. That's the best way. This place makes you forget you're an adult. Yeah, we should go to the President on equal terms and tell him what we want."

"What YOU want," corrected Jake.

But talking about facing the President was one thing and facing him was another.

"Brother Bruce has been getting disillusioned with his mission, sir," Jake faltered as Bruce quaked beside him. "He's been talking about finishing early and becoming an English teacher."

"Oh, has he?" said the President, stifling a laugh. "And just who do you think is going to get you a job?"

"I have friends who are teachers, sir," said Bruce. "They said they could get me a job. There are lots of jobs." He saw the President's look of incredulity. "Apparently," he added.

"With a few phone calls," said the President, "I could inform every language school in Nagoya that you are not for hire. Brother Bruce, have you ever heard of the word commitment?"

FROM UTAH TO ETERNITY

"Yes, sir."

"Mission work is all about commitment and sacrifice. If we all left as soon as we got bored with it, we would have no mission."

"No, sir."

"Off you go and that's all I want to hear about this matter."

Bruce was dismissed.

The President looked gravely at Jake. "Brother Jake, has Brother Bruce mentioned anything like this to you before?"

"No, sir. It came right out of the blue. I mean he sometimes used to get a little bored of walking around all day but we all do from time to time. I think it might be the fact that we can't go out alone that gets to him."

"What about that weekend in the mountains? Did he seem unhappy then?"

"No, sir. I don't recall he said anything. He enjoyed that weekend." (That, at least, was true.)

"I mean we try to keep you boys entertained with the trips and the picnics. We know it's difficult but it's supposed to be a challenge. I mean it's not exactly a prison here Why did he leave it so late to decide to leave? If he hated it why didn't he say so at the beginning?"

"Maybe just now he's begun to get bored. Maybe it'll pass."

"Keep an eye on him then! Try to talk him around!"

Things got worse by Sunday, when Bruce refused to go to the sacrament meeting. The President told the others he was sick so as not to cause any consternation. He was not given any dinner that evening and on Monday morning he was ready early to go out. The President had had severe words with him.

Bruce was despondent throughout the week, but this suited Jake. They would do a few calls and then spend the day in cafés talking over Bruce's problem. Jake was glad he didn't have to work hard these days. Now he was a Muslim, he felt a hypocrite preaching something else. He still held back from telling Bruce though, since Bruce had enough problems of his own.

That Wednesday, Julie and Brian provided a sympathetic ear. James now had a class at their meeting time. But they were as taken aback as Jake had been that Bruce wanted to leave right away.

"There's no rush," said Julie. "Our company always needs people."

"What's the point in wasting time?" asked Bruce.

"It takes time to arrange anyway," said Brian. "You know, to get your contract together, your references."

"References?" said Bruce. He hadn't thought it out too well.

"Don't worry about that," said Julie. "We can get you references."

"Well, don't give the whole game away," said Brian, nudging her.

"It's OK. Listen we'll tell you what they do. If you've got no degree or anything, all you need to do is take someone else's certificate, tippex out the name and photocopy it."

Bruce laughed. "Who would do that and give up their degree?"

"I know loads of people who do it," said Julie. "I've lent people my TEFL certificate before."

"Doesn't the company get suspicious?"

"No, they haven't noticed so far. As long as they have *gaigin* to send out to the companies, they don't worry."

"It wouldn't work," said Bruce. "I'm too young to have been through college."

"It doesn't matter. We could forge that as well."

"No, I don't think we want to get young Bruce involved in all this corruption," said Brian. "All we need to do is organize some privates for you and you'll be in business before long. Who knows? You could set up your own company."

Suleiyman arrived and Jake rushed over to talk to him. He didn't know what to tell him first, so he began with Bruce's tale of woe. Predictably, Suleiyman advised it would be wise to stay on to the end of his mission.

"There's another thing," said Jake, trying to sound casual.

"Yes?"

"*As-salamu 'alaikum.*"

Suleiyman looked blank for a minute. "Oh you learned that? *Wa alaikum.*"

"Why don't you finish it?"

"When we are talking to non-Muslims we don't complete that particular greeting."

"Who says you're talking to a non-Muslim?"

Realization dawned on Suleiyman's face. "Are you saying you've taken *shahada?*"

"Yes, I made the decision last week. I did *shahada* alone. Is that valid?"

"*Subhana'Llah!*" Suleiyman was elated, and Jake had to calm him down. He didn't want the others to know that anything exceptional was going on.

"Of course, of course it's valid," Suleiyman reassured him. "It's between you and Allah but we would love to give you a party or something. Ramadan is coming up anyway."

"I've started to pray but it's a little difficult during the day. I have to keep sneaking off."

"Don't worry too much about that. Do your best, but if you can't manage, you can do them all together when you get back home."

Jake told him the story of how it happened and how he had had his conscience jolted by George's letter, also now by Bruce's decision to be true to himself. But Suleiyman advised caution and told him for the time being to conceal his true feelings but try not to get involved too much in non-Muslim rituals. "Anyway, Allah knows your intention. Think of this. You're like a new baby, all your sins washed away and you can start again. I'd like you to make *du'a* for me in your prayers, that I become a stronger Muslim and that I pass my exams and that I find a good wife."

"I'll do that," Jake said.

Bruce spent the next couple of weeks making arrangements for his escape. He was determined not to be intimidated by the President, who was treating him like a naughty schoolboy. He was given computer work to do every evening and was not allowed to watch TV. At church on Sunday he was given the menial chores to do and was not allowed to socialize with any of the visitors. The President had already contacted his Bishop back home and found out that his parents certainly hadn't sanctioned any of this behaviour. He was told to take a long, hard look at what he was doing if he didn't want to end up a disgrace to his family and his ward. It was difficult to keep the ugly atmosphere from the other missionaries. Dave and Lewis were both concerned that something was wrong but Bruce was not allowed to go into their room. They asked Jake when they had a quiet moment before the study circle.

"Is everything OK with Bruce?" asked Dave.

"So-so. He had an argument with the President."

"What about?"

"I'm not sure of the details, but the President is mad at him and he's giving him a lot more work to do as a punishment."

"What could he have done? Did he do anything when you guys were out working?"

"No, not as far as I know."

"Did he break the rules or what?" asked Lewis.

Jake was giving nothing away. When Bruce came in they went quiet and made as if they hadn't been talking about him.

"I know you guys have been talking about me," he said, flopping into his chair. "Well if you wanna know, I'm leaving the mission."

"Leaving?" Dave stammered. "But why, what happened?"

"Bruce," said Jake. "You wanna make it worse?"

Bruce didn't care. "It was nothing dramatic, OK? Just simply being here in Japan. I wanna be an English teacher and live here on my own. I don't wanna be part of some big organization that controls my every move."

"It's only a few more months," said Lewis.

"That's what everyone keeps saying," said Bruce in exasperation. "But it's not the time. It's the idea. Why should I spend my time doing something I don't wanna do?"

"We all have to do things we don't like from time to time," said Dave, "but if you want benefits you have to put up with it."

"What benefits?" asked Bruce.

"I don't know. Career prospects?"

"I want to major in psychology. How can this help?"

"Mission work could probably teach you a lot about psychology," Lewis remarked, logically enough.

"Yeah, but it's not what Dave is talking about. He's talking about that whole church hierarchy thing. I'm not into that, so it doesn't matter."

They knew he'd met a Japanese girl from the time he'd brought her to church.

"Is it the girl?" asked Dave tentatively.

"That's part of it," said Bruce, "but that's not all. I wanna choose how I spend my time and who I spend it with and I wanna do a job I like where I can use my brain."

There was no arguing with him, so they fell silent, and waited for the first-years.

The President, meanwhile, was putting a lot of pressure on Jake to take responsibility for Bruce and to keep tabs on him and report back to the President on what he said and did during the day. Jake hated this procedure of missionaries reporting on each other one by one. Why were the mission authorities so paranoid? Why was the church so regimented? It was claustrophobic. One day he suggested to the President that if the rules were relaxed a little, people might not feel so compelled to rebel but the President said that Bruce's case was very unusual and the missionaries were all at a very impressionable age and had to receive guidance. This was the age when they began to ask questions and go off in their own directions. Didn't Jake just know it! This was why they had all these study circles and 'heart-to-hearts', as he called them, to voice their concerns. And the President kept harping on about how they went out of their way to organize trips and entertainment for the missionaries. He made them feel as though Bruce was ungrateful.

Jake had other concerns as he began to prepare for Ramadan. He read as much as he could about it. It looked difficult. No food or drink at all, including gum, from just before the break of dawn until a few minutes after sunset. Suleiyman had encouraged him and he was determined to try. For him it was like a test of endurance and he jumped at the chance to put his new faith into practice. Suleiyman had given him a timetable with the times of prayers and the start and finish times for the fast. Meanwhile, the brothers in the hostel were dying for him to come and visit to hear about his conversion. The problem was how to get a night off. Now that he was team leader, Jake had a bit more freedom and a bit more trust, but the President would probably need him to watch over Bruce. Jake had an idea, and invented a Japanese language seminar. He said that all the people who took the exam had received letters inviting them to a special language seminar at the university to talk about further exams, courses and correspondence courses for overseas students. The President was so preoccupied he didn't even listen properly and gave Jake permission. He could even take the car. Of course there was no question of Bruce going with him and none of the others had taken the exam so the story would probably be OK. That gave Jake a couple of hours at the hostel. He arranged it for the third day of Ramadan.

The fasting began and Jake was aware of it every minute. He'd never thought about food and drink so much before. It was easy to skip breakfast in the Ericson household because mornings were so chaotic, but what would he do at dinner? He could maybe drop it in his lap like anorexics did, thought Jake to himself. No, he would have to find a permanent excuse to skip dinner at the usual time and delay it until after sunset which would be about 7:30 or 8 o'clock. He was parched by lunchtime and his stomach was groaning, but his mind was working overtime on how to keep his new practice from Bruce. The first day he slipped his sandwiches into his pocket. Then that evening, at dinner, he feigned sickness and went up to lie on his bed. The day had gone fairly easily except for a nagging headache, but the last half hour was the worst. At last, when he was sure it was sunset, he crammed his sandwiches into his mouth and filled up his cup from the sink over and over with water. The longed-for food and drink were only really wonderful on the first mouthful and after that it was as if he'd never been hungry. His stomach seemed to have shrunk. The difference in the heart though was really noticeable. It felt light and in touch with the spiritual side of things. Fasting made you detached, as you went into a dream-like state where physical things didn't matter so much. But this was not enough food, Jake decided, and he staged a partial recovery, saying yes, he could probably manage some bread and a little bowl of soup. It was recommended in the *Sunna* of the Prophet Muhammad to eat a light meal before dawn to prepare for the fast. It was said to be full of blessings, so before bed that night Jake managed to raid the refrigerator for his *Suhur* meal. He felt like those kids in the schoolboy adventure stories getting up in the middle of the night for a feast. Jake sat up in bed munching his cheese and crackers, watching the greenish light playing on the carpet. He felt in touch with the past, with his body, and with the world. Millions of believers all over the world did this the same way and they had always done it this way, for 1400 years. Even before Islam people had been commanded by God to fast because it taught such valuable lessons. He felt the same way when he prayed. It was amazing that so many people for so long had done these same movements and said these same words. The practice was truly timeless. At any one time, he wondered, how many people were facing Mecca and echoing the same words? Probably every second, someone was saying, '*Allahu Akbar*' - 'God is Most Great' or '*Bismillahi'r-Rahmani'r-Rahim*' - 'In the name of God, most Gracious, most Merciful.' All the time, somewhere in the world, the Qur'an was being read.

The next day Jake had a brainwave. He told the President that he and Bruce should work longer hours every day to encourage Bruce to work harder on his mission. Maybe that way they could catch more businessmen at home and would get more people interested. Maybe Bruce would feel happier about it if he thought he had the responsibility to talk to the businessmen. The President liked the idea. Jake knew Bruce would hate it, however, so when he told Bruce he had to make out that the President had made the new rule to continue his punishment. Bruce couldn't understand why Jake had been so reluctant to go into cafés these past couple of days and seemed to be dragging him on more calls than ever. He thought Jake was trying to impress the President and play by the hierarchy's rules again. Jake decided it was time to take a leaf out of Bruce's book and be honest.

"Have you noticed anything unusual about me?" he asked. "In the last few days?"

"Yeah, I've noticed you've been a real pain, doing all the President's running."

Jake was offended. "I was just trying to do my job. That's all. It's difficult with all the pressure I've had on me. I've been going through a lot lately, Bruce. Haven't you noticed? There's a lot weighing on my mind."

"Sure, I've noticed you've had more work to do this year but that's OK. You can go back and say you had a good mission."

"A good mission?" Jake laughed ironically. "If you mean changing your religion means you had a good mission."

"What are you talking about?"

"This is gonna sound weird but I decided to become a Muslim." It was out at last, to someone else other than Suleiyman. For Jake it was good news and he was bursting to share it, but he feared the reactions of people. The thought of his family made his heart stop, but he would have to tell them sooner or later.

Bruce was still trying to get his head around the idea. "I mean you said you were interested and all that, but to join them? That's a little crazy."

"How is it different from what you're doing?" Jake asked.

Bruce thought for some time and admitted Jake was right in a way.

"Look what you're doing," said Jake. "You've lost your faith. Remember the Temple? It *was* like something out of a theme park. You were right. Now you wanna ditch it and do something else in line with your own ideas."

"I wouldn't say I'd lost my faith, entirely. I wouldn't say I believed in it a hundred percent either, but ..."

"Then what do you believe?"

"I just don't think it has to be such a big part of life, that's all. I mean spending all your time trying to convince people of religion and organizing your whole life round what the church tells you."

"So you want to be a part-time LDS?"

"Yeah I guess so. I believe in God, OK? I believe in Jesus. If I need something I pray for it. I get on with my life."

"But how are you gonna choose what's the right way to lead your life?"

"Lots of things. My upbringing. My ideas. My friends."

"How do people know, though, what's right? They're just people."

'They're all we've got, so we make the best of it."

"We have revelation."

"Yes, I do know that, Jake. I am a missionary too. Anyway, you said you've changed your religion."

"Yes, but I still believe in revelation. I just believe the Qur'an is the revelation. I believe Islam is the religion that teaches us how to live, that teaches God's guidance. It's not even a change as such. It's more of a refinement of what I already knew, picking out the things that were right and correcting the mistakes."

"I doubt your parents will see it that way," said Bruce.

They discussed Jake's change of heart for a while and then moved on to more practical matters.

"So what are you gonna do now?" asked Bruce.

"I'll finish my mission and then go back to the States and see about getting into college. There are other Muslim converts in the US. I might try to find out about a group."

"Your parents will think you've gone crazy."

"Yeah, maybe I will put off telling them for a while, until I get used to it and get home and talk to them properly."

"How can you go on with your mission though, Jake? You can't go around preaching something you don't believe in."

"I can't quit in the middle of my mission."

"Why not? I'm quitting."

"C'mon, Bruce. Isn't that all just bravado?"

"No, it is not bravado. I'm serious. I wanna show them they can't control our lives like this, treat us like little kids."

"Stay, Bruce, for my sake!" pleaded Jake.

"Leave, Jake, for my sake!" he retorted.

Jake had to laugh. It was ludicrous keeping up a façade but it was difficult to convert to another religion. You couldn't be too hasty or your whole life could be jeopardized. You could lose your family.

Bruce reminded Jake of the first Mormons, how they had often had to cut ties with their families and leave their homes to emigrate to the US and join the pilgrim trail to Utah.

Jake gazed at Bruce for a moment, surprised at his using religious teachings to illustrate a point after he'd just said religion was marginal in his life.

Jake thought about the theme at night when he was studying his books. The first Muslims had also been required to go against family, tribe, tradition for what they believed in. It was no joke. He was beginning to see what a serious decision he'd made. He would wait until his faith was stronger.

There was a tense moment the following evening when Christopher asked the President if he could go along to the language seminar. Christopher and Neil had already become friendly with the President and knew how to get around him. Jake resented it because he had never tried to push himself forward during the first year. He had always deferred to Ellis' authority. He also knew that given the choice, missionaries should travel in pairs. The President said that he didn't see why Christopher couldn't go along but Jake insisted that it was specifically for people who had done the exam. He didn't relax until he was in the car on his way to the hostel.

A warm, brotherly reception was waiting for him at the hostel, a combination of informality and spiritual seriousness. When the time for *Iftar* came at sunset they ate dates and drank milk, each saying his private prayer. Then they performed the sunset prayer together.

"This is the first prayer you will do with your brothers in Islam," the Libyan, Sayyid, announced, "and we pray, *Insha-Allah,* that it will be the first of many." Jake had been practicing his prayers from the diagrams in his book and reading transliterated Arabic from a piece of paper. For this prayer Sayyid, who was acting as *Imam,* said the whole thing out loud for Jake's benefit. The experience of praying with others was completely different. Jake felt self-conscious of his mistakes and aware of his surroundings, but he felt very close to the brothers as they all did the movements in unison. Just a few short weeks ago, Jake had been a puzzled onlooker. Now he knew what it was all about because he felt it. He felt sure that God was hearing him. The emotion and joy in the hearts of the Muslims was palpable, in the way they prayed, the way they looked at Jake and the tenderness and concern with which they spoke to him.

They decided to have their celebration meal first since Jake had already done his own private *shahada* ceremony, and then he would read it again formally, partly for the benefit of the brothers, and so that he would have witnesses. The brothers had brought their families in for the occasion and the women sat eating on the other side of the room all swathed in white. The meal was a mixture of all the cultures present, and they ate quietly because they were hungry after the day's fasting. One Malaysian complained of a headache from lack of coffee during the day and the others joked that maybe they should follow the Mormons' example and give it up.

One of the quieter Malaysian students announced that this was the first time he had personally known someone as they were converting to Islam and that it was the most emotional day of his life, especially as it was in Ramadan.

"You see," said a Lebanese brother. "You are not like us. We were born Muslims. We had no choice. You chose Islam so your reward will be much greater."

Jake was embarrassed but flattered. He felt special and pleased with himself that he had become convinced of Islam. He thought about when people converted to the church. There was the same excitement and congratulations but it was somehow a little formal, maybe a little cold. Plus, conversions were so common it took some of the novelty away. He had always envied converts though, for their chance to start off all afresh with their own convictions. Now he knew exactly what it felt like. It was a deep feeling of success.

When the meal had been cleared away, Sayyid took Jake's hand and led him to the prayer area. They all sat in a circle with the women sitting excitedly on the edge and the children, unusually quiet, sensing the reverence of the occasion.

Sayyid began his short speech. He had remarked at the tendency of Arabs to talk too long so he decided to keep to the point.

"*Al- hamdu li'Llah,* our brother has decided to embrace Islam. We are all here to witness him saying the *shahada.* We ask Allah, *subhanahu wa ta'ala,* to guide him and make his faith strong and to keep us all in the straight path. Amen."

He then asked Jake to repeat the words of the *shahada* after him, quite slowly, and then he repeated them in translation. 'I bear witness that there is no deity except Allah and I bear witness that Muhammad is the Messenger of Allah.'

Then everyone sighed deeply with tears in their eyes and the brothers made a line to embrace Jake as though he were a long-lost cousin. They presented him with a little box containing a prayer rug, a personal copy of the Holy Qur'an with translation and notes in English, a compass and a little skull-cap. They reminded him that the only thing he needed in life was the Qur'an, and they told him to keep it close to him always in the physical as well as the metaphorical sense.

The conversation turned to names. They explained how it was sometimes the case that a person took on a new name on conversion, especially if his old name was associated with another religion. Jake was racking his brains for a suitable name that he liked when Sayyid spoke up. "I have a suggestion for you. I think you may like it. It is Yusuf." Yusuf was the Arabic version for Joseph, and it seemed appropriate to take the name of the real Prophet Joseph. Jake liked the idea because Sayyid had chosen it for him, so he accepted it with thanks. It was as if Sayyid had thought of that name before and held in store in the hope that Jake would become Muslim.

"So when will you be leaving?" asked the Salih, the Syrian.

"Well, the mission finishes in the summer so I guess I'll wait until then."

"Brother, you can't continue in the church now you are Muslim."

Sayyid cut in. "I think our brother Yusuf needs time. This is something very big and very important for him. There is no need to rush."

"Yes," said Suleiyman. "The important thing is to do your prayers and study Qur'an and *Sunna* as much as you can and *masha-Allah,* you've managed to fast already so try your best to keep it up."

Jake had to rush to be back in time so he thanked them all again and promised to try and visit them soon.

'How to come back down to the real world!' he thought as he drove back. From an atmosphere of spiritual triumph and warmth where he had been the centre of attention, back to the reality of the Ericson house. Now only his room felt like an Islamic sanctuary amidst the Mormons. The experience at the hostel had been valuable because it made him feel like a proper, accredited Muslim, recognized at last by his peers. How was he going to endure the next few months? He had to have a story ready about the seminar and he asked Suleiyman for a prospectus from the university to show to the Ericsons.

Mrs Ericson was sitting at the kitchen table when he came in.

"My, you look very pleased with yourself. Top of the class, huh?"

Jake smiled self-consciously.

"You must be ravenous. Help yourself from the refrigerator!"

"Oh, thanks, but I found a place to eat on the way." He couldn't have eaten another bite.

Even Sam commented on Jake's demeanour. "What happened? Your face has gone all shiny."

"Shiny?" He put his hand to his cheek. On the way upstairs he examined his reflection in the hall mirror. It was true. His face was glowing. No wonder! He had just experienced the key moment of his life. He climbed the stairs going over it all. He wanted to go to his room and think about what had happened and go over and over it in his mind. The noise of the TV faded. It was grating on his nerves and even the pictures on the stairs now annoyed him. The scenarios of white-skinned angels visiting, of Christ supposedly descending to the Nephites, ancient tribes sailing the oceans, all painted in the classical style with bold colours and definable, realistic figures. They all looked incongruous to him now. He didn't want pictures or images any more. He wanted words on the page and feelings in the heart. That's what studying the Qur'an did for him these nights of Ramadan. As he came to his room he saw poor Bruce through the office window, staring dejectedly at the computer. Bruce looked up as he came in, somewhat cheered by human contact.

"Still here? Tough, huh?"

"Yeah, well. I don't wanna sit downstairs with those guys. How was your dinner? You look like you ate well. That fasting getting to you, huh?"

"We should go to the room. This place may be bugged."

Paranoia had started to set in the more Jake learned about the administration's obsession with keeping tabs on its members.

"If anywhere's bugged, it's the bedrooms," said Bruce.

"You thought of that too? So I'm not just being paranoid!"

"It crossed my mind but I couldn't care less. I don't have anything to hide now."

"Lucky you!" said Jake. He related to Bruce the evening's events in a hushed voice. Bruce seemed impressed with how the Muslims had welcomed and accepted him. Now he realized Jake was totally serious he wanted to know more about the details of how to be a Muslim and enjoyed hearing about the prayers and the fasting. To him it sounded like a tough and demanding religion, and he had thought the Mormons were pretty tough.

"So you've swapped one set of rules for another!" he said.

"The rules aren't supposed to be there to make life difficult. They're to help you be a better person, same as the 'Word of Wisdom'. If you want a healthy body you avoid alcohol and tobacco. Also pork for us. (He felt it strange that he was already saying 'us' not 'them'.) If you want good relationships you avoid gossiping, backbiting, gambling and having sex outside of marriage. Say, if you want a strong economy you avoid interest and monopolies and gambling comes in there too. There's no cheating allowed either, so you see it's pretty logical."

"I'd rather find out for myself, instead of having someone always tell me do this, don't do that. No, I wanna find out myself and if I make mistakes, I'll learn."

"But at the same time you could hurt other people and you wouldn't even know it. You wouldn't know until it was too late. Anyway, you can never really be free from someone telling you what you can and can't do. Well, if anyone's going to tell me I'd rather it was God."

"I thought you called Him Allah?"

"Allah, yes, but I say 'God' out of habit."

"By the way," said Bruce. "Tomorrow's my last working day."

"You what?"

"I'm leaving on Sunday."

"Bruce, you can't just drop this bombshell."

'I've made up my mind. I'm as much use as a dog on this mission. Come with me, Jake! You don't believe any more. You can come and stay with us. I'll take care of you until I make enough money."

Jake brushed his pleas aside. "Have you told your parents?"

"Nope!"

"Have you told the President?"

"Nope!"

"You can't just leave like that. What about your commitments?"

"The church authorities sent me on this mission. No-one asked me about it. So I'm under no obligation."

Jake was becoming exasperated with Bruce's offhand manner. "I don't think you've thought this over, Bruce," he began.

"Would you be saying that if I'd decided to stay? You're only concerned about your own neck. Look, I'm pleased for you, being a Muslim. It seems to have made you really happy. So do the right thing. Give up your mission! You can explain it properly if you want to and then we're outta here."

The confusion of everything coming upon him so suddenly overwhelmed Jake and he burst into tears.

"Ah, no, c'mon Jake. I'm sorry. I didn't wanna upset you."

"It's just all so fast. I'm happy. I really am, but I'm also scared about my parents and everything, everyone back home. They won't understand, I know it. They'll be so upset with me. They'll think I'm doing something un-American."

"OK, OK, you need time. Then I'll be the bad guy. I'll say you tried to persuade me to stay but I wouldn't have it. Whatever happens, Jake, I've made up my mind. I've never been so sure about anything before. The thought of staying here actually makes me sick."

"You're lucky," sniffed Jake, beginning to cheer up. "You've got some guts. I feel like a coward."

"A coward? I don't think so. It takes guts to change your religion or your politics or anything."

Jake sniffed and nodded his head. "Remember George?"

"Yeah."

"He started getting into that *Soka Gakkei* group while he was here but he decided to stay. He wanted to keep it to himself and not mess up his mission."

"I knew there was something different about him. He used to study a lot and he was always talking about Zen or something in Japanese philosophy. But this is what I think. It's down to the individual to go with what they believe in, whatever it is. Too many people narrow their lives down by not following their gut feelings or doing what they wanna do. It's always duty first, country first or career first, and they might wanna go around the world on a motorbike."

Jake looked steadily at Bruce, sure now that he was serious. "I'm gonna miss you, Bruce," he said.

"Then come with me!"

"I can't."

"OK, I won't push you."

Jake wanted to read something to calm his soul and he read a verse from the Qur'an that he had gone over before. It had been revealed when the Prophet was going through some difficult times, and it was to bring him solace and reassurance.

Have We not expanded for thee thy breast?-
And removed from thee thy burden
the which did gall thy back?-
And raised high the esteem (in which) thou (art held)?
So, verily, with every difficulty, there is relief:
Verily, with every difficulty there is relief.
Therefore, when thou art free (from thine immediate task), still
labour hard,
And to thy Lord turn (all) thy attention.

It was true, thought Jake. There was always relief after difficult times. If there were no difficult times the good times wouldn't seem so intense. A song that he remembered Bruce used to play kept repeating itself in his head. 'Should I stay or should I go?' was the refrain.

That Sunday in church was a very tense time for Jake. Bruce hadn't spoken to the President about his intentions but his bag lay packed under his bed. As Jake listened to the words of the service he would change them in his head to bring them more in line with Islam. If the Bishop or President said, 'through Jesus Christ', he would murmur to himself, 'In the name of Allah'. If they said, 'Jesus, son of God', he would say, 'Jesus, son of Mary'. He had been formulating his study circles to be as neutral as possible during the past few weeks, but the new missionaries were always coming up with new points that he found difficult to repeat because they went against his beliefs. A couple of times, to his pleasure, he asked Dave to lead the circle in his place so that people wouldn't get bored with the same face, as he said. For the newcomers there were the usual testimonies from members of the church who had recently joined, which came during the main service. They would explain their reasons, and now Jake found, ironically, that he could identify with them more. He didn't agree with them, but he understood their emotions. Sometimes he felt the urge to speak out and correct something that was wrong. He longed to talk about Islam to the whole congregation. As Suleiyman always said, the non-Muslims had no idea what they were missing. Most of the Mormon testimonies were based on scenarios of the wayward sinner leading a hopeless, empty life who suddenly finds the way, but Jake realized that his situation had been nothing like that. He could never have described himself as having led a sinful life. The church so far had kept him from the worst pitfalls of youth. He had always tried not to lie or cheat. He had always tried to treat his parents well. His life before had been far from empty and hopeless. He had been a man with a mission, literally. He didn't like these corny hard-luck stories. 'My life was so desolate before I found the church' seemed to be all they had to say.

The man who had been speaking was one of Christopher's catches. He ran his own café-bar in Sakae and they were wondering what he was going to do with it. The café doubled as an art-gallery where he displayed the work of his friends, so the Bishop had been trying to help him devise a business plan to filter out the alcohol from his business in measured stages. He sat down looking pleased with himself. As always, such testimonies set the newcomers thinking. Before the next person could begin, Bruce stood up. He scanned the congregation and noted the President and the Bishop's look of dismay. He began his speech.

'We hear a lot about how people convert to the church. That's good because they're wonderful stories, but we don't very often hear of peoples' reasons for leaving and I believe in order to be honest with ourselves we should ...'

There was a commotion as the Bishop stood up and explained in Japanese that this was not one of the scheduled speakers and that he could have his say some other time. Then there was a rather embarrassing scene as the President, helped by Mark and Neil almost forcibly hustled Bruce from the platform as he protested. "Why won't you let me explain at least? It could help people." Bruce was locked into one of the study rooms supervised by Mark until the end of the service, and then the President took Jake with him and stormed in to confront Bruce.

"You know very well," he boomed, "that you cannot just jump up like that without permission and embarrass us all in front of the whole congregation."

"I just wanted to be honest," said Bruce.

"This is not the time to blurt out all your grievances against the church. If you have something to discuss, there are plenty of opportunities either with myself or one of the other brothers."

"I feel that no-one is listening to me," said Bruce.

"I've heard your problem and I've dealt with it."

"Exactly. You totally ignored the problem and punished me."

"I will not have this kind of back talk."

"You won't. My bag is ready. I can have my room vacated within the hour."

The President swung around to face Jake. "Do you know anything about this, Brother Jake?"

"No, sir. It's come as a complete shock."

"Mark, Neil!" he commanded. "Go to Bruce's room and confiscate his things. I want them put in the office cabinet and locked."

Bruce smirked. "This is so childish," he said.

"You'll see how childish it is. You will stay here now until I have time to deal with you."

During the lunch hour before the afternoon's activities, Gregor came over anxiously to Jake.

"Did Bruce tell the President about the weekend?"

"No, that's OK," Jake assured him. "He didn't mention that at all."

Gregor was relieved. "So, what is this all about?"

"All it is, as far as I know, is that Bruce has had enough of the mission. He wants to leave and be an English teacher."

"Couldn't he do that after the mission?"

"He insists he has to do it now. He doesn't want to continue with the mission. He doesn't feel like it has any benefit for him."

"But he's not qualified to teach. He hasn't even been to college."

"His friends have found him some private conversation students, apparently."

"He doesn't know what he's gettng into. He won't last five minutes on his own. He'll change his mind."

"He sounds pretty serious about it."

"I always thought that guy had no sense."

Jake thought that was a little unfair. Gregor had seemed to think highly of Bruce before.

Everyone seemed to be rather on edge that afternoon, listening for scraps of information about the Bruce saga, but the President was determined to allow the day to go on as normal and not to allow Bruce's outburst to disrupt it. Jake had to fend off questions from the men in the study circle and he just said that Brother Bruce had some problems to sort out and urged them to continue with the matter in hand.

"Do you think the church tolerates people questioning or expressing their doubts?" asked Lewis.

"Sure," said Jake. "We all have questions, but in the proper time and place." He was aware that he was speaking like a school-master. "This circle, for example, is an opportunity for people to put forward their questions about whatever text we happen to be looking at."

"Yeah, sometimes you have trouble practicing some aspect of the Doctrines and Covenants," said Dave, "say dating or being bullied by people at school, and then you can talk about it here."

Lewis seemed satisfied with that answer. He said it was impor-tant for new members to realize that questions were not taboo.

Jake thought about that. Maybe he should have been more searching about asking questions first before he went ahead and started doing all that finding out for himself. But what they talked about in the church seemed so basic compared to what he had been studying about Islam. He needed more in-depth answers, not kid's stuff.

Bruce was still stuck in the study room. He was amusing him-self watching promotional videos. It seemed the President was trying to humiliate him, but knowing Bruce, that would only make him more determined.

After the study sessions, the President released him and took him back to the house. Now he made no pretense of keeping the events from the rest of the house. Mrs Ericson was standing anx-iously in the living room and Sam was standing excitedly, watching. The President was now a prison warder and Mark and Neil were his henchmen. He pushed Bruce roughly into the kitchen.

"Where are your clothes?"

"I packed them."

"Where? Where is your suitcase?"

"I'll go and get it."

"No, you stay here! Where is it?"

"Under my bed."

"Mark, Neil! Go and get it and lock it in the office."

"We looked sir. We couldn't find it."

"Look again!" They scurried off followed by Sam who was enjoying the drama.

"Can I call my parents?" asked Bruce.

"Not now."

"They're expecting my call. I just want to tell them everything's OK"

"Why? Have you told them you're leaving?"

"Yes, sir. I said I may be leaving."

"Call them and be quick about it."

Bruce went to the phone and the President went to the living room to try and calm down. Jake didn't know what to do so he just sat in the kitchen waiting for the next move. Mrs Ericson busied herself with the dinner. Jake could have sworn Bruce was speaking Japanese, but then he heard English.

Mark and Neil didn't come down for ages and when they did they looked sheepish. "No bag, sir." they told the President. "He's lying, sir. We put some of his things in the office but there's no suitcase."

Bruce didn't look up from the phone despite the President's gestures for him to get a move on. He seemed to be having a heart-to-heart so the President went back into the living room. Then there was a ring at the door. "That'll be my taxi," said Bruce cheerily. Before the President could move he had slipped his suitcase out from the hall cupboard and he was out the door. "Keep in touch!" he shouted, bounding into the taxi.

"Shall we follow him sir?" asked Mark, like a police sergeant.

"Leave him. Leave him," said the President. "I didn't realize he was so devious. He'll be back. You wait. Brother Jake, you will have no more contact with Bruce, if he tries to call you or have you get together the rest of his things. Do you understand me?"

"Yes sir."

Despite the shock Jake found the whole affair quite exciting. The daring of it! Just to take off like that in a taxi. If nothing else,

Bruce had shown them. He had begun to feel like it was himself pitted against all of them. As Bruce's partner and ally he felt he almost owed it to him, aside from the fact that he was, in his own right, no longer able to call himself one of them. Jake had missed basketball and he felt hemmed in as though he needed some exercise, so he asked the President if he could sit out on the patio to get some air. The President agreed. He was weary and slightly embarrassed because he had been made to look foolish. Jake felt a little sorry for him. The older man went up to the office to make some calls, 'to see if he could sort this thing out', as he put it.

Jake was soon joined on the patio by Sam as he sat gazing at the trees over the garden wall. The same pink landscape as last year. It was a wonderful time to start something new. Sam wanted to practice his catching and Jake was glad of the exercise. Also Sam wanted to be filled in on the gossip about Bruce.

"Where did Bruce go?"

"I'm not even sure myself, but he's been feeling stressed lately. He needed to get away and have some time to himself."

"I wanted to run away once," said Sam.

Jake smiled. "Did you?"

"Well, almost," said Sam coyly. "I got my bag and I told mom I was going camping in the park because I was mad at everyone and she said go after your dinner and then after dinner it was bedtime."

"There's plenty of time to leave when you're older, Sam. Before you know it Phil will be on his mission and then you'll be off on yours."

"My big brother has already been on a mission."

"Yes, well. The time goes quickly. You'd be surprised, so enjoy yourself for the time being."

They pitched for a while in silence.

"Was Bruce mad at us?"

"Oh no, he liked you. It was the job. He found it very hard work."

"Does he like my dad?"

"I think he likes your dad. He respects him a lot but just now he feels upset with him because your dad doesn't want him to go and he wants to go."

"Sometimes I get mad at my dad."

"I get mad at my dad too."

"Oh, yeah. You have a dad back home." The idea seemed novel to Sam who saw his father as the universal father of all Mormon boys, who had so many missionaries come and go under his guidance.

"Will Bruce come back?"

"Maybe. I hope so."

"I hope so, too."

Had he seen through Sam's eyes, Jake would probably have been even firmer in his decision to finish his mission. The poor boy felt rejected enough, but instead events took him over and the scandal of Bruce's rebellion was nothing compared to the new storm brewing.

Jake was summoned up to the office and he was steeling himself for another showdown over Bruce. Instead he was met by the President holding aloft Jake's copy of the Qur'an.

"Will you tell me what in God's name this was doing in your room?"

The way he said 'this' sounded as if he regarded it as something polluting, and Jake was insulted. He didn't like the way the President was brandishing it.

"It's the Qur'an," said Jake, taking it from him.

"I know it's the Koran. I want to know what it was doing in your room. I found it here on my desk with all these books and cassettes. Are these Bruce's things?"

For a split second Jake was tempted to foist the blame onto Bruce. It would have been easier, but instead Jake said. "No, they're mine."

"What do you want with all these?"

"I've been reading them, sir."

"But why? Do you have a Moslem subject you're working with? I mean there are just piles of books here."

"I've been reading a lot about Islam and then I decided to become a Muslim and now I am one, sir, a Muslim." It wasn't as difficult to say as he had feared. It was so liberating to be able to say that. Now the President knew, everyone would know. He didn't care. The news was out in these few words. Jake suddenly wanted to giggle but he kept his face solemn.

"Brother Jake, I've had a very difficult time these past few weeks with Brother Bruce. I don't think I can handle any more jokes."

"I'm really serious, sir. I know it sounds unbelievable but it happened. I've been thinking about it since last spring and I made the decision just this April. I'm sorry I didn't tell you. I was afraid to tell you. I figured you'd think I'd gone crazy or something."

"You're right. What could have possessed you? Is Brother Bruce Moslem too?" He seemed to have difficulty even saying the word, as if it disgusted him.

"Oh, no. That was nothing to do with him. No, it was just me. I suppose you could call it my spiritual journey."

"I'm not in the mood for philosophy. All I can think is that something or someone has gotten a hold of you and filled your head with some kind of nonsense. What is with you two?"

Now the big confession was out, he might as well tell the whole story. "I met an Indonesian Muslim by chance who started ..."

"I knew it," said the President appearing calmer, before Jake could finish. "I knew there had to be someone involved for you to just flip like this. You've always been a very sensible, reliable person. Who is this Moslem?"

"It was a chance meeting, I swear. We were in Donut Heaven in Sakae having lunch and Suleiyman comes and introduces himself. Said he recognized me from the Japanese exam."

"Oh yes, very clever," said the President knowingly. "Chance meeting? Yes, classic stuff."

Jake was lost. "Excuse me?"

"Oh, yes. This is how these people get their new recruits. Just coming up like this, introducing themselves with a 'Don't I know you from somewhere?' Maybe a little flattery and then I suppose he invited you to sit with him, huh?"

"I can't remember. Maybe we asked him and then we just got talking and somehow the subject got onto religion."

"Oh, yes, well, of course. That was his whole purpose."

"I think it was actually me who brought up religion first, telling him about my mission and everything. I even thought of him as a possible subject and then he told me about his own religion, but he wasn't pushy at all."

"Well, that's it. They're too clever for that. They let the initiative come from you. 'Oh, so you're a missionary!' I suppose he didn't know anything about it, huh? Never heard of our church?"

"Oh, he knew a lot about missionaries because they have them over there, but he'd never heard of Mormons."

"Don't you believe it! They probably have a file this thick on Mormons."

"They don't have a mission or anything, sir. It's just a bunch of guys from different countries, mostly students."

"Well, that's how they present themselves so that an unsuspecting person like yourself won't think anything of it. Don't you see? A nice friendly bunch of guys invite you for a talk, maybe a meal, and then the pressure starts. Huh? Was it like that?" Jake's face began to fall as the President went on parodying the Muslims.

"Why aren't you Moslem? Do you know about Islam?"

Jake hated the way the President was trying to poison the lovely image he had of the Muslims which was so special to him, as if they were a group of conniving, manipulative people waiting to snatch his soul. But it was true they had given him that big dinner and made a big fuss of him and told him about Islam. How did the President know all this?"

The President was waiting for an answer. "Well? Was it like that?"

"I guess so. A little. They invited me to dinner once and they told me something about Islam but I'd been reading a lot before that. But Suleiyman never put pressure on me. Really. He just gave me the books and he just left me to read them in my own time. In fact I remember I had been having a discussion with him one time in Donut Heaven and he took a copy of the *Book of Mormon* and he gave me the Qur'an to look at."

"You seem to have spent a lot of time in Donut Heaven."

"Well, that was our meeting place on Wednesday lunchtimes, but we only spent an hour. That was where we met the Brits."

"The Brits?"

"Yeah, we met this guy James on the train. At first Ellis wouldn't sit with him on the train because it was against the rules but he just used to say 'hi' to him on the platform. Anyway after training week Bruce wanted to make friends so we used to talk and then we would go to Donut Heaven for lunch when we were working in Sakae and James introduced us to the other Brits, Julie and Brian, and that's where Bruce got the idea for being an English teacher.

377

They got to be good friends."

"Did they know who you were?"

"Of course. We told them we were Mormon missionaries but they were just polite about it. I don't think they were that much into religion."

The President saw light dawning. "I think I'm beginning to get the picture. They must have tipped off this Suleiyman character to come and introduce himself."

"They didn't even know Suleiyman."

"Well that's what they told you. Jake, you are naive."

Soon the President had everyone implicated in this elaborate plot against the integrity of Jake's mission, but he was beginning to sow doubts in Jake's mind. Maybe it had been too much of a coincidence, Suleiyman turning up like that. But what possible motive would Suleiyman have in jeopardizing Jake's mission? He had no particular personal gain to make in introducing Jake to Islam. He was overjoyed of course that he was a Muslim but he had nothing to gain, in this life, anyway. Everything to gain in the next.

"Not a word of this to anyone, Jake. Do you hear me? I'll be keeping you here with me in the office tomorrow and we'll get to the bottom of this. Now, don't worry. I know this seems serious to you now but you'll probably look back on it as a little spring madness. You see what happens when you break the rules? Didn't we tell you the do's and don'ts? It was for your own benefit. Now you see what it's led to?"

The President seemed to look upon Jake's conversion as a disaster.

"C'mon then. We'll go and have dinner."

"I have to wait, sir."

"No that's OK. We won't discuss a word of this with the others or Bruce's business for that matter."

"I'm fasting sir. This is Ramadan."

The President began to guffaw. "Oh ho, you really are taking this thing seriously. Ramadan? I don't know." He shook his head. "Now come on and eat."

"Nothing will persuade me to eat or drink before sunset." Jake was amazed at the power of his words and his steely demeanour.

The President was subdued by his resolute stance. "Have it

your own way, then." But then he turned around spitefully. "You don't come down until tomorrow morning. Do you understand?" Jake nodded. This was cruelty.

He went into his room and listened for the President's footsteps retreating. When all was clear he went to fetch his precious books from the office. The way the President had spoken about them and manhandled them made him even more protective of them. The books had been his friends over the last few months. But why had he been so careless as to leave them lying around like that? He should have been more careful, then the President would never have found out. Still, it was probably meant to be this way. The choice of whether to confess or not had been taken out of his hands. Maybe it was for the best. He locked the books up in his suitcase and put it under Bruce's bed, keeping just one copy of the Holy Qur'an to peruse during his lonely vigil. The page he opened read *Avoid suspicion because in some cases suspicion is a sin*. What could it mean? He currently regarded every verse of the Qur'an as a direct message to him, Allah's answer to his questions or prayers because there had been some remarkable occasions, time and time again, when he had asked a question in his mind which was answered by a verse he picked at random. It was like an oracle. Should he avoid being suspicious of the President? Did it mean, don't think the worst of him? Maybe he thinks he's trying to help. He went over what the President had just said and remembered the President was trying to make him reassess his contact with Suleiyman and the Muslims as if they had lured him into a trap. That was it. He should follow his own instincts. He had always thought Suleiyman to be a straightforward and genuine person. He had no reason to be suspicious of him or think badly of him.

The time for *Iftar* was coming and Jake thought dismally of the long night without food stretching ahead; and then tomorrow was another fasting day; but he was determined to continue fasting. It had become a matter of stamina, of proving himself. People were faced with greater trials than this. From his readings of the life of the Blessed Prophet and his companions, he had learned many stories of the hardship they faced in the early years, how they made do sometimes with a few dates as food for a whole group for several days. Whatever was available was shared. Even in his most prosperous times the Blessed Prophet never ate very much because as the leader of a struggling community he would never allow himself to eat more than did the poorest among them. Maybe this was a valuable lesson for Jake. He at least had water, and he drank eagerly from his basin. He did his prayers and felt enormous spiritual strength. Men who cracked at the first sign of difficulty were weak. He could have bowed to the President's threats and eaten before *Iftar* but his new faith was already more important to him. For the sake of a full stomach he was not prepared to sacrifice a sacred duty to God Himself. When he finished his prayer he checked his jacket pockets just in case. Sometimes he left things in there to eat. Success! A cookie. He savoured every crumb. He went through the room but there was nothing whatsoever to eat. All Bruce's things were gone. He didn't really miss Bruce's presence because he had been so used to reading late into the night while Bruce slept, but his side of the room looked sad and empty. A solitary tie lay at the foot of the bed. How would they get in touch again?

Jake continued to read but his preoccupation with his stomach was overwhelming. Should he go down and give in? No. He was too proud for that. He would have to endure it and thank God he had water. He got ready for bed and considered eating some toothpaste. It was better than nothing. As he climbed into bed he sat up suddenly, watching the door open in the dark. A little figure came in and laid something on the bedside table. It was Sam. He put his finger to his mouth to tell Jake not to speak and then crept out again. "Thanks, Sam," he whispered. It had taken a small boy, the youngest in the house, to take pity on him. Sam had filled his toy truck with food from dinner, individually wrapped in handkerchiefs: a piece of cheese pie, some bread, a container of yogurt and an orange. It was the best meal he'd ever had. "*Al-hamdu li'Llah,*" he said with real meaning as he finished the meal.

The President came to fetch him the next morning at 9 o'clock. "Hungry?" was the first word he spoke.

Jake nodded.

"Well perhaps you've learned your lesson. Now come and have some toast."

"But I can't," said Jake.

"You haven't eaten for more than twenty-four hours."

"It's still Ramadan sir. I have to fast. It's one of the pillars of Islam."

The President struck his head in disbelief. "You really are determined to be stubborn aren't you?"

"I'm not being stubborn, sir. It's just I can't eat until sunset. That's all."

"Jake, we are not living in the Dark Ages. We have the benefit of the *Book of Mormon* and *Doctrines and Covenants*. All this fasting for forty days and all this nonsense. Nobody has to do that any more." He pushed Jake into the office.

"The Muslims do sir. Actually it's only thirty days."

"Well, that's their problem. If they don't want to benefit from all God has to say that's their problem."

"They have a difference of opinion with the Mormons about that. They believe the Qur'an is God's word and ..."

"Listen, I'm not indulging in theological debate with you, Jake. I don't have the patience. I want to sort out what we're going to do about your mission now that Brother Bruce has gone."

He was totally ignoring Jake's concerns. He was determined to brush it all aside as if it didn't signify in the logistics of the mission.

"I don't think I can continue either, sir, in the light of what's happened."

"You'll just have to. I don't have anyone else."

"But it would be lying, sir."

"You didn't have any qualms about lying before, did you? When you broke the mission rules so flagrantly and continued to break them even when you were rewarded with a position of responsibility."

"I'm sorry, sir."

The President continued leafing through his papers distractedly and Jake watched silently wondering if he should speak. Finally Jake asked, "What's going to happen?"

"About what?"

"My conversion."

"Are you deliberately trying to provoke me?"

"Perhaps it's better if I pack and leave too. I don't want to embarrass you or the mission. Perhaps you could say I got sick or something."

"So now you're attempting to implicate me in your lies! Listen, you'd better get yourself straightened out because the way you're going at the moment your future looks pretty grim. Any chance you had of getting into BYU is out of the question now. You realize that, don't you?"

For a long time the prospect of entering Brigham Young University had seemed less and less appealing to Jake the more he moved away from Mormon values. College was not a priority at the moment, but he did have this gaping hole in his future after the mission. After conversion, what next? Maybe a vacation?

The President took a plain piece of paper and then ordered Jake to tell him in detail what had happened since the mission began. He wanted the whole story of the Brits and the Muslims, where he met them, what they had told him. Jake found it therapeutic to go over it to someone else, making the experience more real and confirming that it had truly happened and had not been some sort of fantasy. Inevitably the deceit over the weekend with Gregor and Maria came out and Jake immediately felt guilty for implicating them in the saga when they had only wanted to help. The President was obsessed with the details of their 'contacts' as he called them and impatient with the parts that were most important to Jake, who tried to explain what first compelled him to open the Qur'an, and the religious questions he had been struggling with. The President made him read and sign the report as though he was finishing a police interview.

For the rest of the day Jake was subject to the standard punishment of data processing. He didn't mind. It kept him occupied and away from the President's endless questions. As for the rest of the household, they had been told not to speak to Jake. The official explanation for his punishment was that he had been party to Bruce's escape. The first-years made a big show of their compliance with the punishment and seemed to revel in it, all except Oliver, who looked bewildered, already intimidated by the rigours of missionary life. Dave and Lewis, whenever they got the chance, would shrug their shoulders or roll their eyes at Jake as if to sympathize with his plight. Dave was put in place as team-leader and the President announced that he himself would be accompanying Jake on his mission until the end of the year.

Jake's heart sank as he began working with the President. It was like a crash course in relearning the Mormon religion. The President, being the President, played it absolutely by the rules. He drove them to all their venues, on the way giving Jake a non-stop monologue on church doctrine and how they had convinced the most unbending subjects. It washed over Jake. The familiar names and stories now were more like well-loved tales from childhood. They were nice stories but they were not truth, and truth had become very precious to him. He looked at the President as he droned on, his confident, wide face and slightly greying temples. How could he have reached this age and still believe in this stuff? Maybe he had himself stopped believing long ago but denied it in himself and carried on just as he was now, parroting the same phrases, absolutely oblivious to Jake and his change of heart. He hadn't even attempted to find out what he believed, but just kept going on about how he had broken the rules.

There was no doubt that the President was a real pro when it came to missionary work, and the surprising thing for Jake was that the language barrier seemed to present very little problem for him. He seemed to put people at their ease and catch their attention, and showed a great deal of interest when they spoke about themselves. It was left to Jake to make the introductory and explanatory statements, by now so well-rehearsed he could have recited them in his sleep. But now he managed to detach himself totally from what he was saying. The President was evidently impressed with the way he spoke.

"You see, you aren't so bad. You keep this up, we might just be able to salvage your mission."

'Sir!' he felt like screaming. 'It's too late! I'm not Mormon. How can I be a Mormon missionary if I'm not Mormon?'

But he remained silent and just carried on trudging after the President on the familiar round. At least he didn't have to think. They had some success, three possibly interested parties during the morning. Jake sat in the car during lunch hour while the President relaxed in the park and had his sandwiches. Jake refused to eat.

The afternoon passed like the morning and then all the way back home the President didn't say a word, so Jake stared morosely out of the window watching the Japanese. He was worrying about Hell. Since he had first starting finding out about Islam he had begun to think seriously about the concept of Hell. At first he had been distressed by the number of times he had seen it mentioned in the Qur'an. The fires of Hell were reserved for the wrongdoers who did not repent and those who refused to believe in God and the Hereafter against all the signs, against all truth and against all the many opportunities they had had to accept the truth. It made Jake fearful for non-believers, especially his family. He got really upset one night thinking how tragic it was that they themselves, who were so certain they were going to Paradise, might instead end up in Hell. Jake looked round and saw all the Japanese people quietly going about their business. It wasn't their fault they weren't Muslims. How could they find out about it with their history and where they were in the world? At first this had been a barrier to his accepting Islam and Suleiyman's stock answer, 'Oh, Allah is Merciful,' did not satisfy him. He was fearful. He was pitying of the disbelievers. He was afraid of Hell himself. Then as happened with all his questions things began to grow clearer to him as he pondered the names of God: *The All-Merciful, The Fount of Mercy, The Just.* If he, a mere creature, could feel this degree of mercy towards his fellow human beings, how much more merciful would the Owner of Mercy be? He realized it was not his burden to worry about who was bound for Hell and who wasn't. This was in God's hands, He who knew every stirring of every human heart and Who had promised that on the Day of Judgment, not an atom's weight of good or bad would be overlooked. Any good deed was judged by intention and would be rewarded out of all proportion to its value by the Grace of God, and a bad deed backed up by a bad intention would only be punished in equal measure to one deed; and even then Allah's forgiveness was greater than the heavens and the earth to those who were sincerely repentant. 'Don't worry,' Jake said to himself. 'Leave it to God. He'll sort it out.' No one would be wronged. Everyone would get what he had chosen. It taught him an important lesson, that life was definitely not a game. It was entirely serious. You had one life and Heaven and Hell were an absolute reality. Whichever one you chose, your choice would be honoured. Free will was just that, your choice!

The President relented that evening, probably in view of the fact that Jake had been good that day and he was allowed to eat dinner later by himself.

"If you keep this up," said the President, "you'll be back to normal next week and we'll say no more about it."

It was strange on Wednesday not to go into Donut Heaven. Jake wondered who might be waiting there for him. Maybe Bruce, or perhaps he wouldn't risk it. Maybe Suleiyman. The President disappeared at lunch time and left Jake in the car. Jake wondered whether he had gone to check out Donut Heaven for himself but then he relaxed when he remembered Suleiyman wouldn't be there during Ramadan. Sure enough, the President came back with doughnuts but no news of Bruce or the Brits. Bruce must be lying low, thought Jake, or even working already.

By Friday evening, the President had lifted the silent punishment and the atmosphere of the house seemed to relax. Sam asked why Jake continued to eat alone and the President said Jake preferred it that way.

At church on Sunday Jake noticed Gregor's cold look as he took his seat on the platform. The President had obviously already spoken to them about the weekend away. Jake felt even more alienated from the church rituals, like a fish out of water. This was no longer his place and he wanted out.

After the long service, during the socializing period, while Jake was trying to avoid some of the newcomers they had met the previous week, Maria suddenly pushed a piece of paper into his hand. He went to the bathroom to read it. 'I know your pain', it read. Jake was stunned. What could she possibly mean? What pain? How did she know? What did she know? Whenever he caught her eye she would nod wisely at him giving a faint smile. Jake found it pretty disturbing. He couldn't stand the suspense very long so when he had an opportunity to talk to Gregor during basketball, he seized on it.

"Gregor, can we talk?" he asked hesitantly, sitting beside him.

"I don't talk to your kind," he said coldly.

Jake shuddered. The hatred that had come into his voice was obvious. "Gregor, what is it? Is it about the weekend? I'm sorry I had to tell him with all this stuff about Bruce and everything, I just got confused."

"I told you I don't have anything to say to you."

"Gregor, what's happened?"

"The President told me all about your lies and what you've been up to."

"You mean about my religious problems?"

"Is it true what he said?"

"What?"

"You know what I'm talking about."

Jake guessed. "Yes it's true if you mean about me being Muslim."

"I don't know how you can even associate with those people."

"The Muslims I've met are real friendly."

"Yeah, I'm sure, when they want you to be like them. How could you fall for it Jake? I always thought you were intelligent."

"That's why," said Jake, ditching a pretense to modesty. "It was through logical argument and reading that I came to Islam. I believe in One God."

"Do you know they destroyed my people?" he said passionately.

Jake was taken aback.

"No, I guess not," he raged. "They probably didn't tell you that side of their wonderful Islam, about the wars and the killing." His voice was raised now and he had attracted attention as the others began to whisper around the gym.

This made Gregor even more angry. "What are you all whispering about?" he raged. "Don't look at me, look at him! Jake the traitor!"

They all stood suspended in the middle of their game waiting for the drama to unfold.

"Here he is pretending to be part of the church when all the time he's been going against the church behind our backs."

"It wasn't like that at all," said Jake. "It's only just happened."

"Can someone tell us what's going on here?" said Dave. "What is it, Jake?"

"I didn't want to tell you in case you got confused or upset. I don't know, it's a complex story."

"What?" said Dave. "What's a complex story?"

"Basically, I've changed my religion. I became Muslim. That's it. It's not a problem for me anymore so I don't know … that's it!"

He shrugged and left them in stunned silence. As he walked away he felt exhilarated, almost wanting to laugh. The situation seemed absurd. The first thing to do was to tell the President that the cat was out of the bag.

The President was livid. "Why couldn't Brother Gregor keep his mouth shut? I only told him because I thought he could shed some light on the matter. Now him and his foul temper! It'll be all over the mission within the hour."

Quite honestly, Jake was grateful. It took away the feeling of schizophrenia, the oppressive feeling of trying to keep a secret. That was always something he'd found very difficult about being a grown-up Mormon. The obsessive secrecy. The Temple rites were to be kept secret and not discussed even when, as in his case, a person had been deeply disturbed by the whole ceremony. Then there were these endless one-to-one interviews reporting on other missionaries or being told things 'for your ears only', quite inconsequential much of the time, but often he would get tangled up with who he was supposed to tell what. Bruce's personality had made him particularly hopeless at this. Now Jake felt strangely unburdened, that he could actually tell everyone what he was thinking.

Events moved quickly by the time the Bishop had got wind of the matter. He felt that the Bruce/Jake partnership had been jinxed and the quicker the mission got rid of both of them the better. Jake was obviously party to influences that could wreak havoc in the mission. Best to ditch one bad apple, was his argument, than to risk poisoning the whole basket. The story seemed to be that Jake had been brainwashed. Before the President could keep the lid on the whole affair it was taken out of his hands and the Bishop had already contacted the authorities in Tokyo. There was some debate as to whether Jake should be sent to Tokyo to receive counselling when the decision was made for them by a telegram which arrived on Monday afternoon from Jake's parents. It read simply: 'Come home immediately!' No explanation. A wave of panic swept over Jake as thoughts ran through his mind. Someone had died! Someone was in hospital! He tried to call several times and only got the answering machine. He would have to go back blind to whatever it was that had happened.

The worst thing about leaving so suddenly was the fact that he couldn't tie up any loose ends. He had to pack in frantic haste without even checking his stuff. He had no chance to buy gifts. He couldn't wind up his mission psychologically by saying good-bye to the towns he'd grown fond of. He liked ritual when it came to leaving. This will be my last train-ride to Okazaki, the last time I'll see this particular town or café we spent so much time in, or the last view of this familiar scenery on the route. It was all left suspended. Worse than the places was the fact of not saying a proper good-bye to his colleagues and the family and the people at church. He had imagined the end of his mission many times, the fond farewells, the good wishes, the ceremony in Tokyo where they would all be sent on their way. The work he had put into this mission and the good reputation he had built up were all wasted now. To leave like this, in disgrace, amidst scandal, it was too much. Maybe he had done the wrong thing by committing himself to Islam. Maybe he had been too hasty. The President was right. He had jeopardized his future. Tears of regret and apprehension stung his eyes. What could have happened at home, at a time like this? There was an awful knot of fear in his stomach as he prayed: 'Please God don't let it be my mother', but even his father or his brother and sisters. It would be unthinkable if anything had happened to them. He hoped it was Alice if it was to be anyone. It was a frightful thought but he hoped it was her. Still no answer from home. What about Suleiyman? He wouldn't even be able to say good-bye and to thank him. For Jake the dearest friend those two years had been his room, and at least he had a chance to sit there for a few minutes and go over the memories of the place and to reassure himself that this revolution of the soul had really happened. He had found truth and real peace of mind during the nights he'd spent here. In some ways, very personally, his mission had not been a failure.

The President had managed to make reservations for Jake to leave early the next morning and he had hardly been able to settle to sleep. The President drove him to the airport for his flight. He didn't allow Dave or Lewis to come along and so they gave him a rather formal send-off at the door. Sam had got up early to see him off and he gave a sad little wave from behind the banister. Jake felt particularly sorry to be leaving this cheerful character who had done a lot to keep his spirits high on the mission. The President seemed glad to be getting rid of the problem and not particularly concerned to discuss Jake's fears that something terrible had happened at home.

"We usually give bad news personally on the mission," he said. "They're probably just worried about you." Jake began to breathe easier.

When Jake came to check in, the President felt compelled to make some kind of good-bye speech. "Well, Brother Jake. I'm very sorry to see you going off in these circumstances. I had very high hopes for you. Really I did. On the whole I was very pleased by the way you worked on the mission. Now I suggest you go home, think it all over in the cold light of day and get rid of all these silly notions. Have a good trip and don't worry about your family. I'm sure they're fine. Good-bye, Jake."

Jake was trying hard not to sob. He couldn't even make his acceptance speech. He just blubbered. "Thank you, sir. I'm sorry."

As he went through the other side he felt like a naughty boy who'd got into trouble. He went to wash his face in the bathroom. He was alone for the first time in his life. Between here and home he could do anything; but he felt fearful and vulnerable. He wasn't as strong and fearless as he'd thought. All his ties with Japan had been cut, all the relationships he'd built up. Instead of being able to develop naturally they had fizzled out all of a sudden. Jake wanted to call someone, to hear a friendly voice, but the mission was out of the question. No solace there. Home? Still the answering machine. He wanted a voice, not just beeps. He would call Suleiyman. He waited an age as someone at reception went to fetch him and then he heard his voice. At last someone who cared about him. "Hullo. Suleiyman? I'm sorry it's so early. It's Jake."

"Jake! *As-salamu 'alaykum.*"

"*As-salamu alaykum,*" said Jake awkwardly, still not quite at home with using Arabic words in everyday speech.

"Is everything OK?"

"No," said Jake quickly. "I'm at the airport."

"What are you doing there?"

"I've been sent home. They found out."

"Oh Jake, I'm sorry. Are you in big trouble?"

"Yes, they went crazy and I got a telegram saying 'come home', just like that, no explanation and I don't know what's happened." He broke down crying again and it took some time before Suleiyman could calm him.

Jake, Jake. Now you've got a long journey ahead. Trust in Allah! Everything will be OK, *insha-Allah*. When's your flight?"

"About forty-five minutes."

"OK, give me your number in the US and I'll call you when you get back. Then we can talk properly."

Jake gave him the number, feeling a bit comforted.

"Now listen, Jake," he said. "Try not to worry too much. You've done the right thing. Allah is with you. Now listen. You don't have to fast for the next couple of days while you are travelling. You can if you prefer but you don't have to. I think two or three days until you get into your home routine. Allah makes things easy for us, OK? Don't push yourself too hard. This is your first Ramadan. OK Jake, you'd better get your flight. *Fi amani'Llah!* May God protect you."

"Bye," Jake whispered.

唯壱

Interlude

This time as the plane took off, Jake felt the same kind of wrenching as before, but now he was being taken away for good, from this place where he had discovered so much and had known so many good times. He felt the pull of the plane as it soared and settled at each altitude, rising more, then settling again. This was what faith felt like. A bit more knowledge and then you settled at a level you felt comfortable with, until it was time to move on to higher levels. The plains of his old beliefs were far below now, receding ever further into the distance, becoming minuscule as he rose higher to higher altitudes and to the rarefied air of unfolding spiritual awareness. There was a verse in the Qur'an that described the process: '*We raise whom We will, degree after degree*'. Conversion was an ongoing process. He decided to let it settle in his heart. Don't be afraid! The best thing to do now was pray.

Jake could hardly believe the extent of the transformation that had come upon him. He had arrived innocent, some would say ignorant, naïve, and thinking he could sail through life by virtue of his being Mormon. Now he was on his way back, alone, cut off, going back to who knew what, with no plans, and no framework to his life. The edifice of his career and his future had suddenly collapsed.

The cabin was tranquil and the view outside was of heavenly clouds below a dark blue sky. Jake had packed his copy of the Qur'an in his hand baggage in case he wanted another conversation with God to put his mind at ease. He opened it at random as usual and there was no doubt the passage was for him.

Do men think that they will be left alone on saying, 'We believe', and that they will not be tested?
We did test those before them, and God will certainly know

those who are true from those who are false.

That was the explanation. It was what he needed. He was being tested. His faith was being tested although it was only a few months old. His responsibility was to overcome the test. It would work out as long as he kept it clear in his mind that his faith was built on the solid foundation of belief in the One God.

As the plane banked towards Los Angeles Jake was growing apprehensive. He had to change planes there for Salt Lake and already Japan was very far behind him and he was going back to the place he knew, but fearing what might be awaiting him there. He had been travelling all day and the time kept receding, producing a sense of heading for the top of an escalator that was going the opposite way. His plane left early on Tuesday morning, so he still had some hours to kill in the airport. Now, since it was still before dawn, he could eat freely. Then when the first light of dawn came in sight it didn't feel right to eat even though he was exempted as a traveller. He didn't want to spoil his record which he had kept up so far despite considerable difficulties. He was probably foolish but he decided to fast anyway. He contemplated the very long day ahead, of questions and worries and wondered if he could hold out until sunset. Yes he could, he decided. In his own home there'd be no problem about when to eat. They would have to get used to it.

唯邑

Salt Lake City, Utah

When he arrived at Salt Lake he went through baggage control and wondered who'd be waiting for him on the other side of the barriers. He prepared a self-conscious smile to meet the sea of expectant faces. There was his dad. He gave a sombre wave and came through to take the luggage cart. His brother Frank was with him and gave him a hasty smile. Jake took a deep breath to control himself. "OK you can tell me now. What's happened?"

Jake's father and brother looked at each other as if to assess whether they thought Jake had really gone mad.

"I think we should go to the car," said his father.

"Dad," he pleaded. "I came all this way worried sick. I couldn't get through on the phone. Please tell me what's happened."

"Don't make a scene now, Jake. People are staring."

Jake complied until they got to the car, and then he blew up. "Now what's happened? I can take it. Just please tell me."

"We got the message from Japan," his father said steadily as if talking to a small child, "that you had gotten in with a Moslem crowd and that you had started telling everyone you were Moslem." His father looked at him as if Jake would put their minds at rest and tell them it was all a big mistake.

"There's a lot to discuss. We can leave that till later. I'm talking about the telegram."

"Uh huh. I sent you a telegram."

"Yes, it said to come home right away, so I assumed something had happened, someone had died or something."

"Oh no," said Frank breezily. "Everyone's fine."

"For God's sake," said Jake, almost lost for words. "I've been worried sick thinking all kinds of things and I couldn't get through on the phone, that damned answering machine."

"Now, don't cuss," said his father. "Calm down!'

"I can't believe this," said Jake. "I get an urgent telegram telling

393

me to drop everything and rush home and when I get here I find out everyone's fine. So why did you call me back?"

"We were worried about you, Jake," said his father. "We were imagining all kinds of things, that you could be taken away or anything."

"Taken away by who?"

"This cult you're involved with."

"What cult?"

"The Moslems," shouted his father, losing patience. "The Bishop came over and told us the whole story from the mission in Japan. We didn't know what to think. Figured the safest thing was to have you back with us."

Jake was still dazed. "What are you all talking about? I don't have anything to do with a cult."

"Well they said someone was trying to influence you. They seem to have succeeded because they said you were going around telling everyone you were Moslem and refusing food and that your room was full of their literature."

"When we get home I'll tell you the whole story, OK? The first thing I need to do is sleep."

"OK, but we have people coming to see you this afternoon."

"Oh dad, can't the visitors wait? I didn't sleep more than two hours. This route from Japan is the worst for jet-lag. It should be evening time for me."

"They're not really visitors. They're people the church are sending over to try and get you straightened out."

He spoke as if Jake's mind was an object to be fixed.

"Well, can't they wait? I wanna sleep and then spend some time with you guys."

"Well, we'll see what the church says," said his father.

Jake's brother didn't speak much. He just turned around from time to time to check on Jake whose eyes were already drooping, and then he would nudge his father and give him a knowing look.

When they got back home, Jake's sister Lisa opened the door looking tense. Jake hugged her and was surprised at her reticence. No sarcastic little wisecracks, just a curt 'Hello'. Joanne was standing awkwardly in the hall looking at Jake as if he had some deadly disease and she was searching for some signs of it. Then he saw his mother standing in the kitchen and he was frightened by the look of pain in her eyes. He went to hug her and she was the only one who seemed pleased to see him. She kept pushing him back to take another look and then held him close again, unable to speak.

"Listen," said Jake, taking control of the situation. He hated this. This was his home, the place he'd always had a warm welcome and now he felt like an unwelcome intruder. "I think everyone is over-reacting a little here. It's still the same Jake. I haven't grown two heads."

The joke fell flat and the family just carried on staring.

"Please," he said. "this is awful. I had to come home because of the telegram. I get here. I find everyone's OK and everyone's treating me like a leper."

"Did you think something had happened?" asked his mother.

"Yes," said Jake. "I thought someone had died."

"Oh Jake, I'm so sorry. Ray," she said to his father, "maybe we should have called first."

"Well, the church seemed to think we should get him home right away before anything worse happened."

"Before we go any further," said Jake, "there is no cult. Do you all get the message? There's no cult. Yes I've been thinking a lot about my beliefs. Yes I've had a lot of questions and done a lot of reading. Now I'm pretty sure I believe in Islam but there is nothing weird going on, OK?"

They all gasped. They had heard it themselves, the confession of faith in Islam, and they realized the people in Japan had not been exaggerating.

"I'd like to sleep, Mom," said Jake, looking beseechingly at her, his ally.

"Yes, I think that would be best. Frank, take up Jake's bag! C'mon and have a bite to eat first Jake."

"Can I just tell everyone," he said, "so there's no confusion. It's Ramadan. I'm fasting. That means I can't eat or drink anything till sunset. OK? Just so you know."

Jake's madness was confirmed. "I think you're delirious, dear," his mother said. "Now go right up and sleep and we won't disturb you till the church people come."

By now Jake was beginning to doubt his own sanity. He was

395

dizzy with jet-lag and full of cramp from the journey. His mouth was dry. He took a shower and got into bed. It was so welcome. His head was heavy and ready for sleep. Any worries could be suspended until further notice.

The horrible dream-like sensation of waking up and finding it still daylight and his mouth still dry confronted him as he saw his brother's face a few inches above his.

"What did you wake me up for?" he groaned.

"Those guys are here."

"Tell them to go away."

"We can't. They're waiting for you." Jake's mom came in to hurry him along. "Jake get dressed! Try to fix you hair and look presentable. The church has sent some men to talk to you."

"Mom, can't they come back to-morrow or something? I have jet-lag."

"They were very insistent. You can sleep later. Hurry on now, Jake."

Reluctantly he dragged himself out of bed and tried to make the best of his grey appearance. He did his ablution and put on clean clothes. He prayed the noon prayer he had slept through and then the afternoon prayer. He was always very careful about his prayers, to wash properly and say them on time. At least he had some privacy now with his own room. He felt bolstered after the prayer and asked Allah to give him strength to face the church people. Little did he know he was walking into his first real battle.

Jake's mother nervously led him into the living room where the two men were waiting. They were both clean-cut and clean-shaven with immaculate suits and shiny shoes. They looked like salesmen. Their faces were quite impassive, although the fatter one had very startling blue eyes. Instead of standing up to greet Jake who went towards them with extended hand, they just signalled for him to sit down, in his own living room. It was not a good start. Jake's father sat awkwardly between the two men waiting for them to take control.

"So this is Jake?" said the large one.

"Yes," said Jake's father. As if proudly introducing his son, he started off telling them that he had just been on his mission in Japan and then he tailed off remembering the circumstances.

"Well, I guess you know some of the details."

"We've done our homework," said the fat guy. "Now I think we should get started, so Mr Carter, if you could leave us now."

Jake's dad jumped up. "Oh yes, of course. You'll be wanting to get started. Now are you all comfortable?"

"Is there another room we could use, perhaps a little more private, out of the way of all the comings and goings?"

Jake felt trepidation. Were they looking for a torture chamber?

Jake's father held a whispered conference with his mother and she showed them to what used to be the playroom at the back of the house and was now used as a sitting room when the children brought friends home. It was a comfortable room decorated in bright colours with bean-bags and scatter cushions to make it more appealing to the youngsters. It was Jake's father who had decorated it for them, thinking that youngsters needed a place to socialize by themselves, as he said. Some of the games from the children's childhood were still stacked on the shelves, and the remnants of fast-food containers and popcorn were scattered about. The men made themselves comfortable and Jake's mother was dismissed with instructions not to disturb them. They would come out if they needed anything.

"OK, Jake," the fat man started. "This is quite a mess you've got yourself into."

"Well, as you know I was called back from my mission all of a sudden ... I'm sorry, I don't know your name."

"I know," said the man coldly, so Jake nicknamed him 'Laser Eyes' and the other one he called 'Sidekick'.

"Do you know why you were called back from your mission?" said Sidekick, speaking for the first time.

"I thought someone had died at first," said Jake, "or that there had been an accident."

"At first," echoed Sidekick.

"Do you know now why you were called back?" asked Laser Eyes.

"I guess it has something to do with what happened over there," said Jake sheepishly.

"Be more specific!"

"I mean maybe something to do with my conversion."

"Exactly!" said Sidekick.

"Do you have any idea what this has done to your parents?" asked Laser Eyes.

"I knew they'd be upset," Jake faltered. The man was very intimidating. "But I figured after I'd explained properly they would be OK about it."

"You say 'upset'," said Laser Eyes. "Let me tell you that your mother is devastated. Did you see her face?" Jake didn't answer. "Did you?"

"Yes, sir." He was already fighting back the tears so he prayed for strength. He didn't want to show his humiliation to this bully.

"Your father is beside himself," Laser Eyes went on. "The Bishop is terribly disappointed in you because he had very high hopes for you. The church has spent a lot of money on you. They trusted you and then ..." He clicked his fingers. "You just throw it all away."

"I would have finished my mission," said Jake, "if I hadn't received the telegram."

"So now it's your parents' fault, huh?"

"I guess they were worried."

"You bet they were worried," Sidekick chipped in.

"You see we see a lot of people in your situation in our business," said Laser Eyes, "kids who've been influenced by crazies and gone off and joined cults, but there are not many like you who have loving, supportive families and a supportive church and good career prospects at such a young age. Seems to me Jake, you had it all and then you just threw it all away."

Jake was determined to get this cult thing out of their heads at once. "Everyone keeps talking about cults. I haven't joined a cult. It's just a personal thing. I read a lot of books, heard a lot of cassettes, did a lot of study and praying and slowly I began to be convinced that the truth is Islam."

Laser Eyes winced.

"But you missed something out," said Sidekick.

"What?"

"You never mentioned the people who gave you the books."

"Person. It was a man called Suleiyman who talked to me at first and gave me the books."

"We understand," said Laser Eyes, "that you should not even have been speaking to this Sullyman according to mission rules which forbid contact with any non-Mormons except Japanese."

"At first I thought he was Japanese," said Jake.

"But he was Moslem," said Sidekick.

"He comes from Indonesia. They look a bit Japanese. Anyway, I assumed."

"But you had broken mission rules before, hadn't you?" asked Laser Eyes.

"In what way?" Jake decided not to give anything away in order to antagonize them.

"You tell me!" said Laser Eyes sitting back. "I've got all day."

"There were some British people we got to talking to."

"Against mission rules," said Sidekick.

"It's difficult to ignore people when they come up to you, and anyway, my partner wanted to make friends."

"You're quite good at blaming other people," Laser Eyes noted. "So this Sullyman. Did you meet him by chance?"

"Yes he came up to me and introduced himself in Donut Heaven. Said he recognized me from the Japanese exam."

"I'm listening," said Laser Eyes.

Jake went on. "So anyway we got to talking and I told him I was a missionary and he said he was studying Japanese and we got onto talking about religion. Then he told me he was a Muslim and I asked a few questions because at first I was thinking to tell him about the church, but his arguments were convincing and they set me thinking."

"Just a casual conversation," said Laser Eyes. "Did he make arrangements to see you again?"

"I told him I always went to Donut Heaven at that time on Wednesday and we could finish our discussion."

"So he was careful not to seem too forward?" said Sidekick. "You were doing all the running, huh? Classic!" he said with a smug smile.

"Oh no. I remember now. At first he invited me to their hostel but I told him it wasn't allowed and that's when we arranged to meet."

Sidekick looked a little crestfallen, his theory knocked down.

"Does your memory often deceive you?" asked Laser Eyes.

"No," said Jake. "But I can't remember every detail of my life."

"I understand he invited you to their hostel again?" continued Laser Eyes.

"Yes, but that was much later after I'd decided to convert. In fact, I'd already converted in my heart."

"You don't seem quite sure," said Laser Eyes.

"No I'm sure because, oh hold on, this is the jet-lag. I'm sorry. There was one other time before I converted they invited me to dinner."

"If we wait long enough I wonder how many more visits we'll come up with," Laser Eyes asked his partner.

"So what happened at the dinner?" asked Sidekick, getting interested in the story.

"It was a really nice meal, too much really. I was bursting and they were all very friendly and welcoming. We talked a little."

"What about?" asked Sidekick.

"Islam. I'd already been reading quite a bit by then."

"Now is this before or after you converted in your heart?" asked Laser Eyes mockingly.

"Before," said Jake, "although I would say by that time I was already half convinced. I just had a few more questions."

"So you went to the Moslems with your questions?" asked Laser Eyes.

"Yes."

"Why didn't you go to the church?" asked Sidekick.

"I was scared of what they might think, plus a lot of my questions were already answered by my reading and sort of in my heart. It was weird."

"In your heart again," said Laser Eyes, stifling a laugh.

"I can't explain what happened. It just did. I'm absolutely sure that I became aware of truths I had never known before."

"So you fancy yourself as the second Joseph Smith."

"No, it wasn't so dramatic. It was a matter of having a question in my mind and having it answered straight away by the Qur'an."

"These people at the hostel. Were they convincing?" asked Sidekick.

"Very convincing, but then they were all practicing Muslims. They weren't pushy or anything like that. They would just tell me what I needed to know. You see the biggest thing for me was thinking about God. I couldn't reconcile my own instincts about the nature of God with what the church teaches and I found in Islamic teachings something that went along with my reason."

"We're not interested in your theological mumbo-jumbo," said Laser Eyes coldly.

"We've heard it all before," echoed Sidekick. "God within, God without. God is everything."

"OK, Jeff," said Laser Eyes. Sidekick was getting carried away. Now he knew his name Jake still liked to call him Sidekick. There was a weakness here in the relationship between the two men. Perhaps if he could exacerbate it ...

"I think your friend here wants to know more about the beliefs," said Jake mischievously.

"Mr Kimball to you," said Laser Eyes, "and don't speak to me like that."

"Well if you're not even prepared to hear me out," said Jake, "there's no point going on." He was getting impatient for the meeting to be over so that he could go and talk to his family and wait for his *Iftar*.

The men carried on questioning him about the Muslims in Nagoya. They seemed obsessed with them, their names, what they were studying, where they came from and what they told Jake. He answered their questions to the best of his recollection and tried not to get too stressed. The fasting at least helped him to feel detached from the whole business; he felt kind of dreamy and uncaring about what was going on around him. He couldn't believe it when he next looked at his watch and found it was nearly 9 o'clock in the evening.

"Could we maybe break for dinner?" he suggested.

"Dinner is when we decide," said Sidekick.

"It's just that I haven't eaten since very early this morning at the airport. Was it this morning? I can hardly keep track."

"We know," said Laser Eyes and carried on.

Jake was beginning to get frantic. How long would they keep him holed up in this room? The lovely room with so many happy associations from childhood was beginning to take on a nightmarish quality.

Laser Eyes focused in on Suleiyman. "So you two got to be pretty good friends, huh?" he asked.

"Yes, we met about once a week. He was very enthusiastic about my conversion and seemed interested in my ideas."

"Did you contact him before you left?"

"Yes, I called him to tell him I had to leave. He said he'd call me when I got home."

"Has he called you?" asked Laser Eyes.

"No, not yet but I guess he'll wait until I recover from jet-lag."

"Strange how he said he'd call and he didn't," said Laser Eyes. "I heard Moslems kept their word."

Here they were again harping on about points like this. Jake was getting very frustrated. Then he wondered why he hadn't thought just to get up and walk out the door. As he rose towards the door, Laser Eyes said, "I wouldn't bother. I asked your mom to lock it. I told you. We'll go when we decide."

"Come on. This is outrageous, keeping me locked up in my own house. I haven't eaten. I need a break. Please." He was pleading now.

Laser Eyes seemed to home in on his vulnerability. "Listen, Jake. This may seem harsh but believe me we have your best interests at heart. When your mind's been damaged like this it takes time to talk you around."

"My mind hasn't been damaged," said Jake, almost sobbing.

"That's the trouble," said Sidekick. "The one who is affected doesn't see anything wrong. It's the people around him who notice."

"What we're gonna do is have your mom bring you a snack and you can get a little sleep if you want. Get you back into US time mode."

Jake was so grateful for the break he said, "Yes, please," rather too ingratiatingly.

He didn't even think twice when Laser Eyes opened the door until he had had his snack and realized he had been lying about the door being locked. Knowing they were in fact liars put Jake considerably at his ease. There was no reason then to trust anything else they said to intimidate him.

He was allowed to wash and go to his room. He realized he'd missed his *Maghrib* prayer so he prayed it along with *Isha* feeling greatly refreshed by the milk and sandwiches. He wasn't tired, just mentally exhausted. Maybe they would give up and go away. Jake's parents came up to see him and before he could ask them why they were letting this happen his dad explained that he had been told to lock him in 'for his own good'. He had fitted a bolt especially for the purpose. What did they expect, that he would take the next plane to Japan to be with his Muslim cult members? Jake laughed at how ludicrous the situation seemed. No-one had yet asked him seriously about why he had decided to be Muslim and why he no longer believed in the Mormon church. Instead they had developed all these hysterical stories of cults and brainwashing and temporary insanity. To regain his bearings he went to his suitcase to get out his books and his copy of the Qur'an. It was always a great comfort at times like this. But the books were all gone. Had he taken them out already? Frantically, he searched the room but no trace. They must have taken his books. Was he still asleep, soon to wake up from this nightmare? It wasn't possible that his own loving family would do this to him. He banged on the door shouting for his books for a long time but no one came to see him. The house was deadly quiet. After an hour of frustrated tears, sleep overcome him.

"Jake, Jake! It's still early."

He sat bolt upright to find Laser Eye's piercing eyes boring into him. "What is it?"

"I thought you'd like to eat before you start your fasting. It's still early."

"How did you know?" asked Jake, confused at his pleasant manner.

"It's my job to know."

Jake ate his *suhur* and prayed for more strength. Then he asked if he could go off to pray *Fajr*. Laser Eyes agreed. Why this sudden change in attitude? Maybe they realized the scare tactics didn't work. When he'd prayed he got back into bed. Laser Eyes appeared like a ghost beside him. "We can talk now," he said.

"Now?" said Jake, "It's four in the morning."

"That's OK. Your body clock probably isn't adjusted. C'mon!"

Jake followed him, bewildered, to the playroom and found Sidekick looking rather grumpy for lack of sleep. His sharp suit looked a little crumpled and he had rolled up his sleeves and loosened his tie. Even Laser Eyes looked more relaxed.

"Don't you guys need your sleep?" Jake asked.

"We're on duty," said Sidekick.

"Oh, I see." Jake yawned. "Well I don't know if I'll make much sense at this time in the morning but anyway what do you want to talk about?"

"Let me tell you again," said Laser eyes with a softening look that reminded Jake of J.R. on *Dallas*, "as I told you last night, we want to help you. You're among people you can trust now, who care about you and who want to help you. Do you understand?"

Jake nodded.

"We have something to tell you that may upset you but I'm afraid we have to tell you."

Jake looked worried.

"It's very hard when you think people are your friends and then they turn out to be con-men."

Oh no, thought Jake. They're going on about the Muslims again.

"You're not the first one to be taken in by this group," he began. "No, there have been others, Americans like yourself, Australians, and some Europeans. They specifically target missionaries, you see. By the way did Sullyman sound surprised when you told him you were a missionary?"

"Yes, he was surprised I was so open about it."

"Well, he knew you were a missionary long before."

"How?"

"He heard from the British teachers who knew Bruce. They were working together."

"But they didn't even know each other."

"Of course, they didn't want you to know that. Did Sullyman make a special point of sitting away from them?"

Jake recalled how Suleiyman always felt awkward sitting with the Brits. He'd assumed it was shyness. "Yes, but it didn't seem unusual," he said.

"Of course not," said Sidekick ominously. "They're very careful."

"You see," Laser Eyes went on. "This group works specifically with missionaries because they know missionaries are very successful. So they try to get missionaries to lose their faith and go to Islam."

Jake remembered how Suleiyman had talked about the missionaries in Indonesia and how they tried to lure people and the fact that he had gone to a mission school himself. The story was beginning to sound more plausible but something wasn't quite right. "How do you know all of this all of a sudden," said Jake, "when last night you were asking me all about them?"

"He's astute," said Laser Eyes to Sidekick as if Jake were some kind of specimen. "It's our job to know," said Laser Eyes and he wouldn't say any more than that.

Jake sat for a while going over his meetings with Suleiyman. Nothing had seemed strange except the coincidences that had been so amazing at the time. Maybe they had never been coincidences after all. But was it so sinister to try and convince someone of your faith if you wanted to share it with people? After all the Mormons had made an industry out of it all over the world.

"They were good guys, though," Jake said finally, trying to take it all in.

"I know, and that's why it's hard to accept they were using you, but those are the facts, I'm afraid," said Laser Eyes comfortingly.

"Can I go back to bed now?" said Jake sounding quite forlorn.

"Yes, you can go," said Laser Eyes.

Jake decided to sleep and then think about what they had told him in the morning. He had to admit he had doubts now about Suleiyman but his faith was still there. Before he slept he did a checklist in his mind of what he did and did not believe. *Al-hamdu-li'Llah,* his faith was still there. It had found a home in his heart, at least for the foreseeable future.

Jake's family seemed much more cheerful when he got up around noon. It seemed the deprogrammers were making progress.

"Feel better, son?" asked his father, as if his Islam was a head-cold he would soon shake off.

"OK, but those guys keep strange hours."

"Well, you'd better get dressed now because they'll be calling you in about a half hour."

"Aw, dad. We've been going around in circles for hours. I thought we'd resolved the whole problem."

"No, well, they told us to be sure and send you in soon, so hurry!"

Laser Eyes and Sidekick, looking spruced up, were waiting for Jake in the playroom.

"Sleep well?" said Laser Eyes.

"Yeah, I was dead," said Jake.

"Yeah, I'm afraid these sessions tend to do this to you. Now are you starting to come to terms with what we've told you?"

"Yes," said Jake carefully. "What you've said sounds fairly reasonable. It's just that I have no way of knowing for sure. The way you describe it, well, it didn't seem that way to me but I guess if you've researched them as you said ...!"

"Yes, we have done our research," said Laser Eyes firmly, "and that is what we came up with. They're well-known. We can bring you examples of other missionaries they've hoodwinked if you wish."

"No, no," said Jake quickly. "That's OK." He couldn't imagine this thing going on much longer. He decided he wouldn't try to argue with them.

"So, what we have to do now is to see how you can possibly redeem yourself with the church and cover over some of the bad atmosphere that's been created."

Jake felt some sense of foreboding. Having half-convinced him that Suleiyman and his friends were a secret group bent on deceiving innocent missionaries, they thought the whole thing was over. They obviously had no idea about faith.

"It's not that simple," said Jake.

"Listen!" said Sidekick. "You should be grateful that we can maybe get you out of this whole mess with your reputation intact."

"The way I feel now," said Jake, "it wouldn't be fair or honest for me to take part in church activities.

"Why not?" said Laser Eyes, aghast.

"Because I would be living a lie. I can't go along and say those words and join in those ceremonies if I no longer believe."

Laser Eyes was getting exasperated. "But we just spent the last day and night trying to convince you about all this Moslem stuff."

"I don't think you understand," said Jake. "My belief in Islam came from God, not from the Muslims. They may have started the whole thing off but I was convinced in my own mind. (He thought it best not to mention 'heart' again.)

"He is nuts," said Laser Eyes, resigned. "He thinks he's in communication with God."

"Is that so weird?" asked Jake.

Laser Eyes laughed, a little embarrassed and merely tutted.

"Well, don't you believe Brother Benson has direct communication with God? He claims to."

"Who?" asked Laser Eyes. Now his suspicions were confirmed. Jake was definitely off his rocker. "Who the hell's Brother Benson? Is he another Moslem?" he said exaggerating the word.

"C'mon guys, you're kidding me," said Jake. But the two men didn't know.

"Hold on! Are you two with the church?"

"What church?"

"Are you LDS, Mormons?"

"No."

"I thought the church sent you."

"Yes."

"So how come you're not Mormons?"

"Does everyone hired by the Mormons have to be Mormon?"

"Well, can I ask you what religion you are?"

"No!" replied Laser Eyes.

"Do you believe in God?"

"We ask the questions." They were back to the tough treatment.

Jake was dismissed while they thought up a solution to this next problem. Jake was told to sit in the living room while Laser Eyes made a few calls. He was not told what was going on until he heard the doorbell and a couple came in. Jake's mother greeted them and they sat down looking very nervous. The man was fairly short with a moustache and sad, brown eyes. His wife was small and slim with very heavy make-up and a bouffant hair-style. They were both dressed very elegantly. Jake's father was asked to sit with them while his mother brought in some juice and cookies.

Laser Eyes began his introduction. "This is young Jake. He's been on a mission in Japan. Got himself caught up with some strange people. Now he's convinced he's Moslem. What I'd like you to do is to tell him where he's going wrong."

The man coughed. "Why you think you are Muslim, Jake?"

"I believe in Allah, in the Prophet Muhammad, the Angels, the

Day of Judgment, Heaven and Hell, Allah's dispensation in all matters." He had prayed earnestly at lunchtime to ask Allah to help him through this ordeal and he felt sure that Allah would help him through this meeting and perhaps inspire him with some good words.

The woman looked embarrassed and blushed at Jake's very open answer.

"You seem to know a lot about Islam, Jake," said her husband.

"Not really. I've only been Muslim a month or so."

"What do you believe about Jesus?" the man asked.

"That he was a true Prophet of Allah," said Jake, noticing his father's expression of astonishment.

"Who filled your head with all this nonsense?" his father said despairingly.

"I read it in the Qur'an," said Jake.

"Why do you believe the Qur'an?" asked the woman.

"Many reasons. It has so many amazing facts in it. It's so beautiful, so moving. There are copies exactly the same from right at the beginning of Islam. It's never changed at all. So many things. I could go on forever."

"Please don't!" said Laser Eyes, obviously bored with all this religious talk.

"We used to believe the Qur'an," said the woman gently, "but now we've found the truth," and she held up the *Book of Mormon*.

"Yeah, and I used to believe in that and now I've found the truth," Jake retorted.

"One of you is wrong," said Sidekick. It seemed that the two deprogrammers had dealt with so many people sent crazy by religion that they themselves had lost confidence in it altogether.

"You see the story about how the Qur'an was revealed is a lot more convincing than the story of the *Book of Mormon*," said Jake. "In fact the *Book of Mormon* is not in any way like the Qur'an. I don't think you can compare the two. I don't know why but never in my life has anyone ever mentioned the Qur'an to me or the Prophet Muhammad or anything about Islam. Dad, did you know any of this? Mom?"

They just shook their heads sorrowfully.

"Why are you talking like this?" his mother said. "It's just not like you, Jake."

Jake was upset to see his mother so distressed and went to follow her to the kitchen to see if she was OK.

"Where do you think you're going?" asked Laser Eyes.

"My mom's upset." He put his arms around her but Sidekick came and sat him down again.

"It's because of you she's upset," said Sidekick.

"Why aren't you drinking your juice?" asked Laser Eyes with a scornful look.

"You know why."

"Tell us!"

"You got me up this morning so I could eat before dawn."

"That was before, when I thought we were getting somewhere."

"Well, I'm still fasting."

"Drink your juice, Jake!" his mother said softly.

"I'm sorry I can't."

"She said to drink your juice!" said Sidekick.

Jake turned on him. "I know what she said. Shut your trap! I'm not drinking it, OK?"

Jake's outburst caused a little consternation amongst the group. Then Laser Eyes said, "Take it away, Mrs Carter. If he refuses to eat, then let him go without." Were they going to lock him up until midnight again, talking?

The debate with the young couple went on and it transpired that they were Turkish. The man had come to BYU to study International Relations on a scholarship and while he was there he had become interested in the Mormon religion and eventually converted. Jake said that one could use the same argument for him, that he was coerced, but the young man denied it and said that the Islamic religion had failed him. Turkey was making advances and those who stuck to the old ways got left behind, and were denied the best schools, housing and jobs. It had been a hindrance to him even though his parents tried to make him study Qur'an when he was young. He always rebelled against it. His wife, whom he had married before they came to the US followed him into the religion but she was eager to give her own theological reasons. She explained how she had always been frightened of

God, fearful to do the wrong thing, fearful of Hell and always afraid of God watching and taking note of every action, even every thought. Then when she heard about the Mormons she felt she was in a totally different world. You did your best but there was no fear of Hell. You did your best to win God's favour but if you made a mistake or did wrong you knew that Jesus would take all your sins away and everything would be OK. Just receiving the sacraments of the Church was enough. Jake told her that he had worried about this point but he believed that Allah was Merciful enough to forgive men anything if they were truly sorry. Also since Allah knew everything, He would be the only One able to judge men's actions and intentions. If Jesus took away all our sins whatever we did, then life was truly pointless and free will was truly pointless. The woman seemed to take Jake's arguments seriously and the two deprogrammers were too busy eating to listen carefully. It was clear that religion bored them, so they let them talk it out. Jake didn't like to delve too much into his criticisms of Mormon theology in order not to offend his parents but he talked about historical proofs and evidence as an important basis for accepting something purported to be from God. Soon Laser Eyes broke up the cosy discussion. At least it had set the woman thinking, thought Jake, although the Turkish man seemed exasperated that he had failed to win the argument.

Jake's mother thanked them at the door and came in looking very drained. She looked tired and ill with the strain.

"Please, I'd like to talk alone with my mother for a while," said Jake.

"Don't you think she's upset enough?" asked Laser Eyes.

Jake hated the way they spoke for her like this as if he were the outsider.

"It's OK," she said. "Maybe it's best if we talk alone. We haven't really had a chance to sit properly since Jake came back."

"I think we know what's best," said Laser Eyes patronizingly. "You're tired, Mrs Carter. Perhaps, Mr Carter, you'd like to take her upstairs. She probably needs to lie down. Jake, you come with me!"

"Wait while I have dinner!"

"I said to come with me!"

Jake blew up. "I'm damned if I'm gonna let you dictate to me in my own home," he shouted.

"Yes, that's right," said his mother in a sudden rage. "You are damned. Think about it Jake. Forever!"

Jake was stunned. His mother had never spoken like that before. Like a child he followed Laser Eyes to the playroom. There followed another session of mind-bending as they tried to convince him he was mad or deluded or selfish, or occasionally they would pick up on some of the arguments the Turkish woman had used that they had half-understood and tried to use them against him, but Jake had no respect for them now he knew they were liars. They didn't believe in anything, so it seemed. They were doing this as a business. He didn't care what they thought so he grew more and more challenging with them and daring, saying there was no point in continuing because they thought he was crazy and he didn't believe a word they said anyway. They sent him to bed in disgust at 2 AM with no dinner, and he was locked in his room with nothing but water, as had happened back in Nagoya. But this time no one took pity on him and there was no midnight caller with a snack.

In the quiet of his room, away from the exasperating attentions of the two deprogrammers, he began to grow fearful. What the Turkish woman had said made an impression on him. She seemed really sincere. It was such a tantalizing thing, that promise of no Hell, eternal happiness with no more effort than just believing in the book and trying to follow the covenants and ordinances, which were not demanding at all. In any case, in the end Jesus would just take all that burden away, whatever you had done, whoever you had hurt, just one word, one affirmation and your ticket to Paradise would be guaranteed. It was like that for Americans on earth. By virtue of having an American passport, all the privileges, all the bounties in the world were open to you. It was tempting to think it would carry on in the Hereafter. But Jake often came back to an image he had once seen on TV of an Indian street-sweeper in Calcutta, who swept and swept and seemingly had none of the bounties and privileges, no home, no family, little food, just a little job. Surely God's plan was bigger than the Mormons would have it. What about the street sweeper and the rest of humanity who hardly laid claim to a crumb? What about injustice? But the prospect was tempting, to have everything taken care of for you. What Jake cared about, however, was, 'Is it true?' He prayed to God to say sorry for wavering after he had been given such obvious signs and pointers in the right direction, but admitted he was still confused. He needed a really clear sign, a kind of miracle. He felt it was childish to make deals with God. He had done it before and failed to keep to the agreement, but this was a crisis point in his life. He needed help. It crossed his mind that the whole Islamic episode might have been a chance for him to really appreciate the Mormon faith and really understand it properly, as if by passing through this stage of unbelief, he would get stronger in the faith, but the old doctrines, the God who had been a man and still had a body, the thousands of separate Gods, ran through his mind and now they seemed like cardboard cut-outs compared to what he had found. It was precious what he had found. This was the Pearl of Great Price they were always talking about. Surely his mind was intact. His faith was built on something solid, but he felt sad as if something was slipping away. Maybe it was his old skin. He went to the window to contemplate the stars and as he drew back the curtain, he saw a perfect crescent moon, the symbol of Islam. He stood in awe and then, overwhelmed with gratitude, he thanked Allah again and again. The privilege, to be given a personal sign, all of one's own! Now he had no excuse. 'I promise I won't ask for another miracle,' he whispered excitedly.

Next morning around 8 o'clock he was woken by Laser Eyes. No more Mr Nice Guy. He had missed the chance to eat. So ravenous, but very happy, he followed his tormentors into the living room. "More visitors?" he said cheerily. He had come to look on the pair as quite ridiculous as they tussled to trip him up. Laser Eyes was grumpy and did not answer.

This visitor needed no introduction. She stormed into the room, threw down her bag and confronted Jake. "Thanks, Jake, for ruining my life," she said.

"Alice, in front of all these people? Can't we go somewhere private?"

"No," she shouted. "I want these people to hear what I have to say. They've told me everything and I think it's pathetic. Do you know how long I've waited for this guy?" she said, facing the audience. "Two years, while he writes me once in a while, speaks on the phone if I'm lucky, and all the time he's becoming some kind of religious nut."

"You didn't say that when I was a missionary," said Jake.

"Did you consider," Alice went on as if she hadn't heard, "how it would affect me and my life to find out my fiancé is going off to be a Moslem?"

"Alice, please. I'm sorry but I need to talk to you about it properly. This isn't something that just popped into my head. This is my life. This is a major crisis and I need time to think it out."

"You bet it's a major crisis," she said. The deprogrammers seemed to be enjoying the row. "I get all my wedding plans. We decide where we're gonna live. We talk about it for years. I watch all my girlfriends going off to get married." This was the point where Alice broke down and Jake's heart went out to her. It must be very hard for her and the angry bravado was just to cover up the hurt. Maybe she'd even begun to wonder long ago whether Jake was really committed to marriage. He wanted to comfort her but he knew she would shove him away in front of everybody. Instead, Jake's mother and his sister Joanne led her away to continue sobbing in the kitchen.

"Well," said Sidekick smugly, "Look at that poor girl!"

"Just butt out of my family and my business!" said Jake. Then he decided on a plan, which if it was to work, he had to play it cool. "Listen, I'm sorry. I'm just very upset right now. I hate to see everyone so upset like this. Just let me go to the bathroom and freshen up and we'll try to sort this thing out."

Laser Eyes looked hopefully at his companion as if to say, 'Finally, he's cracked. He's seen sense.'

Full of adrenaline, Jake dashed to his room and packed his bag. He wanted to find his books and he went to his parents' room. As he guessed, in his mother's favourite hiding place at the back of the wardrobe, were his books. When he had prepared a light backpack, he crept down the stairs and out of the door, as stealthily as he could. No-one was in sight. He was a young man and it had taken him this long to run away. He smiled when he remembered Sam Ericson's story about trying to run away from home. He broke into a run, exhilarated. He was free from the pressure. Where would he go? Anywhere in the world. The first thing to do was visit the bank, the second to get out of Salt Lake City.

Some of the bank clerks recognized him and started a cheerful conversation. "Sorry, I have to run," he said as he distributed the money in safe places about his person. He headed for the Greyhound bus station and decided to head for San Francisco. Even though Bruce probably wouldn't be there it felt somehow familiar.

·

唯邑

Interlude

After the excitement of getting away, reality dawned. What next? Deciding that he would wait until he got there, he leaned back in his seat and watched the featureless landscape go by. There were a few disapproving looks when the bus stopped at a rest station and Jake laid his mat on a grassy area to do his prayers. But he couldn't care less. He had survived the deprogrammers. Who cared about embarrassment? The worst they could do to him was haul him off the mat. He remembered the story when one of the people who hated the Prophet Muhammad's message came and dumped animal innards on him while he was praying. What could be worse than that? What was exhilarating for Jake was to be a stranger here and right from the first, known as a Muslim. He noticed a few nudges and sneers in his direction as he got back on the bus. The old man who had been sitting next to him seemed to shrink away towards the window.

唯邑

San Francisco, USA

The first thing he had to do in San Francisco was to find a place to stay. He found a cheap motel and felt quite daring as if he were acting in a movie. He had never travelled alone before, except that time when he was sent home from Japan, and he was a little uncertain as to how to arrange practical things. Still the place was cheerful and it was home for a few nights until he worked out his future. There was never a time in his life when he had felt the truth of the phrase more: 'Your future is in your own hands.' Well, he had started well. His mental and spiritual construction was in place. All he had to do was build a life around it.

The next day he decided to call his parents so they would not worry. His brother answered the phone almost instantly.

"Hullo!"

"Frank, it's Jake."

'Mom, Dad, it's Jake.' His brother didn't even answer him. He heard voices coming towards the phone, a little scuffle over who should answer and then his dad.

"Jake! Where are you?"

"Don't worry! I'm safe."

"Where are you?"

"It doesn't matter. What matters is I'm alone. I'm safe. I've got money."

"Jake, why are you doing this to us?"

"Dad, did you see those guys, how they treated me? If I'd have stayed another day they would have really run me crazy. I had to get out. All I wanted to do was talk to you, Mom and Alice. But those guys ..."

"Well, they're gone now. So come home and we can talk!"

"Dad, we won't get anywhere until you accept what's happened. I'm not going back to the church. I really believe this, Dad." He wanted some response. "Dad, this is really important to me."

"OK." His dad had to get off the phone trying to stifle his tears and Jake's mom took over.

"Jake, what's happened? Why aren't you coming home?"

"Mom, I love you. I don't want to hurt you or Dad but I couldn't stand the pressure with those guys."

"Oh, I know, Jake. I wish they'd never come and interfered and we could have had all of this sorted out. Jake, please come home!"

"I'm not coming back to the church, Mom. I don't expect you to accept me as a Muslim. That's too hard for you right now. We both need time. I'll stay away for a little while until we come to terms with it."

"Jake!" Now his mother was crying.

"Mom, I would have been on mission anyway until the summer. Put Frank on, Mom and let me explain the practical details. I love you both. I love all of you. Tell the others! OK?" Jake could almost hear her nod.

Then Frank's calm, composed voice came on. "Jake, Mom and Dad are both crying."

"I know, I know. That's why I want to explain the practical details to you. I'm a Muslim, yes. No, I'm not in a cult. I don't know anyone here at all. What I'm gonna do is look for some kind of unskilled work. I have money. I'll find a safe place to stay. Right now I'm in a motel. Tell them, please don't worry! Imagine I'm still in Japan. I'll call or write every week."

"What should we tell the Bishop and everyone at the church?"

"I'm more concerned about mom and dad. Just tell them those two guys they sent were just trying to make out I was crazy but I know I'm perfectly sane and I needed to get away and give my family time to come to terms with all of this and for me to start standing on my own feet."

"OK then, Jake. Well, rather you than me. Speak to you soon!"

He was glad to end on a happy note after the high drama of the last few days. He remembered when he left Japan and didn't have a friend in the world, and he felt afraid and alone. Now he was in the same situation but he felt quite the opposite, liberated and optimistic. He did the same thing he did then and called Suleiyman. This time Suleiyman recognized his voice at once.

"Jake, *as-salamu 'alaykum.*"

"*Wa-alaykum salam.* Good to speak to you."

"Jake, I tried to call you so many times and your family just said you didn't want to speak to me. They said you had realized you had made a big mistake. I was so worried."

"Well, I just had a terrible few days but now it's all over, thank God," and he gave Suleiyman an outline of the events.

Suleiyman laughed heartily when he told them the theory the deprogrammers had presented to him about the Muslims in Nagoya, and Jake kicked himself for even thinking it was a possibility. Suleiyman reminded him that the Jews and the Christians, as it said in the Qur'an, would never be happy unless you became like them. All they wanted was for him to give up his religion and they would be happy. Suleiyman was delighted that Jake felt strong in his faith and that he was making a new start.

"The next thing to do is find a job," said Jake "It has to be unskilled because I don't have any special training. So I'm gonna walk the streets and look for something."

"You could try Donut Heaven," suggested Suleiyman jokingly.

"Oh, great idea," said Jake. "I'd love to work there."

"Are you serious?"

"Sure, it would be a good place to work. Anyway I'll let you know how I'm getting along."

"Try and find a mosque, Jake. You'll need some support and somewhere to go and pray the Friday prayer."

"Will do. *Salam alaykum!*"

Jake strolled into Donut Heaven and confidently asked for the manager. He said he was looking for a job immediately and he wanted to work there.

"Well, that's great," said the manager, "only we don't have vacancies right now. Have you tried our other branches?"

Jake went around to the other branches and drew a blank. The people working there looked almost affronted, as though he was after their jobs. He said he would call again. For the next few days he called back at each of the branches to ask about vacancies. He had enough money to tide him over for a while and have some leisure time. He felt he needed a vacation. During the daytime he would go to the bay, see the sights and sit in the library reading, and in the evening he would hang around in burger joints and diners and drink coffee, which was horrible, but it was his right. He felt absolutely content. He called Bruce's parents, being careful not to give anything away, and they said he was still in Japan but had decided to leave the mission. They didn't seem too worried. He left a message for Bruce when he called home to say that Jake was in town. Then he called Dave's parents but they were anxious to get him off the phone, having heard the whole story from their son, as if they were afraid he might contaminate them with his foreign religion. He didn't even get a chance to give them a message for Dave that he should look him up but then he was glad in case it should get back to his family on the Mormon grapevine.

During that first week he also tried to find a mosque. Under 'mosque' in the phone book he had come upon 'Muhammad Mosque Number 12.' Sounded promising. So he made his way there. It seemed to be in a poor part of town. Coming to the block he walked up and down, unsure if this could be the place. There was nothing looking like a mosque there, just boarded-up doorways. There was a feeling in the neighbourhood also that people were watching him and wondering what a white man was doing around here. Jake felt anxious because he had heard all kinds of hysterical stories about black neighbourhoods, especially with Utah being so predominantly white with few minorities of any kind. Until 1978, he remembered, black people had been officially excluded from the Mormon priesthood. But now he was here, he should do the business he'd come to do or it wouldn't look good at all. He asked an old man who was sitting at the foot of some steps, where the Muhammad Mosque was. The man squinted at him and signalled towards the heavy door behind him. With trepidation, Jake opened the door and started up the stairs. Coming towards him was a young black man. He was wearing very formal dress with a bright white shirt, dress pants and a bow tie. He spoke politely to Jake.

"Can I help you?"

"I'm looking for Muhammad Mosque."

"This is it. Did you want something?"

"I'm looking for a place to pray."

"I don't think this is the place you're looking for," he said simply. "Maybe you need the *masjid*."

"Um, I guess so."

The young man directed him to the *masjid* and Jake went off bemused. Why was it called the Muhammad Mosque and why wouldn't they let him in? Maybe the guy didn't believe he was a Muslim.

The lobby of the *masjid* was a little more grand but it looked more like a community centre. This time two young men in long white robes were sitting at a desk. One of them, who looked Spanish, looked inquiringly at Jake.

"Is this the *masjid*?" Jake asked.

"Yes, what do you want?"

"I've come to pray."

"Are you Muslim?" he asked suspiciously.

"Yes, I am."

"OK, sign the book!"

His companion, a black man with sad eyes and round glasses seemed a little more welcoming. "The *masjid* is upstairs. The *wudu'* area for men is on the right."

"OK, thanks," said Jake.

He went up to perform his prayer but found it hard to concentrate in the huge, empty room with the lovely green carpet because the two young men had followed him upstairs and were watching him pray. As he raised his hands to make his *du'a*, he heard them commenting on him in Spanish, criticising the way he did his prayers. He wanted to get out as fast as possible.

The voice of an older man called to him as he passed by the office. "Is everything OK?" he asked. He looked kind and fatherly.

"Yes sir, I just came to pray."

"And you're a Muslim, *masha-Allah*." The man was obviously African-American but he said a little prayer of praise in Arabic and seemed to pronounce it very naturally. "How did you become Muslim?"

"In Japan, sir."

"Oh, are there lots of Muslims there? By the way, we are Muslims. Call me brother!"

"Ah, not really but there were a few students who got me interested in Islam and I decided to convert."

"How long have you been Muslim?"

"Just over a month."

"That's wonderful. It's good to see so many Americans

embracing Islam."

"How about yourself?"

"Oh, about twenty years. Yes, I came to Islam here in California, Los Angeles, in fact and then we moved here about fifteen years ago to set up the *masjid* and we have our own *madrasa* for the children. Do you live here?"

"I've just arrived here. I'm from Utah originally."

"Oh, Utah. Were you Mormon by any chance?"

Jake decided there would be no harm in telling him the story so he pulled up a chair and explained the events of the last few weeks. It was good at last to tell the story in detail to someone who really understood and really appreciated it. Although Suleiyman's English was nearly perfect, there were certain nuances that only an American would understand and certain special things that only a convert would appreciate, like the half-dream about getting up to open the drawer and read the Islamic leaflets and the miracle of the crescent moon, the way also that the Qur'an seemed at times to be an overwhelming personal message to him. Abdullah had known the same dawning realization of the wonder of the Qur'an and had experienced odd chances of circumstances which lead him further along the path. He insisted on using Jake's Muslim name. He said Yusuf was a far better name and that he should be proud of it. He explained the dynamics of the Muslim community in the US, San Francisco in particular. He explained that Yusuf had accidentally stumbled on the Black Muslim mosque of the area, which was run by a black separatist movement who called themselves Muslims by virtue of the fact that they didn't drink alcohol or do drugs. But other than that, they were as close to true Islam as the Mormons, preaching a fairy tale story of a black scientist who slipped up and created an evil white race who wreaked havoc on the earth. As usual there was the Johnny-come-lately prophet, so often a feature of the new religious movements in the US, whose name was Elijah Muhammad who invented many rituals and had managed to bring a lot of young people to his group who were looking for a change in the unjust society. These people might otherwise have been attracted to the real Islam. Yusuf found the story fascinating, especially the story of Malcolm X, who had had the courage to explain how he had been wrong in joining the separatist sect and preaching for them, and now he had found the true Islam, the true religion of Allah, the One True God. Yusuf remembered, back in Japan, when Gregor had talked about his wife and said, 'brave people convert and the really brave ones convert twice.' He hoped that wasn't true in his case.

Brother Abdullah told him that by the grace and guidance of Allah, a lot of young Americans, especially the African-Americans, were finding the true Islam and taking the responsibility into their own hands of trying to build a better society based on servitude to Allah alone.

"You see," Abdullah explained, "those at the bottom of society may seem the most miserable and hopeless but with the right faith they are the strongest and the most feared by those in power because they have nothing to lose at all and everything to gain. Islam spreads among the poor because Allah loves them most. Someone like you, Yusuf, you always have to be on your guard that you don't get complacent. Islamic faith has to be kept alive. It's easy for a person like you to fall back on his old support system."

Yusuf found Abdullah's attitude more challenging than that of the Muslims he had known in Japan. He was less inclined to praise him and flatter him for coming to Islam against very difficult odds. He saw this as inevitable, seeing that the truth of it was so glaringly obvious. It was a privilege and an honour of the highest degree to be guided by Allah and it was the Muslim who should be grateful. Abdullah didn't regard Yusuf as particularly special, just another convert like himself. He would only become special if he followed the Qur'an and the *Sunna* to become a more compassionate and decent person. Now he had this opportunity from Allah like all the other Muslims, converts and non-converts alike, to do his best. "Stand on your own two feet and do what you can!" said Abdullah. When Yusuf left and thanked him, he knew in his own mind that Abdullah was right. Ego, thinking you were special, was a killer of faith. Thinking you were better than other people due to birth or colour or circumstances or status was something that ruined belief. It was a hard lesson to learn so early in his Muslim career, but a useful one.

Yusuf had just begun to enjoy his leisurely routine when his job at Donut Heaven came up. At first he was assigned to the bakery at the back of the store, with a view to moving up in the world later. He was determined to put his best effort into the job. From the start, he had introduced himself as Yusuf and enjoyed the questioning looks and gradual probing into his personal history. Although foreigners were commonplace in this city, someone with a name like Yusuf who looked and sounded as home-grown American as him was an oddity. He simply said he was a Muslim from Salt Lake City. Everyone seemed to think that was quite something and it wasn't long before Yusuf became the object of some curiosity as he performed his prayers in a small storeroom at the back of the restaurant, ate his first food on the stroke of sunset and didn't swear or joke about girls or go drinking in the evening. For Yusuf, it was fun to be a saint among heathens. Brother Abdullah had advised him to grow a beard according to the *Sunna* so he was glad to be able to go through the stubble stage in the bakery. It made him look older and more mature.

He found himself a room in a small apartment block owned by a Chinese lady. It was near the Chinese part of town. He had already been looking for *tatami* in the Japanese district but found it hopelessly expensive. Instead he invested in what passed for a futon in the US and tried to give his room a Japanese flavour. Brother Abdullah had also told him to watch for the special night towards the end of Ramadan which came once in a year, which was the anniversary of the night the first verses of the Qur'an were revealed. In the Qur'an, this night was said to be better than a thousand months, a night to make supplications to Allah, to ask for forgiveness, to be thankful and to reflect. It was the night when hosts of angels were in attendance. It was a good night to spend as a vigil in prayer or recitation of the Qur'an. The catch was that no-one knew the exact date each year, only that it would be one of the odd-numbered nights in the last ten days of the month. The 27th was said to be a particular probability, and it was to be noted that in the Islamic calendar, the night comes before the day. Since Allah loves His servants to call on Him, it was a chance for Muslims to make vigil and pray on all of the nights to be sure that *Lailat al-Qadr,* or the Night of Power, would be spent in the best way. Yusuf decided to do a private vigil on the nights of the 25th and 27th of Ramadan. Personally, he felt a charge in the air on the 25th night, a special motion in the sky, a tremendous feeling of being closer to God. He preferred to do the vigil alone this time. He didn't feel ready to be among other Muslims yet.

Brother Abdullah had invited him to take part in the Eid celebrations at their community hall, but Yusuf had to work a shift. Moreover, he had still never felt welcome at that *masjid* whenever he had gone along to pray. There was something akin to hostility, except on the part of Brother Abdullah who always treated him well. He had been told of another mosque nearer his home which was used more by foreign students. Yusuf decided to go there and check it out. So after his shift he went along for Maghrib prayer. He had had his own little Eid feast at work of doughnuts and more doughnuts. There were surprisingly few men at the prayer, mostly dressed in ethnic clothes. They all shook hands and wished him *Eid Mubarak,* but none of them asked him what he was doing for the festival. Disappointed, he went back to his neighbourhood and stopped by the supermarket to stock up on goodies. He took his booty back to his lonely room. All San Francisco was oblivious to this happy occasion and this felt so different to Christmas. He felt like he had really deserved a feast and some fun, but it was flat. He made himself a little cracker out of coloured paper and placed some dates inside. He pulled it apart with both hands. 'Happy *Eid!* Table for one sir?' And he sat down to eat his solitary banquet.

Yusuf preferred Donut Heaven to anything else in his life at that time, even the mosque, because every time he went to the mosque, despite hanging around pretending to look at books or bulletin boards, he would just get handshakes or greetings but no conversation. His colleagues in the bakery were atheists to a man: two Jewish atheists, one Chinese atheist and one African-American atheist. They enjoyed teasing Yusuf during Ramadan, trying to tempt him by wafting doughnuts under his nose and eating their own lunch with relish. They thought he was extremely eccentric, but for Yusuf it was nice to be different from that crowd and he didn't find their remarks offensive, but fairly good-natured. An atmosphere of camaraderie prevailed in the bakery backed by a good degree of rivalry with the front-of-house staff. Katie, who was a born-again Christian, often caught the tail end of some or other theological debate as she swept in and out to collect refill trays. Morris, the African-American, asked a lot of questions about the Muslims and had a certain degree of respect for them, the way they abstained from alcohol and drugs, and as he said, 'the women knew their place, and they didn't lie or steal.' Yusuf tried to explain that there was much more to it than that. With the others, it was just a matter of dealing with the basics: God!

"God, I don't believe in you," one of the Jewish guys, Michael would say. Then he would look up. "See, no thunderbolts or lightning. I'm still here. If you're up there, God, why don't you strike me dead?"

"Allah gives men a lot of rope," Yusuf would explain, "to make mistakes time after time. If he punished us straight away, there'd be no-one left. Don't you know the Israelites used to say the same thing to the Prophet Moses in his time? 'Why doesn't Allah bring on the punishment now?' Moses would tell them that Allah was very forbearing with men."

"Moses didn't call him Allah," said Josh, the other Jewish baker.

"Allah is the true name of God," said Yusuf. "It means *the* God."

Cyril, the Chinese baker sometimes looked up from his work with an ironic smile. "I can't believe in this day and age, right at the end of the 20th century, you guys are still falling for this stuff."

Then there would be long debates about the origin of the universe and space exploration and other scientific arguments, and Yusuf would pull verses from the Qur'an like rabbits from a hat to refute them. He felt invincible in his arguments. Sometimes Cyril and the others would listen for a moment when he would talk about cosmology and embryology in the Qur'an, but as soon as he mentioned the words 'scripture' or 'prophets' or the 'Day of Judgment' they would all switch off again with condescending smiles. The manager would quip, 'the only profits I'm interested in are the ones from doughnut sales. Get working!' He too enjoyed the banter from the bakery.

Sometimes the conversation would turn to politics, where Yusuf found himself on unfamiliar ground. He had taken to reading *Time*, *Newsweek* and *The Economist* on a regular basis to try and educate himself, especially on the Middle East.

"Why are those guys always fighting each other?" asked Josh once, referring to Muslims in general. Yusuf could not answer these questions and they troubled him. Sometimes he would say that San Francisco at night was more dangerous than any Muslim country. He saw the behaviour of Muslims as a slight against the religion, but the Muslims in Japan had explained to him that all Muslims were by no means practicing and that the power of most Muslim countries was in the hands of people who certainly didn't deserve the name. Sometimes Yusuf felt afraid that he was supposed to be on the same side as these people who always looked so threatening in the magazines and on TV. Maybe it was best to keep out of politics. Other times Josh would bring up the subject of Palestine.

"My father says those are Jewish lands and that all Jews should return there."

"Then what are you doing here?" Michael would say. He supported the Palestinians who had been thrown out of their homes. He had been to Israel himself, unlike Josh and had seen the situation first-hand.

"But the Jews were thrown out of their lands," Josh would complain.

"And so were the Africans," said Morris. "What do you think I'm doing here?"

"If you look back far enough, what about the Native Americans?" Michael would add. "Everyone's got a grievance."

"But the Jews have no homeland!" cried Josh.

"Sure you have. You live here in San Francisco," said Morris.

Most of Josh's half-understood Zionist arguments ended up flattened like this, but he always took it in good humour. He couldn't look to Michael for support because he was from a non-observant Jewish family, and Michael's own inclinations were towards international socialism. He would only sit up and listen to Yusuf when he expounded Islamic theories of finance and economy and social justice, but he was totally against charity, which was a pillar of Islam. For him, social equity was the responsibility of the state and no one should have to ask for charity. Yusuf told him that charity in Islam was of more benefit to the giver than the receiver because it was like building up credit in the hereafter and it made him less selfish and less attached to material things. But as soon as the talk drifted into the realms of the eschatological, he had lost Michael.

At the beginning of his adventure Yusuf was sure to call his family once a week just to tell them he was OK and to stave off calls to come home. He promised a meeting in the near future, but as he got more involved in San Francisco life the intervals between the calls got longer and the tone of his parents' voices became more and more resigned. Yusuf began to feel he didn't need them any more. Their lives were so different to the lifestyle he had carved out for himself in San Francisco. It would be nice to see them, maybe to visit, but his life no longer revolved around them and a longing to win their approval and aspire to their ideals.

Yusuf continued to go to the little mosque near where he lived and got to know the men who came regularly for prayers, but they were always very quiet and left right away. Those who did stay would sit in circles speaking Arabic, and Yusuf always pretended he was too busy to stay and join in. But now weeks had gone by and he hadn't talked properly to anyone. Why wouldn't someone at least ask about him? He obviously looked different, but they just seemed to accept him with no questions asked, like Brother Abdullah had done. A couple of times when he had gone back to see Brother Abdullah and ask his advice he had not been there and the watchmen in the lobby and some of the other brothers cast such doubtful glances on him that he stopped going there. This was why he longed for work rather than to be alone on his days off in his little room with the Japanese overtones. Since he had left Japan he hadn't even looked at his Japanese language texts and the calligraphy he used to find so fascinating. Instead he put all his time into trying to teach himself Arabic from a book of exercises. It was hard going without a teacher and he would go over and over *ba, ta, tha,* and then get fed up and glance over the rest without trying to learn them. This stood between him and the Qur'an which he'd so far only read in translation. He noticed that whenever Brother Abdullah quoted from the Qur'an he always used the original Arabic because as he said: 'Other than that is not the Qur'an but a translation of a conjecture on the meaning of the Qur'an', far removed from the Word of Allah itself.

One day after Friday prayers, when the crowds were quite large in his local mosque, Yusuf decided to take the initiative. It was no good him complaining that no-one ever spoke to him. He would have to make the first move. Tentatively, he approached a circle of men whom he recognized who had often greeted him. '*As-salamu 'alaikum* Brother', they choirused, and were about to leave it at that when Yusuf hung around for a while and they all made room for him to join their circle. Their conversation broke off as they looked at him expectantly.

"I thought it was about time I introduced myself. I'm Yusuf." He was proud of his new name in this kind of company.

"*Masha-Allah!*" said an older man with a large mustache. "Glad to meet you brother. My name is Ibrahim." Then he went on to introduce the others.

No one seemed to know what to say next so Yusuf said, "I'm from Utah."

"Oh," said Ibrahim. "That's nice. I'm from Lebanon." Then again around the circle announcing countries. No one was particularly interested in the fact that Yusuf was from Utah.

"I haven't been Muslim very long," he said. "Just a few months."

"How did you learn about Islam?" asked another Lebanese called Ishaq.

"I met a Muslim in Japan who gave me a copy of the Qur'an."

"*Masha-Allah!*" A few more phrases of Arabic. "Why were you in Japan, Brother?"

"I used to be a missionary. A Mormon missionary."

"A missionary?" More whispers round the circle. "So what made you embrace Islam?"

"I believed it, I guess," said Yusuf. "It seemed logical." His dramatic story sounded a little pathetic put like that.

The men continued smiling and asking more polite questions, but despite the fact that their English was good, Yusuf never felt that they were as curious about him as he would have liked. If they had seemed more enthusiastic he would have told his story in detail but somehow he couldn't be bothered. As the conversation fizzled out he felt as though he should have a reason for coming over to bother them, so he said he was interested in Arabic lessons. They gave him the address of a college which ran night classes and offered to help him as much as they could. Yusuf thanked them and they went back to their pow-wow.

So this was the reality of being a Muslim for Yusuf. So much for cults and people eager to draw him into their influence. The

Muslims he'd met so far had been at best mildly interested in him as a person, at worst, quite indifferent. There didn't seem to be any group he could be part of. Where were all the other converts he had read about? Where was the community? It was a lonely life.

As his sense of isolation as a Muslim grew, his personal zeal did not diminish and Yusuf was eager to proselytize anyone anywhere. It wouldn't take him long to twist the conversation around to the subject of Islam. At least that could be his goal, to spread Islam far and wide. His landlady was not as patient as his co-workers at Donut Heaven and when he went to sit with her family she would often tick him off. 'No, we're not interested in your Islam stuff. We are not religious people. We had enough with the born-agains before you and now we've had enough. I'm an honest woman and I try to make an honest living and I keep out of people's way. I can't do any more than that.'

"I used to think the same as you", was Yusuf's refrain, although it was not strictly true. He had really moved from Mormon zeal to Muslim zeal with not much in between in the way of godlessness.

"It's people like you cause trouble in the world. If they just leave people be, these religious people, everyone get on with their own business and everyone be OK." Mrs Chan ate sunflower seeds all the time and would punctuate her sentences with a "pah" as she spat the shells into her ashtray.

During the evenings when he had driven Mrs Chan to distraction and went to spend an evening alone in his room, the video was his lifeline. He didn't care much for TV because it was so difficult to really concentrate on something before it jumped to another topic. So Yusuf filled many an hour with video movies, sometimes watching three, back to back, through half the night. He would stave off the moment when the lively motion of people in his room would fade, leaving an empty silence. He and Mrs Chan shared a love for the television serial LA Law and she lent him her prized cassettes of episodes of the series, each one lasting about an hour, recorded one after another. It was not unknown for Yusuf to watch three episodes one evening followed by three the next morning before work and then rush back to get through the last four that evening. It was almost like a job, but he got to love those characters and care about them and analyze all the ethics of each individual case and what he himself would have done. Otherwise Yusuf chose movies of every type to while away the evenings, always being careful to check the morality of the movie first. In a way he built up a personal education around the films. There was a lot about life, even American life, he had never seen or known. He watched the ills of a godless society played out and drew lessons from them. He watched the breakup of families through careless behaviour between men and women and lack of concern for the integrity of relationships, the loneliness and despair of people who had either been left out of the rat race or who had won it and seen there was no prize worth having. He saw the consequences of poisoning the body with alcohol and drugs, the wars of greed and exploitation, and class struggle, now and in the past. There was no movie from which he hadn't been able to draw some lesson and become more convinced of the wisdom of God's guidance to man. He admitted that he was lonely himself but that was because he had no real friends and his family relations were suspended, but since he had embraced Islam he had never known despair. He longed to lecture the people in the movies about what was wrong with their lives.

At work the guys had started putting pressure on him about girls. Why didn't he come out with them and 'look for girls', as they put it? Only Cyril was married, but the others did not have regular girlfriends and often went to bars and clubs in the hope of meeting someone. Yusuf had explained that he had broken up with his fiancée and that unless she became Muslim it was unlikely they would end up married. As far as he understood it, as a Muslim it was marriage or nothing. There was no concept of casual relationships or girlfriends. You had to commit yourself to marriage if you wanted a relationship. Yusuf was used to the teasing from non-Mormons at school but the endless questions about the lives of Muslim women, the four wives thing, the modest dress, left him floundering. It was his movie education which helped him to explain that if women dressed decently and did not try to flirt outside marriage and did not act friendly with any men outside the family, and if men treated them properly and didn't try to harass them, marriages would have a better chance of staying intact and the relationship chaos which now prevailed in the US with all its consequences for children and the health of society in general would not exist. Katie, in her brief chances to catch parts of Yusuf's arguments, was impressed with them but the men still thought he needed to 'lighten up', as they put it, and come out with them.

Yusuf had never in his life been to a place resembling a bar or a club and as a Muslim he didn't have any inclination to do so, but he was lonely and he liked his co-workers, so he didn't see any harm in accepting their invitation to a steak and rib restaurant. They had been careful to meet with Yusuf's requirements that the place should serve fish as he had been trying to avoid non-*halal* meat as much as possible. The other stipulation was that none of the group would drink alcohol at the table. But when they went into the restaurant he knew right away he was in the wrong place. Their table was an island of abstinence in a sea of ribaldry. Tables of college students and groups of young people were tucking into huge steaks and racks of ribs while waitresses dressed as cowgirls kept them supplied with huge pitchers of beer. Other drunks lined the bar at the far end of the room and they were all shouting at each other over the results of a football game. There were busy pinball machines all around the room and loud country and western music throbbing from the jukebox. Josh and Morris didn't take long to get into the spirit of the place, chatting to the college girls at the next table and offering to pay for their desserts. Inevitably they started asking if they could order just one beer each because they were parched.

"Have water!" said Yusuf trying to stay as jovial as possible over his shrimp.

"Water? We need beer." said Josh.

"C'mon, you guys. You promised."

"Yeah, you guys," said Michael. "He told us he could come along if we didn't drink. Can't you go without beer for just one night?"

But soon the girls began to order drinks and asked about Yusuf, whose face betrayed his embarrassment.

"What's wrong with the guy with the beard?" asked one.

"He's Muslim," said Morris proudly. "He doesn't drink."

"That's OK," said the girl. "We're not asking him to drink."

"No, he doesn't even approve of drinking," said Morris.

But the girls' persuasion was too strong and Josh and Morris ended up at the bar. Yusuf was mentally kicking himself. He should have known. They respected his religion insofar as it didn't infringe on their pleasures. He was a minority of one and he felt it. What to do now? He could leave and make an angry scene, or leave politely, or sit and protest, or sit and put up with it. Which was the Islamic way? He knew very well the Islamic way. It was to leave politely and it took all the courage he could muster to stand up, apologize, thank them, wish them a good evening, put his jacket on and leave.

The second influential Muslim in Yusuf's life he also met in Donut Heaven. Cyril had a local garage where he went to have his car fixed, and he knew of a Muslim there called Aziz. His parents were Jordanian but he had lived in California for most of his life. Cyril had been telling Aziz about Yusuf and his funny ways and Aziz was interested to meet him. So they met over coffee and doughnuts in Donut Heaven and at last Yusuf found a Muslim who was fascinated by his story and seemed genuinely interested in him as a person and not as a convert specimen. What was good for Yusuf was that he was the key to the so-far secret world of the convert community in San Francisco and all manner of study circles, socials, discussions and classes about Islam. Aziz was definitely an 'Islam enthusiast' and the first thing he did was to invite Yusuf to his family home for a proper *halal* meal, the first he'd had since Japan.

Aziz's house seemed warm from the minute they opened the door. The interior was of a very pleasant temperature and was lightly perfumed. The couches were low and very soft in the living room which was adorned with beautiful rugs. As Yusuf was introduced to Aziz's father and older brother, beautifully-dressed children of varying ages kept appearing at the door, peeping at him and then running away. 'Come and say Hello to Uncle' said Aziz. It seemed the house was home to a large extended family including Aziz's grand-parents, parents, two brothers and two sisters, as well as one brother-in-law, one sister-in-law and their children. 'Big family!' Yusuf remarked as Granddad and the other men were brought in to welcome him. Granddad had everything explained to him in Arabic but Yusuf could tell by his warm handshake and tearful expression that he was very moved by Yusuf's conversion and he sat down wiping his brow exclaiming all the time in Arabic. First they had little glasses of fruit juice, and then they all went to sit on cushions around a low coffee table. One by one the dishes came in, small plates of olives and delicacies, salads, pickles, pastes, then next up, several varieties of decorated rice and then an array of meat stews and roast meat platters crowned by a stuffed leg of lamb. They left the best till last. Only then did the women file in and sit down at the neighbouring table, often jumping up and down to attend to some request from the men.

"This is a lot of work," said Yusuf. "Thank you so much. I wasn't expecting all this."

"It's nothing," said Aziz's father. "But you are our special guest."

Yusuf remembered the dining etiquette from Japan. Don't eat too quickly unless you wanted your plate refilled *ad infinitum*! Say '*al-hamdu li'Llah*' at least three times to refuse!

Aziz's female relatives were dressed in varying colours and styles. They all had head-covers on except one who was Aziz's sister-in-law. She had very thick, curly hair and an abundance of of jewellery. The women were occupied with fetching and carrying and seeing to the children who had become bolder and were now wandering around with bits of food scattering it all over the carpet and coming up to inspect Yusuf more closely. Aziz's relatives wanted to know the full story of Yusuf's experiences and he was only too happy to tell them and relive all the most precious moments. For them the highlights were the fact that he had been so impressed with the verses of the Qur'an which seemed to speak directly to him, and the fact that he was sent home from his mission. That he had been tested like this so early in his career as a Muslim was, in their eyes, a true indication of his mettle. Most dramatic of all was the rejection by his family and the terrible days with the deprogrammers. Here the women fell silent and listened intently.

"*Insha-Allah*, Allah will guide your parents," Aziz translated for his grandfather. "I am sure they are good people."

"It's bound to be a shock for them at first," said Aziz's brother Ma'mun, "especially as they are already religious people."

"Slowly, slowly, they will come to accept it, *insha-Allah,*" said his father.

When Grandfather asked for an explanation of the intricacies of the Mormon religion, Yusuf could tell he was shocked to think that people could hold such beliefs. Aziz said that he couldn't believe someone could deceive so many people.

The discussion then turned to some of the charlatans who had tried to deceive Muslims over the centuries, creating little sects around themselves. Yusuf had read a little about the *mahdi* who was prophesied by Prophet Muhammad, peace be upon him, who would unite the Muslims once more. The *mahdi* would bring no new message and would not deviate from the *Sunna* of the Blessed Prophet. He would just be a unifier. The prospect of the coming of the *mahdi* gave free rein to several impostors who claimed to be him, such as the Qadiani leader in Pakistan who had been encouraged by the British Raj. However the lifestyle and the words of these people, their behaviour and actions, usually discredited them in the eyes of the majority. A few people however were led astray and it would be left to their children to find their way back to the true Islam.

Grandfather was concerned that Yusuf should do *da'wa* as much as possible with his family to set them straight. It was a shame to leave such good people, who cared about their son, wandering in the dark.

"Allah will guide them," said Aziz's father, "if they are searching for the truth."

Yusuf talked about the isolation he had been feeling, and when Aziz's mother heard about his lonely *Eid* she was very upset. "If only we'd known," she kept saying, "we'd have invited you. Everyone was here." They had some knowledge of the other mosques in the area and communities, but apart from Aziz and his brother, they tended to stay in their own circle.

"You'll find this a problem wherever you go," said Hasan, the younger brother. "Lack of unity. Whenever a group of Muslims get together, within a few years you'll find three or four mosques."

"It's OK to have meetings in your own language," said Aziz, "as long as you get together regularly and work together. Trouble is everyone's always talking about unity but it's always unity with them in charge. Then the other group says, 'Hey, wait a minute! We wanna be in charge.' That's how you get the arguments."

"Take the people of Granddad's generation," interjected

Hasan. "They're pretty much into being Arab. They don't know much about other Muslims, say from Pakistan, Malaysia or Africa but here we're all brought up together. We mix a lot more and we understand each other because we were brought up in the same culture."

"Granddad's not nationalist," said Aziz, affronted.

"I didn't mean he's nationalist," said Hasan. "I just mean his generation. That's more their mentality."

Granddad started to ask for an explanation but they didn't want to offend him, so Aziz's father asked Yusuf how he had managed with Arabic.

"Actually, I'm trying to study it now but it's so difficult from books. You really need a native speaker so I'm thinking of enrolling in a class."

"I'll teach you," said Aziz.

"Yusuf needs to be taught properly," said his father. "I think the classes are a good idea. What about your plans for the future?"

"Well as you know I'm at Donut Heaven now." He made it sound as though he were at Harvard. "I'm in the bakery and they say I can probably go into the front in maybe six months or so."

"You must come and work for us in our delicatessen," said Aziz's brother-in-law firmly.

"No, no." Aziz's father brushed him aside. "Yusuf is an educated person. He doesn't want to spend his life in shops. No, you must go to college."

"Well, yeah. Before I became Muslim I always thought I'd go on to college after my mission. I had the possibility of a place at BYU I was interested in studying economics but of course I've lost that now."

"There are other colleges," said Aziz.

"You know the University of Indiana?" said Aziz's father. "They have a very good Islamic centre there. Ask for the prospectus! See what they have! You never know, there may be a place for you there."

It seemed worth a try. All thoughts of college and career had been suspended in Yusuf's mind up until then. He had even been considering what kind of career structure might be offered by Donut Heaven, but Aziz's father was right. He couldn't just drift on in a dead-end job in a city where he had no ties and no purpose.

Soon he would have to think about focusing his energy and his skills.

The meal was wonderful and not too spicy for Yusuf. It was great to eat a whole meal without worrying about what was in it. Mrs Chan knew about his eating requirements when he had an occasional meal with her and her family but he didn't know how fussy she was about frying pork in the same oil as food for himself. He was never sure if somehow bits of pork or swine products could somehow find their way into his food. The meal at Aziz's house was perfect in taste and variety and the atmosphere and conversation were exactly what he was looking for. The table was cleared and put aside while they prayed all together. Then the coffee and desserts were brought in. Yusuf explained how, as a Mormon, he had not been allowed to drink coffee and that he had just started to get used to it.

Aziz's father made a point of saying that in Islam, it was as wrong to forbid something that Allah had made lawful for people as to allow something that He had forbidden, such as usury or alcohol. So he said Yusuf should enjoy his coffee. Hasan said that since coffee and tea were not around in the time of the Prophet he had received no ruling on it, but Aziz's father said that Allah knows the past, present and future and if He had intended, He would have made it unlawful in some way. But the argument for smoking brought up by Ma'mun, who was a smoker himself, was refuted when Aziz said that although smoking did not exist at the time of the Prophet and so was not forbidden by name, yet Allah had forbidden all things that were harmful to health and in this respect smoking in Islamic law was considered despicable, though not expressly forbidden.

"Don't confuse poor Yusuf with fine points of *Shari'a!*" said one of Aziz's sisters. "He has enough to learn."

"Oh, that's OK," said Yusuf. "I have so many questions about *Shari'a*. It's really useful for me to get to know the practical things."

Everyone was very impressed that he had been able to fast the whole of Ramadan even during the deprogramming session. They felt that this was sure to strengthen his faith from the very beginning and set him in good stead for the future. He asked how he was to pay his *zakah* which he had not yet paid formally for the year but they all laughed at his conscientiousness and said if anything, being new to Islam, this year he would be entitled to receive *zakah*.

When Aziz had dropped him back home Yusuf went over the evening again. It had been a really happy time from beginning to end. Aziz's mother and father were the perfect parent figures to him and the atmosphere of the house with the children and the activity and stimulating conversation made him sure that this was exactly the environment he had been looking for. They were interested in him and impressed with his leap of faith. At that time, though he feared it was a bit self-centred, it was what he needed. He needed outside approval from other Muslims as well as their encouragement. He laughed when he thought of the fuss they had made at the end of the meal when he began to stack the dishes. The look of astonishment on the face of the men had been hilarious, but Yusuf had always lived in households where men did their share of the chores. When he explained to them, the women heartily approved and reminded the men that the Prophet himself, peace be upon him, had always helped with the domestic work when he was at home with his family. They said the men had fallen into traditions which had drifted away from Islam, but after a lifetime of being waited on, Granddad assured them that he was not going to start interfering in the kitchen at his time of life.

The advice from the family spurred Yusuf on to make some plans. First he enrolled for the Arabic classes at the summer night school and then he applied for information about the University of Indiana. He didn't know why he couldn't be bothered to try for any other colleges. He just knew that he felt good about the prospect of Indiana. It was encouraging to have some goals set now after this period of drifting.

Yusuf became a regular visitor at Aziz's house. He always felt welcome there and got the feeling that Aziz genuinely enjoyed talking to him. Soon they felt able to be more informal with him so that often he would drop by and watch TV with them in the evenings for an hour or so. He liked having somewhere to go, and then he felt cheerful about going back to his own room. It didn't seem so empty any more. His knowledge was increasing very quickly now he had begun to get a wider perspective on the realities of modern Muslim living. He became aware of the gulf between the Islamic ideals and the painful reality of many Muslim lives all over the world. There was never any shortage of people who needed help or support, or someone to speak out for them.

At the Islamic circle on Saturday afternoons Yusuf met for the first time a Muslim whom he could regard as similar to himself, a white convert whose name was Rashid. He came from San Francisco and had converted while working in the Middle East. He had been a Muslim for two years and had experienced some changes similar to Yusuf. The big difference between them was that Rashid came from a nominally Christian family and his family's attitude to his conversion had been lukewarm but not hostile. He was enthralled when Yusuf told him the story of the storm that hit him when he first came back home from Japan. Rashid's family had found out gradually as his lifestyle and interests began to change but they just put that down to his being influenced by his trip to Dubai. Also his conversion had been a fairly gradual process, a progressive dawning that what he was hearing about fitted his instincts very well and everything seemed to fit neatly into place. There were no unusual mysteries to be unravelled as there were with Christianity, and as he put it, Islam covered the whole world and the whole of history. For example, Rashid explained that the Jews had the Middle East covered from the time of Moses onwards, but what could you say about the people before Moses and those in more remote parts of the world? 'Are we saying God just forgot them?' he said. 'Then with Christianity you get this retrospective salvation thing for those who lived before the time of Jesus, so that Jesus died for people's sins even before he appeared on earth. Then we've got the Buddhists and the Buddha only came to the Far East so that's not fair, and besides he only appeared five hundred years before Jesus whereas Islam covers people from the first creation on and covers the whole world. No, there were no holes in it for me. I tried to think of arguments against it but it's absolutely watertight, one hundred percent. Isn't that amazing?'

"Same with me," replied Yusuf. "Of course I was terrified when I first began to read it and it made so much sense. I thought there had to be a catch and so I did the same thing, coming up with all these arguments and possibilities but I would get the answer right away and I kept saying to myself, 'What am I gonna do? This thing looks like it's true. Are you gonna keep fighting it?'"

438

Rashid had a girlfriend whom he had known before he went to Dubai and when he told her he was interested in Islam she was interested too, and quite prepared to hear all about it if it was important to Rashid. But when she heard some of the implications for her becoming Muslim and some of the commitments that were required of her if she embraced the faith herself, she began to get cold feet. They had decided to separate for a while and wait to see if Marie could see herself committed to Rashid and Islam, but Rashid wanted her to love the religion for herself and not because she wanted to marry him. Otherwise if their marriage began to go wrong she would probably throw out Islam along with the marriage. But he was hopeful and Marie still came to the woman's circle from time to time to talk to other American converts and to be reassured by them.

It was Aziz's father who first broached the subject of marriage with Yusuf. He told him that there were plenty of women looking for practicing Muslim husbands and he only had to say the word and arrangements could begin to find him a suitable wife. When it was put like that, Yusuf felt scared and couldn't help imagining himself married off and on his honeymoon within a week with a woman he knew very little about. The Mormon system had been similar to an arranged marriage system, but it was different if the families knew each other and the girl was someone from the neighbourhood with the same outlook. Yusuf thought about Rashid and could see himself marrying a convert American who spoke the same language and had a similar type of background and maybe more enthusiasm to work for Islam. He wanted someone with a sense of humour. When he considered the matter properly, however, he decided marriage was something he was working towards, but which could be deferred. First he wanted to set himself on course, see where he was going in the world and then start thinking about family life. Aziz's father accepted his decision and agreed it was good to do his studying first and get a good job, but he advised him that in the meantime if he met someone he felt was right for him, he shouldn't hesitate. Yusuf agreed because he had seen what delay had done to poor Alice. Every time he thought of her, he felt a terrible pang of guilt. Even though it was for the best in the end, it must have seemed to her that her life had come to a halt when she found out that the focus of her life for the past few years had vanished like an illusion.

There were some American Muslim women in Yusuf's Arabic class and he was keen to talk to them and see what things were like from their perspective, but they kept their distance from him and always left right after the lesson to go home. Two of them seemed older but there was one younger one who wore a head scarf but no Arabic *jilbab* like the others, just an ordinary Western-style skirt and jacket. Yusuf wanted to speak to her but she was always with her friends. Then one evening as he left the building behind them, he saw her get into a car with a Middle-Eastern looking man. She looked too young to be married. Well, that was one prospect gone!

As far as the women at the circle went, he never saw them as they always sat on the other side of the partition. They would listen to the talk given by the brother who led the circle and would then have their own discussion. Judging by the number of children running around, it was likely that most of them were married anyway. Yusuf asked Rashid if he knew of any single convert women but he said that most of them were either married or engaged to Muslims or were dating Muslims, as this was a very common way for women to first hear about Islam. There were plenty of stories of American women who fell in love with Muslim men who if they had been practicing Islam properly they probably would never have met. The man would try to teach the girl as much as he knew about Islam, but after marriage things would start to go wrong. The woman would expect to retain the same lifestyle but the husband would expect her to behave like the women back home and follow his traditional culture. In many cases the woman would build up a resentment towards the religion, but in others she would be motivated to find out more about it, and thus came upon the true spirit of Islam. In the best of scenarios she would succeed in encouraging her husband to practice Islam properly, but in the majority she would fail and the marriage would flounder, or else she would carry on putting up with a less then satisfactory marriage and try to raise her children as best she could in Islam.

The only woman who was happy to talk to Yusuf, apart from Mrs Chan, was another of the students at the Arabic class. Patricia was not a Muslim but was planning to travel around the Middle East and wanted to get a start by learning Arabic. Yusuf found her a bit tiresome because she kept questioning him and coming to sit with him during the break when he wanted to speak to the teacher. She was a heavy-set woman with a lugubrious face and she seemed to have a fascination with converts. For her, these were people who had gone over the edge and dived right into a culture that she was just content to explore from the sidelines. She had already wearied the Muslim girls with her questions, and now she was asking Yusuf all about Islam. But no matter what Yusuf said about Islam being a universal religion she was only interested in the Mid-East connection.

"Now I could never imagine actually taking on the religion and the culture and everything," she mused. "Was that weird for you?"

"At first it was hard to get used to, the prayers for example."

"Like you mean you pray like that on the floor facing Mecca and everything?" She giggled.

"Yes, that's the way Muslims have always prayed."

"That's pretty neat. I've seen pictures of it and everything, them all praying together but I've never seen any women in the pictures."

"Sure the women pray but in a different part of the mosque."

"Yeah, I heard from Aisha and the girls. So why aren't women allowed to pray beside the men?"

"It's distracting I guess, also the postures. The women prefer to pray in their own groups."

"By the way, you can have four wives now." She sniggered into her coffee.

At the moment Yusuf was wondering whether he'd be able to find one wife. The four wives thing was always a favourite question for non-believers.

"It's still unusual for a man to have more than one wife but it's a possibility that's there for him. It can be a good thing in some cases like if one wife is infertile or very sick or wants to spend more time on her career. Anyway, a large percentage of American men have several girlfriends at the same time or a wife and a mistress and people don't even think that's strange, plus he doesn't have to keep them or provide for them or take care of the children. In Islam you can't get away with that lack of responsibility."

This made Patricia think for a while. Yusuf could see the

thought processes moving across her brow.

"Yeah, I guess you've got a point," she said slowly.

They sat for a while and Yusuf thought she had run out of questions. Then, "Have you been to the Middle East?"

"No, never."

"Are you going?"

"Maybe, *insha-Allah*."

"I suppose you'll end up there in the end, being a Muslim."

"Not necessarily. A Muslim can live anywhere."

"So why are you studying Arabic?"

"Because it's the language of the Qur'an and I want to read the Qur'an."

"Yeah, I know about the Qur'an. I've bought a copy to take with me." She fished in her purse for her little leather-bound copy.

"Can I see?" Yusuf took it to look. It was a beautiful little copy. "There's no translation," he said.

"So, I'm learning Arabic."

"But how will you be able to understand the Qur'an?"

"Oh I probably won't read it myself. It's just to carry around with me so when I meet people they know I'm interested in Islam."

"It's really worth reading and studying for yourself," said Yusuf. "Would you like me to get you a copy of 'the Meaning of the Holy Qur'an' in English?"

"Is it pocket-size?"

Yusuf laughed. "No, does it have to be?"

"Well I'm gonna be travelling real light. I don't want to overfill my bag."

It was probably a dead-end effort trying to get Patricia into Islam at this stage in her life. She was too preoccupied with her trip. Better let her enjoy her travelling, and who knows, she might learn something really important, maybe even meet someone spiritual.

"So, what's you itinerary?" he asked, and here Patricia was onto her favourite subject as she pulled out her maps.

"I'm starting in Morocco," she said, "heading right across North Africa through Egypt, then up into Israel, Jordan, Syria."

"Do you have visas for all of these countries?"

"I'm planning that now. Don't worry! I've made very careful plans. I have several guide books and lots of telephone numbers and stuff."

"You must be pretty excited, but what's it like for a woman travelling alone?"

"It'll be fine. I'm a pretty confident person. I know how to be assertive because I've heard you have to be really firm with some of these salesmen and guides and everyone because when they see a westerner on their own they see dollars and they give you a lot of hassle. I'll maybe team up with other travellers along the way, say if we have to cross the desert. That's also why I need Arabic, to bargain with drivers and everything, also to avoid unwanted attention."

Yusuf could imagine Patricia wending her way across the Sahara with her purse and her Qur'an, being assertive in Arabic. He hoped it would be the dream journey she'd been hoping for.

Now Yusuf had his own friends and some structure to his life, he didn't have to rely on work so much for entertainment. After the episode in the restaurant his co-workers were happy to go alone on their outings. The manager said he was pleased with his work and that by October he could probably go onto the counter. But there was one condition: 'You shave off your beard!' Yusuf said it was a matter of principle to keep his beard but he would think about it. Whatever happened he would probably have left by the Fall.

In the summer Yusuf received notification from the University of Indiana that there was a place open for him starting late September. That was the good news. The bad news was the cost of the tuition. His savings were modest and most of his salary from Donut Heaven went on his living expenses and the Arabic course. There was quite a sum to find if he wanted to go to college. Then he remembered that his parents had set up a fund for him to go to college. Would it be possible, if they heard he had a place, that they would let him use the money for Indiana? In any case, it was certainly time he called them and found out a way of seeing them again.

Most of the times they had spoken recently the conversation was quite matter-of-fact, trying to stay on vague subjects. Until now, he had not told them where he was, but he told them he had a good job at Donut Heaven and was studying Arabic and that he had met some people. They seemed quite reassured when he told them there were other American converts like him. This time he would invite them to visit.

"Hi, mom."

"Jake, is everything OK?" What would she say about his name?

"Yes, mom, going fine as usual. How are you and Dad, the family?"

"Fine, we miss you, of course."

"I miss you. That's why I've been thinking it's time you came to visit."

His mother was flustered and he could hear her discussing it with his father in whispers. It sounded like his dad didn't see why they had to put themselves out.

"Your father's not sure about work," she said.

"Well, come on a weekend!"

"Well, Jake's there's church."

"Oh of course." He'd forgotten. "Well, can't you go here?"

"Well, I guess ...". Another conference with his father and then his father came to the phone.

"Isn't it about time you told us where you were, Jake?"

"Yeah. It was just I was scared, Dad, after those guys treated me like that and what with the church going crazy. Anyway I want you to come and visit now. I'm in San Francisco."

"So you think it's easy for your mother and I to drop everything to come and see you?"

"No, I don't but I'd love to see you and I'm afraid to go home."

"We'll think about it. Give me your address and number." Yusuf took that to mean that they would come.

Since they had taken the trouble to come to San Francisco, Yusuf booked them into a comfortable hotel for the weekend and made reservations for dinner on the night they arrived. He was waiting for them in the lobby. They looked troubled and strained with worry, but were eager to see how he'd changed.

His mother did a double take as he went forward to hug her. "Oh God, Jake, your face! You've got a beard! But it looks so scruffy. Jake why did you have to do that? You had such a nice, fresh face."

"It's part of the religion Ma," he said.

444

They checked into their room and Yusuf waited for them in the lobby, and then he showed them into the dining-room.

"Well, Jake. This is really something," said his father. "You taking us out to dinner. Do they pay well at Donut Heaven?"

"You deserve it," he said. "I know you've had a lot of headaches over me."

"Headaches?" said his mother. "Jake, I almost had a nervous breakdown. I truly thought you had gone crazy."

"Well, as you can see I'm still here, the same old Jake, plus a beard."

"But what do you do here?" asked his father.

"Well right now I'm in the bakery at Donut Heaven as I told you. I'm just trying to make a living. I stay at Mrs Chan's. It's quite a nice room. I have my Arabic classes and a few friends."

"So you're not involved with the Moslems?" said his mother hopefully.

"Well, there's Aziz and his family. They're really good to me and I go to a circle on weekends and we have discussions but I feel I could do more. I feel I have a lot of energy waiting to be used which is what I wanted to talk to you about."

"Yes?" said his father. "What is it?"

" Well, I have a place at the University of Indiana to major in philosophy."

"Philosophy?" said his mother. "You were never interested in philosophy."

"Do you think philosophy ever got anyone a job?" asked his father.

"Well, you know my interests have changed and I figured if I did a general degree I would have a bigger choice of career."

"So what's the attraction of Indiana?" asked his father warming to the idea now he saw his son seemed to have plans.

"There's a good community of Muslims there. They have a lot of activities for converts, a lot of publications. I've even thought of going into publishing."

"If you had told me all this a year ago, I would have arranged it all for you," said his father. "We could have pulled a few strings and got you into publishing." He sighed. "Jake. I wish you had said something."

"Dad, it's not that sort of publishing I'm interested in. Not just any old publishing or church stuff. I want to work with the stuff I believe in."

"It's not any old publishing and you used to believe it," said his mother looking at him searchingly, "until you got in with these Moslems and then … " She shook her head and continued with her salad.

"I'm convinced my change would have come anyway. Somehow. I really believe God guides people. Really. I've experienced it."

His parents gave him a faraway look, wondering if they were talking about the same God.

"So what do you think of me going to college?" said Yusuf, bringing them back to the point.

"Seems OK," said his father. "Not exactly what I would have wanted, but I keep telling myself it's your life."

"This is a little difficult," Yusuf said, "but you know the fund you built up for me, the college fund? I was wondering if I could have it now to pay the tuition. I have a deadline."

Now his father sat back and nodded vigorously. "I knew there was something else," he said. "Oh, yes. I might have guessed there'd be an ulterior motive for dragging us down here."

Yusuf looked alarmed. "No, it wasn't the money, Dad. Please believe me!"

It seemed to have been the catalyst his parents had been waiting for, to let out all their bottled-up emotions of anger and hurt and rejection.

"Do you know what it's like, Jake," said his mother, "to have your child reject everything you've ever taught him and throw it back at you? Your upbringing, Jake. The way we tried to raise you. We tried so hard. We thought we did everything right. Your father followed all the advice and did everything he could to raise you properly. It hurts me to think you don't value it at all." She was crying gently now, desperately trying to hide her face from their fellow diners.

"Do you want to go up to the room, dear?" said her husband.

"No it's all right. We haven't finished," she sniffed.

"I know it feels like that now," said Yusuf, "as if I've rejected everything you've ever taught me, but it's not true. If anything, since I became Muslim I've learned to appreciate you more. All you've done for me. You raised me to value faith but for me it has to be something I'm convinced of myself. I can't accept a story I don't believe in or a book I don't believe in any more. I just can't. I couldn't live my life like that. I'm seriously convinced that what I do on earth will have consequences after death and so I have to do the right thing. I have no choice."

"I was always there for you if you had questions," said his dad. "I could have answered them. If you'd maybe just waited and thought about it before going off and joining some other religion. Maybe you just didn't give yourself time."

"I had questions and I found answers myself. I didn't have to ask anyone. The answers just came to me in my reading. But there was nothing wrong with the way you brought me up and what you taught me. Well, you really believe it was the truth so that's all you could have done, but you are not going to answer for me in front of God. I have to speak for myself."

His parents were calmer now and they were trying their best to start listening to him in this new identity he presented them with.

Yusuf wanted his parents to see something of his little world, and he introduced them to Mrs Chan the following morning.

"Yes, Yusuf very funny boy," she said bringing through some lemonade.

"Is that your neighbour Jake?" asked his mother.

"Oh, er, that's my Muslim name," he said awkwardly.

"Jake you changed you name! How could you?"

"It means Joseph," he said quickly, "in Arabic."

"I suppose it's not so bad," said his mother.

"I told you he was a funny boy," said Mrs Chan. "Always going on about religion and prophecies and what not. Then there's not eat this, this OK, can't eat this."

Yusuf's mother smiled affectionately at him. "Yes, Mrs Chan. We're just trying to get used to the new Jake ourselves."

"I always ask him why you no get girlfriend, go out, have good time instead of always moping around the house? But he says Islam is marriage or nothing and I say, where you think you're gonna find a girl to marry you? You have to go to Arabia." She cackled over her sunflower seeds.

"How is Alice, by the way?" Yusuf asked quietly. "Is she over the break-up?"

His parents looked at one another and it was left to his mother to be the spokesperson. "Well, of course you can imagine. She was very upset at first. She had waited for you a long time but she used to tell me she never felt much warmth coming from you. There was always this kind of reserved feeling and she noticed you weren't like that with anyone else. Anyway, the fact is she's decided she can't build her life on the hope of one person, so now she's engaged to Tyler Brentford."

"Tyler Brentford?" said Yusuf aghast. "She's engaged to someone else?"

"Well, what did you expect?" said his father. "She should stay single all her life because you dumped her?"

"I didn't dump her," said Yusuf. "But this is so sudden."

"Apparently Tyler had had his eye on her for a long while but he never told her because he knew she was engaged to you."

"So now they're engaged!" said Yusuf. "Well, that's really thrown me."

He knew he had no right to be upset after the way he'd left Alice hanging in the air, not knowing what was happening and in his heart of hearts he had always feared she was not the right one for him, but somehow it annoyed him and made him look foolish. Had she agreed to marry Tyler to make a point to him, maybe to get back at him for making her look a fool? Alice and Tyler? Now the pictures he had often envisaged of when they were married looked alien. They wouldn't be together after all. He didn't know why he suddenly felt sad.

Yusuf managed to resolve a few matters with his parents during the visit. They were a little more reassured about his personal happiness, sanity and safety. They didn't like what had happened any better but they understood it a little more. His attempts to try and argue religion with them or try to discuss actual beliefs fell flat every time. It was too much to expect that they should suddenly see the light and join him in Islam, although he had heard of other converts who were joined soon after by other family members. At that time it was his dearest wish but he knew only God had the power to change hearts. He knew the story of the Prophet

Muhammad, peace be upon him, who tried so hard to convince his beloved uncle Abu Talib of the truth of Islam; the uncle who had supported him throughout the hardest times of his life. But even he, the Prophet of God, could not change a human heart. You could only do your best and there was time enough for that. For now, Yusuf had begun to rebuild the ties. As he waved good-bye to them at the airport, his heart went out to them. He really did have good parents. A few days later a letter arrived addressed to Jake (Yusuf) Carter, and inside was the cheque for his college tuition.

"What the hell are you doing in San Francisco?" came the familiar voice towards the end of the summer.

"I'm leaving it," laughed Yusuf, "in about two weeks. We have to meet up."

The happy reunion with Bruce took place according to tradition in Donut Heaven.

"My God, your beard!" laughed Bruce, pointing at Yusuf's face. "You look so old."

"Thanks. You look exactly the same," said Yusuf.

"What brought you to San Francisco?"

"Well, when I escaped from SLC, it was a case of putting a pin on the map and getting there as fast as I could. I called your parents when I got here at first and they said you were still in Japan."

"Yeah, they said you'd called but I couldn't get through at the motel and they had no forwarding number."

"Yeah, I remember I was a little paranoid the first few weeks. I didn't want anyone to know where I was. Anyway when I called your parents last month they said you were coming home on vacation. It's really good to see you."

"I can't believe you're here in San Francisco. Why did you come here?"

Yusuf told him about the ordeal after he was sent back from the mission and how he had taken the first Greyhound anywhere

"But how did the President find out you were Muslim?" Yusuf remembered that Bruce knew nothing of the events after he had left. Bruce sat open-mouthed as he explained what happened, how the President had found his books and then had tried to sweep the whole thing under the carpet and rehabilitate him, and finally how Gregor's temper had spilled the beans.

449

"I still don't know what made him so angry," said Yusuf. "He was saying something about what your people did to our people. You know how easygoing and friendly he always was and then this day he was like a monster, snarling and saying he didn't want to talk. I tried to explain because I figured he'd understand. He seemed to be quite a spiritual person. I don't know. We never spoke again after that. At first I thought it was all about that weekend in the mountains, that he was mad at us for telling the President."

"I never said anything to the President."

"Yes, in fact that was me. The President made me give a full account of what had happened and sign it. So that came out. But I don't know. He seemed to be more crazy about me being Muslim. He was calling me a traitor. Really, it was terrible."

"Was Maria the same?"

"No, I remember now. That was so weird. She passed me a note before the argument. I remember it clearly. It said: 'I know your pain.' What do you think it means?"

"I don't know. It's like that movie, *Field of Dreams*: 'If you build it, he will come.' Isn't it?"

Bruce repeated Maria's phrase in a deep echoing voice and they both laughed.

After hearing Yusuf's saga, Bruce felt that his own story seemed rather tame in comparison. He had gone to the apartment block where James and Julie were living, and camped on James's floor for a couple of weeks while he established his little business. He taught people either in their homes or in James's room. Some were at fairly cheap rates because they were students but others were prepared to pay a lot more. He cycled to every job to save money and took every student he was offered, including weekends. With careful saving he was able to add enough money from loans from Fumiko, Julie and James to put keymoney down on an apartment. It was called an apartment but it actually consisted of one *tatami* room with a tiny bathroom and a couple of burners for cooking and a refrigerator in the one *tatami* room. But it was in a lively part of town with plenty of other English teachers in the building so he was able to build up contacts quickly. After a few weeks of working at that rate he was able to pay off the loans and then he had a steady income for living expenses and small savings. One thing he found about the other teachers which he didn't approve of was the incredible rate at which they spent money. They were all well paid by the language companies they worked for and from their supplementary work but most of them went out nearly every night and spent about forty dollars on entertainment. They used to laugh at him and call him 'tight-wad,' but he didn't see the attraction of wasting so much money on food and drink and movies.

Yusuf was pleased to hear that Bruce had never succumbed to alcohol yet, and saw that part of the benefit of being frugal was that the other teachers couldn't lead him into bad habits. After that he had started going to Fumiko's every Saturday to meet her parents and have dinner and they seemed to like him, but Fumiko was disappointed in his lack of interest in *gaigin* social life. She would complain he was only interested in work and money, but Bruce kept reminding her that his living depended on him working very hard. If he worked hard, he could start to relax later. Soon they drifted apart and Fumiko met another American who was willing to give her an entrée into the world that attracted her. By then, Bruce had fallen out of love with her and was preoccupied with his thriving one-man language school. He picked up as many tips as he could from his friends about teaching and language but on the whole most of his 'students' were content with unstructured conversation. They were just happy to practice English with a real-life native speaker. Since the fees were often high, Bruce felt obliged to try and make a better job of his teaching. He sometimes felt a fraud, being no more than a high-school graduate with no formal training, but his customers seemed satisfied.

What he had enjoyed more than anything else was the freedom and independence and the sense of achievement he had gained. He was working for himself. He had no safety net so he had to work long hours but he could choose when he wanted to work, which students he accepted, and whether or not to go out with his friends. In the mission it was a case of not being allowed to do anything. Now he had the choice for himself, he found himself following a lot of what the church taught, but this was his own choice. That was the big difference. The only time he'd been in touch with the mission was to ask them to let his visa run its course and for the return portion of his airline ticket so that he could come back home for this short vacation. He had not given an address, but he had asked them to send the ticket on to his family who then mailed it right back to him in Japan. He had never seen anyone from the mission since the day he left. Now seeing Yusuf, he wondered how they all were. They both had a good laugh at the first-years who had became the President's lap-dogs but became nostalgic about the old days of Ellis and George, Dennis and John. They thought about George's conversion to *Soka Gakkei* and how he had managed to keep it secret.

"What is it about that place that gets people to change religions?" asked Bruce. "Maybe it's Japan. I know a few teachers who got religion in Japan, Buddhists, born-again Christians."

"I don't think it's Japan," said Yusuf. "I think it's the age-group and the experience of being away from home. That's when you start to question what you were brought up with and make decisions for yourself. I mean that's actually what happened to you, although you didn't convert to anything."

"Yes, I did," said Bruce. "I converted to independence."

Bruce's plan was to return to Japan and continue the classes he had built up, and then, when he had saved enough money, to travel. He still had a plan to study psychology at a college in the States but that could wait. He was in no hurry to be tied to a schedule or to have his life mapped out. Right now he was relishing the chance to grow in whichever direction he pleased.

It was good to have an old friend like Bruce to see him off to Indiana. Bruce got to meet Yusuf's co-workers at Donut Heaven, and Aziz and Rashid from the study circle. They did their best between them to try and give Bruce a crash course in Islam but for the time being he was happy to observe them from a distance. He put it like this.

"Right now I feel I've got to the top of one mountain and the view looks pretty good. I can see other mountains in the distance that look higher and who knows maybe I'll climb them. But now at this time in my life I'm happy where I am." He agreed with the Muslims though that their evidence was pretty convincing. "Yeah, who knows?" he added. "I may look into it more closely one day."

"Don't delay too long!" said Aziz. "Wherever you are, death will find you out."

"Oh, very cheerful!" laughed Rashid.

"But it's true," Aziz insisted. "No-one ever knows when death is coming. The sooner you straighten out what you believe in and act on it the better."

Yusuf felt pretty smug that he was OK on that score, but he wasn't worried for Bruce yet. His face was full of vitality and his head full of plans. It was the older generation he worried for, above all his parents. At the end of each of his five prayers he was saying a prayer for their guidance.

唯壹

Interlude

In this way, the end of September found Yusuf once more at an airport, headed for a strange city where he knew no-one, cutting his ties again. This time the farewell party at the gate were all friends, no family this time, no fiancée. How much his life had changed within these two years!

唯己

Indiana, USA

The most difficult part of college life during those first few months was the time he had on his hands. The philosophy course was organized in such a way that there were few actual classes or seminars, and a great part of the course was devoted to individual study. For most of the students this was spent in extra-curricular activities, be they politics, sports or other pastimes. Yusuf had expected to be spending a lot of time in the Institute there getting involved with Islamic activities, but the Institute was fairly small and the people who worked there were all graduates at least, most of them extremely well-qualified and much older than him. It wasn't a matter of walking in and being given something to do. It was a case of 'come back after you get your degree!' In fact, he could have done the course anywhere. When he wasn't in the library reading about philosophy or in the common room reading Islamic books from the Institute, or in the gardens reading newspapers and magazines, he was looking for something less intellectual to do.

There was an Islamic society at the university and they had a small prayer room which was used as a mosque. A few brothers from diverse countries were regular in prayers and on Friday the place filled up with people including one other convert called Abdul Qadir who spoke Arabic very well. Abdul Qadir was quite aloof with Yusuf and just asked him a few pointed questions: How long had he been Muslim? How did he become Muslim? Did he fast Ramadan yet? Could he read the Qur'an in Arabic? Had he ever been to a Muslim country? Abdul Qadir's own credentials were impressive. He had become a Muslim seven years earlier while working in Singapore as a computer analyst. He studied Arabic in Saudi Arabia and Islamic studies in Pakistan and he had memorized quite a large section of the Qur'an. He had travelled widely in the Middle East and was now lecturing in computer science at the university. His wife was Omani. When Yusuf made a joke about his difficulty meeting women Abdul Qadir didn't smile. It was as if he resented Yusuf somewhat for stealing his thunder as the only convert at the university and the object of much attention and '*masha-Allah's*' from the Arab and Asian brothers. He told Yusuf about some Americans he had known who toyed with Islam for a year or so, maybe after living in a Muslim country and being dazzled by the culture, 'but it didn't last,' he said knowingly. Yusuf was sure he was trying to hint at something and it made him defensive. He would show him, he thought, that his Islam was not just a passing phase. Abdul Qadir felt obliged to invite him once in a while to his home because he was alone. His apartment seemed strangely quiet and empty and there didn't seem to be anyone else home. Yusuf heard doors slamming and was shuttled into a room on the right. It was empty except for cushions on the floor and looked very appealing. It reminded Yusuf of the *tatami* room back in Japan. He would have loved a room like that but his clutter had already started to build up. Yusuf heard the front door a few times and two other brothers came in. Abdul Qadir greeted them warmly with bear hugs and lots of Arabic. Yusuf was listening carefully to try and understand. Presently there was a knock at the door and a tray appeared from a ghostly hand.

"Oh, is your wife home?" said Yusuf breezily.

"Excuse me?" said Abdul Qadir, scowling.

"Oh, I'm sorry. I didn't realize your family was here."

"Are you married, brother?" asked one of the other guests.

"No, not yet."

"Plenty of time," he smiled.

"Are you?" Yusuf asked.

"Yes, of course," he laughed. "My daughter is now fifteen."

"Oh, you don't look old enough to have a daughter that age."

"In Saudi we tend to marry young," he said.

The meal was tasty as was usual in Muslim homes and this was the first time Yusuf had eaten with his fingers from a common platter. It was a good experience. It made you feel that food could go a long way like this. Occasionally the Saudi, Muhammad, would tell a *Hadith* from the Prophet (peace be upon him), to do with eating. One said that food for two will serve four and food for four will serve eight. Yusuf would make little jokes about not being used to eating like this but that it was a good experience. The others would smile patronizingly at him and then go back to their serious conversation, often lapsing into Arabic.

"Maybe the brother cannot understand Arabic," remarked Ibrahim, the other brother, who was from Algeria.

"Oh, that's OK" said Yusuf. "I like listening to Arabic," and they would continue, although he knew very well there was a *Hadith* that Muslims should not talk privately in front of someone without including them in the conversation.

Yusuf got bored after a while and decided to go to the bathroom giving him a chance to explore the house. Abdul Qadir did not seem too delighted that he couldn't even hold on for a couple of hours but he led him to the bathroom and all the doors were shut. From the bathroom, Yusuf could hear the voices of women and children in the other room. He hadn't realized they had been there all the time. It was strange that he hadn't even glimpsed a woman arriving. He preferred Aziz's home with the family atmosphere. The women sat apart and had their own conversation but they didn't make a big show of it. Apart from Aziz's sister-in-law, they all dressed in the Muslim way and acted modestly but they did their best to make him feel welcome. In this house, he didn't feel so welcome, just tolerated, as if Abdul Qadir was just getting a duty out of the way. Yusuf was astonished to find he was waiting for him in the hall to escort him back to the room. Dessert arrived from behind the door and then coffee. Yusuf decided against making any Mormon coffee jokes. At the end, he thanked Abdul Qadir for the meal and told him to thank his wife for all her trouble. Abdul Qadir scowled again. It seemed he didn't like anyone mentioning his wife, but it was obvious she had gone to a lot of trouble and it turned out they had a six-week-old baby. When Yusuf asked to see him, Abdul Qadir just said the baby was sleeping.

It made him feel more lonely when he left, knowing that unlike the others he had no family to go home to. He had never felt that at Aziz's house. Even though he had no family, seeing them with all their children didn't make him feel envious. He had always felt part of the household there. With these people as friends, it looked as though life in Indiana would be dull.

The choice of philosophy as a subject had definitely been a useful one. Yusuf's knowledge of the world expanded and his mind boggled with all the ideas that men had dreamt up in the history of philosophy. There were some who weren't even certain of their own existence and of the existence of anything solid because when all was said and done, everything was made of drifting matter. Particles could as easily have come together to form a cup as a fish. The thought of this formless world often actually made Yusuf feel dizzy and sick. He read a translation of Sartre's *Nausea* which reflected just that feeling. The main character would be so struck with the gnawing futility of existence that objects would all gradually ooze into each other in his imagination into a formless mass that made him feel sick with emptiness. There were plenty of philosophers who believed in God but some believed in a distant God who had created the world and then abandoned it to itself. There were philosophers who grappled with the question of whether we know that something exists outside our own perception. This was the 'is my room still there when I leave it?' type of question. Was there any existence outside human perception? The most eccentric idea was the one where the philosopher saw himself as a great dreamer who had dreamed up the whole world and played out the scene in his head, because after all, it was argued, every human is locked inside his own head. For Yusuf it was amazing to learn of the possibilities that had existed outside the narrow confines of Mormon thought. He never knew what ideas and differences of opinion and behaviour there were.

Most of Yusuf's fellow students subscribed to an agnostic philosophy. They said that there was no certitude until we die and find out for sure, so we may as well muddle along as best we could, modifying our behaviour as we go along, learning from here and there until we die and find out. They balked at the idea of certainty when Yusuf would try to argue with them. 'How can you be so arrogant as to think you have the truth?' they would say. 'How can you be certain?' Their minds were closed to the idea of a God who creates and remains involved with His creation, who guides and teaches mankind and gives them the gift of Truth to make the most of life and the hereafter. They were not even prepared to listen to the historical evidence surrounding the revelation of the Qur'an and the person of the Holy Prophet. Yusuf became the outsider of the group who would sometimes join them over lunch in the student union but was never accepted into the ranks of the true philosophers because to join, your only qualification was to be agnostic. No truthmongers need apply.

As an antidote to the excesses of the human mind, and this lack of certainty and commitment, Yusuf would study his religion at home. It was the greatest thing to have so many questions about life and what came after death and to know you could have reliable answers. The Day of Judgment was described in detail in the Qur'an, a day when falsehood and truth would be sorted out, when humans would be struck dumb and their bodies would speak of their deeds, what their eyes had seen, their hands wrought, where their feet had walked. Paradise and Hell were also described in vivid detail, revealing exactly what humans should be prepared for after death. At that time their whole life on earth would be played back to them like a video tape and it would be so fleeting that it would it seem like a day, or part of a day. The reality of the Hereafter, which was the true reality, would make the worldly life seem insignificant. Physical commodities and material goods would be of no value then. Only deeds and intentions would have value.

At the same time Yusuf was learning more about the practical aspect of being a Muslim. He was pleased to find that many of the things he had been taught by his family and the church were backed up by the *Hadith*, especially about honesty, cleanliness and respect for other people. This was a good illustration of the mission of the Prophets which was to perfect and refine faith and deeds, to eliminate what was false and retain what was good. No society was a hundred percent bad, but people needed guidance from the Prophets of God to teach them how to choose between what was good and what was bad. Otherwise confusion would remain and lead to the strange schizophrenia of the many churches in America and elsewhere which were trying to follow the teachings of Christ in a nation where war and violence were the tools of progress, where material abundance was the mark of a man's worth and where the individual came first. Why was alcohol OK for some churches and not for others? Why couldn't churches decide whether celibacy was a hindrance or a virtue? Now Yusuf was getting proper answers to these questions. God had outlawed alcohol and gambling. Usury was an evil practice. Celibacy was considered not a virtue, but a curse. More and more, he was seeing that when guidance came from God instead of man, there was a perfect balance between the needs of the body, the mind and the soul and between the individual, the family and the community. It was not a virtue to forego the pleasures of life for supposed spiritual elevation any more than it was good for the soul to have an excess of life's pleasures. Man could not be considered right-minded if he spent all his time and money on his neighbours while his own family went hungry. Left to man, the bias would always go one way or another, an excess in either extreme. If a balance was to be found, it could only be God who could deal justly with all creatures because only God is free of all needs.

Yusuf didn't get all his knowledge from reading but listened to the advice of other Muslims. He found some discrepancy in what they said but Aziz had told him not to accept what anyone told him if it was not supported by evidence from the scriptures.

One day Yusuf was sitting in the prayer room at the university after Friday prayers studying the Qur'an. Abdul Qadir came over.

"*As-salamu 'alaykum,* Brother. Can I see?"

"*Wa alaykum as-salam.* Here, this is my copy of the translation of the Qur'an."

"The Qur'an can never be adequately translated."

"Yes, I know. I'm just reading it, though to get an idea and I study the notes."

"Yes," said Abdul Qadir flipping through the volume. "It's rather sketchy though, this *tafsir.* I'll try to find you some to supplement it."

"Oh, thanks."

"Yes, you know it's better to say, '*Jazak Allah khairan.*' to a Muslim. It means 'May Allah reward you', instead of 'thanks'."

"I know about that. I just get tongue-tied."

"How's the Arabic going, by the way?"

"It's OK. I can make out most of the letters."

"Would you like to read with me?"

"Well er, I don't know. I feel embarrassed."

"No need to feel embarrassed. Come on. How else will you improve?"

Blushing, Yusuf turned to a verse of the Qur'an he had memorized for his prayers and read it quite fluently.

"*Masha-Allah!*" said Abdul Qadir. "That's very good. Read this one now!"

Yusuf didn't know the next *Sura* but he was stuck now. He had to read it now that he'd said he knew Arabic. He read laboriously syllable by syllable and Abdul Qadir corrected him almost every second.

"Not so good, huh?" said Yusuf, shamefaced.

"Don't worry. You're doing your best. Keep going!" Yusuf got to the end finally with much struggle and it was obvious he didn't know the alphabet as thoroughly as he'd made out. Abdul Qadir went across to the shelves and picked out a book for him on learning to read the Qur'an. There were lots of exercises and they went through it syllable by syllable with plenty of drills. Abdul Qadir worked with him the whole afternoon and then gave him the book and cassettes and some homework to have ready by Tuesday. Abdul Qadir said he had known a lot of converts who after years of becoming Muslim had never taken the trouble to study Arabic properly or learn to read the Qur'an. For him it was inexcusable and he said it was better to do it now while he was fresh to Islam and full of enthusiasm than to dawdle and maybe lose that zeal which spurs a person on to learn. Yusuf knew he was right, and he was grateful he had taken the trouble to sit with him and show him that learning to read Qur'an was not some magical accomplishment but something within the grasp of every Muslim who would take the time and trouble. As he went over the drills and the syllables gradually became more and more familiar, he was filled with the same thrill of achievement that he found with learning Japanese, a language that had also looked so completely different. Learning the two languages taught him that signs on paper were just arbitrary, and to break the code, all you needed was a little patience and application.

As much as Abdul Qadir annoyed him, Yusuf would never forget his efforts to help him learn to read the Qur'an.

Yusuf knew about *halal* meat and had only eaten ordinary meat a few times since his conversion, but he understood it was OK to eat meat prepared by Christians or Jews if no *halal* was available. As far as animal fats went, he tried to avoid sweets and cookies made with animal fats. However, the brothers in the Islamic society were much more restrictive. They distributed a list of confectionery which was no good for Muslims because it contained ingredients derived from animal fats which were not *halal* and so reluctantly Yusuf cut out some of his favourite chocolates and cakes and spent a lot of time in the supermarket checking labels against the list which he always carried with him.

There were some brothers who would often correct Yusuf in his prayers. They would adjust his arms when he did *sujud* because he had his elbows too close to the ground. He felt as though he was on show and could no longer switch off and concentrate when he was praying in front of other people. When praying alongside others, they would pull him quite sharply so that his shoulder was close to theirs and their feet touching. They said it was very important not to leave gaps in the rows when praying in *jama'a*. What annoyed him was that a lot of what they told him, he already knew about. It was annoying to be told to do something right before you were about to do it. One brother reminded him to take off his watch to do his *wudu'* when it had just slipped his mind and he had been about to take it off. He felt like a school-boy, being corrected all the time. He tried to take it well because they were only helping him to do the right thing but these things built up and started to nag at him. There was a student from Bangladesh who came in one time and asked him why he didn't wear a cap while doing his prayers. When Yusuf argued that lots of the brothers didn't wear them, the Bangladeshi said it was *Sunna* to wear one and he should. Another time he was picked on for standing while drinking a glass of water. 'You must sit down when drinking brother. It's *sunna!'*

Instead of thanking them for the advice, he began to get tired of it. He was hearing too much about details and things he was doing wrong instead of more important and more general things like virtues. On one side he was reading things which stretched his mind to the limits and on the other his beard was not long enough or his nails were too long or he didn't have the right kind of toothbrush.

As Christmas approached, Yusuf was ready to take a break. He thought he would go home as he hadn't spent Christmas with his family for two years and he had decided against going home for

Thanksgiving this year. He was afraid of going back after so long but by Christmas he was ready to go. He needed a break from Indiana and he wanted to see his family and the longer he took to show his face in SLC, the worse it would be.

Abdul Qadir asked him what he was doing for the vacation.

"I've decided to spend it with my folks."

"I wouldn't advise it, brother."

"Why not?"

"Christmas is a pagan festival. It is a sin for a Muslim to take part in a pagan festival and especially a festival that celebrates the idea of Jesus being the son of God, *astaghfiru'Llah*," he added.

"Well I wasn't actually going to celebrate. I just wanted to spend the vacation with them."

"Believe me, brother, it's better to stay away. You can't help being drawn into that environment."

"Is it wrong to stay with them while they celebrate?"

"It's absolutely *haram* to celebrate Christmas," said a Palestinian brother by the name of Yunus who had come to join them. "Everything about Christmas is pagan now and against Islam."

"It'll be difficult to get out of it," said Yusuf.

"I know," said Abdul Qadir, "but it's worth it. It's not worth the hassle of going along and saying, 'OK I'll sit with you but I can't eat the food', or if they wanna drink you can't sit with them and if there are other family there, you can't sit with the women. It would be too much hassle and then if you compromise once, they'll expect you to compromise every year."

"But what about keeping up good relations with your family? I mean if you're gonna hurt them by staying away, isn't it better to go along and just not take part?"

"That would probably be worse than not going at all," said Abdul Qadir. "Anyway, you'll be a minority. Everyone will put pressure on you. You know what it's like. 'Go on, a glass of wine won't hurt you. Come and kiss so-and-so under the mistletoe!' You know the sort of thing."

"Not in my family," said Yusuf. "They're Mormon."

"Well in that respect you're lucky because they don't drink, but still they'll be putting pressure on you all the time to compromise your beliefs, and at the end of the day, you're participating in an occasion that they believe to be the birth of the son of God. It cuts right at the core of everything you believe in."

Yusuf could tell by Abdul Qadir's tone of voice that he was expecting that Yusuf would be too weak-willed and end up going along anyway. "Maybe you're right," he said sadly.

"It is hard," said Abdul Qadir, "but faith is not supposed to be a bed of roses. You have some things to do that are difficult and some sacrifices to make that are very hard."

"It's just the significance of the day," added Yunus. "Going to visit your family is important to do *da'wa* with them, but choose another day!"

Yusuf didn't know why he felt pressured by them but he did. They made him feel like he would be a hypocrite if he succumbed and went home for Christmas. One by one the other students in his dorm left for their vacations. It was so easy for them. They just packed up the car, no worries and headed for a warm and welcoming family. Many of the foreign students took the time to go on trips. Some even managed to go home while a Malaysian Muslim on Yusuf's corridor was off to an Islamic Conference. He couldn't invite Yusuf because it was in the Malay language. Abdul Qadir and his friends disappeared without telling Yusuf where they were going. He was left quite alone on campus with only a few obscure computer geeks for company, who relished the peace and quiet to conduct their secret laboratory experiments or raid the library for sought-after books for their research.

Yusuf decided the best strategy was just to treat December 25th like any other day. It wasn't special. it wasn't even the day Christ was born, but as the season loomed he was beset with nostalgic longings. Two Christmasses in Japan had not erased the childhood memories. Christmas memories were the most palpable of all. Christmas always had a special smell, a special atmosphere that couldn't be defined. If you broke the day down into what the family actually did, it didn't seem like much but there was a whole atmosphere that went with Christmas that made you look forward to it year after year. Yusuf took a walk downtown. The residents were delighted with the snow and there were small girls swathed in winter coats carrying balloons from Santa, and small boys in thick ski-jackets rushing to open the car door to pile in the packages. Fathers were picking up Christmas trees and mothers were getting their hair done. Seeing family after family laden with shopping bags of rich food should have been grotesque in a world where people didn't eat some days, but it didn't look that way to Yusuf. He felt happy for the families because they looked so delighted. He had been part of a family like that only a few short years ago. Some would say a model American family, fine, law-abiding, God-fearing, tax-payers with four healthy, well-educated, respectful children. Yusuf comforted himself by buying some Christmas food but most of it had *haram* ingredients. He had bought a few gifts for his family but he knew it was no substitute, especially for his mother. His decision not to come home for Christmas was like another slap in the face for her, just when their relationship was starting to mend. He wanted to make some excuse but in the end he told the truth. His conscience was not easy with taking part in a festival that went against his beliefs. He thought his being there would spoil it for them so it was better if he stayed away. Instead of sounding sincere, it sounded pompous and now he went back alone to his room to survive Christmas as best he could. He had never felt so low since he became Muslim.

On Christmas Eve, he watched TV for a while in the student's common room, hoping someone would join him for some festive cheer to share his pretzels and cheese straws and angel cake, but no-one came and he got tired of the game shows and special Christmas pageant shows. In his room he switched on the radio and heard a beautiful choir singing Christmas carols. He had been unconsciously singing Christmas songs all week but when he realized what he was saying he changed the lyrics to make them more in line with Islam.

God rest ye merry, Gentlemen, let nothing ye dismay.
Remember Prophet Isa was born on such a day.
To guide us all in Allah's way.
Since we had gone astray.
Oh, tidings of comfort and joy, comfort and joy. Oh, tidings of comfort and joy.

The Christmas songs made him long for home and he feasted on the memories of many happy Christmasses and the wonder of it when they had been very young. Why had he allowed himself to be bullied like this? Where were they now, all his Muslim friends who stopped him from going to his family and then left him alone over Christmas? He wasn't answerable to them. He was answerable to God and God would know his intentions and forgive him his weaknesses.

Harry Belafonte came on the radio singing a song that had always been one of their family favourites: 'Oh Night Divine.' Yusuf listened to the song, and cried bitterly.

"How was your vacation?" asked Abdul Qadir when he saw Yusuf again after the Christmas break.

"Pretty depressing. I had nowhere to go."

"You should have said something. I went to an Islamic Conference in Chicago. You could have come too."

"No, *you* should have said something," thought Yusuf to himself. He would have loved the chance to go to a conference. His Christmas Day had not been as bad as the night before. That morning he heard there was a group of Muslims meeting at the campus gate. They were heading into town to set up an Outreach stall in the town hall and Yusuf thanked God for the opportunity for some company on this loneliest of days. They had set up a little alcove with rugs on the floor and a desk with Islamic literature and books. A sign on the door invited passers-by to come and see, as well as posters around town saying; 'Come and find the real meaning of Christmas'. They were not the only people evangelizing on that day but they pulled a steady crowd of people on their way back from church or on their way to restaurants or just strolling after a heavy lunch, who stopped to hear them reciting from the Qur'an. One of the brothers, a Sudanese, was a beautiful reader of the Qur'an and they had set up an amplifier to carry the sound around the lobby of the building. Then another brother, an Indian who spoke with an American accent, read out the translation of the story of the birth of Jesus from the Qur'an.

Relate in the Book (the story of) Mary, when she withdrew from her family to a place in the East.

She placed a screen (to screen herself) from them; then We sent her our angel, and he appeared before her as a man in all respects.

She said: "I seek refuge from thee in (God) Most Gracious: (come not near) if thou dost fear God."

He said: "Nay, I am only a messenger from thy Lord, (to announce) to thee the gift of a holy son.

She said: "How shall I have a son, seeing that no man has touched me, and I am not unchaste?"

He said: "So (it will be): Thy Lord saith, 'that is easy for Me: and (We wish) to appoint him as a Sign unto men and a Mercy from Us': It is a matter (so) decreed."

So she conceived him, and she retired with him to a remote place.

And the pains of childbirth drove her to the trunk of a palm-tree: She cried (in her anguish): "Ah! Would that I had died before this! Would that I had been a thing forgotten and out of sight!"

But (a voice) cried to her from beneath the (palm-tree): "Grieve not! For thy Lord hath provided a rivulet beneath thee;

"And shake towards thyself the trunk of the palm-tree: It will let fall fresh ripe dates upon thee.

"So eat and drink and cool (thine) eye. And if thou dost see any man, say, 'I have vowed a fast to (God) Most Gracious, and this day will I enter into no talk with any human being'".

At length she brought the (babe) to her people, carrying him (in her arms). They said: "O Mary, truly an amazing thing hast thou brought!

"O sister of Aaron! Thy father was not a man of evil, nor thy mother a woman unchaste!"

But she pointed to the babe. They said: "How can we talk to one who is a child in the cradle?"

He said: "I am indeed a servant of God: He hath given me revelation and made me a prophet;

"And He hath made me blessed wheresoever I be, and hath enjoined on me Prayer and Charity as long as I live;

"(He) hath made me kind to my mother, and not overbearing or miserable;

"So peace is on me the day I was born, the day that I die, and the day that I shall be raised up to life (again)"!

Such (was) Jesus, the son of Mary: (it is) a statement of truth, about which they (vainly) dispute.

It is not befitting to (the majesty of) God that He should beget a son. Glory be to Him! When He determines a matter, He only says to it, "Be", and it is.

Verily God is my Lord and your Lord: Him therefore serve ye: this is a Way that is straight.

But the sects differ among themselves: and woe to the unbelievers because of the (coming) Judgment of a momentous Day!

Many of the onlookers stayed to hear the end of the story while others grew impatient and left, and some just enjoyed the beautiful reading in Arabic and then walked on without troubling themselves as to what he was saying. As the Muslims had hoped, they generated a fair degree of interest and discussion. Most of the passers-by did not know that the 'Moozlems' believed in Jesus, but they had the usual arguments that the Qur'an must have copied parts from the Bible. When the Muslims asked where the parts of the story that differed from the Bible came from, they would just say it was made up so the Muslims could be different. Many of them were smug and arrogant in their certainty of Christ as saviour, as son of God, as the only path to heaven. This type infuriated Yusuf more than any others because you couldn't get through to them with logical argument and evidence. They were Republican. They were Americans. They were in the right church and they had a one-way ticket to Paradise.

Abdul Qadir was impressed with the Christmas initiative but he didn't have any notion of how hard it had been for Yusuf to stay away from his family at Christmas. It was then that Yusuf resolved not to take him as his only mentor. In fact he would not follow the lead of any one person. He would take advice from several sources and also trust his own instincts a little more. He had read a lot. He felt like a good practicing Muslim. It was time he stood up for himself.

Yusuf was given some magazines and pamphlets from Chicago which he read avidly. His latest task was to educate himself in politics. All he'd been hearing about recently was the Gulf War and its aftermath. He had had the nagging feeling for some time, only hinted at by Aziz, that the US wasn't as snow-white as he had always imagined. Even back in Japan, the Brits used to criticize US foreign policy and that made him feel defensive and angry, but now, as the facts became clearer, he was starting to get a more accurate picture. Sometimes, the US would invade countries herself to make peace or remove dictators. Other times the US would intervene to save one country from the aggression of another to uphold human rights and democracy. Other times the US would leave countries alone to fight it out. Other times, the US would arm one country to fight another and then criticize that same country for human rights abuses. Sometimes the US would support governments in countries who would abuse their own people. Yusuf did not like to read about or believe the details of what went on in some of those jails. So why these anomalies? He knew the Iranian picture of the US as the 'great Satan' was exaggerated, but what could account for their knowingly or unknowingly colluding in torture and destruction? Abdul-Latif, who had been one of the group of Christmas missionaries, tried to clarify this for him. 'Quite simply, self-interest!' Did he think it was by magic that the wealth of the world was piled up in the West while the Third World could not feed itself out of its own resources for paying off their foreign debts? No, it was not magic but exploitation when many Americans died from over-eating whilst many Africans died of starvation.

"This is why Allah has forbidden usury," he explained. "Whether on a small or large scale, you cannot lend money with interest. In fact, money itself has no value. Can you eat it, wear it, live in it?"

It had never dawned on Yusuf before that money had no intrinsic value. Abdul-Latif's friend Omar had a clever way of explaining things by using metaphors.

"Now I come to your house and I say, 'Give me all your furniture, the food in your cupboard, your clothes and your car. I will give you this bag of money in exchange. Plus here is another bag to help you set yourself up again. This is a kindness from me. All I ask in return is for you to pay the bag back plus two coins for every coin in it until it is all paid back. But you can take as long as you like to pay it back. This is my kindness to you. Everything you get from now on, you will give me a part of it to help pay off the extra bag of money.'" Omar waved his finger at Yusuf. "No word of a lie. Something just like this has happened in the world and it is not funny at all."

Going away from discussions like this, Yusuf would feel a great burden of guilt. How could he right it all? All he could do was try to follow God's will and join the side of the righteous people.

Other times this group of brothers, whom he had started to spend more time with, would talk late after dinner in one of their homes. Yusuf enjoyed their company because they reminded him of the brothers in Japan and they did not patronize him, but sometimes they would criticize the US and laugh at the immorality there and the degradation of the people and the crime and despair, and Yusuf would start to feel it was too close to the bone.

"You don't have to stay here you know," he said to one Libyan who had been in the US for twenty years and hated the place.

"I have nowhere else to go," he said sadly, "and I dream we can change this place."

"I'm sorry," said Yusuf. "It's just that the people aren't all bad. My family are good people. They believe in God and the Hereafter. They try to be good parents, neighbours, honest people. You can't say all non-Muslims are bad people."

"No, that's not what we mean," said a Palestinian, Faruq. "Sometimes the frustration of living here and seeing how the people would benefit from Islam gets to us."

"Yes," agreed Omar. "When you see people walking into a pit, you want to stop them. We know the dangers of what Allah has forbidden but they don't listen to us and then they suffer."

"There is no doubt," said Abu Bakr, the Libyan, "that there are good people in every country, people who want peace and who want to follow the truth but sometimes they don't know the truth and the people at the top are controlling them. They think they are free here. No, they are more in prison than any prisoner. The modern Pharaohs have them just where they want them. They are like cattle. They are docile. They follow where they are led. Allah tells us in the Qur'an that there are some people who are just like cattle. They do not use the will that Allah has given them."

Yusuf thought it was a good image. Sometimes as a young Mormon he had felt like that, herded here and herded there, but not all Americans were like that. "Americans are pretty single-minded people," he argued. "Individual. I mean look at the variety of lifestyles here."

"All sides of the same coin," said Abu Bakr dismissively.

Omar came in with one of his metaphors on the typical American life.

"Come, little American to my school," he said in a wheedling voice, "and I teach you to be a good American, love your country, love your flag. Now you start work. This is your salary. This portion is for me. The rest is all yours to spend in any way you like. You have a choice: alcohol to deaden the brain, drugs to deaden the soul, lots and lots of processed food to give you diseases. This portion is for medicine to make you better again. This is for you to buy your home and you can pay me back that loan a hundred times over but take as many years as you like. When work is over enjoy yourself! Overeat, drug yourself. Watch this movie that teaches you to be a good American. Enjoy yourself! You are free. You can vote for whichever of these two parties you like, who will keep you in the lifestyle you've been enjoying. Oh, by the way, I need just one more portion of your salary. That is for security in case anyone wants to come and take all your benefits away. Goodbye! Have a nice day."

The group were rolling with laughter. The way Omar told it, as this imaginary dialogue, Yusuf couldn't have any argument with him. Wasn't it absolutely right? That was the way with many Americans. It was like something out of *Brave New World* but it was true.

Yusuf got along much better with this group of brothers. Many of them were single so he felt on equal terms with them and they would talk late into the night. They were from diverse countries and full of information about life back home. Some of them were in the US more or less indefinitely while others were getting their degrees and heading home afterwards. They were open-minded, and not as condescending as Abdul Qadir and his friends, and they did not tell Yusuf anything by way of correction or criticism unless he specifically asked. Their talk most of the time was politics, politics and more politics, and Yusuf soaked it up like a sponge.

He made a point of checking what they said in his own reading because he didn't want to be too influenced by a few people again. He wanted to benefit from a range of opinions. What he liked most about these brothers was their enthusiasm for *da'wa*. They often held debates with other university societies or food sales for various causes. Whenever the university had a special open day, they would set out a book-stall and start up discussions with interested students. This was Yusuf's favourite role. He loved to explain the religion and discuss the Bible with them and to answer all their familiar questions. Why can men have four wives? Why do you have to pray five times a day? Isn't fasting bad for you? Why can't non-Muslims go to Mecca? Wasn't pork forbidden then just because it was a hot climate and there was no refrigeration? Do women have to wear a veil? Why? Wasn't the Qur'an copied from the Bible? Yusuf fielded the usual questions with ever-growing ease in a self-assured manner that made the listener often quite impressed and usually wanting to learn more. The most difficult thing was breaking through lifetimes of prejudice and misinformation. Yusuf's friends told him that such misrepresentation of Islam by the media moguls was deliberate so as to stop people getting hold of the liberating force of the truth which would rob those leaders of their power. Yusuf had thought this was a rather paranoid view, but when he came across the same misunderstandings time and time again, he began to wonder.

It was also these brothers who taught him how to read critically. "There is only one Book which has Allah as its author," said Omar. "This is the Qur'an. As far as collecting the authentic *Hadith*, our predecessors have done our job for us, may God bless them and reward them with Paradise. Anything else is open to scrutiny. Who is writing it? What are their aims and objectives? What is their philosophy of life? Who is the publisher?" Yusuf learnt to check a bibliography for sources and to learn something of the philosophies of various publishing houses. This would determine what was selected to be put into a book and how it was presented. He learnt to look with a more critical eye at books on Islam written by interested non-Muslims whose sources were partly drawn from non-Muslim works. Scholars such as these were known as orientalists. The most respected ones had used the standard Muslim sources written by believers while others ignored all the Muslim literature and based their research only on the works of non-believers so that it was inevitable their views would be biased. Yusuf decided to read widely and not be afraid of any book, but to bear this advice in mind, always to assess the aims of the author. This concept again was entirely new for him. Books were like magical things and you tended to be so drawn into the world of the book that you forgot the author was just an ordinary person like you with his own views and prejudices and ways of looking at the world.

On one of the open days, Yusuf had been talking to some Protestants over rice and lamb kebabs. He was working at a stall with literature about Islam. The Protestants were fascinated by his change of heart but at the same time concerned that he had 'renounced Christ', as they put it. He explained the Muslim view of Jesus and that in Islam Jesus was put into his correct historical perspective. He went over the gospels with them pointing out verses where Jesus had said that he could not speak except from the Father and that there was only one God. Their evidence was weak as they repeated the usual verses from St. Paul's letters and the Acts of the Apostles but they were so full of faith and the Holy Spirit, as they explained, that this was no obstacle to them in the discussion. They kept accusing Yusuf of being too rational, too analytical. Why did he not open himself to the scriptures and surrender his heart to Jesus who would take away all his sins? The temptation of vicarious atonement had long ago lost its appeal for Yusuf. He had read and understood that each person will answer for their own actions. Instead, he was left with a sense of frustration. Why wouldn't they see? Why did they remain so stubborn and sure against all his arguments? He supposed they could have said the same thing about him. He looked at them, two vivacious girls with rosy faces and sparkling eyes and their companion with his easy smile and earnest eyes. They were so young and enthusiastic but so misguided. How did you convince people like that? Abdul Latif, who was on the stall with him told him not to worry. Every effort made to spread the message was worthwhile, even one word. "Who knows," he said, "today you may have planted the first seeds in the hearts of those Christians and in ten or twenty years you may find them Muslim."

"I hope so," Yusuf said wistfully

"*Insha-Allah,*" said Abdul-Latif. "It is all in the hands of Allah."

One of the lectures that they had been to in San Francisco had taught him a similar lesson when the speaker asked: 'In ten or fifteen years time, how many of us will still be practicing Muslims and how many of those we despair of now will be the best of believers?'

There were stories from the time of the Prophet, peace be upon him, of people who had vehemently opposed his message and yet had ended up, through the gift of faith, as his most ardent supporters. It made Yusuf shudder a bit to think he might lose his faith, especially at this stage where he didn't have much support or outside affirmation. All his roots were outside Islam. For him, at this time, his faith was largely a state of mind. If he lost his faith tomorrow, there would not be many people to mourn it. His family, on the contrary, would rejoice. This was why every time he said his prayers or read the Qur'an and realized it was the most precious thing in his life, he prayed Allah to let him hold on to it.

At the end of the day at the stall, a small, dark man in glasses came up and introduced himself to Yusuf. He was from the Islamic Institute and his name was Bayram. His family were Turkish but he had been brought up in the States. Bayram asked him about his classes and how it was going and how he liked life in Indiana. Yusuf was complaining that outside of class and a little *da'wa* activity, he was stuck for things to do. He enjoyed open days like this one to give him a chance to do some Islamic work but otherwise he was pretty bored. He told Bayram how he had come to the Institute the year before at the start of his enrollment asking for volunteer work but they had nothing available. Then, to his delight Bayram said that there was a project coming up that he might be able to help with. He had heard that Yusuf was a missionary convert and had first-hand experience of missionary work. He had heard favourable reports about his enthusiasm for *da'wa* and wondered if he would like to combine the two and put it to practical use. Yusuf was more than willing to work for the Institute. It was just the break he'd been looking for.

"I'm afraid we don't have a permanent desk for you," said Bayram apologetically, showing him around the office. "Three people share this desk but a lot of the time they're moving around the building looking up files, working on the computer and using the library."

The office had a tranquil atmosphere with the gentle bleep of computers and rustle of papers. There was very little noise except for low murmurs. Most of the men working in the office looked to be middle-aged, but there were one or two younger men. None of them looked like converts as far as Yusuf could see. Behind a piece of screened glass he could see a few covered women working at desks. As he walked past and Bayram introduced each of the office workers, they would look up, give Yusuf a brief smile and go back to their quiet world of paperwork.

A small room through a partition was used as a prayer-room. It was empty and had a beautiful carpet on the floor and a prayer-niche towards the *Qibla*.

The underworld of the Institute was altogether different as Yusuf followed Bayram down the stairs. Down here was the printing press and bookbinding section. There was a clattering and voices raised above the din, and the sharp smell of ink and chemicals. Around a central workbench, young men were in various stages of book-binding, while in one corner a small, Chinese-looking man with tiny eyes was tooling gold lettering onto a leather tome. Yusuf asked what the clothes line was with pages hanging from it. This, it emerged, was a workshop which specialized in the restoration of rare Islamic books. It was a very skilled and intricate process which involved matching and dyeing paper to match exactly the shriveled pages of the original specimen. The pages had to be washed, treated with preservative chemicals and dyed and then washed again, and the new fragments had to be delicately grafted on to the torn pages. The pages had to be ironed. Then the book had to be rebound in leather and the title tooled in gold-leaf. Yusuf was full of admiration for the meticulous work.

Bayram did not pressure him in any way as to hours or conditions of work. Despite Yusuf's willingness to work as a volunteer, Bayram insisted that to show the value of the work he would be doing, he should receive some payment. To fit in with his classes, they agreed on three afternoons a week. Yusuf's job was to help compile a profile of Christian movements in the USA, outlining how they differed from one another, whether they were active in missionary work and in which countries, and the key points of doctrine that they used to convince possible newcomers. Their aim was to build up a profile of the Christians in North America in order to see how they could best be reached by the Muslims. The more they disagreed with fellow Christians the better, because they could end up disagreeing right into Islam. For example, there were Christian groups who believed that Jesus was not divine. The work was a matter of research in the library and calling the representatives of the various churches to find out their history, their organization and their current beliefs, Bayram wanted Yusuf to start with the Mormons since he had first-hand experience with them. He told Yusuf that Islamic *da'wa* needed to become more sophisticated. It was no good trying to use blanket methods for different categories of people. They had to tailor the approach to different mindsets. The results of the research were to be used to write Christian/Muslim dialogue books to be used as resources for Outreach workers who went to visit churches to tell them about Islam, and also to be used to prepare leaflets for the Muslim communities where the churches had missions. Bayram explained that it was only fair that Muslims heard an account about the church from Muslims before they began to hear the church's own teachings. He also said that it was about time the Muslims tried to be more systematic and organized about *da'wa* work instead of doing it on an *ad hoc* basis. They had a lot to learn from the Christians about getting the message across effectively. Suleiyman would have loved this place, Yusuf thought. He decided to write to him after this long interval to tell him how he was getting along.

Yusuf remained on good terms with Abdul Qadir and his friends because he believed he was duty-bound to keep up good relations with all his Muslim brothers, although he didn't see eye-to-eye with all of them. Some of them did not approve of the work that they did at the Institute because they thought the workers there were prepared to compromise too much to try and reach the non-Muslims. Yusuf slowly stopped expecting too much of Muslims in general. They were human beings, not angels, and they were all doing their best to follow Islam, though some were weaker than others and some harsher and more arrogant.

唯㐀

Jakarta, Indonesia

The car ride from the airport was fascinating, although stuffy. Suleiyman and his brothers had been there to meet Yusuf at the airport and now, crammed into a tiny car, they were on their way to his house which was in a suburb on the opposite side of the city. This was a culture shock, much more than Japan had been. Rows and rows of simple, shanty-type houses by the side of a road lit by a single bulb, some with fires outside. The air was steamy and perfumed. Although it was evening, the streets were alive with people, some riding bicycles, others mopeds. The luckier ones had motorbikes and the kings of the road were in little cars. Sometimes Yusuf saw whole families perched precariously on a moped, none of them with helmets or even shoes. Buses would lumber by, so full that people hung on the doors. The place looked really tropical to Yusuf with its exotic trees and plants. At every corner people were selling things, usually snack foods, and cooking on portable barbecues. Towards the centre of the city he could see more familiar buildings, factories, shops and government buildings which stood out gleaming white in the gloaming. The mosques were very grand with a series of domes, and reminded Yusuf of palaces. Suleiyman pointed out various important places between conversations in Bahasa Indonesia, a language which had a kind of clanging quality to those who could not understand. Yusuf kept hearing sounds like 'bam, bam'. He loved that feeling of listening to a language before you knew a word of it to distract you, and enjoying the sounds and intonation and the animation of the speakers.

When they got to the house, Yusuf realized that Muhammad and Jamal were only two of eight brothers and four sisters. The house was a pleasant open building with several balconies and white balustrades.

It had a little field at the front and was set apart from the other houses in the area. Amid the dozens of little children who came out to greet them was a middle-aged lady in sandals. She was the housekeeper who had been with them since Suleiyman was a baby, and even before. With the size of the family, it was obvious that they needed help. Inside the house the furnishings were pleasant but simple, with plenty of colourful, low furniture and wicker chairs and baskets. All the family members gave the charming greeting where they took his hand in theirs and then touched their hearts with their own hands. Everyone was grinning. That was the first thing Yusuf had noticed about Suleiyman.

Dinner was served on mats on the floor. Suleiyman's mother was a bit anxious about whether Yusuf was used to this, but Suleiyman said he was a Muslim and she should treat him as a Muslim. They ate sticky rice, bean curd soup, chicken flavoured with coconut and unbelievably spicy beef. Then there was jelly dessert and papayas. The atmosphere was sunny, lit by bright personalities and inquisitive children. Most of them spoke English but they would keep their bolder questions in Bahasa Indonesian. To their embarrassment Suleiyman translated their questions. 'He wants to know if you're Muslim'. 'He's asking if you pray.' 'She asks, are there lots of people like uncle in America?' 'Do they eat rice in America?' 'Does uncle like hot food?' 'Is uncle married?' Yusuf took the questions with good humour and answered them all until Suleiyman's mother told them to stop bothering him. Yusuf had often noticed that Muslim children felt free to be more direct with converts and ask them things they would be too shy to ask a fellow born-Muslim. In some ways he thought this was a good thing.

They swapped news over the meal. Suleiyman had returned to work for Honda and had obtained his promotion. He had been married to Maryam for two years and they were expecting their first baby. He only kept in touch with Sayyid, the Libyan, from Japan. He had lost touch with the other Indonesians. He had never forgotten Yusuf and often used to tell people about how he came to Islam. He was pleased that they'd managed to keep in touch for so long, sending each other cards at *Eid,* even if it was just to say that each of them was fine. Yusuf made Suleiyman's mother almost cry with joy when he said he would never forget Suleiyman who had introduced him to Islam, but Suleiyman would play down his role and say that Yusuf did so much study and research on his own. He laughed when Yusuf told him the whole story of what had happened when he was sent home from his mission and how they tried to make him think that Suleiyman and his friends were some kind of organized group. "I wish we were," he said. "I can't believe they made all those lies up to try and scare you." Suleiyman's family were amazed at his bravery in resisting his family. Then he explained that things were a lot better these days. Yusuf had gone back for the Easter vacation after the lonely Christmas despite the warnings of Abdul Qadir. In fact his family did their best to be accommodating. They tried not to offend Yusuf and made sure he could eat the food. They didn't object when he retired to do his prayers at regular intervals and didn't pressure him to take part in any church activities. The unwritten rule, though, was not to discuss religion or argue points of scripture. That was too sensitive a point. They would not object to him practicing his faith as long as it didn't infringe on the family. At first Yusuf had been dying to discuss religion with them and show them where they were going wrong, but he came to realize it was wiser to be subtle. Over visits, through these past few years of his degree, he had managed to put across his message indirectly by talking generally about what he was studying and how he felt about it and the work he was doing at the Institute. His father definitely approved of that. It seemed like a worthwhile place to be, but if ever Yusuf touched on too sensitive an issue, like what he had heard at such and such a meeting or what so-and-so had said about the Gulf War or Bosnia, the conversation would dry up and he would have to find more neutral ground. And so their relationship went on as best it could, with this delicate circling around of issues which seemed too sensitive to discuss.

Occasionally Lisa would come up and browse through Yusuf's books or watch him while he was praying. He would answer any questions she had, but as soon as he began to get preachy she would back off. She was the only one in the family who was open about telling everyone her brother was a Muslim. The others preferred not to mention it. Frank and Joanne were both married now. Yusuf had decided with each one to go to the reception but to skip the Temple ceremonies. Frank was not too bothered, but Joanne had been mortified that her own brother would not attend her big day. There had been tears and fights and a vain attempt by Yusuf to explain his reasons, but to no avail, and his relationship with his sister had never gone above cool since then. What mattered to Yusuf above all was that his parents were secretly proud of him and his achievements. He hadn't turned out so weird after all. He was doing well in college. He had a job already in a decent place. He had plenty of friends and was always going off to conferences and meetings around the States. Now, they would proudly boast to friends, 'Jake is in the Far East again.'

Suleiyman told him the way he was behaving with his family was the best way. Gradually, they would come to respect his beliefs and his conviction, and by the time he had a family and children they would have something new to bring them together. 'You never know,' he said. 'Your parents may be more willing to take Islam from your children than from you.'

The way he said it, it seemed like he was certain that Yusuf would one day have children. For the foreseeable future, he himself didn't see any prospect.

Yusuf had settled down and seen the sights, and had been to all Suleiyman's relatives for dinner. Suleiyman broached the subject of marriage one evening when he and Maryam were sitting out on the verandah in the balmy air. Yusuf was engrossed in the jungle-like sounds emanating from the fields.

"Have you begun to think about marriage?" asked Suleiyman.

Yusuf gave a wry smile. "Yes, I began to think about it and now I've given up."

"Why?" asked Suleiyman, surprised.

"You don't know what it's like back there in Indiana. I mean, the prospect of meeting single Muslim women even in San Francisco was slim. In Indiana I'd have more chance of meeting an alien."

Maryam laughed. "Are there no Muslim ladies in Indiana?"

"No single ones," said Yusuf, "or hardly any. There was one, but she wanted to marry a native speaker of Arabic. She was Indian, raised as a Muslim in the US, and she got interested in Islam as a teenager. She wasn't interested in any of the guys her family had lined up for her and I heard she wanted to get married and that she was looking for someone practicing but then they said she wanted to marry an Arab."

"Did you want to marry her?" asked Maryam.

"Yeah, I wouldn't have minded," he said nonchalantly. "She

wasn't really my type of girl but I thought it could work."

"You don't have to marry just anyone," said Suleiyman, "just because she's single and she's living nearby."

"I know, but you're supposed to marry someone with piety, right, before looks and wealth and prestige?"

"Of course," said Suleiyman, "but you can find a woman who has piety and who you find attractive. It's not necessarily one or the other."

"Oh, I see," said Yusuf, as if the idea was new to him.

"What you need," said Maryam, "is someone to help you arrange your marriage, to help introduce you to someone. Do you have lots of Muslim friends?"

"There are quite a few at the Institute and the university, but the guys at the university, most of them are also looking to get married and the people at the institute don't know of anyone."

"It's a difficult situation but it is already destined who we marry, so we shouldn't worry too much," said Suleiyman.

"There was one girl," said Yusuf bashfully. "She was Iranian American and Waseem at the Institute knows her father. He told him about me and he agreed for us to meet."

"Did you meet her?" asked Maryam excitedly.

"Yes, but I could tell she was really embarrassed. She never looked at me and she left the room the first chance she got."

"She was probably just modest," said Suleiyman.

"Well, I said I liked her. She seemed intelligent too and she'd travelled a lot but she turned me down."

Maryam was almost as disappointed as Yusuf.

"That's not unusual," said Suleiyman. "I can't tell you how many women turned me down before I ended up with Maryam," he said with a grin, and she gave him a playful slap on the shoulder.

From then on, for the rest of his stay, it was obvious that the matchmakers had gone into overdrive. Different girls were sent to serve refreshments to the brothers or to accompany them when they went on trips. Suleiyman would casually let know which of them was single and list their family credentials and accomplishments.

"Look, I appreciate you trying to help me," smiled Yusuf, "but I don't think it will work like this. I'm only on vacation. It wouldn't be easy for an Indonesian girl to uproot herself and come to live in the States."

"I was thinking more of you coming to live here."

Yusuf was taken aback. The thought of living overseas permanently had never occurred to him.

"Do you like my country?" asked Suleiyman.

"I love your country," he assured him. "It's beautiful. The people are gentle. Love the food. Mosques are great!"

"So why don't you live here?"

"I don't know," said Yusuf. "I really don't have an excuse."

It was a wonderful experience to pray in congregation among thousands and thousands of fellow Muslims. During Friday prayers that first week they had stood in the courtyard because the mosque was overflowing. As far as the eye could see stretched rows of men dressed in blue or white tunics, some wearing little caps. Despite the number of people and the busyness of the town, that moment of the Friday prayer was as calm as a cloister. As the Imam finished reciting the *Sura* and said *Allahu akbar*. 'God is Great', for them to bow in prayer, there was a rippling hush on the breeze and not a sound anywhere as they all bowed in unison, each person lost in the worship of Allah.

"You know your sisters?" said Yusuf looking up from his postcard. "I've been trying to match up the kids."

Suleiyman went through his vast family again, giving the names and ages of all his nieces and nephews and their respective parents.

"So the other two sisters are single, right?"

Suleiyman stopped for a moment. "Are you interested in one of my sisters? You could be my brother-in-law."

Yusuf smiled. "Amina seems nice."

"She's too old. What about Khadija?"

"She's not old. Anyway, how old is Khadija?"

"Sixteen."

"Suleiyman," he scolded. "She's far too young for me."

"No, girls marry younger in Indonesia. This is not the US, you know. They don't wait till they're thirty."

"Most American girls marry before thirty. That's just a cliché about career women."

"No, I read it somewhere. More and more Western women are putting off marriage until their thirties and then they can't have babies, or they're too busy for them."

"Suleiyman, that is a tiny proportion of American women. Mormon girls are nearly all married by twenty-five. I was engaged at eighteen, remember."

"Oh, yes I remember . You told me about Alice."

"Anyway," he said. "I've grown up a bit now. I don't want to marry a schoolgirl. How old is Amina?"

"Too old for you."

"How old?"

"Older than you."

"How old?"

"Twenty-seven."

"Well, I'm twenty-four."

"So she's older than you."

"By three years Suleiyman. Remember that the Prophet's wife, Khadija, was quite a bit older than him."

Suleiyman added slowly. "Still I don't think Amina is interested in marriage right now."

"I thought you said they married young."

"Amina has been married before," he said quietly.

"Oh, is she not married now?"

"No, it didn't work out. They divorced."

"Wow, really? Is that common here?"

"No, it's very unusual but from the beginning there were a lot of arguments. He didn't like her continuing at university. He had his own shop but she didn't want to help in the shop. She wanted to train to be an architect."

"Is she an architect now?"

"Yeah, she got her wish but now she's divorced and I think she is sorry; but Mama told me they weren't suited at all. They should never have been matched up like that but my father died right after he'd agreed with Zakaria's father and with all the upset they just decided to go ahead with it, but they weren't happy."

"I'm sorry," said Yusuf.

There was a long silence.

"Will she marry again?"

"I don't know. It's difficult when you're divorced in this country. She has no children, thank God, but somehow people think it was her fault the marriage didn't work out. Maybe she was too selfish."

"Will you tell her I was asking about her?" said Yusuf, and his face looked so full of hope that Suleiyman agreed.

"*Insha-Allah.*"

Three days later there were four on the verandah, in the evening air.

唯邑

Epilogue

Yusuf stepped off the plane into the shocking, choking heat, but the fragant air took the edge off it and the midnight sky seemed absolutely charged with atmosphere. Amina stepped off behind him lightly, apparently unaffected by the heat. Wherever Yusuf took her she seemed to adapt without batting an eyelid. For him the heat was a slap and an engulfment. Amina just walked into the heat and became part of it.

They were shuffling now as their walking space narrowed and narrowed as they were crushed on every side by eager bodies. While desperate to keep himself on his feet and to keep Amina safe, Yusuf sought to relish the moment and enjoy being surrounded by more people than he'd ever seen in his life, united by the same goal. The eyes were all purposeful and oblivious of their surroundings. Every man was looking out for himself and his family. Everyone was eager to get the formalities over with and start the *Hajj*.

Stumbling into the arrivals hall, Yusuf felt the terrific change in temperature. Although mercifully cool at first, it wasn't long before the place began to feel quite chilly, just like the supermarkets back home where you would need to keep your jacket on during a stifling summer's day. The hall was pristine and glaring white and the white of the pilgrim's clothes made it look like a sheet of paper.

A few years ago before he had become Muslim, this would have been the last scene he would have expected to see in the Middle East. The scrubbed Mormons had a mental image of a place where things went rancid in the heat and where people were unwashed and sloppy in their hygiene. Now, when he explained to Americans about the almost fanatical concern with hygiene in Islam, the five ablutions, the baths, the eating habits, it just wouldn't register with them. If they could have feasted their eyes on this scene they would have seen hygiene screaming at them from every corner.

It reminded Yusuf of Abdul Qadir's Middle-Eastern friend, Ibrahim. Most Americans were proud of their clean surroundings, their two daily showers, feast of deodorants and germ-killers and daily laundry, but Ibrahim had treated the place like it was a nineteenth century slum. His wife had scrubbed the place over and over until every trace of the previous residents was gone, every skin-cell and unseen foot-print. They had refused to use the pans or dishes there and had bought a whole new set of their own. They discarded the bed and replaced the carpets. The place was completely aired out. Only then did Ibrahim dare to begin living in that house, fearful of breathing the same air. Even as a Muslim it had shocked Yusuf then to think that Arabs could find their habits filthy.

The other striking aspect of this hall was the smell of after-shave, every possible brand competing with each other. He longed for the perfect climate, a mixture of the first coolness he had felt entering the hall mingled with that perfumed fragrance from outside. By now the cold was really getting to him.

唯芝

Yusuf

First we were herded through formalities. I noticed how rapidly the officials worked. They were not demanding or suspicious as they had been in other foreign countries I had visited. Their job was to facilitate any and all Muslims to achieve their duty and give any and all Muslims the right to enter for their journey to the Holy City. For the first time in my experience I realized that the hidden advantages I had always enjoyed as a western, white, educated male and had begun to think were inherent, in this case would not ease my passage whatsoever, but neither as I'd feared did my origins delay my passage.

Secretly, I expected someone to draw attention to my being a so-called white Muslim, either positive or negative. Although I had my visa, I still expected probing questions which I would answer brilliantly, full of confidence that I had the truth on my side, that my conversion was genuine. On the other hand I had imagined that scenario where the affable guy makes a big fuss of me; '*ahlan wa-sahlan,* an American? *Masha-Allah!*' I would have enjoyed the fuss. I tried to purify my intentions, to remind myself that my Islam was to please Allah and that my *Hajj* was for Him alone.

I imagined, as we crept nearer to the front of the line, how I would answer his questions. A sentence came to me and filled me with pride at the fact that I had come such a long way literally and metaphorically. I wanted to say: 'I'm a Muslim and I'm from Utah.' That had a fantastic ring to it. Or should it be: 'I'm from Utah and I'm a Muslim'? That was no better, because in Islam your religious identity should take precedence over your nationality. 'I'm from Cairo and I'm a Muslim.' 'I'm a Muslim and I'm from Cairo, Geneva, San Francisco, Somalia, Jakarta, Moscow, Montreal.' Why did I think it was special to be from Utah? It was special to be a Muslim wherever I was from. I felt disappointed that even now, I hadn't stripped away my pride at being an

American and at having come into Islam against all the odds when I had been told incessantly and read it myself that Allah guides whom He wills, and nothing, nothing will stand in the way of that.

Perhaps now I could start paying my dues. I had the arena in which to work. Now it depended on what I did with the opportunities I had been given. I had to stop mentally rewarding myself for being Muslim and start earning the name. This *Hajj*, if I started it with a pure intention, would be the golden start to my intentions.

I snapped out of my reverie as I was called to the desk. I smiled apologetically and handed over my passport. As he opened my passport and stamped my visa the official gave me a brief, official smile and said, '*As-salamu 'alaikum.*' I knew the answer to that particular question.

'*Wa 'alaikum as-salam, wa-rahmatu'Llahi wa-barakatuh,*' came my reply.